THE MAN

WHO HAD

POWER

OVER

WOMEN

BY

GORDON

M.

WILLIAMS

 STEIN AND DAY/*Publishers*/New York

THE MAN

WHO HAD

POWER

OVER

WOMEN

To C. J.

Inspiring, bold John Barleycorn!
What dangers thou canst make us scorn!
Wi' tippenny, we fear nae evil;
Wi' usquebae, we'll face the devil!

Robert Burns

Chapter One

Encased in blubber, sealed in an invisible life-capsule which was being carried down a quickening Niagara-approach of gray time marked by the passing of greasy, forgettable days, still not knowing what he was doing with his life let alone why he was on the accursed planet at all, Reaney had recently struck upon a new image for his own thought processes, seeing the scurryings of his mind as a pack of laboratory rats sniffing about in a hardboard maze, twitching and trembling at each corner—would this be the dead-end that produced joint-racking electric shocks, or would it be the elusive trip wire that rang a bell and shot a tiny cube of lard through a Lilliputian trap-door?

Scurrying rat thoughts and God help Reaney when men in white coats needled gold wires into his scrambled egg brains to translate minute electrical impulses into human terms. They would, of course, realise that he was mad. They would discover that Reaney sometimes thought of himself as Caesar, sometimes as an ant . . . prophet, lecher, universal mind, all standard Reaney roles. He sat in the boozing lounge of the cross-Channel ferry and watched people watching him (more accurate to say, he watched *for* people who might be watching him) and wondered if they were watching him watching them. Who, in other words, was more interesting, him or them? Or madder? Heading back to London across the briny, the knowing mad and the unknowing mad.

Do you have stray thoughts which strike you as profound
breakthroughs in human understanding (i.e. the world is
divided into two kinds of people, those who . . . and those
who don't . . . type of illumination)? Frequently, Reaney
told himself. My daily progress through the great human-
city to which I am returning (or which is sucking me back)
is increasingly punctuated by audible monologues spoken
by demented human ants who can no longer differentiate
(or don't bother) between thought and speech: The public
gabblers I call them. Is it necessarily a bad sign that I alone
grasp the cataclysmic significance of the middle-aged
woman who stalks the parks on Sundays screaming abuse
at invisible enemies? The formal man on the Piccadilly Line
chatting away to his briefcase. The pavement mutterers,
the cinema mutterers, minds broken by the great city—not
the *safe* wreckage of bums, down-and-outs, tramps, no-
fixed-aboders, winos, rubbish-collectors and litter-bin vul-
tures (*safe* because these are vital bastions of middle-class
security, their role in life that of measurable reassurance)
no, a growing percentage of the *normal* population going
crackers. Normal nuts.

Do you find yourself thinking that ants are better than
humans because their community-organisation doesn't necessarily produce wreckage as ours does? Nor does an ant
hill boast of sadists, necrophiles, plastic fetishists, nor the
man who went to this Mayfair brothel (high-class) to be
hung up naked on a cross at the end of the orgy room and
one Tuesday night when the place was being cleaned up
they found he'd died of a heart-attack early in the evening,
meaning that a number of people had really done it with a

new twist. Plus Beethoven. Or were there ant-Beethovens? How would we know?

Some passing fool kicked Reaney's outstretched feet and, stifling a quick impulse to lash out in retaliation, he opened his eyes. A little more in control now. Given freedom from the American he might make it home on his own feet. He picked up his black leather travelling-case (impressive brass fitments) and went off in search of the lavatory, or whatever they called it on a ship. He tried to pull his suit into some semblance of presentability. In Paris he had behaved like an infantryman on leave, but England approached now, and a return to the discipline of one's own country. No sign of the American. Perhaps he had fallen overboard, permanently, ending his pathetic Scott Fitzgerald capers—standing on the cafe table reciting Hamlet while trying to kick the waiter in the chops. If only Reaney had learned the secret of saying 'no', of not caring whether he offended people or not, of disengagement. Ah, well, head off through these admirably English iron-innards with suitably grouchy face befitting this obnoxious holiday crowd—rucksack scum. A solid wall of young girls in pale gray blazers, round hats affixed with elastic which pressed into puppy-fat chins, Lolitas in profusion, hot faced little sniggerers doubtlessly carrying lumps of half-masticated toffee in their biscuity-smelling gym knicks.

'Excuse *me*,' he said, pushing at them with his bag. Their teacher was a twentyish creature, blonde and glamorous, cool goddess of tennis court and lights-out erotics, a queen silently showing her minions the correct attitude of distaste a lady should adopt towards foul males, personified by large fat man with greasy black hair pushing whisky-stinking way through fee-proven decency. Ah, my cool beauty, half an hour in bed with Old Reaney will cure any Lesbian on earth.

9

Cure? Sir, he who is tired of imagining two lovely Lesbians on the ehm batter is tired of life. Don't you know which side your broad is battered on? Yes, well, that was the flower of English middle-class maidenhood, but where the hell is the pisser?

Being so contemptuous of his fellow passengers that he could not lower himself to ask directions, he walked round, the collar of his blue raincoat tucked in the wrong way, his heavy black bag occasionally banging sharply into innocent thighs. Yes, and you, too, madam; at the back of his mind the sad thought that in a few hours it would all be over, this last drunken flight into boyhood, this probably pathetic excursion into the sadly remembered adventures of fifteen and twenty years ago. Ah well, Reaney, perk up now, a quick leak and a pork-pie and you'll be the king of the ravers again. He found himself at the back end of the ship, looking through optimistic gulls at the receding blur of France. With a drunk's ultra caution, he surveyed the open deck like a wax-moustached villain of the silent screen before pressing his belly against the rail and unzipping his naughties. Out it went in a fine, wind-whipped spray. His raincoat acted as cover. Or sieve. France, I piss at you. May it form a tiny gulf stream, my little contribution, and heat a square millimetre of your beach, and poison a lobster. Watch out, bird, what do you think you are, a gull bladder? Brushing down a soggy front with a fat white hand he picked up his bag, stumbled slightly, moved off with exaggerated nonchalance in the direction of the boozing place. The whipping breeze made his eyes water, his cheeks smart. Salt-caked smokestacks and brass tin trays. Set sail for England and Sir Harry. Ballocks, get out of the blast. Coming to an opening in the wall or scuppers or bilge-mizzen or whatever they called it on a ship, Reaney stopped to look over the shoulders of some dreary students (army type clothes and infantile scarves hanging to knees) at what he realised was his first view of the White Cliffs of Dover. It was a revelation and he was grateful to the drink for enabling him to understand its significance. The French coastline was low, a shallow introduction to the land mass of Europa. But the White Cliffs were high and dark against the sun and from the ship they had the grainy far-near focus of a long-range lens, with its flattened perspectives. The White Cliffs, the England the outside world knows; a battleship island looming out of timeless sea mists, an impregnable bastion. Up there, behind the grim bulwarks of these towering cliffs, a garrison-citizenry leads its secret life, a whole country like a beleaguered feudal town, villeins and serfs withdrawn behind the ramparts. Reaney knew this was a significant moment in his life, like his first dirty magazine. He felt the madness and the strength and the aloofness England must show to the rest of the world. Leafy lanes and crumpets and stupid village clocks and imbecilic men with splendid hearts . . . no, no, I see it all now, why Hitler would think twice, and Napoleon before him, this island fortress is grim and dark and woe betide those who come unasked. From now on he would think of himself living on a high plateau whose edges were obscured by mist and washed by green, relentless seas. Instead of girls, the lounge now featured a pack of Boy Scouts, home no doubt from woodcraft lessons—in Paris. He skirted the pack with equal distaste, feeling curiously upset at the sight of two larger, bare-kneed Scouts carrying light ales from the zinc bar; the rest of the lounge was given over to beards and rucksacks and annoyingly sexy girls—what the hell could they see in these immature *hitchhikers?*

Reaney put down his bag, proud of its black and brass plush functionalism. So well had his mind been working he was surprised to find that he was still drunk enough not to be able to articulate his order properly. It took a third attempt before the foreign barman understood large Scotch. In a matter of hours he would be faced with the great test. Will Peter Reaney find his manhood? Can he fight his way clear of the woman who is ruining his life? He leaned on his elbows. Journeys are a time for reappraisals, and that is why Great Caesar looks so sad because he has—same again, French nit—to fight the greatest battle of them all within the city walls. No more gray greasy days, no more unhappiness, hated wife. To hell with appearances, what your parents will say, what our friends will say, what anybody will say, this is my *life*. Half of the never-again years gone already (and that's being optimistic, omitting nicotine-rotted lungs, fat-encrusted heart, drunken drivers) and I'm still waiting for even a slight hint—yes, just a hint would be something—that the happy part of life, the good part that every human expects, is due to begin.

This is it, Reaney. Do it now, or . . .

Goodbye, one life . . .

"Hey, there yar fur fuck'sake, yaol' bastar', whurthe fuckyabeen, I been allover, Judas priest, less've a drinkolbuddy, whadya say?"

Reaney's last conscious memory of his return to London that gay Sunday was of buying cans of beer on the Dover Victoria train and of matching the American whisky and beer against whisky and beer. Having had to show a taxidriver an envelope to get him to understand the address, he was unconscious when the cab reached his square in South Kensington, and the driver had to get out of the driving cab, come round to the passenger section and twist Reaney's arm before he would get out. He paid by pulling handfuls of change from his pockets and cramming them into the driver's cupped palms. At the top of the steps down to the basement he tried to steady himself against the rail, missed his grip and plunged down twelve or so steps head first, coming to rest quite comfortably with his face hanging over the last step, the only serious damage being to his trouser-knees and shirt. He was unconscious when his wife came out in her dressing-gown and half-dragged, half-kicked him through the front door of their flat. Reaney was home.

Chapter Two

The peculiar thing about me, Reaney thought as he lay beside his blessedly sleeping wife in the morning, is that the worse things become the cheerier I am. My disgraceful return home last night, the equally disgraceful things which no doubt happened on the way, the fact that I am shortly to be subjected to terrible abuse, and then to go to the office and become involved in one of the slimiest methods of earning a living known to mankind, seem only to make me feel even more hilariously randy. The day they finally confine me to the dangerous part of Rampton, I'll don the straitjacket with a fit of giggles and the biggest erection since the Vickers building. Of course, the man *is* mad. My name is Dr. Hyroschimus C. Brästweiber (Wien and Portland, Oreg.), a leading consultant in psycho-sexual wish-fantasies and believe me, this client of mine, Reaney, P. is a lulu. Let me read you, gentlemen of the Thought-Police tribunal, an extract from his case history:

"In 1981 Britain was on the threshold of far-reaching sociological and constitutional changes, as prophesied by the Venerable Eric Blair. From surviving records we know that Citizen Reaney, Peter, was placed in the sado-masochistic (or main) stream of Brixton Grammar, at 13. He reappears in 1979 as a leading street hooligan in the London Buckingham Flats district (previously the site of the home or *palace* (Old English) of the titular rulers of pre-O'Brien Britain). As primitive dictators were used by industrial powers for political ends, Reaney progressed to a higher power level with the help of the IRA (Inland Revenue Authority) which was then fighting for the state employment monopoly, full control of the Bank of England and Treasury against the old *parliament*.

"Infiltrating as consumer-recruits into the National defence organisation (NAAFI—Navy, Army and Air Force Incorporated—at the time almost bankrupt through low trading figures and forced to pressgang consumer-recruits), Reaney's element was introduced to sophisticated weaponry and took over effective control of London.

"In the six months before the Inner Party police quashed this uprising, Reaney proved himself one of the most ambitious sexual deviationists in all history. This is an extract from his diary:

"Oxford Street today. Sealed off the lot, Marble Arch to Oxford Circus. Thursday, late shopping night. Filed them out at Checkpoint Park Lane, me doing the sorting. Marched 500 of the finest-looking wenches in the world to State Brothel Number One (the old Hilton). Naked by the half dozen under the showers, three in a bed, blackies, Swedish au pairs, daddy, there never was a revolution like it. The elite cadre (my fancy name for the mob) get first whack, then we march 'em down to State Brothels Two and Three (the old Savoy and Dorchester) for non-party types. Next op's on for Bond-street, Monday morning. Only class birds on the street at that time. Just dying to get me mitts on Knightsbridge . . ."

Cheery, anyway. Nobody getting hurt, except maybe the husbands whose wives didn't come home. Probably thank you for it, poor bastards. If they were anything like myself. Let's get out of this pit of awakening hostility.

Her Malevolence appeared in the bathroom as he finished lathering his face. Reaney waited for it. Twenty-five, thirty years ago, he'd waited like this for the old man to come home from work to give him a belting for *being caught* stealing crayons from school. Only he was supposed to be a man now. *Did* you grow up?

"Well?"

He began to draw the razor down the left side, twisting mouth and chin to the right, watching his own eyes in the mirror. This, my cheery friend, is it.

"Well what?"

Eyes hot to feel and hot to look at. General effect—drunken excitement. THIS IS THE BIG ROW. The last. Trump card ready. No more nag.

"What do you mean, well what?"

Put your hands on your hips, woman, don't you even know the cliché posture for shrill, injured wife? Ah, Reaney, the true artist of matrimonial cannibalism, cold as a fish. Not for him that slight weakening of the sentimental slob-husband who sees two toothbrushes hanging together, weakens at such evocative trivia and melts into a humble, forgiveness-begging noddy. He dried his face, patted on Old Spice, pulled his bunchy cheeks this way and that, waited for next move.

"Is that all you've got to say for yourself?" Once upon a time he'd found this stupid Roedean bray rather sexy. Like making love to the Lord of the Manor's daughter.

"I haven't said a word," he replied, pushing past her icily and making as dignified a journey to the bedroom as nudity (fat, white) allowed. Pull trousers over stout legs (cruel symbol of lost-youth, the white smooth skin on the outside shins where hair has been worn away by years of long trousers).

"You've been away four days, you come home filthy, stinking, animalistic drunk and you've got nothing to say? What do you expect me to do?"

"I expect you to piss off out of here, that's all, let me have the extreme pleasure of not seeing your silly face." Check the rise of anger.

"Go on, use all the filthy language you like, YOU PIG, go on." Her voice was near hysteria, always a winning sign, and her face was pushing closer. "You think you can get away with anything, don't you?"

A stupid face. Look at the reddened, strained skin. Like the twisted face of an athlete photographed in motion. Yes, well, that suit won't see any more service. The black shiny effort, she never did like that one. Getting his clothes out would be a problem. She'd probably cut them up or burn them in a great demented performance once he'd left. The hell with it. He would be free. Breaking point about now, what do you think, Barrington Dalby?

"HOW LONG DO YOU THINK I'M GOING TO PUT UP WITH IT?"

Keep calm while all around are losing theirs.

"YOU DRUNKEN PIG, I'M GOING TO TELL MY FATHER THIS TIME. HE'LL SEE TO YOU. JUST WAIT." She's got her mouth open and she's having trouble finding more threats. "I'LL LEAVE YOU."

Icy calm, George Sanders.

"Is that a threat or a promise?"

So far he had not been so foolish as to look into her eyes. Scoop money from dressing-table, typical aftermath of a drunken evening, two crumpled pounds and about four quid in half-crowns and pennies. She was wearing her nylon housecoat. She could be happy only if their whole life was a Gas Board commercial for central-heating.

"YOU'RE NOT GETTING AWAY WITH IT THIS TIME."

She was at the door of the bedroom (having made the decision, not caring if he could talk himself out of it, it was no longer *their bedroom,* just a room with objects). He had no other reason for delaying the inevitable confrontation. Funny, the wild glare in her eyes made him feel almost sorry for the state she had reduced herself to. His throat was parched, in anticipation of a drink. She spread out her arms in a gesture of imprisonment. All right, you blood-sucking, heel-nipping bitch. The flat of his palm. On the cheek.

"Get out of the way, you cow."

She'd wanted that, of course. It was her victory. Maybe she'd clip the sequence and show it again in slow motion on *Sportsview* tonight, the controversial knock-out seen frame by frame. A girl falling against a door, knees slowly slumping, hand scrabbling for support, a sweep of dark hair whipping (as under water) across a distorted face, a man's black leather shoes pointing menacingly at defenceless bare toes.

"Hit me, go on, hit me, does it make you feel better?"

Sobbing now, once-loved face in pathetic, triumphant, *woman's* collapse. The eternal victim-conqueror. Neighbours listening, incitement to conform, keep quiet, hush it up, knuckle down, get on your knees, comfort and hug and promise to change. A bullfight poster from, Jesus save us, a honeymoon. Ruined lives. A fine-boned hand's pressable blue veins. Fortunate are we, who live our lives in a film. Nothing is real, thank God. She was waiting for the great soft centre to drop down beside her, probably weep a bit, take his nagging like a man, say he'll never touch it again. Goodbye, one life? Not this time, madam. Tired of constant reconciliation, I have decided to stop "making the best of it", of enduring.

My last chance to be what I am. I am what I am, the greatest escape clause of the whole human condition.

"I'll always remember you like that, snivelling on your knees," he said registering sarcasm like a first year student at the Royal Academy. True masochist, she knows when she hasn't had enough. She came up on her feet, Kirk Douglas in *Champion*, only this time the ending is happy. *You* die. *I* live.

18

"GET OUT, GET OUT, GET OUT. WE'RE FINISHED."

"You'd think I was trying to stay or something," he said. Pause at the door. Give her last, serious, almost human look. "This is it, Angela. I'm sorry. I won't be back." Christ, don't get too sincere. "You've done your best to ruin my life and I'm not going to let you ruin your own." That's a nice touch; good scripting, Schulberg.

This time she screamed very loudly and as the door was open he could only presume she meant it, because normally she couldn't bear the idea of public scandal.

"GET OUT, YOU PIG," was what she screamed. Reaney shrugged and climbed the steps. The door slammed behind him. He closed the iron gate carefully. Eyes still hot, quite exciting these moments of genuine crisis. We don't realise what television is depriving us of. Mrs. Fanchetti came out of the ground-level front-door. Italian-plump in a pink suit, black hair, the widder woman from the first floor. Did she but know it, she had provided the ammunition for the last two or three times he had managed to copulate with the wife.

"Morning," he said, with a knowing smile and wink. Generous, smiling, big-arsed Mrs. Fanchetti. Downstairs a tense English bitch with a fat husband she hated and upstairs a plump woman who didn't shave her armpits in expectation of the return of a manly nose to those pungent bodegas of the body.

The tragedy of our times, people unable to pick the right people. A national amnesty? All marriages annulled? Now's our chance, lads, a conjugal Paul Jones, all parties freed for a merry re-shuffle?

"The sun is shining," Mrs. Fanchetti smiled. They met occasionally coming and going at the front of the house, just often enough to have evolved "family" jokes. He had already forgotten all about Angela (he told himself) as they walked together towards the Old Brompton Road.

"The sun always shines on England," he said, smiling down at her handsome (just a bit hairy) face. "This is God's own country, as all wops ought to know."

She gurgled hoarsely (all Italian women are hoarse. Very sexy with it, too). Green trees exuding purifying oxygen in the residents'-only square. South Ken stateliness in the morning sun, cheery nods to the respectful milkman who reckons you're entitled to "sir" and "madam" for a couple of pints. Forgotten, entirely, that sobbing bitch stamping her Roedean feet on the wall-to-wall nylon-backed.

"Did you have nice time in Paris?"

"Very boring. It's all foreign over there, you know. All that greasy food. It must be terrible to be foreign—isn't it?"

Beaming, shared joke-insult, a mockingly-indignant nudge with her elbow (desirable joint) and they separated at the pub with the bull's-eye windows.

The Great Sham gave her a leering smile and watched her lickable brown legs shimmer off down the pavement. When, for God's sake, did you grow up? All his life he's waiting for the magic moment of waking up to know he's a grown, adult *man*. Still feels no bleeding difference from when he was eight and wondered what important stuff was it that grown-ups talked about. Policemen looked older and more threatening than ever and he was now thirty-seven. Air hostess walks across zebra-crossing and taxi-driver waits. That's a sexily-severe uniform, my dear, in *my* youth all we saw was a gel's well-turned ankle and that made the old blood boil in the drawing-room, I'll say.

Another flag day! The well-groomed matrons of Knightsbridge seem to have the flags up continually, what? What's it for this time, Duchess? Ah, the Distressed Gentlefucks.

Know them well. I support Dr. Reaney's League for Widows' Comforts. It's a more personal type of charity, you see, guarantees women cut off in their prime (like Mrs. Fanchetti) a decent share of English danglers. Ten inch widows, we call 'em. Can't leave good works entirely in the hands of this blasted Labour Government, what? Still, professional charity is a bit off these days, isn't it? They tell me charity organisation is now taught at business schools. For no reason at all I'm reminded of what old "Chuckers" Mott said when he barred "Windy" Fortescue's Hindu mistress from the Punjab Gold Cup. Windy was livid, although the woman was notorious.

"Don't tell me you're worried about a little gossip?" Windy barked. Old Chuckers looked the creature up and down.

"Gossip, sir?" he says, screwing his monocle in that way he had. "Gossip be demned, sir. Anthrax, sir, anthrax."

They found Fortescue in Wellington lines ablutions, throat cut from ear to ear.

Drive on, cabby.

Screaming.

Spreading.

How long before they find out?

Stay cheery. Think of the dirty work afoot at the office this bright and beautiful morning. Have a little laugh with yourself about Dr. Brästweiber and the rest of your secret army. Everybody's mad. Didn't I catch you, Reaney, recently praying for some form of sexual lobotomy, thinking that *you* are the pornography victim they're always writing about in the duller papers? What is all this misery supposed to be punishing you *for*?

Thinking that he probably looked deceptively normal, he paid off the taxi on the left side of Regent Street going up from Piccadilly Circus, about two streets before Oxford Circus. For the benefit of the public (other people, the masses, the audience) he assumed the face of a preoccupied business executive (which he was) hurrying importantly into a suave office building (which he did) prepared for a day of vital mental effort in the interests of making Britain great again (ah well, all societies seem to need these nonproductive utilities: he was the man who checked the Colosseum lions against size and ferocity specifications).

If there had been low swing gates he could have been in a Hollywood big business or police film of the forties, nonchalant heroes arriving late (always) in the office, grinning casually when homely, devoted secretary/worried, passive side-kick calls out that Frankenheimer's been shouting your name for hours, Jim. It was already after eleven, (sorry, chaps, had to give the wife a quick bashing) and they would already have assembled. He always smiled when he saw the low-level black leather furniture which Felix had installed in the front office—"touch of class, they've got it at Rediffusion"—particularly at the contrast between it and their switchboard-receptionist, a dull-eyed junior from Theydon Bois, name of Linda.

"Hello, my darling. All the big heads here yet?" Note the ingratiation-identification with Linda against the high-powered team now sitting in Felix's office. Common touch, which really *big* men never lose. What would her wedding-night be like? Fat, knowing, hungover man in thirty-five guinea suit looks down on seventeen-year-old fellow citizen and has to laugh. Linda England, millions of them, figure of the age, King Alfred . . . Robin Hood . . . John Bull . . . Tommy Atkins . . . Spitfire Johnny . . . now Linda, million-headed goddess, keeping Reaney in suits and booze.

"Barry Black's in there," she said, lifting the headpiece

off one ear to hear the magic name from her own lips. "He isn't half handsome, isn't he?"

Reaney thought of the futuristic hell in which he would find himself and Linda the sole survivors of a nuclear holocaust.

Chapter Three

Although he was an integral part of the machinations of the men who were already in Felix's office, it was with something of the Budd Reaney, slick excavator of show biz slime, two-fisted *agent provocateur* of slick literary skulduggery, that he walked—with a little mock bound and raised thumb greeting—into Felix's Monday morning meet. Little did these five guilty men know that Reaney was only here on a creative assignment, the FBI undercover-agent who had to take part in the murder so that later he could prevent worse crimes, like tax evasion. The microscope was on them, the pin holding them to the collecting board, the scalpel poised.

"Hallo mate," Felix said, above the pounding din of a record on his slim-line desk record-player, and Reaney nodded appreciatively (left eye closed) at the young lad whose latest contribution to music this was, his big bid for a permanent place in the show biz galaxy. The others smiled or nodded, Reaney acknowledging each silently as he reversed down and into a low armchair. Perry Reaney leaves the witness and points dramatically at the public benches —these are the guilty men, your honour:

ALFRED E. FELIX: age 53, chairman and managing director of the following private companies; Alfred Felix Associates, Alfred Felix Agency, Alfred Felix Promotions, Alfred Felix Publicity, Felix Publishing. A tall, bony man wearing a shiny, lightweight, russet-hued suit, he has heavily nicotined fingers, a negotiable East End accent, a wife and three children and his feet on the desk. This is the head office of his small empire.

BARRY BLACK: age 23, singer, thickset lad, general air of a merchant seaman who's won the pools. Curly hair bleached in a colour his show biz hair-stylist calls "white gold", he wears a thin, white roll-neck pullover, narrow-legged, blue twill trousers, high-heeled fawn boots. A white leather overcoat hangs over his chair. He smokes American cigarettes, sits with one leg dangling over the arm of his chair. Gold bracelet on each wrist. Dark eyebrows contrast with his hair. Has quite a tough face, despite the get-up.

JAKE BRAID: age 48, Barry Black's personal manager. Former dance-band leader. Standing (5ft. 4ins.) with his back to the Venetian blinds (plastic) he wears a dove-gray double-breasted suit with double-breasted red waistcoat and dove-gray suede shoes. Three times divorced so he's got some guts in his private life, even if he's chewing his nails energetically as he waits with ill-concealed tension for reactions to the record.

NORMAN S. MATHIE: age 51, solicitor. He sits in the room's only wooden chair, hands folded in lap, undecorative brief-case between orthodox black shoes. Exceptionally tall, he has not had his chalk-striped trousers pressed recently, and wears thick woollen socks. Gray hair in flat strands. Nose like the North Col of the Eiger.

VAL PRINGLE: age 36, self-employed writer of scripts for television series, radio comedians and small budget films. Sandy hair cropped fashionably flat, light blue eyes, suggestion of freckles, strong brown hands. Wears white shirt, no tie, purple cardigan, elegantly-narrow flannel trousers, down-at-heel shoes of a brown, casual nature. Smokes with cigarette in dead centre of mouth, cowboy style.

Before I go ahead with the indictment, gentlemen of the Grand Jury, let me declare my personal interest in this crew; I despise Black—or perhaps it is truer to say I transfer a good deal of self-contempt on to his bizarre *persona*: I don't even bother to despise Braid, because Felix and I have a little plan to ditch him: I appreciate Mathie's air of harassed professionalism: I am just a little afraid of Felix, who has the power of money over me, but I will bend over backwards to be fair to him, the rat: Val Pringle is my best friend, an old-fashioned phrase which neither of us would be so embarrassingly naïve as to use. At least, I suppose you would call him my best friend. I have many acquaintances.

Sun shines through Venetian slats. Yellow carpeting in the boss's office. Very little on his desk, two phones, one blotting pad, press-down ashtray, endearing picture of Mrs. F. and the three brats.

In every room there is one geographical point of psychological power.

Felix had it.

Felix always did.

More than having his back to the window. An orchestration of perspectives which put everyone else lower than The Chief, a congregation in a semi-circle before him. Silly little Braid had subconsciously grasped this ploy and was trying to break the pattern by standing slightly behind Felix at the window. Even rabbits know enough to run at a slight tremor. Felix's choice of low armchairs, desk position, everything, revealed that even if he had no formal knowledge of these things he had an instinct for making himself The Chief.

Intelligence is always admirable.

Coupled with awareness, it is the hope of the race.

In a moronic world do you hate Goebbels for being intelligent yet unable to comprehend his own perversion, or do you (sneakingly) admire him for being intelligent despite his bestiality?

The record pounded to a climax . . . *aaannd if weee niver meeeet agennnnnnn* . . . boom, boom, boom, tinkle . . . *I'll alllll-wayzz beee alone-uh* . . . bass guitar fading . . . Reaney played with the thought that only instant Pompeii could objectively evaluate their contribution to the progress of humanity. Felix examining an unlit cigarette, Braid watching Felix, Mathie hiding boredom by means of an intense interest in his clasped hands, Val nodding in time with far-away eyes, Barry Black playing imaginary drums with serious *mien* and bracelet tossing.

Six of them dragging down more than a thousand quid a week. Feed a few blown-belly babies on that—don't be so naïve.

Breaking the silence which followed the record, Braid proved himself weak man of the cabal.

"Well then . . ." he took a step forward, hesitated, looked at Felix. Val nodded, agreeing with something. Mathie changed buttocks. Felix lit his cigarette, a piece of business they were supposed to watch. Black leapt orgasmically to his feet, hands out, a rhetorical question on his face. Reaney lit his first cigarette of the day. The record—as these went— was quite listenable. The average number of matches in a box kept dropping, didn't it? They probably made a million pounds extra profit for every match less in a box.

"It's got number one written all over it," said Braid, in an argumentative, challenging sort of tone. Reaney drew on his Senior Service—wondering why they had dropped that slogan which read "PRODUCT OF THE MASTER MIND".

Too many master minds dying in salt-caked iron lungs? He waited while Felix proved that the strongest character keeps quiet longest. Let the minions prate and prance and out of their mouths spin their own hanging ropes. At last Felix seemed satisfied that he was actually smoking a real cigarette. He looked up.

"What d'you think then, Val?" he asked.

Braid looked sharply at Val, then back at Felix, startled and quickly annoyed at being ignored. Val scratched an ear, strictly for effect.

"Very fair," he said, pleasantly. "Yeah, quite nice. Any chance of a drop of coffee round here, my mouth's like—"

Felix waved his hand, cutting Val off with a groan.

"Don't tell me about bird cages again, you're making me nauseous already." Real Jews playing Edward G. Robinson playing screen versions of stage Jews, this was the world Reaney had spent what seemed like a hundred years in, was there any other? It was these guys who were driving him round the bend. Any moment he expected Black Barry to shout "Let's have our show right here, fellas!" and for the conference to turn into a zingy production number from a Cliff Richard musical.

He pulled on his cigarette, hoping it might taste so awful that he could put it out and never be tempted to smoke again, even if it was too late to stop the hellish proliferation of gone-wrong cells. Braid looked as though he might be silently rehearsing lines for a matinee tantrum as Felix went through the business of retailing each man's sugar and milk requirements over the phone to Linda. For once, you sensitive little paranoiac, you are justified in your feeling that everybody is getting at you. Imagine how happy he'd be when they told him his theory was absolutely correct—there had been a universal conspiracy against him! These slights were real. Felix was determined to give Braid the old heave-ho. Braid had come to Felix with Barry Black signed on a personal management contract which gave Braid twenty-five per cent of everything Barry Black earned. After two fairly successful records these earnings were now in the region of four hundred pounds a week. Felix got ten per cent of the gross for being the agent, plus two and a half per cent for publicity. Reaney had a boisterous impulse. After all, as junior partner around here, he ought to pull his weight in the old heave-ho business.

"I've decided to leave the wife," he told Val, loudly.

"Again?" Val replied. The coffee came in. Braid was hopping about. What Felix had in mind was to needle the little man into making a fool of himself. Once Barry Black grasped the idea that his manager was a bumbling idiot whose only interest was to rob him of the rewards of his great talent, then the way would be open for Felix to split them up.

"Now look," Braid said, "we've a lot to discuss this morning and there's no point in every Tom, Dick and Harry making speeches. This is the best thing the boy's done and the sooner it gets a release and a full promotional job the sooner we'll all make money."

"It's a question of timing, you see," Felix said.

"Hear, hear," Reaney added, nodding sagely at Braid. He was Al Capone's tame reporter, the one who ended up dead. What possible bearing did all this tomfoolery have on his own life? His madness was of a more serious *genre*, a thing of greater depth than the twiddle-twaddle of would-be strong men cutting each other's throats in a small room. Was he always to be Third Murderer on the credits of life's wide-screen epic?

Money, you cringing, introspective fool!

What about freedom, satisfaction, happiness?

You mean you want these as well?

Now Braid seemed ready to embarrass everyone by refusing to play the game according to protocol.

"Do I get it that you don't like the record?" he asked
Felix. "If that's how you feel just say so, let's all speak our
minds, cut out this funny business—"

Felix sipped his coffee. He put down the cup and turned
to look up at Braid. He spoke rather softly.

"Funny business, Jake?"

Braid's face went quite red. The effect of all this was to
create a strained silence in the room. Then Felix changed
course. He pushed away his cup and pulled his chair up to
the desk in a businesslike way.

"All right," he said. "The record's fine. We'll go for a quick
release and Peter will go to town on the publicity. Probably about three weeks. Now then, Val, let's hear how far
you've got with this telly idea."

As Val coolly outlined a few hardly original thoughts on
building a TV show round Barry Black, Reaney wondered
what his old man would have thought of this lot. All his life
the poor bastard believed in hard work, the kind that made
you bend your back, Post Office savings, life assurance poli-
cies, respect for betters, hatred of bolshies and workshies, to
him the same thing.

BRIXTON SHUNTER BOASTS
OF SELF-MADE SON

"Drinks more than I earn but
votes Labour"—God told

He watched Val's face. Solid. Integrated. Perhaps he saw
the Barry Black spectacular as a nail in the coffin of the
decadent west. It certainly sounded like the greatest load
of star-spangled shit since plastic gnomes. Norman S. Mathie

had sat quietly all the way. Barry Black followed each speaker with eager face nodding deferentially at each, sometimes contradictory, statement. Give him two months as a real star and he'd be re-writing *Hamlet*.

"Well, that's about it," Val said. Felix had paid him one hundred pounds to think up this drivel. Good for Val, he could tell his comrades how the cynical flesh-pedlars exploit creative talent in this dying culture, and spread the bunce around selected refreshment houses.

"All right with you, Barry?" Felix asked, smiling. "We're working hard for you, lad, you'll make us all stinking rich yet." Barry smiled. Felix made jokes about carving up Barry's earnings. Barry liked that. Braid just carved him up, without jokes. In time he'd see Braid as a bigger handicap than epilepsy. "So you'll knock out a pilot, eh Val, and we'll have another chat soon as possible? Right. Now then . . ."

Val took his cue.

"See you in the boozer, Pete?" he said.

The special mention made Reaney feel warm and wanted. Val was his friend, but even as he raised his thumb he marked down this warm feeling as another sign of personality deterioration. Suddenly he needed friends, like some doomy yid in a Saul Bellow novel? When Val had gone, Mathie wiped his spectacles with a yard or two of handkerchief. Felix motioned Braid to take the vacant chair. Barry Black sat back humbly, knowing what was to come.

"As agreed at our last meeting," Mathie began, "I arranged for someone to see Mrs. Gray. She has signed a document admitting that she sent libellous letters about Mr. Black and retracting the allegations made therein. She agrees that she had no possible evidence or grounds for the allegations made in letters and statements regarding the unfortunate death of her daughter and she also agrees that she made these allegations in an effort to extort money from our client. She has also undertaken not to repeat any such allegations to other parties in the future." Mathie leaned forward and placed the document on Felix's desk. "In other words," he said, looking over his spectacles at Felix, "we have nothing more to worry about from that direction."

Felix read the document quickly and passed it to Braid.

"Norman," he said, putting his right palm down on the desk with a certain degree of hammy acting. "I have to own up to you, I don't know how you did it, but if you'd told me two weeks ago we could've got that old cow to sign something like that I should have bet money against it. What about it, Jake? This is a pretty watertight piece of paper you're reading, no?"

Braid humphed.

"How much is this going to cost us?" he asked, holding up the piece of paper. Reaney lit another product of the Master Mind. The lawyer was a genius of the half-world of men's sordid affairs, older brother who protected naughty little boys from the big stick. What Reaney couldn't forget when thinking about Mary Gray was that she'd been in the cinema for about four hours before the stupid attendant had noticed she was unconscious. Bleeding to death through four hours of Tom and Jerry! The cartoon shapes and colours crashing through their inhuman antics, screen hues reflected on the faces of people in front rows, going round and round again, while the girl was slumped in the darkness, the life draining out of her drop by drop on to the fag ends, the cartons, the ice-tub shovels, the pop-corn bags, the ash and the dirt and the trash and the drip-drip-drip of the blood of a girl of sixteen down there among the feet and the legs and the men and the women pushing past her, the usherette's torch flashing across her lap, maybe even a man who pressed her knee and stroked her thigh when she made no complaint in the flickering cartoon world of the afternoon people. There would be a man, in a dirty raincoat, they *always* had dirty raincoats, moving about in the gloom, face turning sideways, always the pushing knee, the feel of a human face at your ear, and the girl whose head suddenly flopped backwards—maybe as the cat hit the telegraph pole and slid down it, or broke in a thousand pieces and miraculously grew whole again for the next keg of dynamite and the kids laughing and the girl who wouldn't reappear whole and happy for the next reel, the girl whose life ran down under the seat in front. And Braid was asking what all this was going to cost!

They talked, these men, and Reaney said nothing. What was one girl's life? All right, so she happened to die against a rather bizarre background. Humans die all the time. We are not hydrogen bombs that our going off should tear the world apart. Other people are so narrow-minded on this point, and in general. They insist on talking about themselves. Then there would be the newsreels, the last frontier of jingoism—"At Aldershot engineers take a new amphibious, four-wheel-drive, five-man anti-personnel germ-carrier through its paces—oops . . . while at Bexhill the boys in blue launch Britain's newest under-water, intercontinental, lighter-than-air bicycle missile—what will they think of next? . . . meanwhile in Red Square the Red Army brandishes its war machines—they call it the peace parade, these witty Russian swines . . ." Drip, drip. Toffee wrappers.

"So there we are, everything under control." Felix. Had history made his lot a bit like the Chinese, human life cheap and all that? Keep killing them and they'd have every justification. Did Felix think of goys as white trash? Was Mary Gray a file heading to Mathie? Had Barry Black already picked his next teenage mattress? Would Braid turn round and say 'We got away with it this time, son'? Reaney had once, in the first flush of intimacy with a few British household names, shown off fairly badly at home in Mandrell-road, Brixton, where his father had lived, a few doors away from the lager factory. One by one he'd gone through the names of stars, singers, celebrities, politicians, comedians: That one was a lush, this one slept with a Tory MP, that one preferred small boys, *she* would certainly never get married, *he* was known in the business as Trixie ("a bold Ada that one").

"Even if it's all true I don't want to know, do I?" his father had said. "It don't do you no good to know all that filthy stuff, do it?"

"That's all right then, Peter can go to the inquest just to keep us in the picture, eh?" Felix. Mathie nodded. Barry Black fidgeted with his gold bracelets. The sun had moved round. Eddies of gray cigarette smoke (from mouths) and spirals of blue cigarette smoke (direct from ash-growing ends) vertically traversed a dusty lattice-work of narrow sunlight strips.

"Goodbye, one life, eh?" he said. Felix, black shiny Felix, frowned. Braid ignored him. Barry Black and Mathie rose. The sun-strips made a golden fuzz of the outline of Barry Black's head. Who knows, she might have missed a rare, early Chaplin.

Chapter Four

Having helped himself to fifteen pounds from Miss Rimmer's petty cash float, Reaney decided that the conference had been enough work for a Monday, especially as he had the problem of his next matrimonial onslaught to solve. The meeting had dragged on so late he would not be able to meet Val in the pub before three o'clock closing. That should be an example to the accursed unions. However, Val would be spending the afternoon in the New Scheherazade Club. As he looked swiftly through the letters on his desk, Felix came in, left arm poking at his camel-hair coat like a bull tossing the cape. Reaney helped with an ineffectual tug or two at the collar.

"I'm going for a nosh with Mathie and Braid," he said to Reaney, who stood on his own ground now and realising this, knew how insecure his own ground was, an office that seemed to shout out lack of belief. Sometimes he felt like falling down at Felix's feet and grabbing the hem of his camel-haired garment and begging forgiveness: "Father, redeem me, for I have not sincerity." Why, he sometimes wondered, *was* he just a little bit afraid of Felix?

"Include me out," Reaney replied. "I'm pushing off for the rest of the day. Paris knackered me and I think it's come to the end this time with Angela."

"Sure, Peter, take a couple of days away from all this and you'll feel better. You'll manage that inquest on Wednesday, eh? And listen—" Felix looked over his shoulder, body adopting a more intimate line, voice dropping "—if you get

35

any fresh thoughts on pressing the ejector-seat button under Jake the Braid . . . I've had him. OK?"

"Yeah, I'll try. My teeth get on edge just looking at him."

"Sink 'em deep in his throat, mate. Enjoy Paris? Good. See you later."

"How's Dixon working out?"

"I put him on Dorry. If he's going to be with us long, he might as well cut his whisky teeth at the beginning, don't you think?"

In Regent Street the people were tourists and housewives. The office ants—Felix referred to them as the luncheon voucher set—were safely tucked away in their multi-storey human parking lots. A young girl crossed at the lights, dragging a stick-leg in an iron scaffold. She'd sat with her back to the wall at school dances, chatting brightly to her pals as they came back flushed from each dance, and she would cry later in her bedroom. Brästweiber was putting him through the hoop today, for the next corner produced a dwarf man with a very large head. In hangovers he had either a run of excruciatingly desirable women, or a surgical boot day. This was surgical boot day.

Did the eye select according to arbitrary predilection, or was The Great Director in a black comedy mood? Suddenly the city streets would be thronged by cripples, deformities, hump-backs, hare-lips, young chicks with elephantiasis, squints, acnes, psoriasis, men with smoothly obvious wigs, plastic cheeks, plastic noses, no noses, crutches, spastics, twitchers, mongols, bald teenagers, varicosed nylons and mole-bearded matrons.

Flicking eye catches inch of bare brown flesh at waistline of beautiful Indian girl's sari. Remember kissing Angela's back (dead white, of course) on that soft hollow just above the hip bone? Red buses, black taxis, flashy airline offices, single-deck Greenline bus on way to secure dormitory-outpost, no, not Greenline, no LT markings, thin metal bars across windows. Inside, men in civilian clothes, something about the way they stared at the outside world, excitement and hunger on their faces. Of course, criminals on their way to some gaol. Nothing like taking them in an open-carriage through the centre of the city, poor buggers. Look hard, oh felons, and when the first cold mists of an autumn Sunday sniff into your cells, sit sadly and think of Regent Street in the sun. But always try to see the bright side, the bit you'll laugh at years later.

CONVICTED MAN WALKING ACROSS GAOL YARD TO HANGING SHED: "You'd think they'd shelter you from the rain on your last walk on earth, wouldn't you?"

PUBLIC HANGMAN: "I don't know what you're worried about, me son, I've got to come back this way."

This is where gay, sophisticated Peter Reaney, public relations executive, turns left into the gay, sophisticated square mile of the continong right in the heart of London. Or human rat-hole. Streets where pound notes bought time from people's lives. In the window of a striptease club the full-length photograph of a young Negress wearing sequined knick-knacks, at the door an earth-faced Cypriot chatting to a man wearing a bowler hat. Three men watch, over newspapers, a doorway, pretending they are standing around idly while all the time they are waiting desperately for some other shame-face to trot out of the doorway so that they can nip in for a seven-minute, two-quid stir into some automated bag—sorry, fellow human being with dire complexities of her own—before nipping off to little wifesy in Surbiton. East Grinstead, Epsom or Theydon Bois will do as well. Over it all the sun, sinking towards the west, a last ray cutting through jumbled rooftops to glint in a tobacconist's window. On pavements and gutters the yellow and green trash, decaying, soggy remnants of the vegetable market. In a doorway a girl in a ludicrous Hussar uniform, heavy invitations to defensively deaf, hastening men, like to meet some nice girls, Irish accent, Catholic ignorance and feudal poverty of the Free State despatching battalions like her across the sea, a trade in live horse-human flesh, a green slave-ranch sending its yearlings to Rome, male-muscle, female-flesh. A Rome whose circuses are held in musty side-street rooms. And the noblest Roman of them all, crossing a street at the angle which gives him reflection, in shop window, heavy, bear-like, roly-poly-like, only the dark head retaining senatorial authority. Push open the door of the New Scheherazade Club, Patrician, and hope the goddam geese sleep undisturbed tonight.

Solid, sober Val at the bar, useful arms almost cuddling a pint. The club, a darkened room, mirror altar of never-drunk fancy bottles, the never-failing excitement of anticipation of new drama, even if he knew that to draw the curtains would reveal a dusty, man-grubby room with all the exotic glamour of a dirty toenail. Men in the club, hard-looking faces containing the secrets of selling cars, of winning on the greyhounds, of where to see a dirty film show (*dirty*, as in all too-human), of all the greasy utilities which make up the commerce of men. And women, too, but they are furniture. Val wasn't greasy. He could swallow his beer and there was no skinoil to kill the froth. Val—and Reaney hoped to God he was of the same category—was an amateur dabbler in this late-afternoon, curtained world.

"Pint?" asked Val.

"Yes, a good honest English pint," Reaney replied, easing his bulk beside Val at the black chrome bar, blowing away cigarette ash to protect his black, shiny elbow. "If foreigners drank wholesome English ale—"

"—and played cricket—"

"—and didn't soak lettuce in oil—"

"—and stood in queues—"

He thanked the woman Cynthia for the pint, hoping she thought of them as out-of-the-run customers, men she could really see had a touch of—don't make me laugh—*poetry*.

"How was Paris then?" Val asked, prepared for the moment to give him his full attention, to listen as long as he was entertained.

"Hot, rude and nasty," he replied. "No, I'm being unfair. The French agency blokes paid for everything, they wouldn't let me spend a penny, and they took me to some interesting places. One funny thing—have you ever noticed in Paris they've got bits of sacking lying about the gutters? No? They have. They clean their gutters by pumping water up through drainholes. The sacking is used to send it down one direction or the other. That's a pretty crude arrangement, wouldn't you think, for the world's most sophisticated city?"

"Remarkable," said Val. "Museums, art galleries, old masters, young lovelies, and all you notice is how they flush their gutters. I suppose you were lying in them at the time. You'll be asking me next what they use their damned bidets for, Carruthers."

Reaney had no fantasy capacity at that moment. He drank some more beer. Val spent most of his time at a typewriter. He liked a bit of action when he got away from the typewriter and the wife and the children and the cats and the tortoises and the hamsters. The chances of a serious talk with him were poor. Reaney needed to think aloud. What was he going to do about Angela? He'd left her once before. Putting a toothbrush, shaving-brush, razor, Old Spice and face-cloth in a brown paper bag, he had stomped out of their flat (they were living in dreadful Cricklewood then, in a damp house owned by a black-toothed Pole) with the intention of kipping with some bloke he knew, and the soggy paper bag had cascaded his toiletries over the floor of the Bakerloo line, and he had gone back, frustrated and highly embarrassed. But this had to be the end. Somewhere in the rag-bag of his philosophy was the notion that one had to endure pain before any action gained significance. Floating through life on a sea of booze meant slithering, unmemorable days. Stop the clock, my purpose has not been revealed and I am almost too old to have a purpose. Pulling out the roll of notes his hand touched a bulk of paper and he suddenly felt quite cheery. It was a story torn from a French magazine. He'd torn it out in anticipation of this dependable moment with Val.

"How about this little yarn then?" he said, smoothing out the page on the bar. "It's the awful truth of what Our Beloved Queen found going on in the attic of Buckingham Palace."

Val smoothed it some more and read with concentration. Then he looked up for Cyn, the necessary audience.

"Come here, my darling," he said, beckoning with secretive nods. Reaney studied Val translating for Cyn's benefit. According to utterly reliable sources, Buck House was the scene of orgies unrivalled by Caligula. Some intrepid French reporter must have been under the breakfast table for there was, reprinted word for word, Her Majesty's vitriolic denunciation of lesser luminaries whose squalorous relationships had made "Elizabeth's eyes blaze with anger".

"All good stuff, eh?" Val said, stretching his arm to hold Cyn's hand, broad brown fingers against red and white. "How about it, Cyn my lovely, why should these Royal bastards have all the fun? Get the doors locked and let's be up the stairs and have it away lively, what?"

Cyn, being a true drinking-club patriot, was shaken.

"That's terrible," she said, addressing Reaney. "How do

they get away with printing all these filthy lies? You'd think their government would stop them, wouldn't you?"

A red-faced man wearing a floppy suit brought a small, bright-faced woman to the bar on Reaney's side. As Cyn served them she kept talking to Val and Reaney.

"That's your typical foreigner for you," Val said. "They don't have our sort of standards, you see. Hitler and all that. Thank God we're English, I always say."

Reaney waited but the couple did not respond, even when Val went on with some daring slanders on General de Gaulle's sex-life. The man had long hands, reddish fingers that would always look cold. The shape of his thumb was particularly nauseating. It was a certain type of male thumb which had first come to Reaney's attention as a boy when he saw a man on the bus from Brixton to Westminster tap tobacco into his pipe with a thumb which had a very large ball and a remarkably thin connecting section. He had tried to explain this feeling to other people, discovering the near impossibility of describing human features with words alone. He could never explain the repulsion this type of thumb caused him. He understood it well enough himself. But that was the story of his living failure.

". . . but I'm going down Portsmouth and I won't be seeing Fred, take that as gospel," the man was saying. The woman watched him intently. "They're always waiting for me to drop in on Fred but I won't, you see? I just never do, do I?"

"I'd like to come to Portsmouth with you," the woman said. The man nodded in agreement.

"I always expected you would come with me," he said. "But you know who we're not going to see there, don't you?"

"Well, no need to tell *me*," she said, with a smile. "But all the same, they expect it, don't they? Doesn't it make things a bit awkward afterwards?"

41

"Oh yes, they expect it, all of them," he replied. "But I just keep myself to myself on that score, and that's no exaggeration. It could be embarrassing but I'm not the embarrassed type, am I?"

"I wouldn't say so," the woman laughed. "You—the only one who goes down Portsmouth and doesn't see Fred!"

"Exactly," he went on. "If you had to see Fred every time you went down Portsmouth it would be a waste of time, wouldn't it? You'd never see what was going on at all, would you?"

All this was of great significance to the woman. She gazed up at the man with marvel in her eyes. "Will we have time to have a drink down Portsmouth?" she asked.

"That's a funny question, isn't it?" he replied, looking away in apparent bewilderment. "Why does anybody want to go down Portsmouth at all if you aren't going to have a drink? Eh?"

"Good," said the woman. "I'm really looking forward to it."

Reaney thought it was as well he was sober or he might have butted in to find out what family epic was behind this. He was sure they weren't married.

". . . the general replies, of course, I have Roman letters on my cap, I'd look bloody silly with French letters, wouldn't I?" Val laughed at his own corn and Cyn made that little facial gesture of naughty-reproval which requires the top teeth to protrude over the lower lip and press it flat.

"Give us two more pints, stewardess," Reaney said. Might as well sink away into oblivion now. I am at the crossroads of my so-called life, he could have shouted at Val. You are the man with a thousand glib plots for the cardboard caricatures you call characters. Give me, your best friend, a glib plot for my cardboard life. Write a twist that will take me through the pain to a happy ending. Give me a line for which there is no answer. Knickers. He knew the sort of line Val would give him—"okay, Angie, we've hadda coupla drinks anda coupla laffs, let's leave it on a high note, I'll never seeya agen, kid, but we'll never forget what we had together."

The white rats have beaten the maze all right. The goddam thing is, Pavlov fruity, they now know how to get to the electric shocks and they *like* it.

"How about young Barry Black then?" Val asked, tiring of games with Cyn, with whom he was always talking about having a "decadent" screw. "For money I'd write a musical round Guy the Gorilla, but do you see him operating at that speed? It all seems a bit ambitious to me."

"Don't knock the client," Reaney said. "Anyway you've only got to bash out some rubbish on paper. That boy has involved me in a much more degrading form of activity, believe me."

Even as he recounted the latest about Mary Gray to Val, he found his eyes flicking back to the collecting box for London spastics. Its tattered paper-covering, encrusted with the dinge of once-eager hands, bore a slogan: LOVING CARE COSTS MONEY. Above the box, glued to the wall, was a letter from the fund secretary thanking Cyn and her husband Allenby for £1 11 10½d. The fingerings of impulsive drinkers had put a shoddy patina on the green paint, a soiled smearing which filled him with tremendous loathing.

It was a sad, sad box. He knew he'd hear three pennies and something Ceylonese rattling if he shook it. Turning away from the sad box he found himself close-focussing on Val's left profile. Sandy hair, healthy, if slightly open-pored skin, small neat ears. He felt grubby himself, conscious of his skin, as if a thousand tiny itch-spasms were poised to drive him mad. Remember—look properly rueful—a 21-year-old iconoclast leaning on the mantelpiece of some crowded room at a local paper party?

Late, and the other young people had sunk down towards the floor like the male chorus in a second rate Broadway musical, bodies hanging like wilting flowers.

WHAT EVERYBODY LACKS IS WILL. NEUROSIS, COMPLEXES, THAT'S ALL A TRICK. FREUD KNEW NOTHING ABOUT THE INDIVIDUAL WILL. WE ALL HAVE IT. And so on until some Scottish fellow wanted to beat his head in. Ah, to be that age again and know what you know now.

"Don't laugh, lady, your daughter may be inside," said Val, sadly. "Still there is one thing in their favour, these kids are all hetero, aren't they? That's a bloody change for bloody show biz."

"Queers worry you, don't they?" Reaney replied. "All this chasing round for stray shaftings and all this nonstop gabble about sex, it's all a put up job, isn't it, come clean now, in your heart of hearts you're as stoke as hell, aren't you?" These were just words. The tongue ruled. Like a fridge. It starts as a functional aid. Soon you're buying stuff just to justify that expensive fridge. You've never even liked cold, canned beer. Soon you're keeping bread in the damned thing.

Val did a little jig.

"It's all true, I admit it," he said. "Cyn, my gorgeous goddess, you've known all along, haven't you? Ah, age-old wisdom of eternal woman, you guessed my secret."

"What're you on about now then?" Cyn asked. The people in the club began to acquire, in Reaney's eyes, a new glamour now that the afternoon was dying. Remember when they used to moan about workers letting the country down by attending Wednesday afternoon football? Ah, dear distant days. This ripe collection, the drinking club set, the new

44

morality: If you saw this lot at a football match you'd cheer them for returning to the old Spartan values.

"So what's all this about Angela then?" Val asked. "You're really swallowing it this time?"

Reaney finished his pint and ordered two more. This was being grown-up, no doubt about it. Divorce and all that.

"Yes," he said, tendering an adult pound note. "It's impossible to go on any longer: It's ruining both our lives—"

"You mean, it just hasn't worked out, baby, it isn't your fault, it isn't mine, we're just two little people who—"

"Do shut up, Val, for two bloody minutes."

"Sorry."

He lit a cigarette to give his temper time to diminish.

"We had a right ding-dong this morning," he went on. "I had already decided when I was in Paris that it was time to chuck it in. Even you don't know what a matrimonial hell it's all been." He gave a large, cheerless smile. "I turn to you as a friend. Please do me the favour of not turning it into a brisk little impromptu cabaret turn, will you? Thank you. All I want from you is warmth and understanding and the use of your spare bedroom for a few nights. Just till I see how things work out."

"Be my guest, dear boy," said Val.

"How about Jody?" he asked. "Can you, I mean . . ."

Val drew himself up, indignant.

"I say what goes in Pringle Towers, buddy," he said. "I'm the old-fashioned type of husband, believe me."

Reaney laughed and put his arm on Val's back. Little did the luncheon-voucher set, scrabbling as they were now for seats on buses, realise what went on in the action-spots. *They* went to the films to see this kind of thing. Val was filled with indignity at the crippling effect the wrong woman could have on a man. For the purposes of this new-found grievance, he enthusiastically dismissed his own Jody as the biggest nag since the wooden horse of Troy, and this made Reaney laugh even more, for Val was just as capable of saying that without Jody he'd be a bum sleeping on hot-air grilles in Drury Lane. Val viewed his marriage in the light of conversational requirements. He was younger than Reaney, younger in manner particularly. A young, crazy bloke who made Reaney glad to be alive. At least one young Englishman wasn't a smooth rat in a business suit.

"When I see happy marriage portrayed on our silver screens I want to stand up and scream 'It's all lies'," Reaney said. "I firmly believe every married couple I know are ripping into each other's guts out in the kitchen and then putting on the big act for the guests. We did a lot of that, you know, low-pitched violence in the kitchen so's the guests wouldn't hear."

"She wasn't your bloody type, that's the top and tail of it," Val said, sagely, shaking his head.

"I wish you'd told me that before I married the bitch," Reaney replied.

"I did," said Val.

"Not very strongly."

"Christ, the first time I even hinted she was a stuck-up, miserable cow you were going to smash my nose all over my face."

"Did I? Actually, you'd suit a broken nose, you know. Give you that essential pugilistic quality. Very fashionable these days."

It was true. They'd all told him she was a bitch. Love, he supposed. Her hands, that was the trouble. Thin, adolescent. Had anyone else noticed that spinsters often have inadequate hands? She was a spiritual spinster. Ballocks to her and all like her, he was going to be free!

"I think I'll pour a few sixpences into the relentless maw of that clearly-rigged robbery device, Cyn," Val said, handing out a ten bob note. Reaney was happy. Val was on his side. He, too, changed ten into sixpences. They stood by the fruit-machine. Val was a fiend for them.

"There's Jolly Jack Goddings with a new bird," Val said, pulling the handle to produce another combination of use-less—and strangely-coloured—fruit symbols. Reaney looked cautiously over the top of the machine, which he noted was manufactured in Chicago. We weren't that short of dollars. Goddings was a gray-faced man of around forty, a smalltime agent who sent battalions of would-be stars into dreary halls in southern England for mid-week engagements at fees of twenty pounds or less. Some malformity of his upper lip interfered with his ability to smile, or he might be playing Humphrey Bogart. Either way, he didn't smile. He was the kind of conversationalist who made men literally desperate to escape. Like many of his type, he went to some lengths to ensure he was accompanied by good-looking women and girls, bait for his conversational trap. How he secured the company of these women Reaney could only conjecture, although he was sure Goddings' advances would make in-teresting tape-recordings. This girl was blonde with broad cheeks, a solid sort of girl all round.

"Well, well, if it isn't Vulgar Val and Reaney the Rude," Goddings cried in his usual unconscious parody of the show business manner. Ten per cent of twenty pounds made him one with international stars and millionaire impresarios. "This is Maggie, Maggie, meet two of the biggest rogues in the business."

Normally able to clear Reaney out of a bar quicker than an attack of diarrhoea, even Goddings, on this exciting eve-ning, was assimilable.

"Howdo," was Reaney's greeting to the girl.

"Where do you find them, ratface?" was Val's response.

"I suppose I'll have to buy you two bums a drink," Goddings said, building up bogus camaraderie for the girl's benefit.

"It's about bloody time," said Val. "You've been here for at least twenty seconds." Reaney winked at the girl. Something about the way the light from the fruit-machine panel caught their faces in the dim drinking club made him think of ghouls at a black mass. The girl stood easily, smiling with the fixed ease of the natural aristocrat. She didn't say much as Jolly Jack fetched the heavy glasses from the bar. Goddings' philosophy was that if he bought a round he was entitled to hold the floor until those drinks were finished. Then you'd buy a round and he'd go on talking anyway. Men began moving towards the roulette table. It was an evening for action. Action—the key to the whole problem. All this damned introspection and going mad, the result, pure and simple, of the sedentary life. As he sipped the pint he had visions of his new freedom, of wild parties, of strong poker sessions, of impromptu car trips to Hertfordshire road-houses, of drinking sessions lasting three and four days.

"What's your angle then, Maggie?" Val asked, "Mine's finding the system that'll make me the Nick the Greek of one-armed bandits." He pulled viciously. Rolling colours, click, click, click, a lemon, an orange, and a fruit unknown to Reaney, in tasteful electric blue.

"I don't know," the girl said, looking at Jolly Jack.

"D'you hear about these two GIS who go to Paris for a dirty weekend?" Goddings said, ignoring Maggie. "One speaks French, the other doesn't. It all happens for them, two lovely pieces, back to their flat, drinks and then they pop into the bedrooms. In the middle of the night the one that doesn't know the lingo wakes the other up. 'Hey Mac', he says, 'what's the French for soixante-neuf?' I literally fell about when I heard it. Maggie's got a very fair voice. I'm trying to talk her into giving it a go."

The girl obviously didn't see the joke. She didn't say very much and Reaney, excited by his own decision to become a man of action about the hot spots of town (ringside seats at boxing matches, days at the races, different women every night), did not share Val's enthusiastic instinct to use her as a fresh audience for personality projection.

"You think *I'm* hooked on these things?" Val said, now bright-eyed, to the girl. "Listen, I know a bloke, plays trumpet in a band, he's really hooked. On his day off he comes in here, gets ten quid of sixpences and sits here from three o'clock. I've seen him go through that ten and another ten, plus what he's won, and still be at it at nine. You know what, it gets so bad his eyes can't stand the glare from the lights, so he puts a newspaper over the window and just pulls the handle, doesn't even see if he's won or not."

They moved back to the bar, pulling high stools into a semi-circle. Reaney found his elbow on a copy of the *Evening News*. As the people round him chatted about the things that make an anthill bearable, he glanced over the paper. Sammy the Snake had been found and life in East Grinstead could go on again. Commuters will be irritated by another go-slow, and will sign petitions against these grasping railwaymen, although if it had been floods the good old blitz spirit would have been welcomed back. Police with tracker dogs searching yet another Essex common for yet another missing schoolgirl. Wouldn't anybody ever get up on his hind legs and tell these kids what was what? No, that would be downright embarrassing. Better by far they learned the hard way. Jolly Jack was now on spastic jokes. He turned inside.

THE CASE OF THE OFFENSIVE BLACK CAP

The black peaked cap worn by a 20-year-old Londoner

*is an offensive weapon, Southend magistrates decided yes-
terday. They ordered it to be destroyed.*

*The cap had 32 studs in its front and back, with chains
over the top and sides. A PC said the man was also carrying
a paper knife, shaped like a Japanese Samurai sword . . .*

*When asked about the cap and knife, the man said, 'All
my mates carry them. The cap is not meant to be an offensive weapon.'*

Down in Merrie England something stirs. On the streets
it was surgical boot day, and the papers seemed to be printing special editions to suit his mood.

BOY, 17, DIED AFTER SEEING TV HANGING

Val was now on about strange sexual perversions. He
had a funny idea of how to win the heart of a fresh-faced
young English miss, to be sure now . . . "well, the wife goes
away and forgets all about the bathwater and when she
goes back, there's the husband drowned, still tied up in his
chains. The law comes and immediately sees it as murder,
well naturally, but no, she says, she ties him up in chains
in the bath every night. And if they think that's kinky, she
takes them out in the garage where there's a perfect replica
of a Boadicea-type chariot. On Sundays, she says, she has
to harness him—completely starkers—in the chariot and whip
him round the lawn. And how about—yeah, I'm not kidding, this is all factual stuff—how about the barrister they
found hanging from his own chandelier in ballet tights . . ."

Covering a grin with his hand, Reaney looked back at
the paper. Good old Val, wonder what sort of parental chat
he'll give his kids when they're at an age when they ought
to know.

*A fantastic research programme has been launched by
American scientists. They have built a robot President with*

a computer brain. It may be able to tell the real-life Mr. Johnson how to act in the world crisis.

The robot would be able to tell the President the next Russian move in the deadly game of brinkmanship . . .

He threw a pound note down in a puddle of beer, motioning Cyn to set up the same again. The girl was drinking gin with pineapple, and ice, which suggested a certain innocence. Goddings was no hand at factual anecdotal material. He liked the formal joke . . . "so they bury this nigger in the sand up to his neck and let the lion out. The Roman punters are raving. The lion rushes across the sand and leaps at the nig-nog's head. By a miracle he ducks and it misses. It comes again—and again he dodges it. On the third time the lion leaps, the nig-nog ducks, and as it passes over him he stretches up and bites off its ballocks. You know what the crowd shouts then? 'Fight fair, you black bastard'."

Reaney studied the girl's reaction. She was either very thick—or so high-minded she didn't deign to laugh. He'd once sat through some dreary public meeting staring at a baronet's wife. She'd kept the same, vague, well-mannered smile on her face for two hours. They probably learned it at their finishing schools. Same sort of thing as the Royal Family. In public you'd often see them lean across and speak to each other and smile. His old man had once told him that what they actually said was "one two-three". His old man was an authority on Royal secrets. Then, a headline of our age . . .

OUTRAGEOUS, VIOLENT, SEXY . . . AND
SUCH SPLENDID ENTERTAINMENT

"Well, cheers, Petey my boy," Goddings said, raising his whisky.

"Yes, good health to you, my friends," Reaney said. And

directing a smile at Maggie—"I couldn't help overhearing the filth these sewer-rats have been subjecting you to. If I were you I should marry a black man. No daughter of mine would ever be allowed to marry a stinking white man. You foul-tongued villains, hanging's too good for you, what you need is a good slap in the face."

Goddings had no sense of humour, miserable bastard.

"He'll be telling you he thinks of you as a daughter next," he said, rather too bitterly, to Maggie. Val put his hand on his hip and tossed his head.

"He's been a luvvly father to me, cheeky mink," he lisped, looking down his nose at Goddings. Jolly Jack was uncomfortable. He wanted to get back to his jokes. The girl held up her handbag, rummaging about in a way Reaney recognised. He waited until her ten shilling note was on the bar.

"You're not actually going to let a young girl buy the bloody drinks, are you, Goddings you tight bastard—beg your pardon, my dear. Tuts, tuts, Jack, I thought even in those damned state schools a chap learned how to treat a white woman."

Oh yes, a merry evening. All action.

"I think I'll have to love you and leave you now," Goddings said. Reaney put his elbows on the bar and beamed at the girl. Would Jolly Jack say what was in his mind, that she was supposed to leave with him? Jolly Jack shuffled a bit, waiting for Reaney to coax him to have another drink, or Maggie to say she had to go, too. She didn't, not immediately. Ah ah, so he hadn't got very far with her.

"Cheerio then, Jack old man," Reaney said to Goddings, noting at the same time the arrival in the club of a plain-clothes sergeant he'd met there before.

In the twilight world of the afternoon drinkers you got all sorts.

"It's a raid," he bawled cheerily across the room. The

policeman waved back, not altogether ecstatic at this public announcement. Reaney had an impulse to drag him into the party. But Maggie picked up her handbag from the bar and before he could resume control of the situation she was leaving with Goddings. A man of action could not be thwarted so easily. He put his hand on her shoulder.

"Maybe I could help you, I've got my contacts, you know," he found himself saying, let her smile patronisingly, she didn't know what life was all about. "Here's my card. Give me a tinkle." Pulling out his card he spilled the contents of his inside pocket on the floor. She took the card and said something. Val was down on his haunches to lift up the scattered papers and it seemed like a good laugh to pretend to pin his hand to the floor with his shoe, as in the films. Unfortunately, he really did jam his instep down on Val's hand. The girl gave a little wave at the door, behind Goddings' back. Val leapt to his feet with a great shaking and rubbing of his hand.

Reaney made a sweeping gesture with his right arm, with some idea of pleading innocence, instead knocking a pint glass off the bar.

Beer flowed in many directions. Reaney had a perfectly good apology to make, but found difficulty preparing the words. Cyn wouldn't even look at him as she mopped up the drink. Miserable hypocrites, that was your typical English bloody drink-sellers. Flog you the stuff all night, but dare get drunk and you'd think you'd committed some awful crime. Ah, get stuffed. He could not be sure if he thought or said this. Later he and Val were on the pavement outside, swaying about among the pavement gawkers and the kids and the dirty old men and the lonely Indians and the frustrated emulsion paint salesmen, looking for they knew not what. Or knew and wouldn't get. Val and him, the last of the real people. A bloody good time to go back and have it out with the bitch, finish once and for all.

"I'm not even half-drunk," he said to Val, who nodded seriously and staggered back a step bumping a man who looked like a wrestler. Reaney felt big enough to belt any bastard, but the wrestler went on his way without incident. "You're all right, aren't you?"

"Swinging," Val said. "Where's the women?"

Reaney strode out into the street without fear to stop a taxi. He had trouble enunciating the address and the driver looked a bit offish as he went back to the pavement and got hold of Val by the elbow. Home, James, it's a great night for a bloodbath.

Chapter Five

Well, lads, there's your freedom, that surging mob of out-of-town gawkers desperately looking up at the Guinness clock and the BOAC ad. Stand on that island long enough and you'll meet someone you know. Hub of the Empire. Gordon's Gin, the *Daily Express* and Martell Brandy. The neon suits us soldier-citizens. We are a hard people. Not for us your effete trappings of eye-pleasing aesthetics. We're fly bill-posters on the empty shop fronts and brick walls of the world. Spiritual litter louts and prahd of it . . . *goodbye Leicester Square* . . . humble, devout worshippers queueing to pay their devotions at the temples, standing all parts . . . fountains in Trafalgar Square and the stereophonic whistling of a million braggart starlings, our soul-mates in the bird world. Instant Pompeii reveals vehicle of the time bearing two male citizens in near recumbent position, freemen going about their lawful business when the white ash fell . . . it's dusk and the throngs still press against the palace gates, desperately seeking nearness to their titular rulers, who are engaged in nothing more mythical than watching the fictional goings-on of an imaginary slum street on television . . . drive on, noble hackney navigator, to destiny . . . I am the very first to see the meaning of the White Cliffs . . .

He came round to the driver's voice, shook himself, woke Val, and paid off the man. Holding his wrist up to the street light he tried to make out the time, but the light was poor. High noon in Detroit, though.

"D'you want to stay here?" he asked Val, who was searching his pockets for his cigarettes.

"It's your party, Pete," Val replied, and he seemed now to Reaney to be perfectly sober. The taxi ride had done them both good. He could handle it on his own.

"That's a pub on the corner you could wait in," he said, pointing down the street. "Just a minute, no, that corner. Got my bearings all wrong, what? I'll only be ten minutes. You will wait, won't you?"

"Are you calling me a liar?" Val asked, suddenly pulling out his cigarette, throwing it angrily over the railing. "Lit the damned thing at the wrong end. Worst taste in the world. Yugggh."

Reaney banged the heavy swing gate to announce his fighting return. The key refused to go in the lock, forcing him to kneel. The door opened. The hall was in darkness. He swept the wall with his palm to find the switch. Silence. A heavy buzzing in his ears. Nothing moved in the hall. She'd be watching television, prepared to put him through the silence treatment. Just wait, miserable cow. It was cold in the basement. Cold and silent. He walked through to the lounge. It was in darkness. He went back to their bedroom. Nothing there. The kitchen. No. The bathroom, no. Playing funny girls, eh? Moved into the small bedroom and locked the door? We'll have you out of there, doublequick. Taking a firm grip on the doorknob, he turned it and hit the door with his shoulder. It swung with the weight of his body and he sailed helplessly into the unlit room, coming to a halt when his knees hit the single bed and he fell, thinking even as he banged his head on something hard that this would make *them* think he was drunk again. He got up.

"Where the hell are you?" he shouted. The flat was dead. He went to the front door and ran up the stairs, missing his footing only once.

"Val," he shouted, fumbling with the blasted catch. "Hey, wait a minute."

He ran along the pavement a few yards shouting for Val. Instinct made him look between each parked car, and in each gate. Sure enough, Val's familiar silhouette was there, against a pillar.

"Hallo," Val said, aggressively. "Can't a man have a quiet piss without all this bawling and shouting?"

Reaney grabbed his arm.

"God almighty, you drunken swine, you got no bloody sense? Come on back, she's not in."

"Just a minute for God's sake," Val protested, pushing Reaney away with one hand and fumbling at his trousers with the other. They went back to Reaney's gate. Reaney descended first.

"She's not here, look for yourself," he said to Val in the hall. This time he noticed a sheet of paper on the wire-leg telephone table. He read it slowly.

"I HAVE GONE AWAY. YOU HAVE HAD YOUR LAST CHANCE. DON'T TRY TO FIND ME, YOU HAVE HAD YOUR LAST CHANCE. YOU'RE NOT A HUSBAND, YOU'RE A DRUNKEN ANIMAL. I CANNOT TAKE ANY MORE. THE BIN HAS TO GO OUT TONIGHT."

He read it again and realised what it was. He turned to show it to Val, but he had disappeared.

"Hey," he shouted. "Where the hell've you gone now?"

"Wassat?"

He read the note to Val standing beside the bathroom wash-basin into which his best friend was being sick. Val didn't show a proper degree of excitement. He shook his shoulder.

"She's gone!" he said. "You deaf? *She's* left *me*!"

"Aaaahooogh," was Val's answer. Reaney sat on the edge of the bath. Val shook his head like a wet dog. He felt for the cold tap. He eventually straightened up, face very pale.

He wiped himself from head to knees with the face towel. Reaney waved the sheet of paper at him.

"She's left me a note," he said. "*She's* left *me*."

Val took the paper and read it carefully.

"Congratulations," he said. "That's solved it all then, hasn't it?"

Even in his elation Reaney felt some disappointment and as Val helped him throw a few essentials into his black and brass travelling case, he felt his brain clearing up, not that he'd been really drunk, it was typical of the world's most truly miserable woman that after giving him all those years of hell she'd deprived him of the proof of his own new personality. After packing he went into the kitchen and drank a pint of milk. It was still only nine o'clock. Val was being solid again.

"Well," he said, looking round the lounge, "if you know anybody who's looking for a good flat with two years' lease still to run, only a hundred and twenty quid a quarter plus rates . . ."

Val was looking at his shelves of paperbacks.

"You'll be wanting it yourself, won't you?" he said. "If I was a bachelor this'd do me nicely. Save you the bother of finding another place."

"No, mate," he replied. "I hate it. I couldn't stand being in it. It's all to do with her, if you get me. Once we're out of here tonight I never want to even see it again."

He locked up and they went to Brompton Road for a taxi to Val's house in Holland Park. He found he was shivering slightly. Relieved of his liquid burden, Val was now in a mood of relaxed hilarity. They both laughed occasionally at the note.

"Don't try to find me!" Reaney chortled.

"The bin goes out tonight, Peter Reaney," Val sang. Kensington and Church Street were warmly-lit places beckoning him to enjoy his new life. Notting Hill Gate was alive, throbbing, pubs promising gaiety, excitement, adventure. He hadn't felt like this since God knows when, seventeen years to be exact when he'd come home from demob and every night had been a face-tingling sally into an exotic unknown.

And it was all her fault, the change. He hadn't come home slobbering drunk in the first years of their marriage, maybe an occasional Friday night with the boys, nothing a normal, broad minded woman wouldn't have welcomed. She'd turned him into a pig, drinking to ease tortured nerves.

"Tortured nerves," he said, as the taxi turned off the main road.

"Me, too," said Val. "Living in the shadow of the bomb, that's my excuse. Men kept shoving glasses of whisky in my hand, your honour. Just here, driver. Right then, here we go into the blue horizon."

Jody Pringle was not, at first, overtly excited at the prospect of Reaney as a temporary lodger. Reaney, so popular and commanding a personality in the male world of the office and the pubs and the clubs, noticed that with her above all, her red hair pulled back from her broad, high-cheeked face, he was edged into the role of apologetic husband's hanger-on. Outside he thought of Val and himself as a strong team, with Val possibly the junior—and more devilish—partner, but once the man was in his own house he acquired a suggestion of almost gruff heaviness. What the hell, he would sit back in the battered armchair beside the fire and let events take their course, be buggered if another man's wife was going to start putting him through the old routine.

Funny about bloody women, even the best of them instinctively took the wife's side. Jody had never even liked Angela, Val had told him that often enough, but as they talked about it he couldn't help noticing a critical undertone. Luckily Val was in no mood to knuckle down to domesticity. In fact, now they were in a good light, the man still looked slightly drunk.

"Will we go out to the pub or do our guzzling here?" he asked, seemingly addressing Jody and Reaney, although Reaney took care to let her make the decision, noting, as he sat neutrally, the subtlety of the question. Jody had returned to the big sofa, strong legs doubled up, where she had been comfortably perched before their arrival.

"I don't mind," she said. "There's plenty in the house."

"I'm easy," Reaney said. "What about the kids?"

"We'd better stay in," Val said. "Although these bloody children get it too easy. When I was a tiny lad my old man would tie me to a lamp-post with a bit of string round my leg and swill pints in every spit-and-sawdust bar in Bristol. I'll get the provisions, you two try and cheer up while I'm gone."

Reaney smiled to Jody as they sat in silence. He liked their house and its child-proof furniture. The house had cost Val ten thousand (or deposit thereon) but the decor was worn and battered with stained wallpaper and cigarette-burned carpets.

"You're an awful man, really, Peter," Jody said, throwing her magazine in the general direction of a pile of colour supplements and newspapers. "I mean, I can just about handle Val when he's in one of his breaking-out fits, but you'd drive me to suicide."

Reaney threw her his packet of cigarettes. Angela had often said the same thing about Val, only more nastily. Jody was now safely categorizing them as naughty little boys. Irksome, but better than resentment.

"You think so?" he said, flipping the matchbox. Val came

back, holding a bottle of Teacher's, three glasses and a jug of water to his chest.

"Yes, I'm sure of it. Oh my God, Pringle, give me that, you can't carry drink inside or out."

With a few whiskies in her Jody found it all highly humorous and when, glowing this time, not lurching, Reaney left them on the upstairs landing at two in the morning he felt he was already enjoying the fruits of freedom. So easy to be nice and popular when there was nothing personal at stake. As he lay on his back in the hardly adequate single bed in the spare room, the whole day seemed to have been a fog out of which loomed the iceberg, the great favour the Gods had bestowed on him. Finding that his vision kept sliding from left to right, he reached across to the bedside lamp and switched it off. Lucky, boy. In my cell they never turn the damn thing out at all and that's the cruellest part of the whole ghastly business. If you try to cover your face with a blanket the wardress peeps through her little spyhole and bangs on the door until you uncover your face. Rank sadism, just proves you could recruit an English Belsen staff in one day with the right ad in the personal columns. We cons do say that the one ray of humanity in the whole dirty rotten prison system was the surprise appointment (Labour Government, got to do *something* radical) of Colonel P. J. Reaney as governor of Holloway.

"Girls," he began his introductory speech to the assembled victims, "I believe that putting anybody in prison is a vile conception wished upon us by sadistic property-fetishists. To my regret I cannot open the gates and send you home, but I will make this a prison of love, if nothing else. Incarceration *can* be fun. Fitted white Persian rugs in each cell—or boudoir, as I propose to amend the nomenclature—are only a beginning. Regulation dress will henceforth be gauze harem pants with halter-neck chiffon bra. Being, alas, one poor male, I cannot compensate for *all* the deficiencies inherent in your tragic—and to my mind sadistic—imprisonment. I shall do my manful best. Emission for good conduct. Star prisoners allowed a confinement. Governor's rounds will acquire a magic thrill HM Prison Commissioners never dreamed of (or probably *do* dream of). Closed circuit TV will mean that the period between cocoa and lights out is not only enjoyed by those prisoners whom I shall have—ehm—carpeted. Out of a firm belief in minority rights I have reintroduced the birch, give your names to my secretary afterwards. Hangings? Well, girls, I notice *The Naked Lunch* is the library's most popular book, so we all know what fun a good hanging can be, but I'm afraid the more extreme forms of progress must wait until we know each other more intimately . . ."

When Jody Pringle quietly opened the door, maternally checking on smouldering cigarette ends, fresh vomit and other mishaps common to her husband's male friends, she saw, in the diffused light from the landing, Reaney's fat white arm dangling to the carpet, blankets slipping in the same direction. She threw them back on Reaney's chest. Back in her own bedroom, she shook her head at the sight of Val, still wearing shirt and trousers, sleeping heavily where he had fallen across the blankets.

"Just like a lot of greedy little schoolboys," she said, lifting his feet onto the bed. She had to lever at his sack-heavy body to make room in the bed. In the morning his breath would smell like bad meat. She pulled the wall-light cord.

When she had gone, Reaney eased his body. Tomorrow would have its problems, like working on how to make the most of freedom. A nasty thought kept intruding, and try as he could to shove it down, there was no getting away from the fact that *ménage à trois* with Jody and Val would be the ideal arrangement. Why in hell were they all so inhibited? At his age a ready-made family was probably the best he could hope for. Tomorrow he'd get them to the pub and work round to a proposal to put real meaning into their friendship.

Chapter Six

Of course, when you really thought about things, nothing was actually new. I, Reaney, or Reaney the God, can remember being able to reach up for the first time to the switch in the lavatory in Mandrell-road. I can remember the first time the cycle didn't topple but moved forward, oh ecstasy. I can remember the very first words I ever read, on the side of a bus: Don't be vague, ask for Haig, which I did, later. I was three then. Always a year ahead of my age at school. But apart from these things, everything is an echo in reverse—as you grow older you hear louder reverberations and then one day you hear the original noise. Like sex. Maybe that's why I'm a man with a built-in geological fault. (My crust keeps cracking.) Yes, I've never forgotten what it was *actually* like to be a child, what I thought when I was four, my first day at school, high pissing contests in the lavvy. In fact, I may be the only man in the world who knows that children are superior to adults. They have a much clearer conception of right and wrong, of what is stupid, they can smell a grown-up telling a lie. Contempt. Grown-ups were heavy, fat, stupid, lazy, dull, treacherous. They still are. Remember Trevor Makins? Had three different coloured pens in his blazer pocket and nobody needed to be told he was a show-off. And more bloody important, they accepted instinctively that showing-off was bad. God knows what kind of kids that Flies fella had to teach to give him *that* impression. Of course, certain boys in the class were occasionally sent to Coventry and no doubt they went home blubbering to their mums and thought they were hard done by, but it was always for some grievous offence against the common good, like cheating on the exchange rates of marbles or comics. *Ménage à trois* at schools would be a matter of fact sign of friendship, not an intrusion into the selfish privacy of property. And now he knew something which had been with him, nagging away at his subconscious for years: He was desperately, painfully in love with Jody Pringle. She was everything he had ever wanted in a woman. No, that wasn't true. She was everything he wanted in a woman *now*. There had been a time when he'd tended to laugh at Val and Jody for the lunacy of their meeting and marriage. Val had been married before to a mascara-ed girl reporter and sleep-around; her name was Karen and when Val began to discover that she was a lazy malcontent, he'd gone on the booze something terrible. He'd been working on the well-known trash magazine in those days, what was it, seven, eight years ago. This Karen—whom Reaney himself had poked a couple of times; he had left the same magazine some years before to go into public relations—was a good bit older than Val and Reaney knew damned well she'd conned him into getting hitched up because, like all slags who're approaching thirty, she'd begun to panic a bit. Well, Karen had gone to, believe it or not, he still couldn't imagine *her* getting an idea like that, some marriage guidance outfit. About Val's drinking and staying out and all that. Naturally they wouldn't take her side of the story automatically and they'd got Karen to arrange for Val to meet this guidance woman. Who was, of course, Jody. By the time Val had given her his hard-luck story they were on lusting terms and next thing Jody was The Other Woman in Karen's divorce proceedings.

Sometimes he suspected that Jody—five years and two kids later—was beginning to wake up to the fact that Karen hadn't really driven Val to drink at all, he was like that anyway. However, second wives always have to be a bit more understanding, knowing that what's happened before can happen more easily the next time, human habit capacity being what it is. Or was he just reading the situation in the best possible light for his own devious purposes? No, come off it, Reaney, you wouldn't be that much of a rat. The bedroom door moved. He twisted his head to look. Jody's oldest, Mark, was peering round at him. Fair, like his father.

"Hallo, kiddo," he said, the gay uncle. Mark ran away, shouting to his mother that naughty Peter was in bed. Never having much hangover on the second morning of a two-day guzzle, Reaney washed, shaved and dressed in a cheerful mood. It was just after eleven. His suit trousers were specked with fluff and had lost their knife-edge crease, his white shirt had beer stains down the chest; from his black bag he took a black sweater and went down to test the current temperature. A tin scooter on the stairs, a torn drawing-book in the hall, a pram parked at the kitchen door, muffled clicking of Val's typewriter. He decided to visit Jody first. She was breast-feeding the second child at the kitchen table. She smiled and made no attempt to cover her breast. Reaney could well imagine himself making one big bound across the room onto her lap and being held at the other breast. *Executives, you can't relax? Try the latest thing for the man who needs everything. The in-thing, wet-nursing for worried businessmen.*

"It's Roger the lodger," she said. "If you want any breakfast you'll have to cook it yourself, the maid's on strike."

"I'm not really hungry," he said. He poured himself a mug of coffee from a white enamelled jug on the gas. "I'll leave you to this scene of natural bliss. We don't want it developing infantile trauma, do we?"

66

"Her!" Jody said, looking down at the dedicated guzzler. "Not *it*."

"How can you tell? Don't tell me they start nagging at that age." He sipped at the mug as he walked through to the small backroom where Val worked. He looked more than ever like an artisan sitting before the little portable, middle fingers tip-tapping the keys, short sandy hair on broad-templed face, a labourer's shoulders and arms.

"Sit down and shut up," he said. "Amuse yourself or abuse yourself but keep quiet till I've finished this load of crap."

Reaney lifted a bundle of papers from the seat of an old-fashioned, wide-armed easy chair and sat down. Through the French windows he could see the scraggy jungle Val called his garden. It was another warm, sunny day, the Gods sending him good weather to mark his rebirth. It was funny to think of Val learning to write and reading all the books in these toppling mounds and all of it being boiled down to write moronic drivel for an illiterate cretin. At least, in *his* case, there was no talent for anything better. Well, there really was talent, but life had denied him any chance of using it. That was a thought, now he was free he could chuck in his needlessly lucrative employment and have a bash at this artistic nonsense. If bloody Val could do it, he certainly could. Tomorrow, the inquest. How terribly symbolic, it would really be an inquest into his own past life. If he was a writer he'd use all these fantastic thoughts. Anybody could do the typing bit and thinking up stupid plots, it was whether you had the kind of mind that saw through the trivia of humanity down to the hard core of fundamental truth that counted. He drank some coffee and stretched down among the litter on the floor for something to read. What the hell was Val doing with women's magazines?

I'm a young man who's forced to believe that 90 per

cent of girls are just out for a good time, no matter what it costs a man. I've had lots of girl friends but they have all drifted off after a few weeks, and I'm sure it's because I don't earn enough money. Character and affection mean nothing to them; they're only after the things money can buy.

And the happy answer? "Stop pre-judging people, like them for what they are—and they'll start liking you."

He looked up his stars in Leon Petulengro. His birthday in September fell within *Libra. Lively, interesting week: excellent time for a holiday. Good omens surround visits but don't overdo things. Show affection to the one you love. Be careful with money. Week-end developments turn out well.*

It must have been happiness week, for no matter what birthday he looked up everyone was promised success in romance and other excitements. Val had hit a winning streak, typing ferociously. Reaney chucked away *Woman's Own* and picked up a piece of yellow paper. It looked interesting, like a secret memo from the War Office for the eyes of colonels and above, the kind that told you interesting things about aerial reconnaissance of Russia. It was headed REDIFFUSION TELEVISION LTD.

"THE UNUSUAL MISS MULBERRY"

One-hour television series (taped)

INFORMATION FOR WRITERS
General:

A series about the adventures of KAY MULBERRY, a blonde dish who is a partner in the LYNN-MULBERRY private inquiry agency. The other partner is an ambitious young ex-CID officer, GERRY LYNN.

On the surface he and Kay are about as friendly

as the devil and Holy water. Each would like to buy
the other out. At least, that's what they say, but
you don't have to believe all they say (see below
for character notes). Kay's father Fred Mulberry,
founded the agency. She inherited a half-share when
he died.

The format is being kept deliberately loose to
encourage imaginative writing. It can include almost
any kind of story that would somehow involve private
inquiry agents . . . industrial sabotage or espion-
age (stealing of patents etc); fraud of all kinds
(including confidence trickery and phoney share
deals); embezzlement; divorce evidence (but involving something like a high society or political
scandal); the tracing of missing people; kidnapping
(say, of a ward in Chancery); blackmail; even some
kind of White Slavery (perhaps involving au pair
girls). And so on. . . .

But bear in mind that LYNN-MULBERRY are private
inquiry agents, not policemen. They have no official
status, no powers of arrest etc.

Your story must be dramatic and credible, but
the style should be high and flip.

It is not the style of the old comedy-thriller.
We're after something cool, sophisticated and
faintly way out. But not cold. We want our principal
characters to come alive as human beings, not a
pair of walking gag-books. And MISS MULBERRY is
very, very human.

There are no current examples of the kind of
style we want, but let's say we'd be much nearer the
high-style of BURKE'S LAW than the realism of NO
HIDING PLACE.

Unusual settings and the right kind of produc-

tion can contribute to this style, but the guts of
it has got to come from the writing. And that means
you.

-+oOooOOOooOo+-

KAY MULBERRY (played by Diana Dors). Aged
about 29. Tried a number of jobs (air hostess, store
detective, fashion model, travel agency courier)
before joining LYNN-MULBERRY. She is intelligent and
shrewd, but wayward and with the usual feminine
extravagances (hats, clothes, jewellery and mad
schemes for redecorating the office in blush pink).

She won't accept a job she's not interested in
or a client she doesn't like, "not even for money"
as she sweetly tells GERRY LYNN.

But once she is interested, things start happening fast--and she gets results, even if her methods
are unconventional and intuitive.

She's essentially feminine (with just enough
muscle to lift a dry martini). And if anyone asked
her if she knew Judo she'd probably say, "Judo who?"

She says she'd rather face a lion than a spider
("Well, a small lion").

She has a flat in Knightsbridge and a tiny dog.

GERRY LYNN, Reaney discovered, was elegant, tough, educated, sardonic, witty, cool, hint of ruthlessness that women
find attractive, plenty of brains, practical, and liked listening to string quartets. Their helper was FLINDERS, a coloured
man who once worked for the Jamaican Police—"a quiet intelligent man with a sense of humour (but not one of those
"comic" coloureds). Can be a useful investigator in areas
where a coloured man would attract little attention—and
certainly wouldn't be suspected of being an inquiry agent".

Reaney pondered this and plumped for Selma, Alabama, after dark.

LISA, on the other hand, was an Austrian refugee speaking German, French and Italian—"useful when dealing with foreign contacts or with Interpol". Val seemed to be spewing *his* stuff out without pain. It all sounded very difficult. CHALKY WHITE was a Chief Inspector at Scotland Yard, friend of Kay's father and "if he were younger and if he had that kind of nerve he would ask Kay to marry him."

All this would be celebrated in a converted Regency house in Westminster with a back mews. Ah yes, those Regency houses in Westminster.

After production notes—noting that this hour-long drama would actually run for 45 minutes—he turned, also noting that he was not personally familiar with the two chirpy lads who'd written the memo, to what was headed

ADDENDUM

KAY'S CHARACTER:

Her preference for only doing jobs that she likes (referred to earlier) shouldn't, of course, be taken too literally. It was meant to indicate an attitude.

Clearly, there could be times when she has to take on a job she doesn't like (perhaps under pressure from GERRY).

Apart from the other jobs KAY did before joining LYNN-MULBERRY she was also a cabaret artiste for a couple of years. This might be useful occasionally-- providing it works for the story (but we don't want any song-and-dance episodes).

OFFICE

On the wall is a big and somewhat hideous photo

of KAY's father, Fred Mulberry--stern and mousta-
chioed.

This is simply a prop for playing an occasional
scene against (if you want it).

Two obvious ways of using it are:-
1. GERRY wants to remove it. After all, Dad's
    dead and gone . . . KAY insists on keeping it.
2. Either GERRY or KAY can, when alone in the
    office, have a mad or despairing conversation
    with it.

GENERALLY

Try to get some bite into scenes between KAY and
GERRY. There's almost always something they disagree
about--even if it's only Dad's picture on the wall.

Don't force it, of course, and have them
quarrelling madly all the time. But a nice snide
crack dropped here and there will always be welcome.

-=ooOoOOoOoo=-

Val pulled a sheet out of the machine and, without reading it, banged a sheaf into shape on his desk and dropped
his arms behind his chair.

"Thank the bloody lord that's me finished with that," he
said, blowing and stretching his neck. Reaney looked at his
solid, blonde, pixie-like friend. Marvels. Such industry and
application and loneliness all for a nice snide crack.

"I've been reading about this new idea," he said, holding
up the yellow paper. "It would frighten me to even start
thinking of how to meet these specifications."

"Is that the Diana Dors thing?" Val asked, turning heavily
in his chair. "They made some and then decided not to show
them. I don't know why. It was Flinders the non-comic coloured who interested me. The one place I could think for
him was a Ku Klux Klan meeting."

A ring-necked pigeon ponced across Val's lawn.

"What's that you're working on?" Reaney asked, beginning to see new dimensions in Val's occupation.

"A load of ballocks about this astronaut whose wife gets done for shop-lifting. I wanted to make him the first alcoholic astronaut. I thought of this scene where they tell him to change course or something and he radios back, I can't, I've just drunk the space-compass fluid. They wouldn't wear it. Do you like this line—'It was as noisy as two pound notes clapping'."?

"Very good. What does it mean?"

"Christ knows. It just sounds good. If you think it's weak you should see the rest. No wonder they have to pay five hundred nicker a script. My God, if only I could get shot of this junk once and for all and get down to something that didn't make me spew."

"Sell the house," Reaney suggested, brightly.

"It isn't paid for," Val said. "As you well know. My God, a man can hardly exist these days on less than a hundred a week."

"Lucky for you you don't have to try."

"Isn't it? How about a stroll to the boozer? You know what they say—a Teacher's a day keeps the lousy apples away. I feel like getting on the juice again. Come on."

Val pulled a suede jacket over his white pullover. It was almost one o'clock. Jody was at the front door dealing with the nappy-wash man. Val had his hands solidly in his trouser pockets. Reaney had no idea marriage could be this free and easy. It would be fun to live with them. He and Val could run about naked together, with Jody watching! Quick —get me a line to Brästweiber . . .

"Hey, kid, we're going for a drop of sherbet," Val said, dodging like a boxer in front of his wife in the hall.

"I'm not surprised, Pringle," Jody said, looking him up

73

and down. "If all I could write was that rubbish I'd want to drink all the time, too."

As they reached the gate, Jody called after them:

"If you're not coming back before midnight give me a ring, Pringle. I might ask Frances round tonight."

Val did a little dance.

"If she's coming I won't be back till Friday. Bye."

Reaney decided the best thing would be to ask Jody to recommend a wife, someone just like her.

Chapter Seven

When the Notting Hill Gate pub closed at three, Val said they would go to see a painter-bloke he knew. Reaney had always believed that his own semi-official afternoon sessions were a mark of "having made it", but now he realised that there must be in London a whole world of people who had sessions during the day without having to report to an office for even a nominal morning's attendance. The painter turned out to be a junkie, and for Reaney this was again contact with the reality behind his own previous pontifications on the subject. Arnie was his name. He lived on the top floor of a dingy big house reached after a short walk from the pub. Val said a bottle of whisky was invitation card, acceptance letter and life membership in one, so they took two of Bell's. Holding the tissue-wrapped Scotch, he felt guilty as they passed men digging up the road. He and Val probably looked like hairy Marie Antoinettes to these rugged delvers, but that was life. The tall terraced houses were shabby and unkempt. The first room they entered was completely bare, except for a rusty bicycle roped half way up a red wall. Val hadn't knocked and he walked straight through into a sort of living-room, in which there was a small crowd. Reaney followed, feeling a bit square-looking in these obviously avant-garde surroundings. The painter was a very big man with a pock-marked face, wearing a fisherman's oil-wool sweater. There was a small man who looked like a Chink. He seemed to spend his time nipping back to the kitchen to inspect a king curry he was making.

There was an American air force Negro, very long, thin legs stretching across the empty fireplace. The oldest-looking woman had long black hair. She wore a Chinese slit dress but when she spoke it was Glasgow. She was Arnie's wife. Three younger girls were grouped together on the floor under the bar window and because of the smoke and the facing light he couldn't tell much about them. The painter was sitting on a high wooden stool, heels on the highest rung. It all looked to Reaney like a meeting of some kind, with the painter Arnie playing big daddy. There was no carpet on the floor and the only decoration breaking uniformly white walls was a poster advertising a concert in New York featuring "Albert Ayler and the New Thing", which meant nothing to Reaney.

There were two large glass flagons of wine on the table, and Reaney noted that Val put down only one of the Bell's beside the wine, the other remaining a happy bulge under his left armpit. The painter Arnie stopped whatever oration he was making to welcome them in a quiet, tactful way which reminded Reaney of church sidesmen conspiratorially ushering latecomers in at the back during hymn-singing. He could see no place to sit and was not affected enough by what they'd had at lunch time ("let's stick to light ales for a bit") to feel like flopping on the floor. He stood with his back against the wall, very boorjoyce, while Val poked about on the table for cups or glasses or jam jars for their whisky.

"The fraud of art in any society, so-called Communist or so-called capitalist, is that it alienates man from the art of his own existence," was the first of the painter's statements to take Reaney's attention off the three girls under the window. A few minutes later one of the girls asked the painter if he agreed with some baffling statement from Kierkegaard.

He wondered how his philosopher joke would go down with the gaunt Arnie and his acolytes: "I'm walking down

Oxford Street on a Thursday evening and which philosopher do I see? You don't know? Schopenhauer, of course. You don't get it? Don't you know that on Thursday Oxford Street has a late shopping hour—Schopenhauer, get it?"

He thought not.

Val ferried whisky after whisky across the room. Reaney met the Chinese-looking fellow on one of his trips to the lavatory.

"Wotcha," was all he could think of.

"Val says you know the Swinging Rocks," the Chinaman said, in a strictly London lisp.

"Know 'em?" Reaney found himself saying. "Yes, I know them. I used to do their publicity. Why?"

"God, how fabulous," the Chinaman said. "What are they really like?"

Reaney gulped at his cup of whisky.

"They're a shower of monsters."

The Chinaman sadly picked his nose. Reaney sang:

"Everybody's doing it, doing it.
Pickin' their nose and chewing it, chewing it . . ."

Reaney headed back to the main gathering, but on his way saw inside an interesting room, which he entered. This was life. The room was an incredible mess of papers, books spewing from crazy piles, sheets of hardboard covered in daubs of yellow and red paint, tubes of paint, old trousers, an army kitbag (*that* must have been a military phenomenon), a naked baby sleeping in a pram which stood beside a chest of drawers, the top drawer pulled open. In this, laid out neatly—the only neat arrangement in the whole place—was the junkie's paraphernalia, which Reaney recognised in a flash; little white pill-boxes, hypodermic needles resting on cotton wool, a bottle of white powder, the whole damn collection looking steely and medical and white. Reaney shook his head. Thank the good lord whisky was his lot. A display of white obscenity. Medical and white and filthy. He felt sick.

In the other room, Arnie, the owner of this snow-white gear, was explaining something to Val, who had pulled himself up on the edge of the drinks table. Reaney moved round nearer the three girls. Two of them were similar enough to be sisters—dark hair and neurotic eyes—and the third looked like a Scandinavian child goddess. Her face was exquisitely child-like, her hair thick and cream-coloured, her tits sticking out of her thin black sweater, worn under a black leather waistcoat, like shelves they were, stand a cup of tea on them you could. Reaney felt randy enough for a regiment of Mongol cavalry, his favourite expression. He gave part of his mind to the conversation, but this bloody girl—even her feet were lush.

". . . Hyde Park corner is a symbol of non-freedom," the painter was telling Val. His wife nodded in agreement. "You're free to stand there and say anything you like, but the fact that you are there makes you a clown. Power elites have always understood the diabolical cleverness of the licensed court jester . . ."

Reaney had heard all this bunk before, but seldom had he wallowed his eyes in a pair of thighs like the ones the young fair beauty was shoving out across the floor. She was the one. There was a Somerset expression—first told him by old Ted Cutler in the mob—which described exactly how he felt about the girl—'Oi wouldn't mind hangin' outa your guts, me dear'.

". . . yes, but what are you proposing to substitute?" Val was saying. "A junta for junkies? A cabinet of addicts, government by the biggest habits in Britain? Come on, Arnie, you're always on about what's wrong, but what've you got to replace it?"

She sipped her glass of red wine and looked up at Reaney. He nodded. She put a magnificent finger to her whitened lips. She was digging all this bullshit. Ah well, me dear, just wait till you've had eight steaming inches of the Reaney universal panacea (cures skin troubles, nervous disorders and restores falling hair), you won't be bothered with all this crap. Now, how was he going to get in there? If the Chinaman was so excited at the idea of the Swinging Rocks, they all might be mad about beat groups. Like to come to a party I'm giving, just a few friends, the Rocks, the beat elite, all your favourite groups in the flesh? Meet my mates, the whole moronic menagerie in the flesh.

". . . we need new cities, built to a specification which will enhance the soul, shining cities on plains where mankind can live its own art form . . ."

Life *is* art and you my dear are the spoils of war, the booty, the plunder. In your body I will ease my pain and on your pneumatic flesh I will roll and thresh like a leaping salmon, and the hell with this rubbish.

". . . just a plain, straightforward answer, I'm not knocking your concept, who is going to create these cities of the soul on shining plains, or shining cities on soul plains?" Val had a habit when getting into the meat of an argument of pulling his fair, square head into his shoulders. Reaney saw fair people as essentially evil. The cowboy-gunman in white, not black. Robert Shaw in *From Russia with Love*, Nazi death doctors, and a drawer of cotton wool and jabbing needles, medically, hygienically poisoning the body. Reaney was reaching a stage where he would *have* to say something, profitably impressing the girl. A few more dollops from the bottle and he'd take over the joint. Change mankind and keep your child next to the drugs! He found himself rapidly identifying with the hard-faced commissars who had these monkeys bunged in nuthouses. He got down on the floor, not too near the girl. Arnie the painter was now on about some rubbish involving the use of home-made tape-recordings to subvert the population. Arnie's wife stood behind him, arms folded, nodding with proper wifely support. The sun was going down over the rooftops of Paddington.

". . . and I believe implicitly that violence, as Mailer says, is the only hope of the human race . . ."

"Ballocks," Reaney said. Nobody seemed to hear him. "Ballocks," he repeated. The blonde girl turned her priceless head. Arnie, consciously adopting the lines of Rodin's thinker, the daft, drug-eaten poseur (Reaney's joke was that Rodin's thinker was really trying to remember where he'd left his clothes), said nothing, which was supposed to crush Reaney.

"Violence, the typical cry of the would-be Hitler, the impotent clerk, the seedy failure, every rotten little lavatory masturbator," Reaney said, sneering hammily, holding up his glass to enjoy the effect of the sun striking the whisky. He lowered the glass and stared the great Arnie in the face. "Blokes like me went to fight a bloody war to get rid of all that," he added, suddenly speaking out for millions of right-thinking, patriotic veterans. How about that, fatman Reaney developing an attack of the old soldiers? Good for a laugh in any company. He'd been called up in 1946.

"Who is this man?" Arnie said, looking round his flock. "Don't tell me we have found a genuine man of the people, an upholder of traditional values! Tell me, man, you would be a Labour voter, wouldn't you?"

Reaney laughed.

"It's my habit," he said. Val gurgled as he twisted round on the bottle-infested table to grab the whisky bottle. Giving the world's most desirable woman a sideways glance, Reaney went on: "Tell me, man, you would be a diabetic, wouldn't you, judging from the hardware you've got out there?"

Arnie was not particularly angry, but his wife was doing an impressive imitation of a woman jumping up and down without moving her feet. Val pointed at Arnie.

"Face to face with the masses!" he exclaimed, gleefully malicious. Arnie's big-boned face slowly registered amusement. It gradually dawned on Reaney that the man was excessively sleepy-eyed. His knowledge of drug-taking was largely comprised of Frank Sinatra writhing in Kim Novak's bedroom and various Sunday paper series. Having established himself as a definite personality in his own right, Reaney rose to fill his glass with an awareness that the girl was now quite interested in him, having seen her big daddy prophet cheeked on his own ground. Through all this the American had sat motionless, day-dreaming, perhaps.

"I didn't know you'd joined the British Legion," Val muttered as he stood beside the table. Reaney grinned. He had come to Arnie's house as a diffident tourist and suddenly he was the people's candidate. Would Huey Reaney get the girl—as well? Was Val to play John Ireland to his Broderick Crawford? He stood by the table with his glass in his fist, defying Arnie's wife to attack him.

"Who's the blonde piece?" he asked Val. "I fancy her like mad."

Val didn't know. Like a true high priest, Arnie was not to be ruffled by scuffles among the mob. Serene. A big man with a big face and a big flaw, pontificating in the nightmare decor of the beat temple. A dope pope. The junkie flunkey of anti-Christ. Reaney thought of his own mind as a spark-crackling electric wire, operating at top output. Brilliant insights sizzled across cranium connections. The Chinaman minced in from the kitchen with all-too scrutable motions, queer feet yearning for air between heel and ground, bearing his steaming concoction in a pot. Arnie sniffed the incense, deigned to put lip to sample spoon, gave serene approval. The three girls still sat on the floor, content to play furniture. Arnie's wife, Reaney thought as he watched her hover behind the master, probably reserved her cooking talents for heroin stews in teaspoons. Angela would have *loved* all this. A slight churn of the stomach. Where was she now?

It had all happened too easily. The room had its shadows now. Reaney knew about rooms. The bomb sliced the three-storey house and he'd seen the bee-cells revealed, fireplaces in the rain, instant bombing shows the pathetic dimensions of our stages. Odysseys in a rabbit hutch. The mistake he'd made with Angela, he knew now, was to have been too available. Crashing into made courting, centring all his pain-ful drives on one object and never stopping to think that the object could have a life of its own. But he'd learned now as living beings could only learn, through pain. Blonde Bertha on the floor would have to come across of her own volition. The great secret was to make yourself desirable and let the women view tally-ho in the morning. Arnie was a clear case of this. Every time he opened his great gash mouth the three girls and his wife looked as though they were waiting for sacrificial rape.

Maybe Arnie had had enough preaching over the heads of women and Chinese turd-burglars for the afternoon, for sud-denly he was chatting to Val and Reaney, man to man stuff, the army kitbag talking.

". . . you know, man, I had this terrible scare yesterday. You know I got all that shit in the bedroom, but that's all on the scripts, y'know, registered supplies. There's enough horse in there to put the whole population in orbit, but I like a smoke as well and there's always some pot about the place. I'm smoking and drinking and getting ten times higher than Yuri Gagarin and suddenly there's this big van outside. I'm at the window and all I see is these faces in funny uniforms and I'm shouting, it's the law, get the pot to hell out of here. You know what it's like, nobody listens? So I grabbed the lot and thought where the hell do I hide it, these cats got pot geiger counters, so the only place I could think of was the roof gutter, so I lean out the window and flip it up onto the roof. It's safe up there, we're clean, we sit back and wait for the gestapo and then, you know what, I look again and it's the goddam laundry. Yeah, *laundrymen!* Well, I'm high, man, I couldn't tell laundries from marines. So then I'm pounding on the door upstairs, asking these old chicks if I can fish for a sack of weed outa their bedroom window. I tell you, Val, it's a wonder I ever get any work done. I see me here with all this gang, smoking, joy-popping, whisky, beer, plonk, I don't know, man, what's the answer?"

Reaney understood some of this. He compared himself to Arnie. His own clothes were shop-bought, commercial colours. Arnie dressed like a Royal Navy stoker, blue denim shirt under sweater, fawn cotton trousers, white socks and big feet stretching brown casual shoes to near bursting point.

"You know," he said, "I've never even had a puff of marihuana. Still, I suppose that's all I need now, a new poison. Tell me," he added, leaning closer to Arnie, "what's the scene with the blonde bird on the floor?"

Val frowned at Reaney, but he didn't bother to find out why. The First Mongol Cavalry was on the rampage.

"That American boy came with her," Arnie said. "I've been through her a few times. She likes it rough, man. I chucked her, I mean, man, you're flat on your back full of shit and scotch and she's ploughing your face with her nails, wanting another session with the goddam coat-hanger. I said, what's with all you young chicks these days, can't you enjoy your sex without going ten rounds with Rocky Marciano first?"

Reaney looked round and down at the American air force Negro. Happiness was just a pair of droopy eyes. Where the hell was all this black vitality?

"She's called Henriette," Arnie added. "The way to introduce yourself is to kick her on the leg, sharply. She loves all that."

The Chinaman brought in the curry, taking great delight in ladling it out around the room for those who cared. Mrs. Arnie said there was somebody downstairs at the door and Arnie waved his arms above his head and said it was going to be a party anyway and soon more people came into the room. Reaney got Val in the booze corner.

"You still got the other bottle?" he asked. My God, this was living, a crash course in experience, specially telescoped for the senior citizen suddenly free of bourgeois chains. Twist and shout. The sky was now a brilliant dark blue.

Later when the room grew more crowded and Reaney found himself weaving about, chatting here and there to strangers, seeing himself as a big, hard man from the cold hard commercial world able to carve a way through this jumbled beatnik world, occasionally nipping out to the lavatory and leaning out of the window to grasp the bottle which Val had parked on an outside ledge, he convinced Val that it would be a good idea to grab the blonde and one of her mates and rush them off somewhere quiet. This, you gibberish-tongued foreign bastards, is what *we* do behind the massive ramparts, late at night when the guards are mounted and the keep is lit by smoky torches. We don't sip at life, we swallow it, gulp and gorge it, for tomorrow it's over the top for England and King Hal. He came face to face with the girl for the first time as he pushed through the room towards Val. She was talking to a short man with long hair and a woolly red beard. Reaney had already chatted with him in the hall: Reaney had found on his weavings that his name was being spread around as the party's show business representative. He stood beside them, feeling massive.

"I haven't been able to work at all," the hairy lad said. He banged his forehead (probably shaved) with the heel of his right hand. "I've had this block."

When she spoke she had a real London accent, not badly articulated in the Cockney idiom, but the drawn vowels of somewhere like outer Middlesex.

"I'm starting at St. Martin's in the autumn," she said. "It's very difficult to get in there, isn't it?"

"Oh, these art schools—typical," the man replied. Reaney failed to find what they were typical of. Standing, the girl was an Anglo-Saxon Cleopatra, dull-eyed goddess with a typing pool accent. The man with hair saw somebody he knew and disappeared sideways.

"A lot of our groups seem to come from art schools, funny isn't it?" he said to the girl, the voluptuous Henriette.

"Is it?" she replied, quite disdainfully considering she was only some little scrubber with big tits addressing a massive man of the world.

"I see, the bitchy type," he said. "Watch out, little girl, or some big nasty man will put you over his knee one of these days and turn your bum into a zebra crossing."

She looked at him directly now, a flicker of interest in her rather small blue eyes.

"You're married, aren't you? I can always tell married men, they're so spooky."

"Me, married?" Reaney said, putting his hand on his chest. "I've had more divorces than you've had hot sinners." He thought this was crackling stuff.

"Big deal," she said, poor little thing. Body of an imperial concubine, imagination of a fish on a slab. But she was interested in Reaney. "I had my first lover when I was twelve," she went on. "Impress me!"

Reaney dropped his cigarette on the floor and stamped on it. It seemed natural to reach out and twig her ear. She didn't complain.

"I'm too old for all that impressing stuff," he said, airily. "You either drop 'em or you don't." He looked round to see if Val was about. He couldn't spot him through the smoke and the faces and the shoulders. A record player was blasting tom-tom stuff through the flat. Yes, you need a bit of mental attraction, don't you? Mature, sophisticated women with minds, not pea-brain adolescents. Val and he could take off from this weird jumble and get back to the bigtime spots where they were known, where real women were, where money counted and you were glad of it. One thing he didn't want on his first night of freedom was a lot of fencing about with teenage neurotics. Or was he just a withdrawal artist? Cowardy custard, I don't give a monkey's.

"I'm going for a drink," he said, scanning the room. He was circulating the comparatively open space round the walls of Arnie's now jumping flat when he came on her again, talking this time to an older girl who left an immediate impression on Reaney of being hard-faced. Henriette stopped Reaney.

"This is Hilary," she said. Reaney nodded. "His name is Peter."

"He's big enough," Hilary said. She had *thin* teeth. "Is it fat or muscle?"

Reaney was on his way to bring Val and himself a cup of whisky. He wasn't going to waste precious Scotch on these two twits, the action was where the men were, warriors, you see, too busy fighting to develop fine arts, storm, burn, rape and pillage, that's us, you lesser breeds. Maybe we ain't done so much storming lately, but we've been at it a long time, you must admit.

"Excuse me," he said, convinced he was icily formal, the man who could drink forever. "I am on my way to see a man about a dog." The light was none too bright. He marched on to the lavatory, on the seat of which he found the thin American Negro sound asleep, mouth open, scrawny black neck pulled back like that of a plucked chicken, exposed for the axe.

"Pardon me, coloured American gentleman," he said, courteously, as he edged his knees into the narrow space between seat and bath. Feeling his hip against the American's head, he leaned out of the window to reach for the bottle. His hand touched it and then it wasn't there and he heard a smashing of glass down below in the unseen backyard. Ah well, that was life all over. Time to move on. He decided he might as well dispose of the cup, too, and it went soaring out into the night. More of a tinkle with that one. The Yank slept on. It seemed highly amusing to rip the toilet roll out of the holder and, unrolling it with disobedient fingers, wind it round the American's legs, shoulders, neck and face. He wiped his hands, patted his hair in the mirror, winked at himself and went back among the assembled dementia.

Shoulder, men. Sorry, lady, I mean, sir. Hello Arnie, you old bastard, great party, swop you my whisky habit for your drug habit, yeah, I'll take wine, great man, hey Val, let's get the hell out of this rubbish the whisky's gone alas like my youth too soon how about pushing off and getting some more I know a good place plenty of wimmin yeah come on hey there's Henriette and Hilary bet they're having an aitch of a time we're off into the night ha ha you coming? Of course, you're coming, I'll spank your little botty black and blue if you don't, I know your type, hey Val, amazing, in't it, find 'em, fight 'em and forget 'em, come on my little darling, me—drunk? Never, just the fresh air, hey Val, see any hansom cabs, where do you kids live, never mind, TAXI! I spy with my little eye one dirty great flat-footed copper, shall we dance? What's he saying?

". . . you wouldn't like people dancing and singing outside your house after midnight, so just watch it . . ."

Who the hell does he think he is, bloody coppers. Stop pulling me, Val. TAXI! Half a sovereign, my good man, if you transport us to—where the hell is it? Sit by me, little nubile lady, Uncle Peter needs to rest his warrior's head on your ivory-white shoulder, Val's my best friend in the world, hey Val, you're my best friend in the world, aren't you?

"You could have had us all run in, you noisy bum."

What's he on about? My head's going round. Warm little body . . . I'm all right, I'm tired, that's all, where are we, never know where you are these days . . .

It was still cold when Reaney opened his eyes and found himself staring at a dimly-lit wall. Where was he? His eyes were *drained*. He felt his trousers, his pullover. He tasted vomit in his mouth. He was on a bed, with newspaper under his head. He got up, standing on a straw mat which he felt slipping as he took a step. He sat down on the strange bed and held his stomach. No, he was all right. Seemed a bit shaken. He went to the door of the bedroom, opened it, found himself on a stair landing. There were three other doors off the landing, the first of which took him into a bathroom. He looked at his face. Eyes desperate and crusty. Hair wild at the back. Mouth pulled down by invisible fingers. Val? Where the hell was Val? Where the hell was *he*? He could remember saying they were going to leave Arnie's. When was that? Something in the street, Val pulling him away from some bloke. They had girls with them at that stage. No visible damage to clothes. Some woman's bathroom, nylons on the towel rail. Adventure, man, pull yourself into shape. He splashed his face with cold water. He poked his finger down his throat and decided the hold was empty. Good. Now for the strange unknown. He watered his hair. There's a big bag of face for you. Money? He checked and found his wad of notes intact in his hip pocket. It was dark outside, a few lit windows, above black roofs the upward glow of London's night-light. He dried his face on a perfumey towel. That was better. Reaney faces the world. Which world? Live dangerously, me hearties. He corrected a slight stumble and left the strange bathroom. This time he noticed that the landing was at the top of three carpeted steps which led down to a glass door. The landing was obviously inside a flat. It seemed to be at the top of the house, so it was unlikely he'd just barged in off the street. Two of the doors were locked. He tried the handle of the third. As he opened it, music. Radio Luxembourg, the late-night show, he knew the DJ. Couldn't be very late then. Or maybe it was tomorrow night.

"The monster awakes," Val said, and he found himself looking in on Val and the two girls—what were the names, aitches, what the hell. Val was sitting with his back against a studio couch. The girl Hilary Thinteeth was sitting on the couch and her legs were over Val's shoulders in a cosy sort of way. She was, after all, wearing trousers. Henriette, blonde, sarky, bustful Henriette, was sitting in a big armchair, with her trousered legs curled under her. She was wearing nothing else. Reaney took this in his stride. Val raised a glass in a toast: "To Reaney the unconquerable. I told you, Big Boobs, didn't I? He'd be back. You can't keep a good man down."

Henriette stood up. Reaney's clear eye saw that Val was drunk, Henriette was drunk enough to have dropped her insolent pose and Thinteeth was getting pretty merry, judging from what she was doing with her bare heels.

"Would you like a drink, my lord?" Henriette asked, moving round the studio couch—which like the rest of the furniture in the biggish room was well-worn, *professional*.

"I'll have a whisky," he said. She walked on springs, a small girl really. Up and down, that was. She brought a glass from the mantelpiece on which stood the transistor radio, a framed picture of a family, and above which were pasted a dozen or so grainy blow-up pictures—he recognised Nureyev, the Rolling Stones, P. J. Proby. When she handed him the glass, she put her hands under her pink, naked breasts and raised them for his inspection. "That bitch says they're beginning to sag," she said. "Tell me they're not."

Nothing more natural in the world than to bend and kiss them gently.

"Sag?" he said, toasting them. "You need lead weights to stop them floating to the ceiling."

"See?" Henriette said, turning her head to the other two. "Peter says they're up to scratch."

"Yeah and he's just the boy to be up there scratching them," Val gurgled thickly. The whisky washed away the taste of water-diluted vomit. It seemed like a jolly evening all round. He sat down in Henriette's armchair.

"What happened?" he asked Val, who had his face twisted round into Hilary's lower regions. Perhaps his nose was running.

"You wanted to belt a copper outside Arnie's and you heaved your ring up in the taxi and then passed out and we had to drag you up the stairs, all twenty-eight bloody stone of you. Nothing much."

Henriette came in front of him. She was pulling on a cigarette. She flopped down on his lap. He put his arm round her, after recoiling slightly.

"I feel fine," Reaney said. He wasn't taken in by the atmosphere of permissiveness and calm in the room. Life was hell and it would start being hell again in a few hours and the whole thing was building up into—she was whispering in his ear:

"Do you really like me? Say you really like me?"

"Of course I like you. Where is this?"

"West Kensington. Hilary shares with me. Do you think I'm being naughty?"

"I don't know about you, I'm beginning to feel very naughty."

"I know. But *I'm* too young to be naughty, aren't I?"

"Probably."

It was jollier in company. 'B' Coy in the wog brothel all over again, only this time old Jock wouldn't start smashing the place up and he'd get his moneysworth before the redcaps came. Val put his glass down on the carpet.

"Hey, Val," Reaney called above Henriette's fat little shoulder. "You realise that's the first time you haven't had a glass in your hand for fourteen hours?"

"They need factory acts for the drinking classes," and Val was then too engrossed with Thinteeth to converse further. It seemed ungallant to stick around with gay patter. He finished his drink and smirked at her.

"I think they want to be on their own," said the fair little pigeon, breathing quite heavily for someone who, as far as he knew, had taken little recent exercise. This is it, Reaney. She led him by the hand back to the bedroom in which he had woken up. He should have guessed from her naughty-naughty whispers that she was a complicated little thing. First she insisted on undressing him. Then, that he lie on the bed while she performed a somewhat amateurish striptease performance, hardly made more entrancing by the look of determined, nay grim, exhibitionism on her tight little approval seeking face. But what the hell, Great Reaney, they import these maidens all the way from Galicia, emperors for the pleasuring of. Then she was on the floor, crying. He felt a wave of shame and pity, until he realised that she was going on about being a naughty girl who needed punishment. When he proved reluctant to understand what was required she pulled a wire coat-hanger from under the bed and shoved it in his hand.

"Punish me," she moaned. "Then I'll be daddy's good girl." Reaney stood up, naked and angry, touching her fat bottom tentatively with the hanger. She meant him to belt her severely. Instead he grabbed a handful of long, fair hair.

"Shut up, you silly little girl," he said, savagely, slapping her across the face with the intention of calming her hysteria —honestly, as he later told Val. When eventually she lay contentedly asleep in his arms he realised wryly that sincerity was all, even misunderstood. She was completely satisfied. He was completely frustrated. She would not wake up. What he wanted was of no interest. Naughty girl had wanted punishment from Big Daddy and Big Daddy had given it, unwittingly, and now Big Daddy could writhe in desperation but naughty girl didn't want to know. Big Daddy wanted to get the hell out of it, only he needed the sleep. It was of little surprise to him when, after a few moments, he was awakened by Val and Hilary pushing into bed beside him and naughty daughter. This Hilary now, she was a *very* grasping young woman. He supposed it was some kind of consolation. All the little piggies slept entwined among the hot, damp straw.

Chapter Eight

You've never seen love scenes like these on the screen before.

"Love at boiling point"—*Daily Mirror*.

"Sizzles"—*People*.

"Jet-pace romance among the trend-setters"—*Daily Express*.

"To be judged on two levels"—*Observer*.

Mind you, that was the film version of what really happened to me. You see, I have a theory about the furtive madmen who *really* run Britain and America and Germany: When they could no longer escape the fact that the public realised all too well that nuclear bombs meant hell on earth, they had to find a sophisticated nuclear version of the old Goodbye Dolly Run Rabbit Run and by Jingo rubbish that humourised impending disembowelment in gangrenous mud (rats ate at the face of breathing Tommy Atkins while his intestines steamed in the rain, but don't tell civilians).

Well, they did (as we all know) and to this day every fool thinks he's going to be the only survivor of the nuclear holocaust (a fine big evasive word which covers up the fact that your skull will be in Potters Bar and your eyeballs part of the radioactive cloud hovering over Paris). Nevertheless, it could happen, because Wishgroup are damned clever chappies and when I came out of the deep-freeze in Smithfield market (or the deepest vault in the Bank of England) where I had been happily locked over the weekend, it was to find people talking about green moons and showers of fine dust. I had my conjugals that night and a couple of months later the clinic confirmed that the wife was in the pudding club. I was watching TV with her when they hammered on the door, very strong butch-types carrying sten guns. They took me to an underground Government shelter not a stone's throw from Westminster, a palatial sort of joint where Cabinet ministers, at least, were sure of a luxurious holocaust. That night Mrs. Jacqueline Campbell-Montesquieu, our first female Deputy PM, came to see me. What she told me was a shock. The dust was a dastardly Russian device for the radioactive sterilisation of every male in the western world. I had escaped its effects. The Government was split. One lot—mainly men—wanted me immured in a top-secret laboratory, to be milked of semen by scientific means and fed on high-sperm-count rations, the produce to be artificially introduced into as many women as there were sperms, women being chosen on a rigorous basis of proven childbearing ability and IQ.

The others—later known as the Natural Loveites—wanted none of your artificial nonsense. They wanted me installed in State Love Chamber Number One, fed like a prize bull and kept at it seven days a week, with queues of Motherhood Lottery winners winding all down the Mall.

The Deputy Prime Ministeress wanted to have me for herself first (naturally), for the men of Britain were not only sterile, they were incapable of *anything*. Jacqueline being a queen among women, I was only too happy to fulfil my duties as a citizen. Then came the Cabinet, which mirrored drastic changes in British society by becoming an all-female body. Even after the Civil War when the FSAI Party (Fair Share by Artificial Insemination) took power, the party leaders made jolly sure *they* got their share of Britain's greatest asset in strictly time-honoured fashion. State records show that my greatest achievement was to produce the goods for Britain 113 times in one week, after which my productivity-norm was heavily slashed by the Privy Council's medical advisers. Mind you, being the one man who, as it were, stood between Communism and world domination, I became a little temperamental. Naturally I insisted on male guards. I fought for the right to have one woman of my own choosing every week as a change from my hardly-inspiring scientific routine, and thus I helped many of the world's leading beauties to contribute towards saving our way of life.

But suddenly a man, if he is a real man and I am the only one left this side of the curtain, has had enough of the hothouse. He has to strap on his gunbelt and breathe the fresh air and ride his hoss out of the stinking towns over the great prairies where he can feel *clean* again. Jog jog, old Silver, the wind's in our faces and the grass blows in waves and yonder's the snow-capped range where we'll shoot a bear and sizzle deer-steak on burning logs and wash in icy streams. Very icy streams. Can't escape the cold.

The blankets had been pulled off Reaney, who was on the outside of the bed. He sat up to pull them over his naked body and in the light from a gap in the bedroom curtains saw three sleeping heads, Val in the middle. If there was one thing he did not want that moment it was to have anything more to do with the two girls. If he'd been able to slip off under cover of darkness, still pretty drunk, it might all have seemed like valuable, awareness-enhancing experience. But to chat to them in broad daylight, cold sober, after the many varied events of the night—get out now, men. Take to the boats, lads, and let the women drown. Wednesday morning, Brästweiber, and life has entered new graph curves, new high pastures in the crystal air of the lush plateau. I may even resign from my overpaid job, shout STOP above the roar of London's traffic, think about what

95

I'm going to do with the rest of my hitherto itchy life. I'M FREE. Once I get out of this sweaty conglomeration of human flesh, bingo! I have over a thousand in the bank. Felix —keep on walking sans Reaney. Barry Black, pursue your yowling career without the assistance of my propagandistic flair. Jake Braid, Mathie, Linda—from your dubious purposes and ingrowing affairs include me out. Out of bed and away we go, me hearties.

He shook Val, leaning over the soundly sleeping Henriette, her morning face none too alluring, miserable, selfish bitch. Come on, Val, no noise or undue movement, extricate yourself from this sordid aftermath of drunken lust and let's be hitting the trail.

"Oh Christ, let me sleep," Val said, twisting his face into the blankets. Reaney dressed. He returned to the bed. This time he gave Val's nose a sickening twist, smiling as he watched the cod's mouth convulse and the eyes open wide. He put his finger to his lips and nodded towards the door. Val held his nose as though he might begin crying. He levered himself up onto the pillow, swung his hairy legs over Hilary's head and with one magnificent bound was free. He dressed quickly. Two deadly gunslingers, covering each other as they backed out of the hate-filled saloon. Men can be real friends—women, well, all right for warrior's relaxation, toss a coin or two at the camp-followers and let's buckle on our dringle-drongles and yoicks. The girls slept on, having, indeed, moved close together in the bed. The two men of the world finished their dressing and reached the door. Reaney blew a silent kiss at their erstwhile passion objects, Val shuddered, and they were escaping merrily down the stairs of the strange house and on the big outside pavement.

"I think that was a night to expunge from the records," Val said as they walked towards the main road in search of a taxi in a part of West Kensington which Reaney could not immediately place. Cars under barrage balloon covers and a starkness about the streets. A veritable plethora of empty and notably unwashed milk bottles on front-door landings.

"Are you feeling weighed down by guilt?" he asked Val. It was about seven in the morning and already West Kensington rumbled with passing trucks, industrial traffic kept out of London's suaver areas by unwritten by-laws.

"I don't have guilt complexes," Val said, his clean, young man's face temporarily dusted with frowsy lines. "I'm actually guilty." Reaney felt fine. The therapy of a good roll in the midden. Only we Dr. Livingstones of the sewers know the feeling of true cleanliness. He felt perky. Val would never know he hadn't made Henriette. *That* was a terrible reflection on his virility, by Christ. Good job Thinteeth was a girl of *very* liberal ideas!

"Sir," he said to Val, looking down at him with a raised right index finger. "Sir, for a gentleman to be found in West Kensington is disreputable. For a gentleman to be found in bed in West Kensington with a common shop girl is disreputable and damnable. But for a gentleman to be found in West Kensington with two shop girls is damned unthinkable. What say you, Boswell?"

Val seemed to huddle as he walked, although it was not cold.

"I've been thinking," he said, looking with pain at a fly-posting hoarding covered by yellows, blacks, reds, advertising appearances by lesser-known beat groups at obscure clubs and halls in West London's prole quarters. "What are we looking for? Style! All last night I kept thinking how functional we've become. We like a drink, so we drink the logical way—like pigs at a trough. Sex, the same. Clothes, as near to army uniform as you can get. Speech, direct and basic. See what I'm getting at? We think we're emancipated, classless, but all we are is technicians of life. These tatty kids we're always jeering at, they're looking for a sense of style. Even Arnie is, trying to elevate life from the sheer functional level of a barrackroom."

"I see, you want to be Oscar Wilde. Surely this is the same as building a beautiful cathedral to cater for the visual sensuality of illiterate Spanish peasants? It comes a bit strange from you of all people, wanting high style at the very point in time when all these opiates are on their last legs. It's like being told that Lenin secretly dressed up in voluptuous drag and called for the priest on his death bed."

They saw Baron's Court tube station and decided to travel to Earl's Court and change there for Notting Hill Gate. The tube was mainly patronised by working-class types at that time and Reaney felt, as he had with the men in the street-diggings, slightly ashamed. How to tell them he was on their side? In theory, anyway. He suffered from pains they knew not. You fought to get away from shiny linoleum and ignorance in a Brixton backstreet, so why the hell feel guilty when you saw your old man's like? Couldn't they have fought? Why did you fight? Because you were unhappy. Why didn't they fight? Because they were happy. Therefore, they were better off than you. Maybe he'd be a father now, knees-up at Christmas, ten crates of brown and light in the back of the coach to Southend. A son doing well at school. A cheerful, indomitable wife who went out for a good old Saturday night in the saloon bar, she'd be sexy in that upper working-class way of the middle thirties, a mature London bird who didn't need stupid women's magazines to tell her how not to become a kitchen drudge. Ah yes, well thought of at the union, reads a lot, you know, got it up here, old Pete has.

Instead, he'd made it. Spends more on whisky than father earned in a week!

Brästweiber: "I cannot see why you are so unhappy about your work. Surely you have told me often enough that at least the kind of music and entertainment you promote, while not actively encouraging the development of mankind, does no positive harm? Indeed, aren't you always making a joke out of the fact that the existence of Britain's 12,000 beat groups means that there are at least 20,000 teenagers not engaged in street thuggery?"

Reaney: "It's not what it does to them. It's what is happening to me. Val here takes care of his conscience by diverting some of his crap-earnings to the communist party. I don't even have that dubious conscience salve. I don't believe in communism. I started off by laughing in the progressive manner at the Pope, as a voodoo man in his robes, a witch-doctor sanctified merely by the passage of years. Then I found I laughed at everything. I need a miracle. I don't believe in humanity because I know myself. I'm getting to a stage where I think we're actually worse than the ants. Isn't that madness—to be part of a race and yet be so cynical—or honest—that you realise the only hope for life is that this particular species—my own—is killed off with the minimum disruption of the rest of the planet's life? Isn't that the cue for a miracle? I hated Churchill, yet I cried at his funeral, because it was *real*, to do with history and a world where men died and fought, and it wasn't to do with selling rubbish on television. I look at a picture of the old guard bolsheviks, terrible, grand old men with their droopy moustaches, railwaymen maybe, who thought they were taking over on behalf of the ordinary people and all they were doing was paving the way for a terrible old peasant to have them put against a brick wall in the corner of an unvisited yard and shot, covered with lime, dead. DEAD. Gaston Dominici, the man who was supposed to have shot that British family, a terrible old peasant from the unvisited part of France . . . swop him for Stalin. Swop them all about. Men lie dead. Terrible men lie in wait, believe me. The impotent clerk waits for The Sign, on with leather boots and take revenge in a wire compound, his revenge on all the superior people, the lovely girls who sniffed, the brighter men who got the promotion."

Brästweiber: "I sense ambivalence here. Are you really horrified—or are you the impotent clerk? Why the obsession with historical horror?"

Reaney: "Can I cure myself of always being the man on the Auschwitz operating theatre, the man in the South African island prison, the girl seeing the paras plug in the flex, the man waiting for Hungarian boots? No, I can go back to my adult play-life, my escape from obsession. I am not rotting a life away in a maximum security cell. I am behaving like a normal man. I am making cash, and I try to pretend we've achieved a good life because we're all making (or thinking we're making) more cash than our daddies. Our bankrupt country is going on in great style, as solid, as safe as we're ever likely to be. Why is it I never feel like a man? Why should the funeral of an old worker-despising bastard like Churchill make me weep? I *knew* what he was, a boy playing with toy soldiers. I wanted to kick him, say, 'haven't we grown up? Do we need so-called giants? Do you insult me by saying I wouldn't have fought the Nazis under anyone else? I am finished with being a toy soldier for the Churchills and the Hitlers and the Stalins and the Napoleons and all the unbalanced neurotics you can name'. That's what I always wanted to say. I want to be a man."

Go away, Brästweiber, you embarrass me. The day comes I need a trick-cyclist I'll have my head examined. It's all lies, anyway, what I told you. Go away, there's no place for you on the Circle Line.

"By the way," Val said, as they walked from Notting Hill Gate tube station towards his loved ones, "that was a fantastic game of poker we got involved in *all night,* wasn't it? How much did *you* lose?"

Reaney had a bath while Val described to Jody how they'd played Nick the Greek in a smoky backroom with some of the slickest characters in all London. Reaney made a point of scrubbing his whole body with Jody's nail-brush. Outside the sun shone, and he whistled a cheery selection from his Gilbert and Sullivan repertoire as he rubbed the old corpse with a cold cloth. At least his white cliffs were white.

Chapter Nine

In the office Reaney found Linda with her headset on, reading a paperback which he took from her hand and dismissed with a disgusted grimace, walking into his own room with a merry cry to Felix's secretary, the gorgeous Katrina, who shared a room with the less gorgeous Miss Rimmer. He sat down behind his desk, conscious of the sharp suit, clean shirt, clean socks. The mail was on his blotting pad. First was a letter from Dorry's New York office, from Alterberg. Joe and he wrote often. They'd only met once—on a previous Dorry tour. Joe was a "good" American, small, tired, quiet—when sober.

"Hiya Pal,

Looking forward to The Arrival? The Voice is very excited. We've been visiting the drinking spots of Pennsylvania, fitting in a concert or two when there wasn't any social action. Our boy now has a travelling companion called Franks. You will find him a delight to your jaundiced old-world eyes. He looks like a gridiron rockhead, but he has a male nurse diploma. He was hired to 'help' Dorry, a shield for the sensitive artiste's easily-bruised persona. Your Scotch manufacturers may offer rewards for his urgent disappearance because he sure is a threat to their profits, Dorrywise. He is a male nurse like Jack Dempsey was a male nurse. Watch him, fella, specially if our boy tries to get you elbow-bending. Franks takes a good order, but he lacks flexibility. This is to let you know personally *what the line is on Franks. We are calling him a personal manager. The cameras will pick on him for sure. We don't even whisper the male nurse bit in the john. In the picture? I knew I could trust you, Peter, old chappie. Give my kindest regards to Alfred.*

Memorize the contents of this letter and burn it, I'm typing it myself with no copies. Dorry grossed $340,000 in twelve months through June. As he gets higher and higher he gets hotter and hotter. Funny, isn't it, a couple of old soaks like us should have took up this hyar singin' lark. If D. is anything to go by Scotch makes sweet moosick.

Felicitations from this brash American cousin,
Joe."

Joe wrote a lively letter. Comforting to think of someone else suffering the same pains in New York. It wouldn't be too difficult to find good reasons for a quick trip to New York, see the town with Joe again. Make a note to brief young Dixon on the male nurse. Efficient tycoons are men who learn to write down their problems and solve them in order of importance. Visualise your boss sitting on the crapper and you'll lose that crippling inferiority complex, would-be successful executive. Skim through the letters. *No* on this one, *file* on that, *Attention ASF* here, *stock answer* there. An unopened envelope marked *Personal and Confidential.* The writing. His hand shook as he rammed his thumb into the envelope fold and messily ripped it open. Sinking stomach doth make cowards of us all.

"Dear Peter,

I have asked a local solicitor to start divorce proceedings against you for cruelty. I am living with my parents for the present (but they did not influence me in any way). My father is going to the flat on Thursday morning to

collect everything I want, clothes and personal things,
you can keep the rest or sell it.

I am sorry things turned out the way they did and I am
also sorry that the divorce may be rather painful. You
may or may not believe me but I do hope that you will
find happiness in your future life.

Yours sincerely,
Angela."

He read it again. Not too painful, was it, little scared boy?
Rabbit sniffs air, feels safe for moment, nose keeps on twitching, ready to bolt. Well, that was eight years, that was. No
point in replying. The bitch was only trying to put across
her own version, dignified decency. Goodbye, one wife.
Goodbye, eight wasted years. Wasted for her, too, of course.
Hope you find happiness, too, dear. Well, the war's over and
the Yanks have opened the gates of Stalag XVI, but for
me it isn't the great outburst of dancing and singing I always
thought it would be. Sadness. The couple can't get close
enough to each other, she looks up at him her eyes shining,
they're still holding hands as they inspect Mr. Bravington's
engagement rings, they laugh outside at the free teaspoon
which goes with the ring, they sit on the embankment and
kiss and kiss and intend to hold tight to each other till King-
dom come and it's cruel what happens to them. What *actually* happens? He thought of a night when she lay awake
crying because he'd been flippant about some domestic nonsense or other. To hell with all that. He was free now, saved
from the brink. A wonderful world lay ahead. He could
think of things to do, join a whaling ship for the winter,
hitch-hike round an England he didn't know, learn to drive
and pick up a heap and push off for the Continent, emigrate
to America, dig out that terrible adolescent novel and see
if he could show Val a thing or two, maybe go back into

Fleet Street and carve up those drunken neurotic morons. Women, girls, lovelies, all waiting in the next bar, cool, serene beauties with new, exciting bodies.

He took the sheaf of letters into Katrina's room.

"I'm off to see a man about a body," he said, seriously, because there was a certain anonymosity between him and Katrina and he tried not to yield an inch to her in the way of idle chitter-chatter. "Miss Rimmer, if you would give me ten out of the float . . ."

He stood at the window, hands in pockets and stared down at the pavement while Miss Rimmer—bursting to point out that he'd had fifteen only two days before and wasn't this piling it on a bit thick—went through her precious cash-box ritual. Poor old dear, life had robbed her of Reaney's Universal Panacea and all she had were her teeth-hisses and petty routine. Katrina now, what was her problem? Maybe this prickly, defensive, icy pose was self-protection against dreaded sexual lustings. For him. Of course! She sweated at night thinking about him. Well, dear, I've just got free of one man-eating orchid I'm hardly likely to fall in that direction again. The luncheon-voucher moved in anthill files down below on the pavement, watched by a new, benevolent, relaxed Reaney.

He took the notes with a nod, shoving them into his hip pocket.

"Tell Alfred S. I'll give him a ring if anything spectacular happens," he said to Katrina, whose creamy face, he noticed with a surprising touch of pity, showed hardening lines round the mouth. "Bye."

Down the stairs, hands in pockets, whistling softly, a big man on a mission, possessor of secret knowledge which gave him superiority over the mass, yet a superiority which made him feel almost tender towards these jumbling, harried people. He walked in the sunshine down Regent Street, postponing the hiring of a taxi to enjoy the sensation of calm stomach muscles, looking in large shop windows, faint smile on his inner face. After the court he would probably go back to Val's house, see what the lad was planning for the evening, maybe take off himself on a cheery tour of *his* places. Even as he thought of this a faint worry crossed his mind, for what *did* a freed man do with his time after the initial razzamatazz? Old friends to look up, the pleasure of intended reconciliation with old pals, travel . . . then what? It all came back to women, didn't it? With the right woman a walk round the block was an erotic odyssey. Without a woman . . . ? Don't be vague, ask for Haig.

London passed by the window of the taxi, whose Jewish driver had fallen in with Reaney's mood, making reflective male non-jokes as Reaney gave the address, shouting mildly ferocious comments on other drivers and London traffic in general as they went round Piccadilly Circus and headed through Trafalgar Square and Whitehall for the river. Reaney crossed his left ankle on his right knee. He could feel the whip of a slight breeze off the river, a police launch pencilled a wake in mid-stream, bright new buildings stood out as if on a colour postcard. South of the river it was not so slick and glossy. The people looked scruffier than those in Regent Street, no longer crowd players for the big city technicolour glamour epic, *local* people. Reaney had known this world once. He tried not to think of himself as an escapee. All that escape and superiority business was over. Pity the old man was dead, for they could have come together now in a way they never did when he was alive. Funny, the old man had been dominated by his old woman, he was still, he supposed, dominated by his old man. That was life, people dominated by people, dominating others in turn. The domination game. Were you *ever* free? Politics, now, there was a thought. Remember those nights in small front rooms, the ward committees, Labour's foot soldiers? How the parties changed as he moved away from Brixton, from the practical men of action who wanted the Party *in* and then we could let the longhairs gabble about their fancy ideas, changing to the elderly Austrians who seemed to dominate ward committees in Earl's Court, gray-haired old gentlemen whose attention was so easily diverted to reminiscences of Dollfuss machine-gunning the Karl Marx flats. And the smoothies, more terrible when they were women, practical intellectuals who were going places, who told the young and the dissatisfied and the rebellious that the only way to reform the country was through the Labour Party and the only way to reform the Labour Party was from the inside and once you were inside—bingo, this isn't a theoretical debating society, time for ideas once we're *in*, get out on the knockers and get *me* in and you'll have done your bit for The Cause. Maybe the time was ripe for Reaney to step back into that hot little world and use his knowledge to be the first nonsmoothy, bring back a touch of old Nye, (before the Judas episode) back to the passion, away from the ambition and the relentless drive for position and self-aggrandisement. People, I am your man. Here is a letter authorising you to shoot me without fear of prosecution if ever, by foul corruption touched, I do you down as all the dirty rotten bastards who got into power in *our* name have done us down. Soak the fat boys, spread it out thin, say that in a modern accent: The Stock Exchange was abolished yesterday, one hour after we won the election. All land has been nationalised and all people own the houses they now live in. All the bombs have been defused and sunk in mid-Atlantic. Bombers are now winging their way with stock-piled wheat to India. Democratic elections are being held in every factory in the land. Vocational rehabilitation colleges are now set up to help millionaires, landlords, entrepreneurs, press lords, dukes, bishops, heirs and Graces learn trades so that they can joyfully join the fluid labour force they used to tell us so much about. All the food is hereby made free, with Food Boards being set up on the lines of water boards. Murder is still our most heinous crime, but murder of men's minds joins the list. All churches are hereby converted into schools, all church money diverted to education. Religion is still allowed—anything is allowed except exploitation of mind and body—so long as the officials of these religions follow the same pattern of life as the Carpenter they kept beating our ears about. How to sum up my programme? The Human Being Movement? People before property? Would you care, two ladies getting off the bus with your shopping bags? Or would you duck your heads in the sands as you have done before? Why, I cry into the black howl of eternal space, did our Earth life bring murder from the mud, indestructible murder-chemistry planted in the very cells? Maybe, indeed, there was or is a God, because no man with love in his heart could have with such viciousness computer-planned the senile hate that eats into our fibres. Only a God could have sunk so low. Old peasant Jehovah-Stalin, do you sit up there eating babies to the music of screams from mangled bodies? No, this wasn't madness, it came from a doubtlessly bogus welling of sentimental love for a human race whose only justification seems to be its superior ability to exploit. Ah well, let's give up politics, Reaney, that love programme of yours will require the execution of about a million people in the interests of humanity so the hell with it.

"Thanks a lot, mate," he said, handing a half-crown tip.

"Ta, guv," said the Jewish taxi-driver and even as he drove away Reaney knew the diseased motives of his liberalism, look what a good guy am I, you ain't being gassed in this country, me old matey.

A small knot of youngish men stood outside the red brick coroner's court. Judging from their scruffy hairstyles and not-quite-Bohemian clothes they were reporters. Once he'd reported an inquest in this very same South London coroner's court. All very dreary, those days. At least in his business one was concerned only with drugging young minds, not projecting human misery for mass circulation titillation. At least. One of the young men looked at him with passing interest, hand cupped over cigarette. Reaney went into the court. They wouldn't print the bloody truth if he swore an affidavit, and he was, from now on, a free man who carried no crosses for nobody.

The same narrow public benches, the same air of dusty Dickensian functionalism, the same Works Department colours, the old wood of the witness box, knots left raised above foot-planed planks. Usual representatives of the great unwashed, brown shoes, black armbands, three spades, women in black, one sobbing, the others patting her with embarrassment as the copper looks on. An older woman with a man's arm round her shoulders. That would be Mrs. Gray. Who would the man be, didn't look terribly grief-stricken? Probably the lodger, Mary's father had run away with a mother of four from the same street when Mary was about nine. Reaney wondered what they would say if they knew he knew so much about them. He watched Mrs. Gray, a woman who had done a deal with Mathie's legman, cash in exchange for silent complicity, a woman now acting out the supreme tragedy of a mother's world. They loved it. To-day, Mrs. Gray, you are no longer ordinary, unknown Mrs. Gray. You have a real life role, Grief-stricken Mother. You have Lost Your Little Loved One. Cry and weep and sob and sniffle and wail and all in public and the people will love you for it and they will care for you and hold your elbow gently and help you off buses and give you sad, sympathetic smiles and for once Ted the rogering lodger will make you a nice cuppa instead of pushing off dahn the boozah. You're queen today, Mrs. Gray, A plum part. A daughter you didn't even like had to die to give you this life-enhancing moment so make the most of it, old cow, Ted looks sickeningly healthy and it might not come again.

The young reporters slid into their allotted bench, the sleek coroner took his raised seat, and the copper-clerk read out some guff and another copper took the witness box. Dickensville, that box, with its high brown walls. The coroner now, what attracted a man to that kind of work? Listen every day to precise accounts of many splendoured death? Society, it must be admitted, catered for all tastes. Old queers sublimate in the scouts or run choirs. Hair fetishists become barbers, foot fetishists fit shoes, but what makes a man a coroner? (Or a dentist?)

". . . on forcing entry I discovered the deceased lying on the floor close to the bed. From her position I assumed she had been attempting to get out of bed and had fallen. I ascertained that she was dead . . ."

Or what, indeed, makes a man a Press Agent (we prefer the "public relations" bullshit, but it all boils down to infiltrating their stupid names into the stupid papers)? The woman was 78 years old.

"What are these scratches on your face, Constable?" asked the coroner, a smoother-looking dietician than anyone else in court.

"They were caused by the old lady's cat, sir. When I bent down to examine the deceased the cat attacked me. It was mad with hunger, sir, and subsequently had to be destroyed. Actually, it had eaten quite a lot of the deceased's face, sir."

"Thank you, Constable. Was there anything else to give some indication of how long the deceased had been dead?"

"She had stopped taking her milk in five days before the neighbours reported it, sir . . ."

Reaney watched the reporters giving each other knowing looks. Naturally they didn't bother to take notes about the cat. Couldn't let the great unwashed vomit over their sunshine breakfast foods. Old lady doesn't take in milk for five days. Lies on the floor, beating her feeble old arms feebly in the still, stale air, for a day or two. This is London, matey. Who cares? We live here to cut away the Lilliputian strings, not poke our noses into other people's business. She used to complain about noise. The other tenants weren't going to panic because she kept quiet for a few days, were they? The old bitch probably preferred her cat to any human, anyway.

". . . the woman was found on the floor of the kitchen. She seemed to have been trying to put the pan of burning fat into the kitchen sink, sir. With the help of a fireman I carried her outside. A neighbour asked me if I'd seen the children. The fireman could not gain immediate entry to the house but when the fire was brought under control a complete search was made of the house. In a cupboard in the kitchen we found the bodies of four young children. The cupboard was latched on the outside. They appeared to be unharmed by the flames. It was my deduction, sir, that the mother had put them in the cupboard when the pan went on fire and then she had been overcome by smoke. She was a Jamaican, sir."

"I know, Constable," the coroner said, and Reaney thought it was just possible there was a note of rebuke in his voice. The reporters scribbled hard during this one. We like to hear stories about stupid spades, eating catmeat sandwiches, stealing our jobs and drawing National Assistance (at the same time), running six whores, pink Cadillacs and trying to marry our daughters. It's well-known, matey. Now we've proved how dim they are. We search through this dreary procession of inquest-worthy death, misery unlimited, looking for—what? Confirmation of our prejudices? It-might-have-been-me thrills? Serves-them-right triumphs? From the slums and the bed-sitters and the streets and the sheds comes the incessant flow of last chapters, half of them so revelatory about the awful things that can happen to people that they cannot be printed in the public sheets. A good publicity job on coroners' courts, mateys, and they'd soon have ticket touts outside. Don't read second-hand stuff about Nazi doctors in the Sunday rags—come along to your friendly local death show and hear the real stuff.

An Irish dishwasher, at Stockwell tube station, had fallen between the carriages, so drunk he thought the gap was the door. Hanging head down in the deserted station, he probably yelled and struggled, but the guard was at the other end of the train, view blocked by the curve of the platform. The train moved off, the dishwasher kicked, then his hanging-down head hit an upraised obstruction. A woman standing on the platform shortly afterwards saw a face peering up at her from the rails, just where the artificial light of the platform merged with the damp blackness of the Northern Line tunnel. The body, sir, was found two hundred yards up the tunnel. The dishwasher had no known address. He had worked as a casual at a cafe for a month, but nobody there knew much about him. No traceable relatives. From papers in his pocket it was established that he had died on his birthday. Post-mortem revealed the remains of a pork pie and approximately ten pints of beer. Other distinguishing features (i.e., distinguishing him from other human beings, not ennobling him) were a cleft palate and varicose veins.

He watched the coroner making notes, trying to discover some reactions on the man's face. Reaney had not thought of his own matrimonial, sexual or occupational problems for at least an hour. Humanity was paying a heavy price to take him out of himself. Thanks, old lady, spade mother, dishwasher, you died in the Great War against Peter Reaney's narcissism. Will your deaths have been in vain? Too early to say, really. The human mind seems to have built-in shock-absorbers to cushion it from bulk horror. Mrs. Gray now, spotlighted in a series of dusty shafts of sunlight angled from high old municipal windows. Heads down, gentlemen of the press, scribble, scribble, this is the one, beat groups mentioned, might make the nationals, lads, starstruck girl bleeds to death in news cinema? He examined the latest trend of the white blotches on his nails. Not enough greens, mac. Not enough oats, mate. Gustavus conquered the world, the dishwasher drank ten pints and ate a pork pie, Angela went home to Daddy, a teenage girl wanted beating, a coroner went home to a well-laid dinner table, Mrs. Gray hammed it up in the box, poor little Mary, quite contrary, ran away from home, so did her daddy, now Mary's gone, alas like my youth, too soon. Don't listen to this guff, your honour. Is it truth you're after? I am a guilty man, I wish to reveal all. The business (as we in the business call the business) is all to do with making money out of young girls. We excite them—but we are husbands and fathers, your honour, we are not monsters. Of course, some of the lads will have their fun, like shoving lengths of hosing down their trousers to make the twelve-year-olds in the audience think they are seeing something. Does it do any harm? We always say no, your honour. We don't wage war, or hang people, or steal. We are decent blokes, really. I mean, we don't take this seriously, do we, we men of the world? Just one thing, your honour, if you want to see what we do when we're making money, book for the first house. At the second it's ten to one your seat will be wet. Yes, off-putting, I admit. But, your honour, the Mary Grays are an infinitesimal proportion of the whole. It's like Woolworths, your honour, everything's on display, the idea is that the goods *are* near, so *available*, that the shopper's basic resistance is already weakened before making a conscious decision. A very small proportion accept the invitation *too* logically—they reach and run. Mary Gray is like a shoplifter, you understand? We try to keep them apart, but the forces at work are very strong. This is why, in the business, you'll hear men like myself saying they're happier dealing with queer merchants. The girls can't tell the difference and there's not so much mess. Look at it another way, your honour, it's something in Barry Black's favour that he's normal, isn't it? The white patches on my cuticles are equidistant from the cuticles, which, if I can find out how fast nails actually grow, is a good clue to the dietary deficiencies which caused them. I could remember what I ate just before they appeared, get me? I don't think I want to hear the doctor on these details, really. It's enough to put you off sex for life. One swift insertion of the yak's hair fly-whisk and next thing a woman can be dropping out on the floor between her own legs.

Reaney bent his head and covered his eyes with his left hand and looked at his knees and at the shiny knots in the floor. It was as if the evidence about Mary Gray, her mother, the landlady, the doctor, the CID man, factual monotone, unemotional, was a message in code.

The maggot was eating into his brain again. This was where *he* was leading the people. Little, cold, dead, pathetic. She could have been engaged, starry-eyed, altared in white, pregnant, mother . . . only he had told the people about the coming of Barry Black and she had been suffered to come unto him (or he had been suffered to come into her). If it comes to that, I would have avoided the dishwasher, joked about the unmarried spade mother, probably watched the milk accumulate with the best of them.

He found his face beginning to twist, the eyes close involuntarily. Death as a result of a haemorrhage following an illegal operation, coroner's martian comments on morals of young girls, adjourned for further inquiries. Mrs. Gray stooping out of court on arm of sponging lodger, sniff back the nose-run, blink the eyes clear.

He sat in the court as the next case came on. Suicides under trains, car-drivers identifiable only by bridgework on false teeth, stillborn babies found at bottom of flatblock incinerator, the mangled, the crushed, the diseased, the starved, the demented, dancing jerkily across his brain, the city gives up its dead, I *know* now.

It has all been made clear at last.

Rejoice, ye sufferers, one has been saved from self-love. There is no God. I *know* now. My tears. They are genuine. I came to listen, to study, to earn money, to fulfil my function. It was no accident, people.

Fellow human beings, this has gone on long enough.

Chapter Ten

It was almost five o'clock when the coroner finished his last case. The fresh air helped to make Reaney feel less numb. He stood momentarily on the pavement, not knowing whether to pose as a solitary man walking in search of self-truth, or whether to leap in a taxi and head back across the blessed river to Slicksville. The youngish reporter who had taken note of him when he arrived also came down the three little steps in an undecided manner.

It seemed ordained—as in a dream—that they should speak.

"Quite a varied selection," Reaney said, nodding back at the court. The reporter had thick, almost frizzy, fairish hair. It seemed strange that a young man of his type should spend his life moving about in South London writing down little stories for the benefit of the people. Underpaid afternoons reducing humanity to slick paragraphs.

"It's always like that," the reporter said. "The good stuff is unprintable."

So that was it, all human life in a shrug. Reaney looked up and down the street. The coroner's court was in a small municipal enclave—which included a very small park and a red-brick building which he presumed was the mortuary—set down amid small shops, garages, pubs, chemists, betting shops, greengrocers, electrical fitters, builders' merchants, gents' outfitters, slashed-price supermarkets, easy-term furnishers, gents' barbers, ladies' hairdressers, probably round some corner a terrible little pet shop with a stock of faded goldfish, two budgies, one terrified rabbit and in the window a writhing litter of apparently dying kittens. But all these things presume stability, do they not? Little men creeping out of their anonymous holes to realise their ambition, every man's ambition, to have his name up before the public. Little men with flags for every possible invasion. Little men who think they're free, capitalists already.

"I used to work round here on one of the locals," Reaney said, but it was not nostalgia in his voice, only regret for the wasted years.

"I'm on the *Post*," the reporter said. "Were you related to somebody in there?"

The rising inflection, interest, possible pars, possible double-column leads, possible off-the-diary human stories, possible world scoops . . .

"Yes," said Reaney. "All of them." He walked off. He had thought of striking up a casual conversation, but he had surely learned something now. He would walk through this illustrated street map, this nostalgialess conglomeration of human nothingness, but it would not be a pose. Once, not far from these streets, he had taken part in the public humiliation of a man. Get a few exclusives for the nationals and you'll soon make the move to Fleet Street, they always said, and when the reverend gentleman upped and ran with the Sunday school teacher, wasn't it young, ruthless, intuitive Reaney who had traced them and pieced it together from neighbours and eventually forced his way into their furnished love-nest in Balham? Please give us a chance to live our own lives, the girl had said. Duty of the press, I'm sorry. Or the woman with a hundred cats? And the love life of these parts, in those glorious days of youth! The club where they all went on Friday afternoons to drink away the troubles of low wages and frustrated ambition? She was quite old, actually, in a fur coat, one of those women you find in afternoon drinking clubs in South London, they're always called Mrs. Smythe, Mrs. Something, never a husband in evidence. By eight o'clock she was a beauty and it was no trick for the high-capacity youth to buy her a drink, say what a coincidence, they got the same bus home, get on the bus, walk her home, kiss her aged face in the shadow of a South Norwood hedge, work her up to the just one coffee, mind, stage, of course I loves yer, age shall not come between us, into the doggy hall, a coffee, a fiftyish widow reborn to the thrills of courtship, a barnyard cockerel looking for flesh, a kiss, an armchair, the floor, a threadbare carpet and a leaping dog that wanted company, and the mask of powder worn off to reveal the lines and the knocking at the door, my God, it's my son come home early, he'll kill you, of course, the son is thirty-bloody-six, and helpless laughter as he fastened his flies in the little back area and climbed on a dustbin to reach the top of the garden wall. Crash on the pavement, hurry off into the night, what a story to tell the other young cockerels.

The reporter caught up with Reaney.

"Excuse me," he said, ingratiating, plausible, disarming, slimy. "I didn't quite understand what you said. Which particular inquest were you here for?"

Cheap clothes in a nasty window light, all the stock's on display, a rotten plum on the pavement, prices slashed, we've lost our lease, buy now, fantastic bargains, strong youths jostling home from work, tea, wash, out into the adventure of the night, the adventure always in prospect, never experienced. A man who earned his crust by hanging about, asking questions, printing iceberg-tip "stories", a man trying to walk away from all this. Maybe he shouldn't walk away . . .

"I was joking," he told the young man. "I'm not related to

anybody. I was just passing, wondered if inquests were still as horrible as when I was a reporter."

"Is it all right to ask you what you do now?"

Scramble for the bus, people. Life's too short to stop and think what it's *for*. A black driver, eh? You see, our second-class citizens are beginning to rise in the world. Their children will have English accents. A gradual process, my black friend. We English will accept anything if it comes slowly enough, even justice.

"I'm a company director," he said. "Isn't everybody?"

"What sort of business?"

They were at a corner now, a pub corner. To go in or not to go in, the story of his life. In *there* you forgot all *this*. He saw, wonder of wonders, a cruising taxi. He walked to the gutter and waved at the driver. The reporter followed.

"You don't have time for a drink then?" he said.

"No, I'm short of time," Reaney replied. The taxi pulled in to the pavement. In these streets the man who hailed a taxi was of interest, for this was London Transport territory. They probably thought, those ill-clad people, that the big man in the sharp suit was a bookie or a gangster, one of the aristocracy certainly. Where to go?

"Regent Street, please," he told the driver.

"I've a feeling you are somebody," the reporter said, crowding close as Reaney opened the door.

"Aren't we all?" He got in, sat down, reached to pull the door.

"But who *are* you?" the reporter asked. Reaney wondered if women, any woman, could fondle a man with frizzy fair hair and dandruff. He looked the young reporter in the eyes, holding the door open for a moment:

"That's what I'm trying to find out."

He looked back through the darkened rear window. The reporter was watching the taxi go away. Other cars obscured Reaney's view. It all depended where you stood. Perspectives, you know. Cut to eyes of man seeing taxi grow smaller, cut to man in taxi being borne away from it all, cut back, does "it all" still go on when you leave? Tomorrow's *dance macabre* would go on, but would anyone sit at the back of the court and bleed?

Reaney let himself into the office. There had been moments when the office floor, after hours, had seen more of the action than a Paddington whorehouse, but now, in the shadows, quiet, it was a funny little place. He turned on his own delayed-action neon tube, hung his jacket over his padded, swivel chair, sat down. If he didn't do something now he never would, he'd go out there and start off again on the old rampage. He opened a drawer to find some flimsy. He saw the corner of a newspaper cutting. He lifted papers to see what it was. Oh yes, Reaney's Revenge. What had he had in store for the poor old dear before he began at last, after all those years (my God, if anyone else knew about this they'd say he *was* mad), to tire of tormenting the old bitch? . . . his own insanity lay before him, reply coupons culled from all sources, sent off (for the last ten or eleven years) in the name of Mrs. Pugh, notorious Welsh landlady of Earl's Court, an evil old bitch who had evicted Reaney and Charlie Hughes in provocative circumstances (a party, one of those where some clown thought it was a good joke to pour wine into the telephone) and who must have become, in the eleven intervening years, the woman on whose door more salesmen knocked, and through whose letter-box more circulars, brochures, pamphlets and details popped, than any other man, woman or child in the western world. Embarrassed, he tore up the remaining coupons and dropped them in his metal waste-bucket. He sat, thinking of those days. Charlie was last heard of emigrating to Australia. Angela never had liked him, but then, which of his old gang did she like? Twilight of the gods, he said, looking over his shoulder at the great expanse of darkening blue sky under which mighty London was but a speck of dust. He decided to write to Angela.

". . . I am also very, very sorry. Your going away that night was, perhaps, a shock that I needed. I am glad you have seen a solicitor for there is certainly no possible point in us ever even contemplating seeing each other. It was probably all my fault, and I don't want to make any excuses. I'd be happy, however, if I thought you really were convinced that we were just two unlucky people who found we'd married the wrong partners. I am sorry for all the pain I caused you, really I am. I wish I could take it all back. I am not just pretending now. I . . ."

He finished the letter hurriedly, noticing how the big I-I dominated the lines. Of course it was her bloody fault. Nagging bitch. He typed her parents' address on the envelope.

It was very quiet. Outside the dull rumble of London, not specific noises, just the never-ending sound of a human city in movement, rose up past his window, and he wondered how far into the sky this gulf stream of London noise reached before it was blasted off into all space by howling winds. He put another sheet in the portable and typed on the top left, *Dear Alfred,* then sat, hunched over the machine, waiting to determine his own emotions.

"I was at the inquest on our departed fan this afternoon and frankly I came away sickened. I have decided that whatever else I may be, I am not going to be involved with the likes of Barry Black and all the other assorted personality defects we call clients. I wish to resign from the firm, relinquishing my directorship, and to sell back to you the shares you have been kind enough in

the past to vote me. I am not saying that what we do in
this office is wrong, just that I no longer want to be part
of it. I am writing this not as a cowardly way out, but
merely to make it formal, so that I cannot be talked out of
it in the morning. I am sure you will understand . . ."

He typed the envelope, sealed it, then looked at it, white
and neat. He put it down on the blotter. It wasn't a declara-
tion of independence. It was a plea for another chance. The
grave was waiting for him, too. Getting nearer. All he could
do was run. Where? Anywhere. He was fat and heavy and
tired in a success room high above a success street and all
he felt was a threat of tears. One moment looking back
through the reversed telescope of memory, he was young
again, walking quickly through inviting streets, starting out
on the adventure and the next moment he was in this darkening room, half way house of the whole adventure now
turned from anticipation to dread. These summer nights in
parks, in Naafis, in the exciting new world of pubs, going
with the boys to the doggies, to the football, teatime clean
up, waiting for girls, knowing that life ahead was to be an
eternity of new days, new pleasures; a small boy plays football in a public park, tomorrow the big treat of a day at
Hastings, today the big man, seen it all, the treats forgotten,
only the grind grind GRIND of a stomach that says worry,
worry. Once the pleasures, now the needs. Somewhere out
there a man and a woman who lived more vividly each day
in memory turning slowly to wet earth. Go back to streets
where a small boy was totally forgotten—and there was nobody to remember. Look for a girl called Barbara and ask
her, do you remember *me*, Barbara? Only the face and the
body have changed, I still want to meet you tomorrow
night, to wait in anguish at the Town Hall corner. Where
did I make the mistake, Barbara? I sit in this room of black

leather and stale tobacco and I can smell your perfume, I can turn on tears, a sweet agony of memory lurking at the back of my head, the torture of what it might have been, instead of the dreary hell it is. Can I not snap my magic fingers to end this misty dream, which is reality, and stop this stupid nonsense of two real people turning to wet earth when they should be back by the fire in Mandrell Road waiting for *me* to come home? Run to the tube, Northern Line to Clapham North, run, run, home, home. But it's too late. Wet earth claims more of us every day, crash, mangle, crush, poison, every day some more gone who might remember and the new ones who'll never know what I was. Slipping into the grave, the man who never really lived. Stop, for Christ's sake, Reaney, get among people quickly, man, before you go over the edge. He put the envelope in his pocket. He picked up the outside line and dialled Val's number. Jody answered.

"It's Peter," he said. "I'm still at the office believe it or not."

"Having a quick one on the floor?" Jody said.

"I wish I was."

"Well, I know you don't want to speak to the dreary wife. Val went up your way about an hour ago. He said he had to meet somebody from television in some club, he said you'd know which one if you phoned."

"Yeah, I know it."

"Listen, while we've got a chance for two quiet words, what are you doing about Angela?"

"Angela? Nothing. She's seen a lawyer. She wrote me a letter today, said it's final and all that. Why?"

"I wondered. What about your flat?"

"The hell with the flat. I never want to even see South Ken again. Maybe I can get somebody to go down there and clear out the stuff. That's the least of my troubles."

"I can imagine. Well, I don't suppose you'll be too drunk by closing time, try not to start a riot when you come home. Bye bye."

Bye, bye. Home, to the lodger's room! He locked up and walked down Regent Street, noting with some contempt that despite all the day's revelations, he was already quite excited at the prospect of walking in on Val and the New Scheherazade mob. But this could be the body's doing. The first sign of alcoholism? The body is used to the shock. It now needs the shock. Today a booze-up, tomorrow the heavy social stuff, the next day, shriek of my fears into that great purple sky as I crash about my cheap hotel room screaming for more drink, bottles empty, quarts of light, triangles of whisky, white gin labels, try perfume, lavatory disinfectant, anything, give me another drink, slobber it over my lips, put it down my flabby chest, just another drink, be vague, *anything*.

In the club, standing in a semi-circle round the bar, Reaney found, to his surprise, a group which included Felix. There was also Val, and that girl with Goddings from the other night, what was her name, and Goddings, and Seldom Seen Fred—as Reaney had labelled Kelsey, a song plugger, on some forgotten joking day. And, well, well, that was why Felix was taking a night off from the azaleas, Mister Big himself, the Tsar of all the Tam Ratings, Reaney's favourite hate figure, Teapot Dome, which was the nickname *he* (oh yes, there was a time when he had revelled in all this and had seen himself as a poor man's Runyon of the scene) had given to the tall, drooping-faced man with the smoothly brushed graying hair and the pencil-line twentyish moustache. His real name was Pemberton Mobley. He was the big wheel of Commercial's light entertainment mess. Drinkies, Pemberton, one of my chaps has an idea, can't do any harm to hear what you think of it, have a noggin or two anyway, love to.

They'd obviously said all there was to say about Val's brilliant idea for Barry Black's *own show*, and now Seldom Seen Fred and Goddings were jousting in the heats of the heard-this-one stakes, as Reaney could see instantly from the placing of heads as he approached the group.

"Hello, Peter," Felix said, warmly.

"Hello, Reaney," said Pemberton Mobley, graciously. When Reaney had first met the bastard he was somebody's bumboy in a film company known to the trade as Bumph Inc. This year he was dressing like the rat on its way to a carnival and speaking like the Delphic Oracle, which was how Reaney considered tv life went, pompous con-men hiding infantile yearnings behind sixty guinea suits.

"Hello," he said, quite formally. "Hiya"—to Val. Nods to Jolly Jack and Seldom Seen Fred. A smile full of artificial surprise as he pretended to recognise the girl. He sensed that Pemberton Mobley would shortly be taking off for less sweaty surroundings. He affected a distaste for low jokes. Reaney found, in his company, that he liked them, the filthier and less witty the better. Pemberton Mobley got his dirty laughs from daily dealings with his ulcerated staff, his illicit thrills from playing puppet-master to eagerly cringing artistes.

It was Seldom Seen Fred's turn. The borrowed nickname suited him only when you were paying for his services. Otherwise he was every bloody where.

". . . this little bird's sitting in class when the teacher sees a pool of water spreading out, under her chair. Brenda, she says, all disgusted like, why didn't you put your hand up? I did miss, says Brenda, but it came through my fingers . . ."

Jolly Jack laughs the statutory two seconds (joke tellers,

Reaney had long since realised, didn't find jokes funny at all: they liked the technique: they were true folk artistes, uncommercialised, almost innocent in their grubbiness. Tot shows dropping proudly to Mum). Jolly Jack commands, by his raised hands and angled head, attention. He starts joke, but Felix senses mood of Pemberton Mobley and they change the angles of their bodies so that without moving their feet they have left the group. It was, of course, Val who bought the actual drinks, although Pemberton had said, loudly, that it was his shout.

Reaney felt better with a whole pint inside him. He was relaxed. Now to explore the possibilities of this exciting little lay gathering.

"Well, Pemberton," he said, moving in close, "you're doing your annual bit of slumming I see."

Pemberton Mobley felt to see if his pencil-thin moustache was still in position.

"Always a pleasure to come down from the clouds and see the picture from new perspectives," he said. Reaney actually liked, no, enjoyed Pemberton. He had put on new coats of arrogance and pretence since they'd first met, but it was still possible to budge him into a self-mocking grin. Just as there must have been *somebody* who was allowed to remind Stalin of the good old days. Or was there? That was why he'd had them all embalmed in lime.

"Pemberton thinks there might be something in our idea for Barry Black," Felix said. Big men, sipping necessary drinks, successful men who rationed their minutes.

"I should think he would," Reaney said, in mock indignation. "He's got the best taste for crap in the network. That's why they keep promoting you, isn't it, my good man?"

Pemberton laughed, or allowed his upper lip to curl just enough to reveal his teeth.

"You should get on one of these BBC programmes, Peter, I've always said that," he replied. "You've got just the right kind of bitchy non-wit they go for. I'm sure there's a fortune waiting for the next Gilbert Harding. You've got the weight for it."

Reaney thought of the court. Roll on, great march of misery, scream your miserable ends away in the dark.

"Some day they'll storm your citadels and tear you smooth-suited reptiles to pieces, a frenzied mob of maddened viewers," he said. "Worse, they may even sentence you to hard labour for life watching your own programmes."

Felix obviously sensed that he was edging towards a non-humorous area. He shifted his feet and changed the subject.

"Is it true what I hear, that your budgets are being cut again this year?"

Pemberton toyed with his Cinzano. He cleared his throat and addressed the hall:

"They attack people like me because we don't give them intellectual programmes, but if only they knew the battle people like me, serious TV people who know what this medium can do, have inside. Sometimes I feel that we are thought of by the companies as mere time-filling machines, churning out pulp to bridge the gaps between the commercials. It's a matter of fighting inch by inch for what we believe in. Criticise the programmes by all means, but believe me, if there weren't a whole lot of decent, dedicated creative minds working in TV, you would really see a triumph for the forces of ignorance."

"Ballocks," said Reaney. "Of course you're only there to fill in time between the commercials. Christ, Pemberton, don't say you're even beginning to believe all that turgid bullshit? For God's sake, let's be honest among ourselves even if we go on kidding the great unwashed."

Pemberton shrugged. Reaney decided that this was an

historic occasion. He had actually witnessed a point in time when a man—Click!—was finally brainwashed. Or was it the moment in time, trapped for eternity in amber, when he finally freed himself from the last trace of self-delusion? For Felix's sake, he decided to ease things a bit.

"However, I must say, Pemberton old fellow, you're the only stuffed shirt in the whole racket who can still take a joke. There's hope for you yet."

Pemberton laughed, and Felix followed suit, looking relieved. Reaney noted that Val was making good time with the girl, what was her name, it went with the broad face? The letter in his pocket. Go on, give it to him now. Cowardy cowardy custard. Then Pemberton said he had to push on to see some dreary Americans at the Hilton and Felix said he was off, too, and Reaney had the letter in his hand.

"I'd like you to read this letter," he said to Felix. Then the bony nicotined hand was slipping inside the jacket and the white envelope was lost to Reaney's view. Ah well, nobody could make the accusation, least of all himself, that he had done it in drink. They went off. The group closed up. Reaney called for drinks, beaming all over Cyn as she took his money, giving her decadent hand a squeeze. He decided to call Cyn back and ordered an extra double whisky, for himself. He only wanted to catch up with the others, nothing so hellish as being more sober than other people, dangerous in that it gave you the idea *every* night was as pointlessly dull, stupid and infantile. He drank the whisky in one breath-catching swallow. Then he buried his lips into the pint.

Now we have the scene where young ambitious girl stands in circle of older men. They kid her, play up to her, actors playing jolly uncles, roguish fathers, understanding brothers, just waiting to trap little sister, whereupon the mask is whipped off to reveal the face of cruel lust. For the flesh, that's what it is. The flesh, soon to be crippled and bruised and minced, needs other flesh. But the girl is no bride of Christ. She knows where she, in her completely self-devoted, narrow little mind, is going. Which man can help in the great cause of helping her? This is a great cause. It is all she knows. Yesterday, dressed in mummy's frocks, she flaunted and turned before a mirror, today she's mature of body but her grasping, self-wrapped soul yearns to dress up again, to be the pampered little girl again, with grown ups loving her, loving her, loving her. Who is to be trusted in this laboratory breeding cage? Like the mouse who volunteered for space research because he was tired of cancer. Why? Human rats sniffing, nibbling, twitching—rat hairs on end, minute screams, gradual love, love, love *for the shock.* Into Subject Reaney's brain they wove their delicate gold wires and soon the white-coated rats looked in amazement at the computer's blotted English, each maniac scientist suddenly aware that his own private writhings were shared by Subject Reaney, looking at his fellow torquemadas with dawning awareness that all this secrecy was for nothing, we all had this bubbling mud-beach at the bottoms of our brains, good night, mad Reaney, obliterate this gold-wire slime-carrier, he threatens us all in the safety of our sterilised rat playpens. Felix would definitely think he was daft when he read the letter, but that, Alfred S., is only the tiniest melt-drop on the tip of the tiniest icicle on the tip of the tenth of the iceberg. And as that is what we see above the surface, guess what the other nine tenths are like? Ghostly screams of a primeval prime-evil nature fill the bone-carpeted dungeons. Reaney shook himself. At least in the nursery level madness of the New Scheherazade one was safe, temporarily, from the greater, all-consuming madness of the mighty machine outside. Temporarily. They had their jokes in Belsen, too, you know, the pyjama-clad stick-humans. It's a debatable point as to which of them, the blonde girl with the solid cheekbones, or the fawning men, was more to be feared, but it seemed uglier in a woman.

She had all the attributes. Fair hair (is it naturally blonde? Yes, well why did you dye the roots black?) three hundredweight of dark green eye-shadow, tits like Forth Bridge spans, an arse like two cats in a sack (they all turned to watch as she went to "spend a penny"). Did she have a good voice? Almost all human beings have good voices. Only a few are so tone deaf that they can't string two notes together. But only a tiny minority are obsessed with the need to dress up in mummy's dresses. Quite shaggable, too, actually. At this time in a drinking club Syphilitic Sal would look shaggable, mac. In the morning she'll be a real case of the galloping Helena Rubinsteins. Val was making good time with her, she kept laughing louder at him than at the other two. He had little chance. He felt bitterly rejected. He took the next two or three pints with a gloomy face, which the men ignored. There was a certain dignity in standing back from the ring of hungry wolves, he supposed. Notice in films how male stars never chase girls, always vicky verky? That's me in the mirror, stranger, name of Reaney, hired gun in from Tucson, go on, reach for it, stranger, I don't tote this hardware for fun.

"Hey, what's wrong with buggerlugs then?" Goddings asked. Soon he had allowed himself to be drawn back into the circle.

"I think you're a woman hater," the girl said. He blinked so that he could determine the expression, if any, on her encrusted features.

"A woman hater?" said Seldom Seen Fred Kelsey. "Like Lloyd George, you mean?" No, that wasn't sharp enough. He came up with another. "He's a woman hater like Casanova was a woman hater."

"Anybody with the slightest acquaintance with the works of Sigmund Freud knows that that is exactly what Casanova was," Reaney said, magisterially. The girl smiled, or rather her facial crust cracked in different directions.

"Maybe Pete will deign to handle your publicity," Val suggested. "Maggie's been telling us she's a sex singer."

"Oh yes," said Reaney, George Sanders to the core. "If I may ask, which sex?"

He was on his way now, all right. The way it worked with men and women was this: Men chase a woman: She rejects them: They save face by calling her a whore. The girl called Maggie smiled. Reaney wondered if that kind of make-up might come off in one (as King James the First was supposed to be proud of his ability to peel an orange with one hand, keeping the peel in one piece) if he got his fingers under the edge and lifted.

"Tell me," she said. "Do you drink to forget or because you've nothing to remember?"

Easy to get laughs from a bunch of half-sloshed jackals, my dear.

"I spill more than I drink," he said. Laughs all round. Friendliness restored, Reaney willing to offer himself, power through submission.

"Would you do my publicity?" Maggie asked.

"I don't think so," he said. "I'm practically—pardon—finished with it all. Publicity, lubricity, what's it all about, eh? How did a nice girl like you get into a racket like this?"

"You make it sound like whoring," she said.

"All show business is a form of whoring," he said. "At least whores let you touch them for the money. Show business is respectable prick teasing. Ask these esteemed gentlemen, they'll bear me up, hey isn't it correct that most fan mail for instance, is unpublished filth?"

Jolly Jack had many obscene facts to relate on this score.

Reaney was silent for a while. A new thought? All over the city there were men who knew a little secret or two. This man knew that actresses often get little lumps of human excrement in the post. Another knows how many incurable venereal maniacs there are in locked wards in Surrey hospitals. Another can recite a list of household names who happen to be raving alcoholics. Here and there, everywhere, little secrets. But what about the Great Secret Collector who one day will know them all? Suppose he pieced all the secrets into a Central Office of Information booklet? They'd ban it, of course. We must protect us people from our own secrets.

Later Cynthia seemed to have disappeared and he had his elbows on the bar. The girl was beside him. Goddings was chatting to some blokes he didn't know. Val had changed ten bob for tanners which he was feeding into the bandit. Seldom Seen Kelsey was somewhere around. Reaney opened his fingers to let a shower of coins fall on the shiny black bar. Still no Cynthia.

"What'll you have, Maggie?" he asked. "This fucking club —I beg your pardon—this bloody club gets like the Marie bloody Celeste when you want serving. What's your other name, Maggie? Mine's Reaney. Hey Cynthia, where the hell's the service around here? Yeah, Reaney. Insidious sort of name, don't you think, eh? Insidious, that's Reaney. Preeny, tweeny, sort of thin oil I always think."

"Isn't it Irish?"

"It is, I'm not. How about that? SHOP. Hallo, you terrible woman, where've you been all night, men are dying of thirst out here. What's it, Maggie? A pint for me, Cyn dahling, and, what's that, Maggie?"

"Gin and ice and pineapple, please."

"All in the same glass? Jesus wept, you ever been asked

for that before, Cyn? I should think you haven't, you bold thing."

Goddings returned. He wanted Maggie back again. Reaney bought him a drink. As he handed it to Goddings, he leaned down beside the thin-faced man's left ear.

"Isn't it time you went home, Jolly Jack?" he murmured. He winked as he straightened up. If the bastard didn't take the hint he'd make a big fist of his right hand and shove it in his face and ask him where, exactly, he wanted it. Heydey hey, chaps, Reaney's on a rampage night.

Some time later Reaney watched Goddings leave, conscious that there had been some kind of unpleasantness.

"There he goes, your manager," Val said to Maggie, waving in the direction of the door. "Out he stumbles into the Soho night, lurching off into God-knows what scenes of paralytic stupidity, vomit dribbling out of the corner of his mouth. And that's when he's sober."

Reaney found this extremely amusing. He roared with laughter. He banged Val on the back, a little too strenuously.

It was all fun and friends. Revels. Power through best bitter. Reaney, man of our time. Action. A camera whirls in a 360 degree rapid turn of blurred pictures, people, bars, glasses, lights, cars, streets. Cut. The great weight of the cathedral towered above him, dark and massive, a triangle of warm light thrown on the pavement from a small door set under a low arched entrance. Walking slowly, he went through the door, into the great vault. He had been there before when the sun was diffused through tall stained glass windows high above the saints' statues. He would kneel at the great altar, like a Crusader praying all night, forehead on sword. Pray for peace. The expected hand on the shoulder. Follow me, my son, we are glad that you are here, a candle flickers over a stone wall and shadows of a thousand years dance over smooth-worn stone flags. Yes, I have made the decision, under this great vaulted arch, a tiny being, take me to the cells of peace, low arches, cold corridors, stone tunnels, iron doors staggering open, to the small, white-washed room where the sheets were coarse, clean, cold, the blankets of woven wool, smelling of pale flowers. He had known, there would be a pitcher of water. It was cool and safe and he slept in joy. Then the hands. I am a mere novice, it is my first morning, let me rest on this first morning, tomorrow I will rise in the early dawn for prayers but this first morning let me sleep.

"What are you mumbling about?"

A red, candle-wick dressing-gown. He noticed that as his eyes opened. A blonde girl. Looking down. A mug of coffee pushed close to his face.

"Hello, hello," he said. "What am I doing here, wherever this is?"

He raised his head. The walls were completely unfamiliar. It's a wise man who knows whose bedroom he wakes up in.

Chapter Eleven

She straightened up, pushing hair back from her eyes with her fist. No make-up. Square, pale face, largish head. Pale blue eyes. Regency striped wall-paper, light gray carpet, a bogus-looking abstract. He was wearing his socks, shirt and underpants. She sat on the end of the bed, looking at him. He eased himself onto his right elbow and lip-tested the coffee.

"I feel great," he said, the first words to come into his head. He felt ill and excited at the same time. Always did. He drank for the hangovers, "I don't remember getting here."

"No?" she said. "That's very convenient for you, isn't it?"

"Oh yeah? Was it that bad?"

"I've seen worse. You were upset because I wouldn't sleep with you. You kept running into my room." She did not appear very angry. He smiled and risked some coffee.

"Indecent exposure in front of young girls, eh? That's a sign of middle age if you like. I trust you didn't see anything that shocked you."

She raised an eyebrow. She was wearing a man's red silk dressing-gown. It fell away at the neck to reveal the usual swellings. He felt quite hilarious. Cuddly-bear head, honest blue eyes, gone the muck and the artifice. A different girl altogether. She sits at the crossroads of her life. Will it be mascara and expensive abortions for show biz great Maggie? Or will she marry the boy next door and give up fame for babies? Or will she slump in a news cinema while the rabbits and cats and canaries and bears leap and prance and the blood goes drip-drip-drip onto a public carpet?

"I see myself as a debauchee's debauchee," he said. "A satyr's satyr, a despoiler of virgins *en masse*, a devil about whom Aleisteir Crowley would have said 'This is going too far'. My mind is a wide-screen panavision infernorama. At this moment I fester with images of you and I mingling our flesh in every position known to the sex-priests of the most ancient and obscene Indian religions." Did he actually say all that to her? She was a very self-possessed girl. She drank her coffee. Her hand was useful, square.

"Last night you kept on about cities being machines that feed on people," she said, smiling. Men will have their little thoughts, won't they? "I couldn't make head or tail of it."

No, she wouldn't, for the prime requirement of her ambition is a ruthless, one hundred per cent devotion to self.

"All actresses are failed women," he said. "And no real man would ever disport himself in public. Did I tell you that as well?"

"You were gabbling on so much I lost track. I like listening to people, actually. I think it's the only way to learn, don't you?"

"It depends," he said. "How about passing me whatever crumpled remnants of fags there are in my jacket and we'll turn ourselves on, nicotine-wise."

She fished in his pockets, producing a sat-upon packet of Piccadilly Tipped. He watched her move, solid hip-buttock buttresses filling out the dressing-gown. His flaw was that his appeal—there must be *some* appeal or he wouldn't be here—was to their sense of humour. Terrible thing to realise, women only agree to a quick wrestle in bed because they think you're a bit of a laugh. She held her flattened cigarette as if it was her first, between the middle fingers of her right hand, eyes screwed up. Gene Kelly once said the test of a real dancer was to do it smoking. Whatever happened to Gene Kelly's musicals?

"Did you really write your resignation yesterday?" she asked. He wanted violent lust and here they were, gabbling like a comfortably married couple. It was ridiculous. They'd reached the bed-chatting stage in one leap, cheating him of bruising passion. Stop. Withdraw five paces. Start again. I'm not a fairy. I don't make *friends* of women.

"I did indeed. I may become the new Schweitzer. It's funny, we cross on the time graph as you are entering the great world of reality. I found God in a star-to-be's boudoir."

To make love to her would be to accept that daft little world's stupid conceptions all over again. He had found a measure of truth, and it had to be preserved from the delusion of love-making. Today he had an idea. How to start.

"You kept telling me to marry the boy next door and forget I'm a singer," she said. "You're a bit crazy when it comes to this business, aren't you?"

"*I'm* crazy? Why are you so obsessed with the colour problem, says the wasp millionaire to the nigra shoeshine kid? The class war is over, says a million-acre-owning Prime Minister. I'm obsessed because it is there, like Everest."

As he explained about wasps, he thought that Brästweiber would be watching and nodding cynically. The trouble with you, Reaney, is that you don't even sound honest to yourself when you're telling the truth. Dr. Dichter taught Madison Avenue to sell the sizzle not the steak and Dr. Goebbels sold the sizzle not the gas ovens, but compared to Dr. Reaney these were cherry tree choppers. Her comment on the conclusion of the wasp dissertation was that she would love to go to America, "even for a holiday". Reaney realised that she already saw herself on the Ed Sullivan show.

"Would you like me to wash your shirt?" she asked. "It would be dry in an hour if I put it in front of the gas fire."

Well, that would be nice and cosy. Why wasn't she ripping into his naked flesh with scarlet talons, burning her initials on his bare arm with a cigarette end, spurning his prostrate body with a rapier heel? Or vice versa.

"Listen, Maggie, what's wrong with you anyway?" he found himself asking. "Last night you were going at me like it was Insult Week or something. Your mush was like a technicolour cement factory. If anybody had asked me I'd have said there she goes, mate, the original hard-faced show biz pusher." Talk, talk, talk. It is all unreal. Out there is real. Real pain. Real people being tortured.

(Note from Dr. Brästweiber: Subject Reaney is in a situation where he has to show active male aggression if he is to have sexual relations with the girl. His ideal situation is one in which a masterful woman takes all the initiative. Without close study of the subject, one can only postulate, from the girl's manner, that she requires an aggressive and positive man. People like this, if matched, have every reason to feel that the cookie has crumbled most unfortunately.)

"You think you know everything, don't you?" she said. "Take off your shirt and I'll wash it in the bathroom. You don't have to get up. That's my friend's bed you're in. She's gone home for the week."

She left. Reaney sank down into the bed. Through the window he could see chimneys. He still didn't know what part of London he was in. Operating at 110 per cent power in a hangover it was easy to accept the situation. But what would he be thinking of in four or five hours when the booze had worn off? What sort of bird was this Maggie, anyway? There must be an angle here somewhere, Marlowe. Tall, suave Philip Reaney lies back in strange bed and clasps hands behind head. What is the secret of the cool, mysterious, beautiful Maggie? No, not furs and a belting from the other bloke. We banned that one to make sure it would be more widely read. You see, we mandarin class of the power elite realised just around the end of the Second World War (yes, we were agitated by the surprising defeat of our front man Churchill) that long term research was vital. Television we saw as a short term answer. No, what we needed went deeper than that. So we hit on masochism for the masses. Now, a lot of our own chaps were bitten by the bug at school, but for the masses we realised that the cane in the hands of a man would never become a sex symbol. And so we banned a few trashy but still fairly erotic (to a dull mind) works, which was guaranteed to make them desirable reading matter in the minds of males who normally would read only the sports pages of cheap newspapers. We promulgated the idea in films and plays. By the 1970's I doubt if there were fewer than 8,000 whores in West London alone catering for masochism. I used to sit in the club of an evening thinking of all those ghastly little bedrooms with those ghastly females swishing canes, swinging whips, chaining, tramping, lashing, binding and beating and I used to shudder. Still, we achieved our purpose. You think I'm being far-fetched, Montmorency? You may laugh. Our psychiatrists told us it worked. Men with that sort of guilt on their minds don't rush out and look for trouble, I can tell you. They keep damned quiet, sir, damned quiet. We could tell from the voting figures. A man gets obsessed with ghastly tricks like *that* and the only way he can rationalise his fears is by a defence-mechanism. The more a man thinks he is mentally breaking up the stronger he is for law and order, discipline, obedience. All he has left to cling to is what he knows. Some damned Socialist Johnny comes along telling him about challenges and adventures and changes and he's frightened out of his wits. Mind you, we had our set-backs. That fellow, what was his name again, yes, Reaney, that's right, Wat Reaney. A throw back, of course. An out and out sadist, sir, right under the very noses of our whole set-up. He'd made his money and kept it pretty quiet, of course. If he'd been content to keep it quiet we would probably never have touched him, but to buy London Zoo and turn it into nothing less than a—well! Impudence. You know, he advertised in newspapers quite openly. I forget the wording, something like *Women of England, are you tired of wearing the trousers? Do you yearn to be treated savagely, brutally, by a* real *man?* You know, Montmorency, I read that file and I was shocked, yes sir, shocked. These women were paying this Wat Reaney one hundred pounds a week to be locked up in cages in the Zoo. He treated them like dirt. Oh, I won't go into all the ramifications, believe me, it was damned messy. *Legally* there was nothing we could do, was there? They were paying him for the privilege. When we sent chaps up there to question them not one wanted to leave. Not one. Fella had them eating out his hand. Women from good families, too, I may say. Naturally, we couldn't let him go on. The whole country would have got to hear about it. These brain fellas, they said it was such an explosive idea it might undo all the work of ten years. It could have led to a complete swing the other way, just as we estimated that well over half the male adult population was so masochistically brain-washed it was ready to vote against *anything* that looked like radicalism. *Anything.* What did we do? Well, Monty, old chap, I can't say I'm proud of the method, but we had to think of the country as a whole. We arranged a surprise for Wat Reaney, yes, a very large surprise. One evening when he was doing his tour of the place he was due to pay a call on what used to be the polar bear enclosure. It was dark, and I daresay the fella was tipsy. He must have had a terrible moment when he found he was in a damned cage with polar bears and not four bank managers' wives. Quite a shock. Ah well. The Universal Mind allowed itself a self-indulgent smirk. Since The Universal Mind had returned from Paris—how long ago was that now, three million beer years?—great truths had been put to him, great layers had been ripped from his awareness, and as long as the imagery didn't run to Peer Gynt ripping off onion layers to find that it had no heart, it was all part of a pattern.

He had seen. He knew.

Seeing and knowing didn't make him, personally, any happier.

In fact, they made him downright depressive.

But personal happiness was nothing.

His happiness would come in doing something about It All.

THE CITY IS EVIL. WE HAVE BEEN FOOLED. WE HAVE BUILT *Their* PYRAMID.

IT IS TO *Their* GLORY. THE BUILDINGS ARE *Theirs*.

THE BIGGER THE BUILDINGS, THE BIGGER THE CITY, THE BIGGER THE PYRAMID, THE SMALLER ARE WE.

they made us ants.

it was *deliberate*.

the bastards *deserve* to die.

but who the hell *are* they?

they are *not* Mary Gray.

they are not *me*.

HAM BURGER, D.A.: "TO YOUR KNOWLEDGE, MISTER REANEY, HAVE YOU EVER HELPED THEM??????"

PERRY MASON'S OBVIOUSLY INNOCENT CLIENT: "YESYESYES-YESYESYESIAMASGUILTYASALLHELL.

inasmuch as I saw evil and preserved my own fat.

inasmuch as I connived in the purposes of men who see other men as objects.

inasmuch as I blamed the system, other man, lazy men,
corrupt men, exploiters, sadists, dictators.

inasmuch as they were all me.

Reaney decided his feet needed a good wash as he placed
them on the mat by the side of the bed which belonged to
the friend of Maggie.

As he traced his missing objects of apparel he noted the
general atmosphere of the flat. Men living without women,
he had always known, tend to create a state of unmitigated
filth. Women living without men produce a silly, almost pathetic look in their rooms. No synthesis of objects and space.
Clean but pointless. Having covered his unattractive feet,
Reaney ventured into the nether regions of the flat.

The bathroom was empty, his shirt hanging from a string
over a brown-stained bath. He distinctly remembered her
saying something about a gas fire. It was quite worrying.
He had a momentary distrust of his own memory. No, simple, she probably ran out of shillings, gas-ring-bed-sit-girls
always ran out of meter shillings.

He found her at the gas stove end of another room, which
also served as a bedroom, her own, doubtlessly delectable-
smelling bed standing, unmade in its cooling glory, by the
wall. She was now wearing black slacks, flat-heeled shoes
and a sloppy brown sweater. Yes, yes, again yes, there is
something brave and sad about the lines of a woman's body
working over a sink or a cooker. Had he said that before?
Once he had prided himself on never repeating a joke to
anyone to whom he had told the joke before.

"Hello," he said. "I am resurrected on the second day."

She didn't look round from the frying pan.

"I hope you like pork sausages. It's all we've got. We
never remember to get in enough food."

Neither did Charlie way back in Earls Court, when the

world was young and Reaney looked forward. Remember those breakfasts of baked beans and pickled onions?

"Do you shave your legs?" he asked. It was the sort of question twentyish, iconoclastic Reaney used to ask. The whole scene in Maggie's flat made him feel like that.

"I *beg* your pardon."

"Nothing personal. I just wondered if you had a razor on the premises, so that I could shave my iron-hard stubble. I *will* admit that the idea of putting the same razor that you apply to your lovely limbs on my ageing cheeks is not totally without excitement."

"There's one in the medicine cabinet. But there's no shaving soap. We don't often have men for breakfast."

He scraped heartily. In those days they often woke up in strange flats, beside various bints, and shaving without lather had all seemed part of the great adventure. He watered and combed his black, black hair. They ate at the formica-topped table in her bedroom-kitchen. Four large pork sausages each. Plenty of brown bread. Young Reaney felt thrilled beyond all measure. Old Reaney couldn't help a slight sneer. She was one of those "generous" women who liked to see Her Man—or just A Man—Eat Well. Reaney knew those women. They ate Their Men for afters. She didn't hide the fact that she liked a good nosh-up. He had always known that he gulped his own food in a manner hardly short of disgusting, but she didn't suffer from any of the raised little finger business either.

"I have to see Jack today," she said brightly, when Her Man had eaten well. This obviously meant something. Reaney was thinking of two things. One, that it would be nothing short of geldingsville to leave the flat without giving her a swift tumble. The other, that he might start off with a swift spanner in the sick little workings of the Barry Black axis. It was difficult to see how this would *actually* help, but it would be a start on the right road. He had to prove he wasn't really part of all that.

"And what do you have to see Jack about, my little Mrs. Beaton?"

"You always sound so sarcastic. Don't you think I could be a good singer?"

He lit two cigarettes. She liked that. He felt that she might be another starting point.

"It's not that I don't think you're a good singer." He folded his arms, footballer style, hands under arms, dangling cigarette, head slightly askew to make smoke miss slightly screwed left eye. All right, Reaney, let's hear The Word, what has The Great Prophet distilled out of his sojourn with the ravens? "Just tell me one thing before I tell you what I think. Just one thing. Why do you want to be a big star and all that? Why?"

"It would be fun," she said. "And I'd make a lot of money. I could buy things." Little girl smile.

"Yes," he said. She had firm, white arms. They would form an honest circle round a man. But not him. He was breaking all circles.

"I know you're going to make it all sound rotten," she said, making a sad little face, then smiling again. Time to grow up, little Miss Sugarkins.

"Marilyn Monroe had thirty odd plastic surgery jobs done on her to make her look the way she did," he began. "That's a good symbol for a start. You see, in the old days, they had the right idea. All entertainers were classed as gypsies, tinkers and rascally vagabonds. They came in by the rear door, they left hurriedly so's not to befoul my lord's residence. Then they rose a social level, they became on a par with good-class whores. That's why it was such a scandal for a noble fella to marry an actress. Theatres were closely associated with whoring. Today things have changed. We sneer at our politicians, and we respect the whores. Give this illegitimate, neurotic, hysterical bird a face-lift, pump foam rubber into her oversized tits to take out the natural sag that goes with that type of deformity, straighten her nose, change her name, dye her hair, scrape her teeth—or replace them altogether—sandpaper her legs, shave her armpits and she's a symbol for the whole world. Not *just* a sex symbol. Every man wants to have her, every woman wants to be her. No, no, extreme cases prove the point. The world takes its lead from individuals who only become famous because they have personality flaws as deep as the Atlantic Ocean. Would you put a mass murderer on the high court bench? Now then, where does that leave young Maggie, who has a good voice and doesn't need any foam rubber injections, as far as I can judge? Don't mention it. Do you think you're going up there to *sing*? You are going up there to be ogled by frustrated men who wouldn't care if you balanced tea cups or produced flags of all the nations from your left earhole. You are the raw material of a great masturbation complex. The newspapers print your picture, flying out to New York, flying in from New York, wearing leopard skin coats, plenty of leg, getting your name linked romantically with this queer and that married man, denying, no commenting. You know? Well then, what purpose do you serve? You are flesh. Unattainable, unreal, pornographic flesh. Do you honestly want your own personal body to be printed in a daily newspaper so that half a million strange men can go into a lavatory and masturbate while looking at your picture? They do, you know. That's why they print the pictures. I know, God knows I know. Don't interrupt me, I know it's horrible, but this is probably the one time in your life you'll hear the whole rotten truth. I've seen the whole thing change. Ten years ago I got a right ballocking in Fleet Street for using a picture of a new fashion in shoes.

We only showed the shoe and the model's ankle. The editor bawled me out, said what did I think we were doing, catering for perverts? I hadn't even heard of shoe fetishists then. Today they print different fetishists' pictures in rota, to keep up circulation."

Maggie was making movements of her lips which suggested she wanted Reaney to stop.

"I know it's awful, but you have to listen. You know what we are having? A sexual revolution. Permissive society. Anything goes. Complete freedom. No hanging, no victimising homos, no censorship. This is great. This is what this country needs. But, Maggie, when it boils down to individual people like you, don't you see, this freedom is for bastards to turn you into a mockery. You're not a human being any more, you're a-a-a *thing*. Freedom, they talk about. Have you ever seen freedom being enjoyed in a strip club? That's all we are, one horrible great rotten strip club. The man who watches is degraded. Nobody suggests he has the freedom to have real sexual freedom, like divorcing the awful bag he's married to so that he can find somebody he likes. The girl is free to make good money. But nobody suggests she is free to claim any dignity as a human being, or make the same money without shoving her quim in people's faces. The only man who's got any freedom is the man who takes the money. Everybody else is a masturbating monkey in a cage."

Reaney was breathless. Maggie was clearly agitated to a point where she might either scream or throw up. Reaney of course, had gone too far. Again. In the wrong direction.

"I'm sorry, I got carried away," he cried. "I'm afraid I'm . . . I'm . . ." He stood up and walked to the window. It was Bayswater, he *thought* it'd been Bayswater. Something about the chimneys. He could see Whiteleys, the big store where all good things lay as in Aladdin's Cave. He looked over his shoulder. She stared at him. He walked across and put his hand on the floppy sweater.

"I'm sorry," he said. He might as well have shown her dirty pictures.

She looked up. Bone structure gave her a bigness, but it was, like his own bulk, a physiological joke. She was innocent and she wanted to cry.

"Well," he said. "I'd better be going . . . I . . . thanks for everything." He gave her shoulder the required press of comfort and apology and went to the bathroom to find his shirt. Good God, he said to the mirror, I shouldn't have done that. Why not? It was horrible. Don't be wet, it's a hard world. He saw how carefully the collar had been stretched on the wooden coat-hanger. What innocent, warm thoughts had been in her big blonde head when she'd hung it up? Yeah, man, we're all innocent till we find what it's all about. In the bedroom he found his tie. Dressed for the great highway he went back to the bedroom-kitchen. She was washing up.

"I'm off now," he said, his voice somewhat weak.

"Bye," she said, without turning round.

Of course, he could walk straight over and clasp her in his big strong arms and all that bunk, but why bother? They'd never meet again.

"See you around," he said.

"Yes," she said. She didn't look. He let himself out and descended to the street. All these bed-sitter dumps had the same worn old carpet on the stairs. It wasn't what he'd wanted to say at all. He'd meant to talk about life, death —not about her or stupid show business. He knew a great truth and he couldn't tell anyone else. His brain was scrambled. He felt panicky. The next step would be to join the mutterers. Then the nut house. No, he'd be better off dead than that.

Chapter Twelve

The venom Reaney had put into his gabble frightened him
seriously now. He took the first bus which came along the
Bayswater Road heading east. He felt filthy, sweaty, smelly.
His eyes were not focussing too clearly. Buildings seemed
to float by, as though in a silent film. He had the impression that he was watching himself go through the motions,
as though he was alone in a darkened cinema watching,
watching, handing the fare to the conductor and at the
same time watching himself handing up the money.

He got off the bus at the first stop in Piccadilly. Where
now? For once in his life he did not feel like following his
natural inclination to rush to where there were people he
knew. There was an evil in him and he wanted to be with
it, alone, until he had brought it under control. He had not
been speaking about the girl Maggie and show business.
He had been pulling long-still curtains back from a window
into . . . into what? The rat maze? Foolish, juvenile image.

Beneath the images and the gabble he had found—pulling
it forth like a huge white rabbit from the folds of a cloak
—a *real* badness. He had wanted to insult that girl, to throw
muck over her face and body, the body he knew he would
never possess, because he was not man enough. Thoughts!
Self-defence. Women! Yes, yes, yes, obsessed with something that he could not, would not—ever—understand.

When he found himself at the gate which opened onto
the top step of the stone stairs which led down to his former
home, he was not surprised. In a dream one is never sur-

prised. He had his key-ring and he went into the chilly, stale, dust-smelling hall of the basement where he and Angela had lived for four years of their marriage.

Her father had been there to remove her things. A cup containing an inch of old tea stood in the kitchen sink. It was chilly and silent. In the switched-off fridge there was a half-full bottle of lime juice.

He went to the bathroom. He ran the hot tap, the geyser gas erupting into flame with a small, dull explosion. He put the plug in the hole. He removed his clothes, garments which seemed to have been pasted onto his body for as long as he could remember. Once they'd had baths together. There was soap. A cake Angela had used. Finished, that was it. That was why he carried this resentment and hate for Barry Black, Black above all the others because he was beginning, not finished, and he, too, had killed something. It was the weight in his throat and his chest he noticed most, the dull, dragging weight. Pain. Jesus Christ, *yours* was not the secret Calvary we millions walk to every day. Silent walls. The head seems to fill still rooms.

Naked, face an anaesthetised mask, he climbed stiffly into the bath. He lay down. The water warmed only his hips and shoulder blades. The bath was still cold to touch. Lying flat, the belly was still a whale's back, the male organs an uncovered seabed corpse, the thigh fiords, the smooth-rubbed white of outer shins, the thin bone fan of repellent feet. The same cracks in the ceiling plaster. The running water, the small gas-roar, beyond the silence. Where once there was life.

The water would rise. Hot Steam.

His head was already light.

The knees were now drowning.

To Angela, a final message that *she* was not to blame. To the world, to the people, there are those of us who bear the hereditary blood-poison from some radioactive contamination which blighted the new swamp life back in those steamy days of pre-history.

You are better without us.

It would be easy. The drowsy heat, comfort. Darker now. Drift into sleep. Think of nothing. Warm, mounting warmth, little waves, perfect stillness, no waves, green darkness, Jim Butterworth, there was Jim Butterworth, hello Jim, how long've we got? Jesus wept, this stinking sun, plenty of water thank Christ, no good for drinking, what d'you mean, you useless git? Trust you, Useless, fill up the jerries from a poisoned well, yeah, well roll on, Useless, if you think a bunch of thievin' wogs is going to make me snuff it, you've another think coming, I'm getting down Casa Sin tonight regardless. I'll put a bomb under those maggotworthy gyppoes, give us the bloody Bren and shut your cakehole, I'll get it operational, you couldn't organise a piss-up in a brewery, yeah, come on you wog bastards, fancy slitting our gizzards, do you? Power, power, in my hands, come on, Useless Bloody Butterworth, hold the bloody belt or I'll ram the butt down your moaning cakehole, stroll on, try that, you crawly bastard, this isn't Useless Butterworth it's bloody Reaney now, blast your stinking wog head open I will, die you bastards Old Allah ain't going to help you now-bastardsbastards   bastardsyyyYYYYYEEEEOWWW . . . body convulses, Reaney, what the—he was splashing in water, his mouth swallowing, his hands scrabbling for the sides of the bath.

His feverish movements started an end-to-end tidal wave in the bath and as he sat up, gasping for air, it broke over the edge of the bath, swamping the floor.

Tears came as Reaney dried himself. Tears of wild rage. This was how low *they'd* brought him. He found his underclothes in the chest of drawers. He yelled without shame, bawling oaths and threats, pulling on garments with ferocious movements. His hands shook, his mouth quivered. Anger was all he felt. Anger at himself for the drunken stupidity of what he had almost done, for not fighting the madness. He picked up a bedside table, twee-bugger-bastard-rubbish, and hurled it at the wall, roaring, his face red and twisted with venom.

Frightened of his own bloody flat? What had he been doing, playing big silly girls? My God, this was peasant superstition with a vengeance, frightened of ghosts, he'd never shirked a ladder yet and the hell with this madness that had had him quivering in hidey-holes.

First, out with her gear. Smash the bloody stuff, send it to the starving Indians, God knows what they'll do with framed prints of old English castles, poor benighted wogs, but thank them, burnous-clad buggers, they'd saved him in the bath . . .

Wearing another of his suits, a clean shirt, new underwear, a silk Italian tie, Reaney looked round the place and imagined the life coming back to its two bedrooms, lounge, kitchen-diner, hall, bathroom, and cubby holes when he held his party.

It was now about eleven-thirty. He came up the stairs as quickly as he could move his legs, having also decided to get rid of a lot of this stupid fat, get fit again, harden the belly, buy weights or run in the park or some stupid bloody thing. Already the blood was flowing.

He had forgotten all about Mrs. Fanchetti. She was sweeping the front steps.

"You were making some din, eh?" she said, interrupting her sweeping. Her legs were not so brown and shimmeringly sculpted now that she was wearing fluffy slippers and no nylons.

"Oh yes," he replied, coming up level with her, opening the basement steps gate, determined not to be likeable. He felt . . . powerful. He would go through the office like a dose of salts. She dragged her brush behind her as she came to the front gate.

She wanted to chat. Her legs were all right, even in the flesh. She was wearing a sleeveless blouse, a dark skirt and an apron. Her arms were brown and fat. A bit too much hair about the lip and the cheeks, but what the hell, he had to shave, too. The sun made her squint a little as she stopped for her confidential little gabble. Once, coming home a bit stoned, he'd met her on the pavement and made some pretty obvious hints about having it off with her lively like and she'd pretended to be all shocked. She'd had her chance. He was starving. Maggie's sausages were already digested. Hadn't helped. That's how alcoholism started.

"I'm sorry to hear about your wife," she said, shaking her head up and down in clack-clack Italian granny style. Her hands, round the broom handle, were small and firm and brown. Her domestic uniform pulled tight round her breasts and hips. Two years and she'd sag.

"Don't be sorry," he said. "I'm not."

He was vibrating with a new thought. Parked beside their house was a gleaming blue Jaguar. Its metalwork gleamed in the sun, its paintwork gave off lustrous reflections. He'd buy a car now, Angela had always stopped him because he was liable to climb into it pissed and have a smash. FREE—to walk in and buy one and—power in his hands.

"Not sorry?" she said, squinting up at him. "Ah, such a bad thing. My Alberto, he died, you know. I was so sad."

"It's different," he said. Hands in clean pockets, Reaney in clean body. Empty, ready for re-charging, mind cleared, body purified through emptiness. His attitude was still that of a man whose feet were trying to drag him away. "We've separated."

She was going to gabble on but he said he had to go and get something to eat. Solitary, self-sufficient man-about-town strolls into gleaming cafe, has leisurely breakfast, interests those dreary half-people who hang about such places waiting for the city to finish their demolition, ignores them, walks out into brighter world . . .

"Poor man, I will give you breakfast," she said.

So, what of it? Eyetie women started being over-maternal before they were in their teens.

Whether she had a lot of friends or not he had never known, being previously only interested in her as a handy reinforcement for flagging desire, but she obviously had money. Her kitchen had a tiled floor, and although it was darker than the usual English woman's idea—stainless white chrome and wax-cloth—the dominance of rich brown hues made him feel warm. He studied her hips and legs as she messed about at the oven and sink. The place smelled of her—like sweet gravy. She was about thirty-eight, forty, hard to tell with *them*. Legs thicker than the English ideal, but smooth and well-shaped—he had half-expected them to be hairy and he had never been keen on pursuit of the hirsute. Even jokes yet!

What she gave him was a plate of six small skinless sausages and fried tomato. He had expected spaghetti. Christ, he'd been eating sausages a couple of hours ago with another bloody woman. Forget *that*. Chop this lot into your cakehole and beat it, buster, now she's made herself slightly available she's no longer the sex-symbol in the upstairs flat. Planning, that's what he needed, no more blowing in the wind.

Again, the same proud, sympathetic woman's gaze as he shovelled sausage. What the hell it was about him, he stood six foot, he weighed more than sixteen stone, he looked like Nero after an orgy's orgy—and the only woman who hadn't gone all motherly in the last week was a teenage scrubber who wanted beating.

Out, mac, get lost. Have to get to Felix and sort out this letter.

"Is good?" she said, nodding again.

Partisan leader Pietro ate with his tommy-gun over his shoulder, his boots still muddied from the night ambush of the tedeschi patrol, his face unshaven after six nights on the mountains. But when the wide-eyed women brought him red wine and smiled dark, flashing invitations, he shook his head. After the war a warrior might relax, now there was killing to be done . . .

And yet, even then, fired with his new-found energy, desperate to find an escape into action that would keep this morning's shame suppressed, there was no escaping that brown face, the dark, unwavering eyes, the unimaginable swell of heavily crossed thighs, the iceberg tip of bosom. The excitement of suddenly wanting her made his heart pound.

She made it easy, she had to make it even easier before he acknowledged that he understood. She stood close to him as she began picking up the empty plate and cup. Her thigh was solid against his knee. Her bare upper arm remained in front of his face, inches away, the smooth, voluptuous woman's arm with its little flashes of exquisite bone and muscle tension. Still, he did not move. At least, not unless she had X-ray eyes.

Would she—?

No, she was lifting the plate and the cup and moving away. Ah well, my God, it would have been—

She was coming back.

His mouth hung slightly open. His eyes were hot and

heavy. The pain was all fire, burning, luscious pincers causing unbearable torture.

She wanted to flick crumbs off the dark red table-cloth. His ears buzzed with muffled fuzz-noise.

This time he was looking into her left arm, where it joined the elbow, where the tight, stretching blouse pulled into soft white flesh.

Then she was looking at him across her arm, her mouth slightly open, too, her eyes locked with his, her face poised to smile or—

NO.

Don't drag me down, please!

No more *mess*.

No . . .

She took her weight off her left arm. She stared into his eyes. Slowly she put her hand on his shoulder. He waited for the touch. Even then he was rigid. He saw her fleshy knuckles as though blown up a thousand times on a cinema screen. He didn't breathe.

Then she moaned and closed her eyes and turned into his lap, grabbing at his shoulder, his neck, pulling him.

Kissing was nothing. Their mouths sucked for holds on each other, their hands moved and pulled and moved, aching flesh.

"Ohhh," she moaned. The kitchen was deep brown. Leaves danced like silver. Clip clop on the street. Powerful nicotine-stained fingers on warm woman-flesh.

On their intermittent progress out of the kitchen into a bedroom, he had a close-up of a hair-parting, hidden white revealed by flattened fingers. Dark, dim, blurred room. Untidy fall onto chilly silk coverlet. Drowning hands pulling at woman's clothes.

Sniff, my God, it isn't . . . She had breath like carrion. Like a tomcat's calling card, like deadly gas, like the god-

awful first whiff of an addled egg. He could taste it, poisonous draughts from a white-toothed sewer. Momentum
of agonising relief-seeking pain kept him going, now pressing his cheek on hers, burying his face in her dark hair. Her
eyes, closed in fantasy-producing rapture . . . the fat white
of her widow's thighs . . . his eyes closed, his nose searching for safety . . .

Her smooth knees gripping his hip bones, knowing feet
locked on his shins . . . the desperate moment of location,
the great drive, the great drive, God give me this minute,
her mouth nibbling round his face, his relentless face-press
into her ear, the mouth, the carrion mouth, lipping round,
asking for the woman-assuring kisses, nicotine fingers spatu-
lating on skull, holding it away, the divine, the desperate
insertion . . . and the woman-agitating attack, the crack-
crack-crack of male back, divine, head-splitting, relentless,
whip crack, steam-hammer, pneumatic drill, drill, drill, not
looking, not needing to look, god a minute more, the salmon
leaps, its great silver whip almost, almost, almost . . . there!

The great white whale is stranded in shallows, its gargan-
tuan flips taking it farther towards dry, deadly land, its jerk-
ings suddenly weaker.

So what the hell was all the excitement about? The face
that nuzzled against his chest seemed older, harder, now
that his masculine chin and cheeks had rasped off the
powder. Full lips now, when he looked closely, not so red
and not so luscious. And the sudden, sneaky whiffs of
foul, acidic poison.

Reaney went through the usual guzzling, snuggling, re-
assuring motions, but when, eventually, he was able to get
off the bed, saying he was desperately late for the office, he
needed to scurry.

"Is good?" she asked, shyly, pulling at her hastily-parted
garments.

156

He smiled at her warmly, although not getting within touching distance. Now she was a plump, perhaps too mature, little pigeon of a woman, needing the man to make the gesture of love that would carry her over the woman's post-coital depression, yeah man, I know all the terms, the all-knowing, comfortless Peter Reaney. He pulled his trousers up from his ankles, not having bothered to remove them properly in the Cresta Run of his now curious heat. M'Lord came home after the Napoleonic wars and pleasured his mistress thrice before removing his boots. Now he knew what was required—had he not been married to a walking compendium of every cosy marriage-smoothing hint for eight years? But there was nothing left now but (doubtless momentary) relief and a great desire never again to get within smelling distance of Mrs. Fanchetti's lung-gas. He combed his hair—with her comb.

"I always thought we should've been more neighbourly," he said, grinning at her in the dressing-table mirror, tightening his tie. No, it was impossible to go back to the brink of the sulphuric volcano and perform the second, comforting, this-proves-I-loves-yer mating.

As he went about his escape she kept throwing her arms round his neck, alternately crying and laughing, gabbling on about how this was now his *real* home. He covered his nausea by an excess of post-randy slapstick, but when, after promising to be there again that evening, he was free in the street, there was no suppressing the terrible agony he felt for her. The city-pyramid might devour its slaves, but there were other miseries.

It was after one when he reached the office. As he forced his legs to run up the stairs—the new fitness campaign—he tried to stand back and discover how he felt about facing Felix. Nothing. Neither fear nor anger. Interest. Felix was walking back into his own office when Reaney came into the reception room, vacated by the luncheon voucher spender, name of Linda.

"Hello there," Felix said, with exaggerated pleasure.

"Hullo."

He followed Felix into the office. Now he felt a little nervous. So stupid to be caught in a situation like this. Felix opened his bottom desk drawer, the one on the right which held his shoe cleaners, face-tingling deodorants, electric razor, toothbrush and hair-oil. He polished one laceless black shoe after the other, lifting them onto his swivel chair. There might have been two new specks of dust since the shoes had glinted first in the day's sunshine.

"I'm going to lunch with Pemberton," Felix said, bending over his left shoe, touching it with the yellow duster. "They want to do a couple of spectaculars with Dorry. Maybe you should come along. It wouldn't be too bad an idea to work young Barry in, eh? We've got Dorry, so why not row in Barry as well, can't do any harm, eh? Let them see what a natural he is for his own series, no?"

Reaney watched the tensions play across the shoulders and arms of Felix's jacket as he polished his toecap. Maybe he hadn't read his resignation?

"Yeah," he said, hardly enthusiastic enough even for Felix, who looked at him as he shoved the duster in the drawer.

"Even if you're chucking in, you'll still have to work out some kind of notice," Felix went on. Then he grinned. "What was all that crap about then? The trouble about you, Peter, is you won't fall down when you're drunk, you keep on your feet and do the first stupid thing that comes in your head. It's a good job I know you. Right, let's go."

So that was supposed to be that. Just a stupid drunken idea. His big decision to get out of the whole stinking, corrupting, stupid, rubbish business—dismissed with a song and a smile. They went down in the lift, Felix soliloquising about the need to milk all they could out of Dorry's tour, him probably due to come an alcoholic cropper any of these days.

"Terrible, isn't it, to have talent and money and still want to kill yourself with booze?" Felix said.

"Nobody's perfect," Reaney said. Felix laughed. Reaney laughed, too. He was forgiven, the saved lamb. Who cared about those still in the snowdrifts? Wasn't self-preservation the oldest and healthiest emotion?

Furthermore, who cared that one man now had proof that unseen hands were pushing him nearer Niagara's edge?

Chapter Thirteen

It was what Pemberton Mobley said at lunch about young girls that made Reaney decide that, whatever other compromise he might have to make, he would find some way of making somebody remember Mary Gray.

They'd been in Isow's, Reaney finding that although he still felt half-starved the very sight of food made him seasick, each mouthful of omelette requiring concentrated effort, when a show business columnist called Evan Rahilly had stopped at their table to ask Reaney if they could fix something up for Dorry's tour.

"I could do the whole column about him, the last of the hell-raisers and all that," Rahilly said, looking down at Reaney. "I'd have to get it first, of course."

"I'll ring you, mate," Reaney said. Rahilly's paper had a circulation of around two millions. If exclusives were to be given away the Express or the Mirror were better value. As Rahilly strolled off, looking to Reaney far too well-dressed to be a proper Fleet Street man (hence the automatic suspicion that the chancy bastard was probably taking kick-backs from somebody), Pemberton showed a flash of his old, pre-bullshit days, self:

"If I'd to choose between a hall packed with sweaty twelve-year-old morons and one super-snide in a fifty-guinea suit, I think I'd take the snide, but there isn't much in it, is there?"

Felix munched on, nodding reflectively. In a world of neurotic gabblers, stone-deaf monologue artistes, silence was strength, whether you were dealing with tiny Jake Braid or panoplied Pemberton Mobley. (How did you ever find out if you, too, had bad breath? That was the one thing your best friend would never tell you.)

Pemberton's sarcasm was a welcome glimpse of pure nastiness now well concealed beneath the usual show biz buffoonery of cheek-kissing and incestuous flattery, but even nastiness could not redeem a big man who thought of children as sweaty morons. Pemberton Mobley—all of them, if it came to that—was being well paid by the pharaohs. Here's a jolly new work-song, slaves, isn't life grand?

Beside the ungathered rice he lay,
His sickle in his hand . . .

But Peter Reaney was no Uncle Tom, he was Prometheus unchained, Ramsay MacDonald reconstituted to detest duchesses, the people's last hope. Before the inexorable forces that were hurtling him to the brink could destroy him he must do something. In action would come sanity.

Having given Pemberton the two Dorry dates in return for a verbal assurance of support at programme planning for the Barry Black series, Felix and Reaney walked back through Soho to the office. There were several telephone messages for Reaney. He hung his jacket over the chair and prepared to restore some order after the dissipation of the last few days. His mind could work at ten levels, if necessary, and it was vital that he establish himself again in the society of men—if he was to act.

First on Linda's list was to ring his bank. What, he wondered, could they be on about?

It was Snead himself, the manager, who wanted to speak to him.

"Ah, Mister Reaney, it's about your joint account . . ."

Joint?

". . . not having had any notification, we couldn't do anything else . . ."

He listened in silence. Figures, figures, he had plenty of loot. What was the old fossil trying to say?

Angela?

"WHAT?"

A simple matter really. Some joint account cheques required both signatures. Others required only the signature of one of the joint signatories.

"You mean, they let her cash a cheque for four hundred and eighty five pounds without even asking me?"

Oh, no . . . oh, yes. Cleared out the bloody account!

". . . on the standing orders there's exactly eighty-four pounds to be paid out, you have eight hundred in your deposit, of course . . ."

Reaney lit a cigarette, resting his elbow on the box as he struck the match. Clear-head, fast-thinking. She'd said she didn't want any money. Her bloody father had been at her, obvious.

"How much notice do I need to draw out the deposit account?" he asked. The pressure was on now, bang, bang. Seven days. How could he make sure she didn't get her hands on it? "We've separated, you see, it's rather tricky."

Bank managers didn't like that sort of thing. If Reaney made a formal order to stop cheques on the joint account the bank would have to stop his cheques as well until the two parties came to an agreement. If there was no instruction, either party could go on cashing cheques. Deposit account money could be transferred—the point was who got to it first? If bloody Angela was out to ruin him she'd have thought about the eight hundred iron men in the deposit, the father-dominated bitch.

"No, there's no application to transfer money from your deposit," Snead said. Dry-voiced old ledger-basher, didn't he ever think of the lives involved? "You could come round here and make an order transferring your eight hundred from the joint account. You can't do it until tomorrow now, I'm afraid."

All right, so what was another twist of the rack-handle? He could cope. Next on the list, a Kensington number, no name, please ring back (woman's voice). Ignore it? Come on, live dangerously.

Buzz, buzz.

"Yes, who is this please?"

Oh my bastarding luck, Mrs. bleeding Fanchetti.

He didn't think fast enough to put down the phone before he spoke.

"My name's Reaney," he was saying, even as he recognised the voice.

"Is Mrs. Fanchetti," she said, gurgling with fond laughter under her voice. "Will you be coming tonight, I have such a lovely dinner, very nice for you."

How the hell was it that every time he was ready to play it hard, look out for number one, the opposition had some pitiable handicap that wrapped round his ankles like a gaucho's bolas?

"Oh," he said. "Well, no, I've got to go out, business, you know."

Be hard. Silence is power.

"Oh," she said. How many tiny silences had she endured? "Perhaps I'll see you tomorrow?"

"If you like."

"I enjoyed my breakfast."

"I enjoy cooking it."

"See you tomorrow?"

"Is very nice."

Push on. One day Gulliver was free of the cobweb. How did she know his number? He phoned a magazine features editor to plant the idea that Barry Black was shortly to become a national sensation—"good angle for you, dearest, he's very fond of cooking, very sexy in an apron, too, if you like that sort of thing"—what next on the list? Dorry was arriving on Sunday, better check with young Dixon.

"He's on the phone," Katrina said when he picked up his own phone to ask Dixon to come in. "It's somebody in Manchester."

"When he's through then," Reaney said, momentarily wondering why, at his age, it took only a suggestion of iciness in some stuck-up, jumped-up secretary for him to feel vaguely in the wrong. Was there any woman who didn't have the same effect?

Time for a quick shufti through the *Melody Maker*, see what the trends were. He noted the views of a singer on whisky . . . *Firewater. A bad chemical to put inside you. A socially acceptable drug which is, in fact, more destructive than the drugs that people put down*. Put that boy in the Top Zen and clap with one hand. Nothing else of note, he flung the paper into the basket. Two cuttings pinned to sheets of blue paper, Felix's habit of passing round chuckleworthy items.

TRIBUTE
TO A
DRUMMER

My friend Bryan was killed four weeks ago in a road accident. He was a drummer in a very popular beat group called the Devil Riders. Please publish this tribute. All the words in capitals are songs the Devil Riders wrote and Bryan played a great part in this.—W. S. POWELL, GERRARDS CROSS, BUCKS.

As long as we live, WE'LL ALWAYS REMEMBER, MINS MINUET, and TWANGING. They were great tunes played by a great drummer, whose TIME came to an end most tragically.

We attended the funeral. SHIRLEY was there and the church organist played SHIRLEY'S TUNE, a nice slow tune called SNOWFALL, we could not get him out of our minds, the good times we had with him when he'd play a CHA CHA FOR SATANISTS then when Tony came in on bass guitar he'd shout out TONY'S GOOD, or how we'd sit by the river and he would be dreaming he was on SWAN LAKE '63 then he would jump up to go home and say "Cheerio—DON'T PHONE ME", which was very funny as he wasn't on the phone anyway.

He loved rhythm and blues, but quite often he would come along whistling TCHAIKOVSKY'S PIANO CONCERTO NO. 1 IN B FLAT MINOR, which was the group's own version of Red Square.

They called themselves the Devil Riders, and they wrote a tune called THE DEVIL RIDER THEME. Well, what more can we say about someone who is missed more than anyone has ever been missed? We can all say to ourselves, Bryan, you'll always STICK AROUND WITH ME.

Drummers, it seemed, did better than dishwashers. On top of the second cutting Felix had written, "Any volunteers from this office?"

'CHASTITY PLEDGE'
SIGNING-ON DATE

A "chastity pledge" for teenagers will be introduced at Reading, Berks, in June, Mr. Fred Jackman, a temperance society secretary, said yesterday.

Mr. Jackman, who announced the scheme last month, explained that those who sign the pledge will renounce sex outside marriage and dissuade others from "going astray".

He supposed that he had made as many jokes about iron lungs as anyone else, but he didn't think it was too bloody prudish to wonder how Alfred had managed, so quickly, to forget Mary Gray. Or did his own tremor of indignation arise from guilt?

Dixon's inch-wide tie matched exactly the pale green of his office door. Dixon was twenty-three, a fact of which Reaney found himself acutely aware whenever in the lad's company. His hair was fair, not unlike Val's in shade, but it was professionally styled, a plastic crew-cut. Dixon was an ivy leaguer, fresh, hygienic, cheery, dedicated, a sort of bleached Sammy Glick, Reaney always thought, but then, he was guilty of romanticising even the most decent and obvious people. Dixon, he had long since tired of hearing, had his head screwed on, would go places, knew what it was all about. He was too damned nice for a start. The only irregular thing about him was the width of nose between his hazel eyes. Room for a third eye in there. He grinned all the time, nothing was too much trouble for him, and the hand which held the Dorry guff was brown and clean in a way that made Reaney's own cigarette-holders feel damper and grubbier.

"Long time no see, Pete," Dixon said, pulling a chair up to the desk. Val without the taste for drink—or the talent. The new plastic man.

"I trust my absence hasn't held up the good work," Reaney replied, shirt-sleeved elbows on the blotting-table, feeling heavy and coarse by comparison with young mister slick. Normally he would have gone for jokes, exaggerating his own excesses. He had a feeling it was time to show young Dixon that there was more to life than twelve-bob hairstylings. "What've we got lined up for Dorry?" He didn't smile—and when he took a cigarette from his packet, he closed it without offering. Let the chill breeze touch *your* knees, lad.

"Oh, I think I've got it all well in hand," Dixon said, grinning the smooth boy's sideways grin, they all thought they were Paul bloody Newman. At least in the First Great Unpleasantness this type had the guts to be cannon fodder. Now they were all button-down collars; tell Dixon about the dishwasher and he'd give you the poor bastard's consumer-research rating. (Z Minus, of course.)

"All right then, let's see it," Reaney said, "unless we're playing poker, of course."

Dixon was slightly puzzled. A new tone. Where was the fat, drunken buffoon? He put his papers on the desk. Reaney rested on his elbows. With a green eyeshade he'd be killing front pages and firing Alan Ladd. But Dixon was fireproof, waterproof, mistake-proof. He had fixed up as good a publicity coverage for Dorry as Reaney could have done himself. One woman's magazine, three radio interviews, all the trades, the usual press party, an optional personal appearance at some big boys' club charity shindig, plus a beauty queen from Manchester who claimed to have seen his last film thirty-seven times.

"Yeah, well that seems fair enough," Reaney said, touching the papers tentatively. The beauty queen had been his own idea. Dixon would doubtless claim the credit, when all he had had to do was get a girl to agree. Hardly the Augean stables. "I've got Rahilly after me for an exclusive, hell-raiser, you know. What do you think?"

Actually, Dixon was all right. He could hardly blame him for being a smooth, unhuman egocentric, plastic man when he had stopped being ditto only in the last week. He found it difficult to concentrate on what was said. The face of the young. Smooth skin. Shining eyes. Belief. Excitement. Clean underpants. His thinking was fair. Rahilly would do it, but they'd be better to give one of the bigger circulations first chance. Reaney had a stray thought.

"I met some *Paris Match* bloke last week, he was going on about cowboy singers, seemingly they're trendy in France. Give that bloke Moscour a ring, eh? Maybe he'll get them to send a photographer over. And about this Simpson girl, for Christ's sake let's not have any rubbish about them falling in love, eh? Whenever the Great British reporter hears about that kind of engagement he automatically thinks the guy is queer. And another thing, Dorry's got a male nurse with him, to keep him off the juice. According to Joe Alterberg he looks like King Kong. I don't think a personal male nurse is good for the image, do you?"

"No," Dixon said, thoughtfully. Nobody *looked* thoughtful in this business. They *acted* thoughtful. Dixon knew the whole range. He probably made love with an eye for camera angles. Or was that himself? "Could we say he's a bodyguard?"

"Why would our well-loved client need guarding?"

"Gangsters?"

"Kinda corny, isn't it?"

"Not in the States."

"Hired to keep English girls out of his hotel? Good angle, our girls have such a wild reputation Yanks are scared stiff. No?"

"Suppose we play it very tight, say we've no comment? Make him a mystery bodyguard?"

"Very good. That's the one. He speaks to nobody. They'll follow him all over the country. Is he carrying a gun? Is it true he saved Dorry's life in Korea? Is he protecting Dorry from bookies' heavy men? Is he . . ."

. . . as mad as me, sitting here, burying my head in the

sand of mindless ant-scurryings? Playing the junior partner in life's great delusion.

Dixon left crisply, papers gripped importantly, imminent activity on his face. Reaney sat back. He felt slightly better for the small flurry. Better? Trying to justify himself in the eyes of men? His wife had left him and was now trying to bankrupt him. Drink and doubt were driving him farther and farther from sanity. In three or four days he had connived at the death of a girl (accessory after the fact), failed to make love (with his sixteen stone body) to another girl after satisfying (albeit unwittingly) her minor's perversion, made yet another girl weep with indecent oral exposure, consigned a love-starved widow to the humiliation of rejection, and was seriously considering becoming a second husband to his best friend's wife. Plus all the other madnesses that floated about in the sludge of his brain, all of it devouring days that might be grim but were the only days he would have.

He had seen beneath the surface of the lie-drugged society and he was still working at the lie. At 6.30 p.m. he was due, he noted from his diary, to attend a cocktail party in honour of some new outburst of telly glamour. Tonight, sure as death, he'd be drunk. For this moment, sitting alone in his pastel-shaded, not-quite-padded coop, he was lucid. In work he found energy. To do what? To bury his head in the sand of meaningless activity? He rang Val, arranging to meet him in a pub near the TV building. The trouble with communion of like-minds is that they deny the necessary art of speech. The wisecrack was our gag, Of Human Badinage . . . he delved under the rubbish in a bottom desk drawer, pulling out a brick-coloured cardboard file on which was written in heavy ballpoint capitals STRICTLY PERSONAL. He'd been carrying some of this junk round for years. Poems, short-story openings, one-page plays. The file on his lap, he leaned back so that his head propped his massive body against the wall and his big, scuffy black shoes were on the desk.

How about this, a play he'd started writing nine or ten years ago when he was on the magazine and rejoiced in being king of type-writer's diarrhoea?

> GREGOR . . . man of the world, shabby but distinguished.
> HARVE . . . also about 50, shabby but common, resentful.
> BARMAN . . . any age, any type, says nothing.

GREGOR: "If she really loved you why did she run away away with me on the eve of your wedding?"

HARVE: "You tricked her, pretending to be rich. I could have worshipped her for twenty years. You ditched her after a week, leaving her stranded in Worthing with the hotel bill."

GREGOR: "Only fools worship women. Sadism is almost exclusively a male concept."

HARVE: "Go on, make a joke. Is everything a joke-- twenty wasted years out of two lives?"

GREGOR: "The real joke is that she was so disgusted with herself she's spent the rest of her life taking revenge on men like you, not men like me. Isn't that rich?"

HARVE: "You know where she is?"

GREGOR: "The whole world knows. Except you, with your pathetic little case of unrequited love."

HARVE: "What do you mean, the world knows? I've searched for her every day."

GREGOR: "Where--in public bars? Greyhound tracks? Football matches? Show me a wasted life and I'll show you a fool."

HARVE: "You must tell me or--"

GREGOR: "Or what? Listen, old friend and supreme imbecile, she's famous. She would make a point of not recognising you if you did meet. Why should she? Twenty years ago you were on the point of laying a social nobody's idea of treasure at her feet--a semi-detached orange box, an inadequate supply of rexine-covered matchstick furniture, and all the primeval lust of a man who had never been bold enough to regard his own naked body in a strong light."

HARVE: "I loved her!"

GREGOR: "Don Juan with dandruff. Passionately he drops his upper plate in a glass, rolls up his meaty socks and shoves them in his shoes, rolls down his varicose bandage, folds up his truss, switches out the light and the earth moves . . . ."

HARVE: "You are making fun of me."

GREGOR: "No! My God, these days nothing is sacred."

This went angrily into the basket, torn and torn again in case the cleaner had a curious eye. He remembered the romantic defeat that had sparked off that leaden outpouring. Now then, here's a bit from T. S. Reaney, typed on waste-end copy-paper.

> *Piccadilly, filter de luxe,*
> *Product of the Master Mind,*
> *Clean white tubes for men*
> *who require an end to*
> *flavour blur. Riding tall*
> *in my kind of country.*
>
> *White tubes in pleasure pack,*
> *But would you swallow*
> *the dead man's gulch of*
> *the afternoon ashtray?*

Kingsize, none so pleasing, a
clever crystal filter sweats black tar.

Sixty a day, the angry cells mutate
And in dark, front stalls the
wrong end stinks my mouth. I never
once walked a twilight beach
with two women, dreams
tailormade by Pearl and Dean.

Wheeze a cough, wheeze a cough,
pumice the skin. The cells are getting
angry, but I'm discriminating . . .
Does Signor Ponti smoke in bed?

Rip, rip, any piece of paper can only be torn to seven
folded thicknesses. My God, the raw evidence of that
golden age of youth fairly made you sweat. How about
SEPTET . . . LINES FROM THE UNDERGROUND? Almost too pain-
ful to read. He skimmed down heavily xxxxx-ed lines. Ouch,
ouch, and double-squirm.

> *. . . Upminster to Hounslow West, forty-six*
> *intervening halts. London is a village*
> *the size of outer blackness . . .*
> *Knightsbridge, where women with splendid*
> *parts may go . . .*

Yes, only the callow years produced this kind of drivel
. . . *the gravy smell of distant rushing winds.* Throw the
lot to the bottom of the basket, hope the cleaner lady has no
time for rubbish-bin research.

Now what? The idea had been boiling up in the left side
of his brain to have a bash at Angela. He put paper in the
type-writer.

"Dear Angela,

Whatever else you may think you have achieved by your recent bit of trickery at the bank, you can tell your father that his brilliant idea has decided me to fight the divorce all the way. I shall counter-sue for adultery, deprivation of conjugal rights and refusal to have children. I shall say your parents dominated you (as they did and always will). I hope your father enjoys the publicity.
Peter."

Into the envelope and off with you, lovely little hand-grenade. Now what? Dorry on Sunday. Party tonight. The bank in morning. Go with Barry Black to the studios tomorrow afternoon. Stay away from flat, avoiding Mrs. Fanchetti. Cut down on drink. Keep alive new me. Maggie. Chance to talk there. Made a mess of it. Ring her up. Apologise? Don't ring. Maybe drop round. Maybe bump into her. Is she important? Nice girl. Why pick on her? Read Guardian, improve mind. First Sea Lord goes because Cabinet rejects new carriers. Indecent verbal exposure. Russia sends dogs into space. Sign of change of life? Premier tells Russia arms race near point of no return. Flash it next in the tube? Cuba orders 82 Leyland coaches. Two bodies found after crash. To die, and thus be popular. Dr. Obote arrests five ministers. Is the truth indecent then? Lifeboat saves crew in fog. So little of it about, sounds dirty. The abortion bill is amended. Can't have serious indignation in flippant England. A step towards one union for engineering industry. The talking computer is on the way. Synagogue fires; two accused. Battle of Pork Chop hill? Can't have, don't want? Can't have, will destroy? Missionary plan to resolve India's Christian unity. She was a genuine listener. Tory bill to help illegitimate. Monks' skeletons found on site. Instant Pompeii reveals fat man reading paper, rat-maze mind behind grinning skull. Books page, a philosopher on prayer. Against Augustine. Protestant Monument. Doctor and Dean. Rewriting the history of Methodism. Tillich. Is God bothered? He's me, I should know. Not bothered. Portia wind ensemble at the Wigmore Hall. Ezra Pounds while Ernest Humsaway. The future of Britain's wet deserts. My belly. Future, very little. Bonn surprised by de Gaulle's tone. Women behind it all? The big kid-on? Big, wide, black, *scuffy* shoes. Belly flat in recline. King Faisal accused by Nasser. King Reaney accused by teddy-bear blonde. Steps by Ghana to avert crisis. I'm Ghana wash that man right out of my hair. Why her, why a young sympathetic girl? Why not Felix —why not a grown man? Copperbelt ultimatum by Kaunda. Stop belting my coppers, you black nig-nogs. Scared of grown-up men? Ten Hungarians face anti-State charges. Magyar Maggie. Singer. Got the needle, you old sew and sew? Whitehall has gloomy forebodings. Who hasn't? Senator Kennedy urges US to face realities. Better than facing charges. Only time you were manly this week was belting that Henriette child. Playing daddy. A daddy man can play domestic Stalins? Be a daddy and ignore the grown-up power game? No arms for Iraqi Arabs from UAR. Judges open way for women to challenge Jockey Club. Playing what with Mrs. Fanchetti—son, nephew, seigneur? Britain the underdog on seabed. Reaney, the underdog in any bed? Insult Maggie to *make* her angry? Subconscious wants to be her naughty son? Directors fined £128,000. Or thirty days. Wants to be Jody's naughty son? Val's naughty son? Spell it m-a-s-o-c-h-i-s-m, in front of the child. Couldn't stand Angela because she wanted him to be grown-up? Protest on Karl Marx plaque. If they won't let you be their universal son, try to change the world? Half-baked Freud? Why lock women in zoo cages? In Holloway? Compensatory sadism for shame-carrying masochist? Ever had a satisfactory relationship with a woman? At school? Hopeless love for too-popular Barbara? In Portsmouth they are not amused. Don't they visit Fred—ever? Hallo Fred, they don't visit me, either. Mutations. In the coroner's list there are none but the tragic. Maybe Mary Gray was an evil-minded, nasty, over-sexed, vicious, greedy little bitch? In death she became a victim? Action equals label equals fraction of the whole truth? Going mad through passive awareness? Better a small practical truth than universal vision? Bury the head? Why not? Am I to suffer for God when they don't recognise me? Girl of 16 wins pancake race.

The phone rang. Is there no privacy? It was a boozy bloke he knew on one of the trades, wondering if it would be all right for him to bring two of the office girls to Dorry's press party, them being great fans of his.

"It's open house," Reaney said. "See you at the inquest."

Katrina had very sexy legs. She wore her skirt a few inches above her white-bone knees. The lines were sharp and shiny and kissable. When she came in to pick up his inter-office stuff, she looked as disdainful as ever, but he noticed that she was not in such a tearing hurry as usual to push off. He sat back, hands clasped on shirt front.

"Are you a virgin?" he asked. She looked at him. A fringe of hair over the left eye. Not a lot of mammary-flesh, but kissable legs. Hard face lines equal grown-up equal desirable power.

"*You'll* never know," she replied, taking his searching gaze head-on. A cool one.

"What a pity," he said. "I'm launching a new PR stunt. Ten grand for the most beautiful virgin in England. There aren't many left, it seems."

Katrina hid her curiosity beneath layers of self-composure.

"How do you prove you're eligible?" she asked. Ah ah, icy dame takes hook.

"Prove it to the judges, of course," he said, feeling chirpy. "Mind you, once you've proved it you're no longer eligible. It's not a very practical scheme, but the judges do all right."

Katrina inclined her head as she pulled at the fringe with an elegant splay of fingers. It was almost half-past five. Reaney let his chair land on four legs. Katrina wouldn't die in any common cinema, that was for sure. She and Dixon would mate well, the stainless steel couple.

"All right then," he said, "don't hang about. We don't pay you to stand around gossiping, y'know." He smiled as evilly as he could and concentrated on his papers.

"Have a nice time at the party," Katrina said, sarcastically, moving towards the door.

"Life's a party," he said, without looking up. "And by the way, get me a tenner out of the float, would you?"

He waited for her to tell him to get it himself, poised for practice in his new power role. She fetched the money in silence. He crammed the roll into his hip pocket. The backs of her knees seemed to quiver as she left. Come to think of it, Angela's knees had played a big part in his pathetic rush into marriage. If only she'd been the type to play that kind of game . . .

In the pub he ordered a large Scotch and waited for Val. He could see himself between bottles in the bar mirror. A funny old world, ain't it. Camera shows mass of slightly blurred faces. Track in. One of the fudges grows larger, larger. We see the familiar cow's lick hair, the small moustache, the angular, clerkish face. Hindsight makes us want to cry out to the crowd round about, "that's him, grab him, kick him to death now and save the world". But when the power came to a man, only he knew what was in store for the others. Heil Reaney. Luckily, oh hastily-drinking com-

176

muters, this ex-corporal is persecuted only by himself, or his revenge would make Belsen seem like a mere portent.

In a fawn-coloured lightweight suit, white shirt and floral pattern tie, Val looked like a Las Vegas bit player.

"I'm glad you called," he said. "Jody has that stupid bitch Frances coming round tonight. I thought I was lumbered."

Reaney had heard a lot about this Frances. From the vehemence with which Val talked about her he guessed she had, at some embarrassing moment, turned down his drunken advances. All he knew about her was that she wrote copy in a big agency and had a first novel coming out—sometime—and was living apart from her slickly successful husband, market research or thought police or something.

"I was looking through some crap I wrote years ago," he said to Val, who could only have got brushed up in expectation of a pick-up. Must be Jody's monthlies. Not that they made any real difference to his moral code—just that he was more conscious of the lack and made preparations. The difference between good guys and cheap guys is that cheap guys make plans. "It was hellish, I couldn't believe how bad it was."

"You're lucky," Val said, rueful. "I hear this all the time, stuff I wrote ten years ago makes me sweat. *I* sweat as I pull it out of the bloody machine. I know it's a joke, but there's truth in clichés, that's why they're clichés—I'm ashamed to take the money." He shook his head. In some vague way Reaney had hoped to put Val to some kind of crucial test. At least try to bring his so-called best friend's mind to bear on his own problems.

"People these days are very narrow-minded," Reaney ruminated. "They insist on talking about themselves. Why, to put it bluntly, do you go round moaning about having to write crap when it's only your own raving greed for cash that's the cause? Tell me, Val, we never seem to discuss life's great fundamentals."

Val shrugged.

"I've got two kids by Jody, the house to pay for and that other bitch to support," he said, in the mock-matter-of-fact way of true English heroes. "I didn't pay tax for three years and they caught up with me. If I make two hundred a week for another year I might see daylight."

"Real artistes starve in garrets," Reaney joked. "Did Van Gogh pay income tax?"

"You're like my bloody agent. He says real writers should be out there in the mire digging ditches, keeping themselves pure to write *Finnegan's Wake*. He doesn't dig any bleeding ditches. The whole thing's a capitalist concept. Starve the artist—easier than shooting him."

"So what do they do in that socialist haven you're always bashing my ears about?"

Val shook his head with the passive annoyance of a long-sufferer. He nodded to the barman. It was a businessman's pub, properly servile and attentive minions. Spruced up, Val nevertheless seemed a little weary.

"Russia, Russia, who needs Russia? How many times do I have to tell you, I'm a bloody Communist only until the red flag goes up over Buckingham Palace? Then I'm on the boat to America. It's a rebellion manifestation, a critical yardstick, that's all. Two large Scotches, please."

No more silent cries for help from Reaney. Now he was rowing hard against Niagara's quickening pull.

"Bang—there goes the belief of a lifetime, shot down in snappy sentences," he said. "What is there left for an old cynic to believe in, if his naïve friends are not to be depended on? Tell me, Val, what is your attitude to the permissive society, naughty-sex and all that grind?"

Val breathed deeply, still longsuffering. He poured the

water. When Reaney looked into his face it seemed older. Hardening skin, hair no longer unruly—flatter, somehow, as though the great push was over.

"A big bore. You know what, I wish they'd come out with something like a voluntary labour idea to build roads in the north of Scotland. They do it in Yugoslavia. They could give you a tax amnesty for a year's pickswinging, I'd be in it, like a shot. I'm fed up."

Reaney drank some whisky and water. Ah well, there goes ménage à trois with Jody and Val. They decided, for want of a better idea, to go to the party, just before seven. Reaney had a moment's revulsion when he saw the edge of the crowd through the door, but soon they were in the thick of it. The party—western man's frontier. The jungle. Eat or be eaten. Fight—with civilised weapons—for women. Show tooth and claw to rival males. He was known, he was regarded as a funny man, other men made a point of talking to him, new faces were introduced, waiters instinctively knew he was worth serving, tray after tray of Scotch, gin or sherry. The rabble-gabble of men in the know. Mao, let me shake you by the hand. Forced labour on farms is what this cancerous strata, this parasitical bunch of juvenile narcissists and money-fetishists, *need*. They are human beings, after all, they deserve better than this. He met a woman from one of the dailies, knowing the face so well, unaccountably unable to recall her name. So embarrassing! He'd know her breasts blindfold, but he couldn't remember her name. She had expensive clothes—not fitting quite right— make-up that would always have the out-of-register look of a pulp colour comic—heavy nicotine. Imagine his brown-stained, pocket-grimed fingers grappling with hers in alleged ecstasy!

"Haven't seen you around lately," she said, eyes flicking over his shoulder, no sooner with one quarry than she was looking for the next. In villages, of course, you *had* to come to grips with thy neighbour. How terribly feudal, darling.

"It's tough at the top," he said. "How's your love life?"

Words, words. People living, dying, hoping, crying, screaming, struggling. She might or might not be available for a swift one at her flat, depending on whether the next hour provided something more glamorous. Reaney moved off. He got beside the bar. Sooner or later Val would appear there and they could shove off. Even the production girls (each legion squad of a hundred men has four camp-following whores, official, whose tent is always struck first, and who service all hundred at each stop) looked uninteresting. At the other end of the room the big wheels were chatting about the new programme. He established rapport with a young Irish waiter.

"I only came in to use the bogs," Reaney said. The young Irishman thought this was the height of gay, London devilment. "Not your kind of bogs, of course." The young Irish barman knew a wag when he saw one. Also he'd seen Reaney talking to the top people. He was no mug. He kept a bottle of Glen Grant under the table-cloth, whipping it like smuggled dynamite whenever Reaney gave him the big wink. What's-her-bloody-name came by. She was on the last round-up, nothing more exciting had come along.

"Going on anywhere?" she said, giving cold fish eyes to the friendly waiter. Nicotined hands feeling well-thumbed flesh. Out there it was real, even the horror of cleft-palated dishwashers.

"Yes," he said. "My mate and I have fixed up these two young birds, luscious, you should see them, they're bent. Do the whole lesbian performance first. Pity you couldn't come along."

"Give you a ring sometime," she said. Off, hardened lady, off into the night, search for some other tedium-reliever.

The party began to thin out. Only the hardened soaks now. The defeated, masquerading as the real guys. Val was in tow with some chick from the publicity office. Reaney knew her, no chance. All chat and heavy hints and a quick dash into the house she shared with mummy. A frightened, frigid baby aged thirty plus. Val was giving her the Max Miller treatment. She loved it, the dirtier the better, hard lines, Val, if your boiling ballocks drag you all the way to Kenton, Middlesex, in chase of that tight little hole. No white man has ever seen the mythical burial ground. Colonel Faucet—the drip—tried, but somebody turned him off. Ha ha. Rape was the only hope for a bird like her. Funny, rape on the National Health. Put her in the legion tent and let them stamp their boots with impatience as frigid Brigid loses her fear of the male organ. Be the making of her.

They finished the Glen Grant. Then one of the publicity blokes, a really nice guy whom Reaney had promised for years to take out on a bender, came round and suggested they adjourn to the nearest boozer.

"Okay, Wilfred, my old china," Reaney said, knowing he appeared only "cheery", outward appearances always one step behind his true state of drunkenness. "I know you're only trying to get shot of us. I know. Don't worry, mate, I'm not a free-loader. Not like some creeps around here. Come one, I'll reciprocate your kind hospitality."

As they moved towards the door, Reaney went back to the bar. The young Irishman grinned.

"Hey," Reaney said, looking round conspiratorially. "Got any booze you want to flog? I don't see why we shouldn't soak these smooth bastards, eh?"

It was gay in London, muther, bejabers. Reaney slipped him ten bob for the bottle. Haig with only one off the top. He crammed it down inside his trousers.

"Cheers, Paddy," he said. "Look after your mates, I always say."

Ingratiating bastard.

It was all go in the boozer. Frigid Brigid was having the time of her life, with Val's hand round her stiff bum, Wilfred setting them up like there was no tomorrow, Reaney giving them the benefit of his massive personality. Not jokes—anecdotes, puns, wild exclamations, hilarity unleashed. It was easy to conduct the orchestra of humanity. They were lucky he was this ex-corporal and not the other, for he had the secret. Life was the real joke, the one they'd never heard before. Strangers waited for his next proclamation, the pub jumped as it hadn't jumped since it was a gin palace. He was the last drunken Englishman, the last bearpit wag, the last tavern brawler, the last ale-quaffer, the last hope of the pale ghosts who huddled, now, behind the ramparts that once told the world *we* were the scourge. Come on, desiccated creeps, throw off your guilt, throw out your chests, you're English. You're feared, hated, never laughed at. Let's light the fire in our bellies. Form up the squares, Kabul to Kandahar, Mad Mullahs, Pathans, Uhlans, Marshal Ney—stuff the lot of them, bloody foreigners, show them cold English steel and they'll run, tonight we rollick and jest and swill our English ale, tomorrow we put all foreign tricksters and knavish monkeys to the sword . . .

"You're in good form," Val said. Reaney looked down. Everything was bright. There was drama in the air. He patted Val on the top of his head.

"What did you do at Agincourt, Daddy?" he asked. "Your country needs you."

"You're pissed." Val didn't seem suitably enthusiastic.

"I am a warrior, enjoying a warrior's rightful indulgences," Reaney replied, pulling Val round against the bar. "Are you with us, oh tiny scribe? If you are not with us you are against us. Same again, mine host, methinks this tavern right jolly."

Wilfred's presence, Reaney knew, gave him freedom to cavort as he pleased in the telly-men's pub. Many were the weird and wonderful sights and sounds it knew when telly-men fell a-roistering, but Sir, Peter Reaney has *never* been drunk. Who was that poet, the one whose standards were "fairly robust—to him you were not drunk unless you were flat on your back in a gutter"? Why worry about any bloody thing, eh? These people thought he was out of his mind, let them, bring a bit of colour into their dreary little lives. Frigid Brigid began making noises about going home. Reaney didn't want Val to leave with her. He needed Val around, stocky, integrated, single-minded Val, keep the party together, not that he was the all-males-together rugger-buffoonery type, oh no, if there was half a chance Val could insinuate his member (and he'd be up her like a rat up a rope) and lose his deposit in a general erection, fine, he'd give him the minicab fare to Kenton, Middlesex, and maybe go along for the ride (as the man said when he saw his mate place his glass-eye on the belly-dancer's navel, "I hate peeping tums"), but frigid Brigid was scared of the old chimney-sweep, surely Val must realise that.

"I hate to break up the party," she said. "It's the trains, you see."

Reaney calmed down. Val had his arm round her waist. Like a lot of thirtyish frigids she had big tits that flounced and quivered like those cats in the sack.

"My tiny friend wants to escort you safely home," Reaney said. "He is a gallant, poor fool. But as his agent, I must ask what's in it for him? Nuffink is for nuffink, y'know. Charity begins in the Charing Cross-road, Moishe, already. As a man of the world, you can tell me, my dear—will the brave young gallant be rewarded in traditional manner at the end of the trek? Eh? Go on, tell me, think of me as a priest."

She was reluctant to go. She liked a good giggle. These men, they're proper cautions, ducks. The things they say!

"Never mind him, divine one," Val said, looking up into her eyes, Groucho and Margaret Dumont. At this stage he'd set off walking to Glasgow at the very mention of a quick jump. Decent Wilfred hadn't had such a good rave up in months, he kept saying. He was dancing about, benign, delighted, a passive kind of lad whose role in life was to smooth the way for livelier bodies.

"Well, just another quickie then," she said. Mummy had told her how evil men were, wanting only One Thing. How right Mummy was.

"Here you are, my darling," Reaney said, wondering if the drink would buckle her knees. They were all such small, slight bodies. They'd fall against him like swallows hitting a lighthouse. He could pick them all up under one arm, smack their little botties and put them to bed. It wasn't all a waste of time and money. He was a voluntary guinea-pig, off into orbit in the interests of science. Val's alcoholic astronaut!

"It's like Christmas, everything's so merry," she said, giving with a merry little "whoopsie" as some of the water splashed on her boobies. Reaney wanted to get rid of her. A stray thought was growing into an impulse. Soon it would be an uncontrollable determination. Maggie. She was the key to the whole thing. Of course! He'd been angry because he loved her. He was jealous. He'd fallen in love with her from the word go. Her singing nonsense involved commitments, ambitions, other men—no *real* male could tolerate a woman with a separate life. Although the separate bit attracted you in the first place.

So he needed Val, because he wanted her to know he

wasn't dropping round for a swift bunk-up. The impulse grew stronger. Get shot of this walking parody, compared to Maggie she stank of museum dust, inadequate hands, isn't it obvious? Bet she and Mummy had a darling cat. Poor people, blasted country with its twisted, neurotic, spinsterish cruelties. Nobody would ever say he was like that. Back to Falstaff, lads.

"You see, my dear, the trouble with old married men like Pringle and myself is that we've no *time* for gallantry, much as we deplore its passing. Isn't that right, Val, oh ye of many offspring? All right, all right, don't get shirty, nobody's saying you're henpecked, I'm just trying to tell this lovely lady that the swift poke is vital if people are to get to know each other better. It's a lonely old world, ain't it?"

What did Wilfred think? Grin, grin, same again, something to tell the lads about. He could imagine Wilfred writing home to his mother in Welwyn Garden City "dear mum, remember you warned me about bad company, loose women, drink, harpies and wreckers. I'VE FOUND THEM!" What was Frigid thinking? Giggle, giggle, but Reaney's subtle message had got home. She wanted out, now. Val's clutching arm was now to be gently avoided.

"What're you doing, for Christ's sake?" Val hissed, showing a threatening fist. "I'm making the scene with this bird, for God's sake." His young man's eyes were glassy now. Frigid had turned her head to speak to some bloke at the bar. She had a heavy neck. Heavy and dull, the synthesis into sexiness never having occurred.

"No chance," Reaney said, nodding disparagingly at her back. "She's lez." Val frowned. It didn't figure, her being lez with tits like that. Reaney nodded in confirmation. "I've got two birds lined up." He mouthed the words almost soundlessly, lips making exaggerated italics, two fingers held up, pointing first to his own chest and then at Val. He got the message. Silly bugger, he'd be only fit for the human rubbish heap by the time he found out it was all lies. Even if Maggie's friend was back, even if Maggie was remotely likely to fancy a four-hander, even anything, there would be no messing about. Not tonight.

With nods and winks he got the message across, pull out. He saw Val looking at Frigid with a puzzled expression on his face. But she was going now, handbag and gloves and little yellow beret, swaying slightly, Mummy we had a marvellous time, really, no, nothing nasty happened, please Mummy, they're not like *that*, why do you always spoil everything? Bye bye, little girl, say your prayers and God will put you in the legion.

Now then, decent, nice, friendly Wilfred, how do we get shot of you? Easy, for a puppet-master.

"Eh, Wilf, you won't think I'm rude, will you, you see," lower voice, look round, beckon him nearer with little finger, "Val and me's got this pair lined up, you *know*, only we've got to get there soon, you know how it is . . ."

"Lucky bastards," Wilfred said. "No chance of a third, no?"

"Sorry. Don't worry, I'll get it fixed up for the next time. We'll have a real night of it."

They parted—at length—from Wilfred in the street. Val was puzzled. He didn't know how the great party had disintegrated so quickly. Reaney waved at passing taxis, the story of his life.

"Anywhere in Queensway," he told the driver. He ushered Val into the back. It was the thing he did best. To stifle any awkward questions he immediately pulled the Haig up and out of his trousers. It was quite warm to touch.

"Have a slug of ballocks-warmed Scotch," he said to Val. He'd find Maggie's place easily enough, there was nothing he couldn't do when he felt like it. Strong, strong, the Scotch that gurgled over your tongue.

"What's about these birds?" Val asked. Reaney shoved the bottle at his face again. As Val tipped it up he gave the Regent Street pavements a disdainful sweep. Only crumbs on the street at this time of night.

"Leave it to me," he said. "It's all go with these two. That bitch in the pub, she's nothing. Lesbian sure as arseholes."

He didn't have much of a pull at the Haig when it was his turn again. This wasn't to be a rave, it was serious. He could imagine the surprise and delight on Maggie's face when he told her why they'd come.

Chapter Fourteen

Queensway, brightly lit, managing at the same time to convey the impression of both warmth and draughtiness, seemed to be hellish busy.

"Foreigners, you see," he said to Val, whose hands were deep in trouser pockets, small hunched figure of the street-chilled wanderer. All very foreign at Queensway. The fifth column, where once they'd have been war-captured slaves, their men yoked, their women given to the warriors.

Very busy. People, all walking the other way, many going out of that way to bump into Reaney. Why is it always me you bump, he felt like shouting. What the hell did nig-nogs have to be so haughty-looking about? No, these were nasty thoughts. Put them down. We are all men and your women are lovely. Ban all male immigration! Will the black man face up to the hard fact that the white man does want, most desperate of all his shrivelled yearnings, his sister?

"Ten years from now a black woman will be the highest bleeding status symbol in this whole country," he said to Val as they stepped along, the one kept buoyant by a lie, the other by the thought of coming re-enlistment in the ranks of good men. Heyday hey, heyday ho, a girl is going to be pleased to see me.

Three foreign-looking youths, their whole greasy manner redolent of the slick plausibility of your average Mediterranean workshy, came towards them, refusing to break line, arrogant sex-mad bastards wanting him and Val to move off the pavement. He went straight towards them, Val in tow.

They did not break ranks and nerve until he was almost in contact. As they dodged round him, he stopped.

"Why don't you hold fucking hands?" he snarled. It wasn't intended to be a snarl, more of the eyebrow raised devastation of George "I wish I had your style" Sanders. They said things in lingo, but they knew one Englishman was worth any ten lesser breeds. Get back to your *cafes!* So where was this scene then, daddy, Val wanted to know. It was at the back of Whiteleys, he knew that, from there it would be easy. Once, at a time when home was a place to which he phoned to say he was not going, he'd begun lusting after the seedy upstairs ecstasy of Soho whoredom. He was usually so drunk by the time he had raised himself to such depths they wouldn't take him on. However, he had found one who must have been fourth division—she kept shop open till two in the morning, when, as is well known, the only categories abroad in Soho are Guardsmen tired of crawling about in public parks with politicians and drunken journalists, so she didn't care if the customer was drunk or whether he was a venereal Pakistani hamburger chef. Yes, Whiteleys, left-wheel, lads. The point was that this fourth-division whore got to know him and as he was more excited by the idea than by the actuality, he rapidly reached a stage where his lurching visits boiled down to paying her three quid for a chat with his trousers down. Once they'd reached some fascinating stage in her reminiscences when it was time for another client and he'd waited in the other room, chatting to the elderly Italian crone who minded for her, until conversation could be resumed. After that he realised the farce for what it was. Why the hell did it *always* turn into cosy chat? What was wrong with him? Jesus Christ, who chats to Soho whores? They're people, of course, just like you and I.

"I don't go for all that people nonsense," he said to Val,

who murmured agreement. "Carry that we're all God's Chil-lun rubbish to its logical conclusion and Heinrich Himmler's your bloody brother. Some people opt out, don't they?"

"Where's these bloody women, I'm bursting for a leak," Val said.

Yes, he recognised the street. About halfway up, that Queen Mary block of Nashville terraced town houses.

"It's one of these," he said. "Better have a snort before we start."

Drink, drink, the glasses clink. Two dark shadows pass the bottle. Over the city hangs a pall of dust. There are no stars over London. Heydey hey, won't Maggie be *delighted*. Two wandering friends, men of the night, bravely battling home from Troy. What *was* her second name?

"Why are all these houses like Negroes?" he asked Val, whose young face looked hard and worn under the tall lamp-posts. Val shook his head while gurgling down whisky, eyes looking at him over the juncture of fist and bottle. "Because they all look alike to me. Get it? They all look alike to me. Ha ha."

They went up the steps to the door of the nearest house. Names on little white cards, about forty of them, they crammed them into these joints, must make a fortune. No name he recognised, although the light was very poor. What the hell, seek and ye shall find, knock and it shall be opened unto you, ring and—they didn't have bells in the Bible, ring all the bells, let's play *Chimes Blues* by King Oliver, bring adventure into their dreary lives.

The door was opened by a man in shirt sleeves, a some-what unhappy-looking individual, probably foreign, lots of Poles run these gaffs.

"Good evening," he said, smiling, inclining his head in a small, formal gesture such as foreigners practised, silly twits.

"Can you help us? We're looking for a young lady whose name is Maggie?"

The man's shirt was of that old-fashioned variety which requires a separate collar. He was not wearing the collar. He had the door open about eighteen inches. Not one of your traditionally hospitable innkeepers, to be sure.

"No," he said. He made to close the door. Reaney put his hand against it.

"She's got blonde hair," he said.

"Clear off out of it," the man replied. He closed the door.

"Rude bastard," Val said. They went down the steps. They had another pull at the bottle before mounting the next lot.

"People are getting frightened, have you noticed?" he proclaimed to Val. "Over-crowding, that's what it is. No, don't bother reading the names, ring the bloody bells, they're only watching telly the stupid bastards. You panic in a crowd, don't you? Everybody panics in a crowd."

"Mob violence," Val said, quiet, serious. "Nasty sight. Lowest instincts appealed to."

"Exactly. Isn't anybody at home? Good God, the sanctity of the hearth means nothing these days. Ring them again. She lives here, I'm sure it's this one. Look at it this way— everybody panics in a crowd. The world is getting crowdeder every day, population explosions, right?"

"Right. A million Chinese born every minute, in front of machine-guns."

"True enough. So what was Hitler all about then? Jews? Racialism? No, no. You can't get away with that one any longer."

"The Germans were never conquered by the Romans."

"Exactly. Oh, good evening . . ."

One nervously peeping woman in a dressing-gown opened the door a few inches on a chain while behind her,

Reaney sensed, built up a small crowd of bell-summoned residents.

"Do you have a girl called Maggie living here? We've come from Australia to see her, urgent family business." He smiled benevolently. The woman looked back into the hall, speaking to the bemused mob at her heels. Reaney prodded Val in the biceps. Boxing clever, eh?

"No," the woman said. "Are you drunks?"

This was very funny.

"Drunks, madam? We're private detectives."

She banged the door. Right in their faces! In the middle of a normal, polite conversation. He turned to the array of cards and bells. He pressed one and then another, thumbing up and down. Cheeky devils, they'd better not come that insolent again.

"Go away," a woman shouted from inside.

"Go away yourself, you old cow," he retorted. He wasn't drunk, just angry. Justifiably.

"I'll call the police," came the voice.

"Call the Pope for all I care."

They went back down to the pavement.

"It's not much of an orgy, if you ask me," Val said.

"Stop whining. Nothing worthwhile is easy in this life. Have another drink and shut up. It must be the next one. Anyway, as I was saying, it's crowded, you see. The world. People are panicking, therefore, ipso ergo, you get mass murder."

"Hitler had good ideas but he didn't go far enough, is that it? I am against Hitler. Is it this one?"

"Mybe it's becos we are Lahndoners, walkin' up an' dahn. Ring the bells, press the buttons, don't bother me with details, I have discovered a very large truth, if you were not too drunk to grasp it. Race murder is only the crowd panicking, don't you see? Give me a drink, you greedy devil, I paid for it. Go on, ring the buggers."

He stood in the darker shadow of the tall porch, watching Val poke at buzzers. He was only little, poor Val. He needed protection. Reaney would see him all right.

A woman opened the door. Hard-faced, he could see that. No room at this inn, JC, mangy bitch in the mangy manger.

"Maggie in?" Val said, shoving forward in an aggressive manner. Reaney put his hand on Val's shoulder, smiling knowingly at the woman.

"Pardon my friend's impatience," he said. "He's come all the way from Maracaibo to see a girl who wrote to him when he was doing life on Devil's Island. All he knows is her first name—you know how it is."

She folded her arms. Fine figure of a woman, begad, face like the back of a bus.

"Maggie?" she said, eyeing them contemptuously.

"A blonde girl," he said. Fortunately he was holding the whisky behind his back. Such women of the *rentier* class were very bigoted.

"Wait here," she commanded, closing the door.

"This is it," he said to Val.

"I don't like it," Val replied. "I thought it was going to be a party."

"I thought you were a writer."

"What's that got to do with it?"

"It's real life, isn't it? The darkened city streets, the cold-eyed citizens, man's eternal quest for the Holy Grail. It's a symbol, we're living a symbol of our times."

This time the door was opened by a younger girl.

"Yes?" she said. The first woman stood behind her. Reaney craned to see if he recognised the shabby hall-carpet.

"You're not Maggie," he said, accusingly.

"She's not in," the girl said. "I share with her."

"Ah ah," he said. "I know all about you. I've slept in your bed."

The girl looked round at the hard-faced woman. How silly of him, that was the landlady, strict rules, no male callers after ten o'clock and all that.

"We've come for the party," Val said. He was really rotten. Couldn't hold it any longer.

"My name's Peter," he said. "I was hoping to see Maggie, rather urgent, you see. Could we wait, will she be back tonight?"

They could have a cosy chat, pass round the whisky, show her that not all men were sordid.

"No," the hard-faced landlady said, coming forward beside the girl. "You can't wait here."

"Why not, madam?" he asked, perfectly courteous. Such universal suspicion, didn't they know we're all on the same side?

"It's the rule," she said. "You'll have to go away."

"Ballocks," Val said. Reaney patted him on the head, smiling in a man of the world manner.

"My friend is overwrought," he said. "He's had an unfortunate life. I assure you, we'll—"

"Go away," the woman said, quite nastily, too. She made to close the door, forcing the girl back inside. Reaney went forward, knowing he could charm even her.

"It's important we see her," he began. "It's a vital message—"

She slammed the door to. He pounded on it with his knuckles. Totally uncalled for rudeness! What was wrong with these people?

The door did not open again. He gave it a kick. Val made as if to charge it with his shoulder, but he held up his hand.

"Don't stoop to their level," he said. "We'll wait here till she comes. Maggie'll see us all right."

They stood on the pavement. There was a surprising amount of whisky left. Val sat on the bonnet of a parked car.

"Let's tie all the car aerials in knots," he suggested. "I don't like them."

Reaney took a much-needed drink.

"Not a good idea," he said. "Have a drink."

"It's not all that, is it?"

"What isn't?"

"This party."

Stupid bastard. Anti-social. Why did he pick a nit like this for a best friend? Where the hell was Maggie? What was it all about, eh? Lot of rubbish.

"Rubbish lives," he said.

"I'm going home," Val said. The car was a Jaguar. Didn't like Jaguars. Company directors doing ninety killing old ladies claiming to be under course of drugs. Drunken criminals. Shoot the bloody lot of them.

At first he thought it was a van but when the two policemen got out and came round the car he realised it was a Black Maria.

"Hullo," he said. They stood side by side, big blokes, coppers, got to be, haven't they.

"Is this your car?" one of them asked Val.

Val shook his head.

"Wish it was, mate," he said.

"Get off it then," the copper said. So much shadow off their peaked caps couldn't see their faces. Maybe they didn't have faces.

Val didn't move.

The copper pulled him off. Val tried to push him away. Reaney stepped forward—to explain about Val's epilepsy. The other copper grabbed his arm.

"I work here," Reaney said. "I can vouch for that man."

Val seemed to be trying to kiss the copper. That wouldn't get him anywhere, stupid nit.

"Come on," the copper who was holding Reaney said. "We'll take you somewhere nice."

"I have an appointment with a girl singer," Reaney explained. "I can make her a star." Only way—impress them with glamour.

But they were determined to take poor Val away in the van so he thought he'd have to go along and vouch for him. The copper was kind enough to help him into the back of the Black Maria.

"Stupid nit," he said to Val as they sat beside each other in the darkness. "They're running you in. What did you have to sit on that car for?"

"Where's the whisky?" Val asked. Then he passed out. Reaney looked through a small window at passing lights. It was all hopeless. Val was just a human burden, no good to man or beast . . .

He remembered—vividly—standing in front of this inspector bloke, Val now recovered, asking him when the beating-up started, Val asking a passing police-woman sergeant when she had a day off for a date, him bending forward and asking the inspector if he could call his lawyer, the inspector making them empty their pockets, Val shouting that it wasn't like bloody Dixon of Dock Green, was it, him having to give their names and addresses because Val said he was suffering from total amnesty, the sergeant giving them something to sign, him saying it was a classic frame-up, the inspector being very stroppy about something, then going somewhere and being put in a narrow room with no chairs and shiny linoleum on the floor.

Nobody came when they banged on the door and there was no lavatory in the cell so they pissed, in turns while the other watched, against the wall and it ran under the heavy wooden door and then a copper came, very nasty he was, power-mad, obviously, raising his voice about the mess. Reaney telling him about the Geneva Convention rules as regards prisoner's toilet facilities, then they were going different ways, him in a tiled cell with a wooden bunk, one measly blanket, what the hell, it was Val they'd arrested, not him, he'd only come as a character witness, it was a rotten, stinking, stupid mistake, every man had a right to call his lawyer, I'll kick your door down, no use, he sat on the wooden bunk, have a fag, where's the matches, bastards, I know your bloody game, leave the fags and take away the matches, psychological torture, get away with murder at night cops do, I'll sue you to the House of Lords, why don't they come? He had friends in high places, thank God he had, too, for England was in a hell of a mess what with the old medieval dancing madness breaking out again (rust in the plastic wheat factories) and Neurotics Anonymous having joined with Alcoholics for Anarchy to make the largest single party MRA (Make Room for All) which was now campaigning for cyanidisation of the water. You were right, Sigmund Reaney, they said, so now there's only one way to save this country from suicide, *your* way, A State of Sexual Emergency. It may be too late, he said, but I'll try, God willing, I'll try. A crash programme of free public brothels—police stations and churches will do for a start. Virginity between consenting adults to be a crime against society. All unmarried or childless women over the age of 18 to be conscripted in National Sex Service, staffing mental hospitals, asylums—the neediest cases first. All television and radio programmes on a wartime basis—Dicks for Dock Green, Bed-Cars, Ready, Steady Come, Doctor Finlay's Blue Book, Grand-Stand, Have a Go, Independent Television Nudes . . . our men must be brought back from the abyss (as the bishop said to the cardinal) of clean-living. The great thing about power is to see your own ideas become reality—the zoos are crammed, Paddington whores vie with each other to earn the new decoration—Heroine of English Labour, backs to the mattress, women of England; lay down your wives, men of England; we are on the brink of general insanity through chastity, the madmen gather their forces but tonight Our Leader gives a Party Political Broad on all channels. My friends, for years they reviled me, saying I was dirty-minded, filthy, tonight I come before you to restore sanity to the bawdy politic. Once this was a green and roisterous land, jolly, ruddy-cheeked Englishmen and wenches shagging in the fields, in the ditches, in the alehouses, in the barns, in the stables, in the street and under hedges. We were a happy, strong nation. Today, in this year of, so-called Christian, prudery, we see the results of fear, of viciousness, of the rule of the prurient, of the old maid. England expects every man to do his duty, every woman to lie down and laugh. Ours is a fertile land. It can be a happy land. This is how. I know many of you know these things only from history books, books written, I may say, when we stood alone and were proud thus to stand. Stand again, England. Inch by inch we shall fight the good fight. Arise, ye sons of Crecy, and they shall say about us in the ages to come, *this* was their finest hour. Stand? I don't want to, what the hell, where's this, what am I doing, tiled walls, who are you, what the—

"He's all right," the copper said. Reaney arose, the single blanket falling about his knees. The light in the cell was strong. The copper was in a hurry to get him out.

"What time is it?" he asked. His mouth was foul, his whole body felt filthy. What had happened? What was he doing in a cell?

"Five," the copper said. "You can clear off now."

He walked with as much dignity as his tousled, creased

appearance would allow. They'd gone looking for that girl, oh Christ, what a mess. He had to stand in front of an inspector while the stuff they'd taken from him was poured onto the desk from an envelope. He signed a receipt.

"Feeling better?" the inspector said, Reaney stood back, shoving the stuff into his pockets. He eyed the man with what he hoped was supercilious indifference.

"You've got to be in court at ten," the sergeant said. "You've got to be there, you understand that, don't you?"

"Why should I?" Reaney replied, anxious to get out of this polish-smelling, centrally heated dump, determined, however, not to cringe to the bastards. Take away the matches, leave the fags! What did they do if they had you for more than a night?

"You have to forfeit two pounds bail and you've still got to appear in person anyway." The sergeant liked saying that.

"Where's my friend?" Reaney asked, not warming an inch.

"We let him go about two o'clock," the sergeant said. "You were sleeping. You made a mess of our floor, didn't you?"

Reaney looked him up and down. They hated that.

"We were put in a cell without a toilet. We shouted for at least ten minutes. What did you expect us to do, drink it?"

He was middle-class, he talked middle-class, he didn't cringe, they naturally wanted to correct any wrong impression he had. He ignored the chatty remarks.

"Where is this court?" he asked. They told him. He was shown to the street by a constable.

"You can get a taxi easy enough around here," the constable said.

Reaney was furious. What had they been doing? It was

the powerlessness. He was in a damned cell, nothing he could do about it, literally nothing. Plucked out of the night, shut away, marched about, spoken down to by heavy-faced, sanctimonious big boots. He breathed angrily through tightly-pursed lips. He eventually stopped a cab, which took him, silently hating everything, along the deserted Bayswater Road through Notting Hill Gate and up Ladbroke Grove. He had no compunction in waking up Val or Jody.

Hammer, hammer, let me in. It was Jody, in Val's dressing-gown, hair all over the place, who let him in.

"I knew this was bound to happen sooner or later," she mumbled as she went up the stairs. He followed. Her white ankles were all he could see in the dim light. Val—imagine walking out, leaving him to rot in a dungeon! Friendship? And who'd told them *he'd* slashed on their floor? Val. The tiny, self-centred rat. Well, he could do something about that. At the top of the stairs he put his hand on Jody's arm, stopping her sleep-stumbling walk to *their* bedroom.

"I love you," he said. He had his arms round her before she replied. He kissed her warm face. He was as strong as a bear. "My darling," he said. "My darling."

He wasn't really sure whether she struggled much or not, but he had little difficulty in getting her into his bedroom. Strike—and don't give them a moment to think. In the dark, one husband was much like another. He kept kissing her as he undressed himself, half-lying on top of her, panting with the twisting effort required to remove his trousers with one hand. Then he was on top of her. He had no intention of letting her go, whatever she did.

"You bastard," she whispered. "You're taking advantage of me." Her hand rested lightly on the back of his neck. He was still angry.

"You need it as much as I do," he said.

He removed his socks by the big toe method mastered by

all desperate men whose love life continually borders on near-rape.

"Is it me you want, or just a woman?" she asked, both hands now round his neck.

"You'll do," he said. "You're here."

But, of course, it had been love all the time. Jody. Staring him in the face. That was why Val was his best friend, the easiest way to be near her. The first time was all revenge. He let his whole massive weight rest on her. He had no thoughts in his head at all, just fire and anger throughout his whole body. The second time was just as passionate, but there was time to kiss her, lips, ears, forehead, hair.

"Darling Jody, I've been in love with you for years." It was true. He waited for his brain to contradict, but there was nothing going on up there, nothing apart from Jody.

"You're just saying that," she said. She had her arms round his chest, hands clasped at his back, strong honest circle round a man.

"All right, whatever you think." Why hadn't he tried before? Hadn't he realised, Val drinking all the time, poor sodden Val, couldn't love any woman, poor writing fool. Drinking to avoid the truth, his passion gone the first time they were in bed. A writing fool. Between the second and third time he took off her nightdress, hands shaping over her generous body, hands that had come home.

Now he was no longer a rutting animal, a stag, but a proud, eager lover. He stroked her hair, ran his fingertips over her face.

"I wanted to do this when you were feeding the baby," he said.

"I know you did."

"I thought I was going mad," he said. To make love without concentrating grimly on the brain's pornography, to make love and mean it and be able to talk at the same time and not to think of angles, escapes, recriminations . . . she was mistress and wife and lover and mother and friend and daughter and all the women he had ever wanted. Safe now.

Dawn light filtered between their faces. He saw her strong nose. He kissed it, taking it into his mouth.

"I feel like a cat that's had too much cream," she murmured, pulling the lobes of his ears. He tried to look into her eyes. She lay, all woman, face in a private smile. Not private—not to him.

"You'd better go now," he said. "My darling." He eased himself towards the wall.

"Throwing me aside like an old boot?" she said.

"For tonight," he replied. "We don't want the children to get upset, do we?"

"What a considerate lodger you are." She stretched as she sat up on the edge of the bed. He'd seen paintings of women like her, strong white bodies which he'd always dismissed as masturbating painters' fantasy projections. He lay, naked on his back. He felt tired and proud and relaxed, the way he used to feel after route marches or days on the assault course. The rozzers, Felix, Mrs. Fanchetti, nobody could get at him now.

She bent down and kissed his mouth, then she was gone into the stillness of the sleeping house.

Such was the body heat generated by intercourse he was able to lie on the blankets without feeling cold. He listened for Val's imminent discovery of the betrayal, but there was no sound after her soft steps ceased. Well, well, Noble Reaney, you've done it now, all right. Was it love? Was it just new trouble? Was he now a *whole* rat?

Perhaps, perhaps. It was a new complication to end all complications, that was for sure. But to have made love and meant it for the first time in your life—*that* was something he wouldn't forget—or let slip—in a hurry.

Chapter Fifteen

Even knowing what he now knew, it was still possible to whizz down a cup of Jody's black coffee with Val in the kitchen before they left on the hungover spree of attending court. He felt more like her husband than Val. Everything about her—her unmade face, her kitchen-roughened hands, her untidy red pony-tail, her greenish eyes—details noticed individually now for the first time, yet the whole adding up to a woman he seemed to have known and waited for all his life. And he felt relaxed and cheery. Val was quite ill.

"Come on, squire," Reaney said, patting Val on the back. "You'll only get weighed off for half a bar on a DD. You look sick enough to be facing a five stretch on GBH." He translated for Jody—fined ten bob for Drunk and Disorderly, better than five years for Grievous Bodily Harm. He felt very worldly.

Jody looked at Val and made a tut-tut sound. She seemed sleepily cheery. He took this as a sign that it had not been a momentary aberration, that she felt the same way he did.

In the taxi to the court Val sat back, hunched more than ever, occasionally letting out a small moan. Reaney tried to cheer him up. He felt he owed Val that much at least.

"Stick your fags down your socks," he said. "You'll be a snout baron."

Val winced. He'd put on a clean white shirt and tie. The snowy collar contrasted with the raw surface of his shave-reddened neck skin.

"You'll be an intellectual among the cons, mate," Reaney

went on. "They'll make you the nick librarian. Look at the great book you'll be able to write."

As he mouthed this second-hand gaol patter he thought of the day ahead. After court he'd have to go to the bank to snatch his own money. At least that was what he'd planned, but now it seemed a very creepy-crawly thing to do. What was he to be coming down to their level? Money was nothing to him. He'd have to go back to the flat and get some fresh clothes if there were any left. What about Mrs. Fanchetti? Mental shrug, Italian-style. Then to the office, the bank, the TV studios with Barry Black. A crowded day. Tomorrow? Saturday—his first free day since God knew when. A good day for lovers!

And then Sunday and Dorry's arrival at London airport and all that jazz. Oh well, it was a great life if you didn't weaken. He'd wait to see how he felt about things when the booze had worn off and the morning hysteria had died down.

He bought twenty Senior Service tipped at a kiosk near the court. Val waited, unhappy, cold—although it was yet another bright morning in this gayest of all cities—falling silently in step as he came away from the kiosk, shoving change into his hip pockets.

"Cheer up, man," Reaney said. "What's a DD rap to a hell-raiser like you?"

Inside the entrance to the court he asked a policeman where they had to go and they were shown into a side office which led to a narrow corridor which led into a largish, crowded room. A bench ran round the walls seating a large number of unhappy-looking men. Policemen came and went through this prisoners' ante-room.

Reaney found a space on the bench. A terrible old bum, wearing an ancient army greatcoat which reached his ankles, moved to let Val sit down. Reaney brought out the fags. The old man watched Val taking one from the new packet. Reaney held the pack to the old man. He looked at Reaney as if to spot the catch, then he took one with blackened fingers protruding from tattered woollen mits. Reaney struck a match and lit all three.

"Ta, mate," the old man said. He took his first drag as if the fag were a precious object being examined by a suspicious jeweller.

"This is a gay little gathering, what?" Reaney said quietly to Val, who seemed to shiver. Standing together were three young lads, wearing short Italian style jackets one of them with a new bandage covering left ear, left eye and right skull. They showed no interest in the older, defeated majority. A young office type carrying a briefcase came towards Reaney, attracted no doubt by their respectable suits. The man on Reaney's side—who wore a black donkey jacket with the name of a building firm painted in yellow letters across its back—pushed at the man on his far side until there was room for the young lad to sit down, clutching his briefcase on his knees.

"What rap they got you on, bud?" Reaney said, offering the fags.

"Oh, no, I don't smoke, thank you," the young man said. He was Scottish—better-class Scottish. Reaney regretted only the time that was being wasted. Otherwise it all seemed a bit of a giggle. He was already in the exercise yard, talking without moving his lips, walking with the old con's yard-step. Val was sunk in depression. Reaney decided that a *real* writer would lap all this up, especially the terrible old men who, now that he thought about it, all wore ankle-length army greatcoats of impressive vintage.

"My mate and I were framed," he went on to the young man. "So why did you get your collar felt, sport?"

The young man seemed desperate to talk—and his lips trembled, as though tears were near.

"They say I exposed myself, indecently," he said.

"Did you?" Reaney asked, genuinely interested. Yesterday *he'd* been near the perverted stage, too.

"I don't know, it's not what I normally do, I mean, I'd had a few pints, you see I'm just down from Dundee for an interview, I met this man and we went for a drink and the next thing I knew they were taking me in, how long will they take, do you know? I've got to get a train back to Dundee at one o'clock, I've only got one day off and my firm don't know I'm down here for an interview."

"You'll be all right," Reaney said. 'It's not what I normally do'! What do you normally do, touch up little boys?

He finished his cigarette. It was not ash-tray territory so he dropped it on the stone floor, but before he brought his heel down the old man had bent forward, thin old fingers reaching for the butt. Reaney took hold of the stretching arm.

"Don't do that," he said. "I might have тв or something. Here, have these." He gave the old man the flattened packet from the night before, in which there were six oval-shaped Seniors. The old man looked at him unbelievingly.

"You're a pal," he said. Reaney felt quite embarrassed. Val looked steadily at his own knees. A writer? The young bloke twitched about as though he needed the bogs. The old man began to wrestle with himself under the great tent of his coat. Bugs, probably. So, a bath and he'd be all right. Poor old bastard didn't look as though he got many baths. Eventually he seemed to uncoil his body. He brought his hand out from the coat.

"Here, mate," he said to Reaney, drawing close in case *they* were listening. He held out his hand, which held a pair of well-worn black socks. "You 'ave these, mate," he said.

"They're good socks. Get half a dollar for them from any-body, you will."

"I've got socks, thanks," Reaney said. "You keep them."

"No, mate, you give me fags, you 'ave the socks, good socks, they aren't nicked, not likely, I got them off this frienda mine, didn't I?"

There was a sneaking impulse to hug the dirty old bas-tard, but this was a man's world.

"I'll tell you," he said to the old man, head twisted round so that he was looking into the hairy old face, with the dirt engrimed on the hairless skin beneath the eyes, "I don't need socks right now, but I could do with a watch. Any chance?"

"Watches is difficult, mate," the old man said. His eyes were gray, the pupils reddish, a smear of excess water on the lashes. "It'll take time, but you leave it to me, mate, I'll see what's goin', don't worry."

"Thanks, mate," Reaney said. The old man winked. Reaney gave him a cigarette. Val lit his cigarette without saying anything. A police constable came towards them, a young fellow.

"Mister Reaney and Mister Pringle?" he said, standing above them. Reaney looked up, hard-faced. No con liked coppers, especially smarmy young coppers. "Feeling better then?"

This must be the twit who ran them in. He wanted to make it all seem very friendly, a joke between men of *their* type, a special relationship in a room of low-class layabouts and bums. Val grunted. Reaney just looked.

"You'd had a few, of course," the copper went on. Reaney saw the three young hard cases in the Italian bum-freezers looking over. He gave them the cold eye as well. "We thought we'd better take you in, you were carrying quite a lot of money, you never know, do you, all for the best really."

"I suppose so," Reaney said. "What's the damage likely to be?"

The copper made a little face.

"Drunk and disorderly?" he said. "Ten bob at top weight."

Reaney shrugged. Maybe he'd been too friendly.

"What was disorderly about us, actually?" he asked. "I don't remember anything like that."

"You'd been at doors," the copper said. "It was the sarge really, he thought your friend here was trying to hit him."

The copper explained that they'd be first in the court and that there was nothing to it. He went away, walking straight through the three young Italian suits, who gave him the minimum of grudging gangway. The old man coughed in a great spasm.

"All right, Dad?" Reaney asked.

"Coppers," the old man wheezed. "Don't go much on them, mate."

"When will I be up?" the Dundee flasher asked Reaney, who was obviously now an expert.

"Christ knows, Jock," Reaney said. "Depends on the beak, dunnit?"

He had to laugh. Here he was in the drunk tank, acting out a tiny scene, having a great time, never felt better. But the old men, they were a sad sight. Pity the bloody prime minister wasn't down here, maybe shake up his bloody Socialist principles a bit, see London's human wreckage, not the hell-stories of the coroner's court, oh no, the living victims, poor old sods, standing in a queue, future candidates for the coroner's little show.

Then they were in a narrow corridor, waiting to go through a door into the court. The same copper stood beside Reaney and Val, giving with the same matey patter. Val grunted occasionally. Perhaps he suspected? No, impossible.

He was fourth to be beckoned by the copper who stood at the door. The courtroom seemed to be a small amphitheatre. A copper showed where to enter the dock. The atmosphere was like that of a busy schoolroom. He faced the beak across the well of the floor. The beak wore rimless spectacles on his nose. The young copper got in a roofed box to Reaney's left. He rattled away in a low voice. The woodwork was brown, an extension of the coronary decor thought fitting for the gravity of society's business, schools and courts, very similar.

"Do you plead guilty or not guilty?"

"Guilty." Was I hell.

"I suppose you'd been drinking and became a bit tiresome," the beak said, looking over his spectacles at Reaney. He said nothing in reply. "Anything known, constable?"

"Nothing known," the constable said. No, you third-rate Solomons, nothing known about me. Nothing known.

"Ten shillings," the beak said. It had lasted thirty seconds at least, the judging of his crime against humanity. He stumbled slightly as he left the narrow dock. He was shown through another door into an office where a police-sergeant took his ten bob and gave him a receipt. He folded it neatly and put it between the fold of his New Scheherazade membership card. A gay souvenir of champagne days. Ah, those boat race nights . . .

He went round into the public seats, but by the time he found the entrance and eased in behind a small knot of men and women who seemed to be waiting for dramatic happenings Val was already leaving the dock. Nobody thought to ask *why*, but why should punishment professionals be interested in why? Nothing known.

"Painless, isn't it," he said to Val. They re-entered the spectator section out of interest in the Dundee flasher. Val seemed cheerily surprised that he hadn't been deported or flogged. He nudged Reaney as they stood with their backs against the panelled wall, nodding in the direction of two well-dressed (not exquisitely groomed, just well-dressed) matrons who sat on the front spectator bench, a box of chocolates open on a lap.

"Good as the fillums, ain't it?" Val said. People moved about the well of the court. He could now see the press bench. He saw a rather luscious piece come in a side door and approach another bench, the two male occupants of which moved along, smilingly, to let her sit. Probation Officers? Oh to be arrested by lovely policewomen wearing fishnet blue and halter-necked tunics! Oh to be given into the power of such a lovely probation lady, to bare his heart to her. Vote Reaney for all-female (non-butch) rozzers.

The Dundee flasher hung his head in the dock, young, red-cheeked in the Scottish manner. A copper gave the facts, nothing but the facts, ma'am. He'd flashed his arse to men and his wendell to women. He had called out various lewd greetings. See a doctor, let you off this time (maybe the doctor will cut it off, Scottish salesman, before you rip asunder the fabric of the nation), don't come before me again, goodnight, sweet ponce, and it's up wi' the bumholes o' Bonnie Dundee.

He had to leave for the flat, to change and get to the bank, but the meaty stuff was coming now.

". . . a watch was kept on the premises for five days, during which time sixty-nine men were seen to enter. Having obtained a warrant I went to the premises. The door was opened by a person in female apparel with long blonde hair, later ascertained to be a male person. In one room we found a number of canes, whips and a large quantity of contraceptives, used and unused. In an adjoining room we found a man and a woman naked in bed. The woman said 'I gave her the twenty-five quid', and the man said 'Will my name be in the Ipswich papers?' The accused was found to have twenty-five pounds in her possession when she returned . . ."

Nothing known, oh naked gentleman, so fear not the papers of Ipswich. The crime is in the offer, not the acceptance. Such is not the case with most crimes, curiously enough, for it's the shop-lifter who's the criminal, not the shop. When is a shop not a shop? When it's a knocking shop, you lucky people. Or, as the young man said to the queer copper, I know the law is an ass but does it have to be my ass?

"Come on," he said to Val. The two matrons craned forward to hear the quiet-voiced police inspector. None of the ragged old bums of the drunk tank were to be seen as they crossed a stone floor and left the court. Swallowed up in the subterranean world they were allowed to inhabit between inspections? So what to say to an ex-best friend betrayed with a kiss? The sun shines on two resting warriors walking the great ashtray we call a city. Peter-Val-Jody. Oh, daughter Jean, you're much nicer in bed than Mummy. I know, that's what Brother Bob says, too. There was not even a need to arrange anything with Jody—it would happen again and such complications as this smallish, square-set, fair-young husband shrivel to nothing in the heat of our certainty. All the world means nothing to a lover.

"I'm going home, I'm stacked up with work," Val said. "It must be all right, being an old tramp with no bloody income tax or anything, just wander about, follow your nose."

So Val wanted rid of his load.

A sunshine street in West London, a gay Friday morning, tatty buildings landscaping our wandering thoughts. Nothing is known.

"I'm in love with Jody, you know that, don't you?" Reaney

said. He looked straight ahead. The mind concentrates, which is the real relief of action, but Boswell wasn't in listening mood.

"The real torture of life is not to want *a* woman," Val sermonised, always the half-mocking quotation, never words on tablets. "It's to want *all* women."

"Or to have bad breath, or a husband who no longer fancies you, or to live in Dundee and fight to keep your hands from your zip fastener?" Was now the time? "Nobody's perfect."

They stopped a taxi, which dropped Val at the junction of Ladbroke Grove and Holland Park Road (he knew nothing and his last thought was that they might have a drink at home that night), then Reaney was being borne in a series of right-angled tacks to his onetime home. He decided against stopping the taxi up the street, away from *her* window. He was really too old for such dodges. He had found his person now, he was strong.

Down the stairs, studiously avoiding the ground-floor windows. Quick, key, work your magic, enter, close Sesame. The flat smelled now, stale, unused, a gentle aroma of departed life. It was dark, too, after the sunshine. He threw the shirt in a corner of the bathroom, ran the geyser, put his shaving things on the basin. A change of socks and underwear, a new skin for a new battle. He whistled to himself as he lathered in the steamy mirror. Notice something? Alone yet relaxed. Security. Knowledge that there is a person. The blade slides, microscopically smooth. The face reappears in neat swathes. Quick splash with hot, then cold, after-shave to tingle, dry on rough towel, quick swab with *her* facecloth round sweaty armpits, dry those, into the ghostly bedroom, clean underwear a-plenty, not so many shirts left, use them up, tomorrow we'll be sober, aggressively stiff striped tie, have to be dark brown sports jacket and dark gray flannels, suede shoes, sunshine clothes for a sunshine day. Nothing known? If only they knew, but they knew nothing. Veterans of Somme, Mons, Wipers and Crecy —we know nothing about you. Sixteen-stone-plus noble Roman dons weekend purple and heads for the bath-house, the forum, what-have-you, thumbs practising the downward jab.

Knock at the door. He knew she'd probably come down and he noted, as he took a last look at himself in the wardrobe mirror, that he not only looked composed, he also felt nothing in the way of panic.

"Oh hullo," he said. She had an eager smile on her face. She was wearing her light-coloured suit. Broad, womanly —but what about that gothic horror from her lungs? He stood at the door. The sun made little reddish rainbows in her shining hair. Beneath the suit jacket she wore a white blouse. Brown, welcoming, womanly flesh. He made no sign for her to come in.

"How are you?" she said. "I saw you come home." She smiled.

Many tints in a Mediterranean face. He stood back a step. Breasts, hips, it was the nacreous shine of the nylons that really did it. He could get to the bank by half-twelve, bit of a rush, meet Barry Black at one, necessary to spend some time with him today, just a feeling—the kind of feeling that came in advance of a new course of action, half-felt thoughts.

"Coming in?" he said, bowing slightly with a nice little sweep of his right arm. She inclined her head graciously. If she'd looked pathetic in any way . . . no, she was the old upstairs Mrs. Fanchetti again, ripe little brown galleon. He let her walk past him into the hall. Ripe calves, plump but smooth. He had an idea.

"Just a minute," he said. He went into the bathroom. He

tipped some after-shave into the palm of his right hand. He heeled the palm on his nose, then thumbed lotion into his nostrils. She had gone on into the kitchen. What did she want now, to feed him up? No time for that, mama mia.

He hung his jacket on a hook behind the kitchen door. Knowing what to avoid, his kiss was on the back of her mint-smelling neck. She snuggled backwards against his body. He ran his hands down her jelloid front. He stood like this long enough to test his own reaction—and the workings of his anti-gas lotion. Seemed all right. Of course, I meant it, Jody, but think of this as an academic test of *me*.

"Not so quick, my bad man," Mrs. Fanchetti said when he started to steer her to the bedroom. She twisted round to look up at him. He breathed out slowly. "You must say nice things before we are doing it." He raised his eyebrows, looking sideways up at the ceiling, a gesture she might construe as a joke but which was merely a breathing precaution. "Do you love me?"

Well, that was a silly question and it deserved a straight answer.

"Love you?" he said, looking down. Perhaps she hated his breath! Too bad. "Of course I don't love you." He put his hands on her breasts. He cautiously drew in air. Yes, there it was, a slender trace. There, Jody, faithful to you in my fashion. "You don't think you've got to love somebody to have a quick jump, do you?"

She pulled away from him, hesitating, then seeing the seriousness on his face.

"You said you loved me that time?"

Silence in the pots and pans. The whirr of the fridge.

"Did I? Well, you know how it is, a man'll say all sorts of things when he's steamed up."

"Oh!" she said. Thank the Lord (dubious as His intervention might be) she was angry, not cringing. He was passing the test!

"Yes, oh!" he replied. "Look, I'm a bit pushed for time, are we going to have it away now or not?" He looked at his wrist-watch, a subtle gesture. She went to slap his face, but he pushed her arm aside. He shrugged. She made up her mind in a rush and was out of the kitchen and through the hall in no time at all, no time at all. The Great Seducer felt thirsty. He let the cold tap run for a bit to bring in fresh supplies. Cold, cold, is the water that sparkles for free, to Jody my true love faithful I'll be, tralala.

He double-locked the front door, climbed the steps, walked in the sensuous sunshine to the pub on the corner, always a taxi in these parts, off to the bank, my good man, and watch me cry all the way. He sat back, relaxed, senses heightened by the coitus that never was. He could feel his skin for the first time in weeks. Nice, baggy skin, make a simply huge hearth-rug for any lion's den. How did the city look now? Knightsbridge, even more exciting when you knew these sleek persons achieved their sleekness through the deprivation of others. How many Lancashire proles punched clocks to keep that exquisitely-preserved matron in facials? How many men's family-supporting wages went to feed that lion-sized dog? That's what it's all about, squares, we've been let down by our revolutionaries so now Baby Face Reaney is gonna blast open every bank between here and Oklahoma City. In prole-town you either rot or get strong. Take one man's money, another man's wife—the rest is all for the birds.

He walked into the bank as Pretty Boy Floyd might have done, cool, hard and mean. The mood lasted until he was shown through dark-panelled (schools, banks, courts) corridors to the manager's office. He wanted to waste no time in chit-chat. His feeling about the afternoon with Barry Black was growing stronger.

"Good morning, Mister Reaney," the manager, Snead, said.

"Morning," he replied. "I'm in a hurry, actually. If I can just transfer the joint account money into the current account . . ."

The manager could see no statutory way of preventing this, but his shiny-arsed soul rebelled against such hints of freebooting. He wanted to hear details, talk around it, jabber, get in the picture. Reaney wondered what this man felt about the years before. Had it been worth it? Roses in Muswell Hill? No more bank exams? Pension? Was it bank managers or accountants who were said to suffer most, as a group, from constipationary troubles? Ten pints a night, mate, that'll shift it. He sat while the manager talked. Actually, he felt quite rosy. He had found his person—at last—and he felt he should spread the goodwill around. He knew, my God he knew, the hell that men went through.

"Yes, I can see all that," he said. "But I can hardly be expected to sit back and let my wife take all my money, can I? What would you do, Mister Snead?"

It was a sly question, giving Snead a chance to play God. Snead was suddenly all fatherly. It was settled that the money would be transferred to the current account, but just in case Angela decided to cash the lot the bank would speak to him first if she arrived toting a large cheque made payable to self.

They parted on mutually best-wishing terms. How jolly to be knowledgeable in the workings of men. He took another taxi to the office. It was now a quarter to one. It was quite hot, but the open taxi windows allowed a fast breeze to evaporate body heat. Luncheon vouchers milled round bus stops, in front of shop displays, teams of clerks and copy-typists filling safe days with an illusion. An illusion? Forgive me. The returning warrior has difficulty in not reacting contemptuously to those who missed the battle. The fortress needs its serfs and villeins just as much as it needs its skull-grinning men of death. Up the stairs in a merry bound. See Felix first.

Short, business-like, friendly, men with a common purpose. Reaney to go with Barry to the TV studios, Reaney to supervise the arrival of Dorry on Sunday, Alfred to take care of the minor business of Rahilly's exclusive, Alfred to take most of the money. Look at me, Alfred S. I am different today. Don't you notice, old stag? You don't seem to frighten me any more, not so much anyway.

An unexpected complication was Braid's arrival with Barry Black, though why should the shark travel without its pilot fish?

He left the three of them in Felix's room to make a phone call to Norman S. Mathie, ostensibly, to check on some vague detail of a contract they were drawing up with the Paris people, the one he had so brilliantly negotiated for the company when he was in Paris. When the hell was that? Only a week ago? My God, the greasy days had made good time while they lasted. It was easy then to turn Norman S. onto the subject of Mrs. Gray's signed statement.

"Brilliant stroke, that, Norman," he said. "How the hell did you actually manage it? I haven't had a chance to talk to Alfred this week, running about like a mad thing, you know."

Mathie, like all men, was always eager to eroticise his own role in life's great drama. Reaney drummed on a pad with a yellow Biro as he stood by his desk, waiting for the revelation.

"Five hundred nicker . . . I thought it would be about

that. Jake won't be too happy about parting with all that loot, eh?"

The moment of truth.

Jake? Alfred!

Alfred S. Felix had paid the five tons. Paid it to Mathie who had it paid to Mrs. Gray, distraught widow and bereaved mother. He knew why, of course. It was Braid's debt. But Braid wouldn't want to pay, he'd be only too happy to postpone that cruel moment. Postpone until Felix knew he was stretched to the limit with investments for equipment in some new group he was fitting-out. Then—bang. Pay up or settle with a slice of Barry Black, a big slice. The big end.

"All right then, Norman, be seeing you."

He went back to join the three mutually interdependent jackals. Felix was addressing whatever remarks he was making to Barry and Jake was hopping about at the end of the desk, poking in his womanish criticisms, objections, feeble-isms.

"Better be off then," Reaney said. "Alfred's told you, I suppose, this may very well decide the series one way or another. Do well today, Barry, and on your door they'll pin a star."

"Yes, but remember, Barry, it's not just how you perform," Felix added, standing up. "It's how they think you'll be to work with. It's all right us pushing you with guys like Pemberton Mobley, but if the directors and producers don't like you they can drop a lot of poison."

"I get it," Barry said. "It's be-nice-to-suits-day?"

Felix said that was very good, Reaney laughed heartily, Jake allowed himself a reluctant smile. They left. Out in the sun, worms, don't worry, just a quick dash across open ground and we're back in the safety of our underground shelters. Important, the seating arrangement in the back of a taxi. Barry first, then push in, make Jake perch on the flap seat, he doesn't like that.

"How's it going then, Jake?" he asked, pushing the snout, released this morning after twenty-five years in the big house, the man who'd kept his vengeance warm for quarter a century—and now found revenge meant very little. Jake took one. He let Reaney light it, shaking his head, waiting till it was on before he accepted this rare invitation to moan.

"Alfred's always so busy," he said, looking at Reaney, acting as if the blond youth were not in the back of the taxi with them. "I've got lots of ideas for Barry, but he's always busy, isn't he interested in anything I've got to say?"

"We've almost got this telly series fixed up," Reaney said, looking at Barry for corroboration, which was given with a serious, slow nod. "Barry's date-sheet's filled up for three months, what Alfred thinks is let's see how things go before we start any more big plans. I'm sure he's not ignoring you deliberately, Jake." Like hell he wasn't. "Anyway, I hear you're pretty tied up yourself these days, new groups and whatnot?"

Jake made a grimace of dismissal.

"People keep bringing me these groups," he said. "But it's Barry I'm really interested in." Not so interested as to speak to the boy, of course. "I don't know if Alfred really knows what potential the boy has."

While little men moan, tigers stalk the streets. Barry was prey and the creatures of the jungle stalked round and round. But a new tiger is on the scene, folks.

"You may be right," Reaney said. "But Alfred has the contacts, doesn't he? Ask anybody in the business, Alfred's only got to pick up the phone and he does more good for the lad than twenty brilliant ideas, eh?"

Barry nodded to that. Jake gave him a side glance of such speed that it was transformed into an almost audible sneer.

The way Reaney saw it, the *new* Reaney, there was only one way into this situation for him. Barry had signed a personal management contract with Jake Braid, tying him to the little man for three years, Jake taking a quarter of everything he earned.

In turn Jake had signed an agency and publicity contract with Felix, for another three years, giving Felix twelve and a half per cent of Barry's earnings. The two and a half per cent went into the publicity company, of which Reaney was a director. The ten per cent agency slice went into the Alfred Felix Agency company, of which Reaney had no share.

The eighty pounds a week which was his average weekly income represented a very small slice of Felix's total profit, yet his activities now so overlapped from publicity into artiste promotion that he was being robbed by not getting a slice of the agency profits. He didn't want to own Barry Black, even if that were possible, which, contractually, it was not; neither did he want to manage Barry Black or have any pressing need even to know the lad. Neither was he all that interested in the difference between eighty pounds a week and, say, two hundred pounds a week.

What did he want? Well, for a start, the time seemed to be at hand to put an end to this amateurish, above-it-all approach to the grubby little affairs in which he found himself playing a part, however unplanned and reluctant that part might be. Half a per cent here and there meant nothing whatsoever to him as a thinking man, but if you were going to play a game it was more satisfying to win than to lose. He could see that now. It was the natural loser in him who had provided this perimeter fence of jokiness, of cynical superiority. Anybody could stay above it if they didn't take a serious part.

So, as the taxi-driver steered aggressively through the carpuscle traffic of Friday lunchtime, he was forming out of his vague impulses the plan of action which would bring him back with a bang into the mainstream of men's commerce, whatever the drop this might entail. The warrior could not live forever on his returning glory. Forget the White Cliffs, these constipated canyons of concrete and glass are Reaney's ramparts. Not all battles can be Agincourt or Alamein.

Having passed Barry over into the excited care of a girl production assistant, he decided to take Jake off for a quiet drink.

"Let's go in the public," he said. "It'll be quieter." Also he couldn't remember how his last evening in the tellyman's pub had ended and there was always the chance (twenty to one) he was barred for some social misdemeanour which could not be wiped off the record by a ten bob fine. Jake, naturally, had a gin and tonic. Reaney ordered a tomato juice for himself. In modern warfare the infantry is too technological to go over the top loaded with cheap rum.

He let Jake moan on a bit about how society's various conspiracies were robbing him of rightful recognition. When that over-worked vein was almost exhausted, he led Jake into a glittering future where the conspirators would be routed and the little man would show the world who was king.

"The real way to make the loot, of course, is to have a sole representation set-up," he remarked. "You manage them and you act as agent, take anything up to fifty per cent that way, all perfectly legal."

Jake had many important things to say about that. Reaney let his tomato juice stand. He could be as tight as anyone else, if it suited him.

"It's the only way," Jake said. "You can spend about two

thousand pounds on a new group—for the risk you deserve more than ten per cent, don't you? Stands to reason."

"Of course," Reaney replied. He wasn't even offering cigarettes now. My, my, how changeable some men can be. "Mind you, some of the sharks in this business go too far. I know one group who were still getting fifteen quid a week on a fixed-wage contract and they had a record at number one. That's laying it on too thick, far too thick."

"Yes," Jake said, not altogether convinced. Perhaps he thought fifteen was too high. He was the kind of mean little monopolist who wanted to own the contracts, the agency, the halls and next year, God willing, the customers. "I'd have put Barry on sole representation, but I didn't have the contacts, not then, anyway."

"You've got them now though," Reaney said, helpfully. Jake began to blossom. He was prompted to say it was his round, even!

"Yes, of course, I'm not as slow as *some* people think," he said, handing over eighteen-pence of tomato juice as if it was his last bottle of Napoleon brandy. "But what chance have I got, now I mean, the contract's signed with Felix, you'd *need* Barry to start it off. The others I've got haven't started earning yet."

Contracts could be broken or wiggled out of. Or bought back. Men with brains could always beat these legal bastards.

"You don't have to tell me," Jake said. "With Barry as a foundation you could have a very solid set-up. How much would Felix, do you think, want for the contract?"

Three years at ten per cent of, say, eight hundred a week. That's twelve grand, tiny man.

"Say ten grand?" he said.

"I haven't got that kind of money," Jake said. "Not available, anyway."

222

No, you'd have some paltry life assurance and five or six squirrel accounts in banks and post offices and maybe half of your house.

"Well, you'd have to find a sleeping partner to put up the readies," he told Jake. Does it all sound very easy, little man? Come on up, the garden path is lovely. "Maybe I know one or two likely prospects, always guys about with capital they need investing, aren't there?"

Of course, Jake knew lots of likely lads with capital that was just lying about gathering dust. Already he was being attacked in the public prints for being Britain's show business monopolist, ruthless little carteliser that he was.

But, to look back at a more practical point in this exciting new venture, was Barry really safe to build an empire on? How about that girl, what was her name again, you know the one? If there's one thing Reaney knows, it's the dynamite factor of a young lad with a dangerous taste in ruinous publicity.

"Oh, he's all right," Jake said. "All he did was stuff the girl. We've all been through that stage, haven't we?" Winks, elbow digs. You mean, *he* didn't fix up the abortion?

"What, Barry! He hasn't the brains to fix a fuse. I did all that! Mind you, that's strictly between you and me, Pete."

Of course. But it's something I wouldn't have the slightest idea of how to fix up myself. Good job you know your way around, Jake.

"Yes, well, you can't be in this business long if you don't know what's what, eh?" Jake was a giant sunflower, opening in the morning warmth. "He's very good, normally, but that silly bitch got up and pushed off half an hour after the job was finished. No wonder she snuffed it. Kids haven't got any sense these days, have they?"

"Jake, I wouldn't ask anyone else this, but now you've mentioned it, ehm, a friend of mine's got this bird in trouble, all right, don't laugh, this 'friend' needs an address badly, ehm, yeah yeah, all right, it's me."

It was as simple as that. Having led Jake a mile in the wrong direction he had nipped in with the vital question and got the vital address. A real doctor, too, the address was in Vauxhall. Squalor, seedy. Sincere sort of nodding face to Braid, personal papers slipped back into the male pouch, smooth down in case ominous bulge attracts attention of thought police. Reaney knows all the secrets—not *all* secrets, but all the secrets of his own little patch on the bottom of the pond.

They went back to the studios, walking diagonally across the sunless street which went round the back of the great telly headquarters, a dogleg, shopless street of the old dimension, made tinily artificial, as if on a film set, by the new dimension of god-provoking Telly HQ.

"Can the island take the weight, that's what I always ask myself," he said as he and Jake went in the factory-like rear entrance.

"Do what?" Jake responded. Reaney gave a short, self mocking laugh. Jake had no interest in metaphysics. Soundless, well-lined lift, soft-tiled corridors.

"We'll let Pemberton take us down to the studio," Reaney said to Jake as they entered the carpeted executive burrow. "He likes to play host."

Pemberton's latest secretary was the usual snooty, would-be general's daughter. She didn't know if he was in or out or anything, but when she came back she welcomed them as if seeing them for the first time and they went into Pemberton's sanctum. Carpets, of course, and the rest, a plasticky, dustless, uncluttered room, hues, not colours, status through the living sepulchre. Reaney felt that his motors hummed in low gear. Nothing known. Just wait.

Usual guff between Mobley and Braid, now he had his

secret and he wanted away, time to think about it, work it out, successful men are those who know the value of a secret. They went down in the same lift, down, down, darkness of the empty lift shaft above and below.

Into the studio, a sort of inspection party from command HQ, introductions, gay banter, technicians deliberately—and noisily—ignore the top brass, pink-shirted side-kicks only too eager to please, wires, trolleyed cameras, hanging searchlights, sense of well-being through tomato juice, life is a studio mock-up. Barry comes out of the ruck, like a slightly embarrassed schoolboy whose vulgar parents have arrived late for sports day.

Reaney stood back with Pemberton as the director, a large, bearded man with a down-to-earth beer gut, spared Jake a few words.

"Funny isn't it," Reaney said, "he doesn't look much, our Barry, but he comes across hot and strong on the box."

Pemberton smiled.

"The camera finds the magic that the eye misses," he said. His hands were clasped behind his back. The studio to him, was the absent landlord's occasionally visited estate. It belonged to him, but he did not pretend to know all the details. "Our production people speak highly of the boy. He washes, too, it seems."

You either had the Braids and the Felixes, noses so deep in the grass they couldn't see the sky, or you had the Pembertons, self-mocking in their parody roles, so far above the grass they couldn't see the ants. Officers, gentlemen, other ranks. He would be the first grass-grubber who could keep one eye swivelled upwards at the sky. Standing here on a Friday afternoon under the powerful lights of the tackle-dropping studio roof, I, Peter Reaney, have come to one of those few chances a man has to decide on his own destiny. It is all a test of myself from here on, of what I am made of.

There can be no regrets if this moment is ignored or wasted. All I need is a sign—which way do I go?

"So you think Barry's likely to land a series then?" he said. Pemberton tilted his head to the right, puckering his lips.

"What do you think of your friend Pringle's strength?" he asked. "We're usually inclined to pick our own writers. He does straight stuff, normally, doesn't he?"

"I think he's very good," Reaney replied. The director was speaking down from his control-room eyrie, asking the people on the floor to prepare for Barry's first run-through. The lights were very bright out there in the middle. You had to give it to the boy, he was the one who actually went out there and performed. Was that *just* an accidental knack? Perhaps not, but what he'd said to Maggie still held water, the knack or whatever it was had no importance for the rest of us. "He could do it standing on his head, fresh approach and all that. Might be a bit expensive, though."

"Oh?"

"What sort of script percentage would the budget have?"

"Half-hour show, guest act and a feature comedy spot? Wouldn't reach above seventy-five, I shouldn't think, not the way our budgets are going."

Val's idea, as Pemberton Mobley well knew, was for something a bit more ambitious than that. Still, suppose it was a hundred, at six shows to begin with, Val could cop six tons for what would probably take him four or five working days to write. Did he deserve it, in the current Reaney scale of self-interested justice? Val was keen, he knew, because he was tired of straight scripts for wooden police series, he wanted to get into the more musical side, bigger money there if you made good. How would Val's luck affect him and Jody? With a new interest he'd be even less involved in his domestic situation. But if he didn't get the series he'd probably take harder to the drink. Did he want a complete break, or a long run of safe afternoons in bed? He would have to spend more time close to Jody to find that out, let alone what her ideas on the subject were. Better not to have any positive influence at all in this case.

"Naturally we want this series to do something for Barry, not just expose him as another pop singer," he said. "He's got a cheery sort of appeal which could be developed. He can speak lines fairly adequately, which by these standards is being Sir Laurence Olivier. I think Pringle's just the right bloke to bring it out. On the other hand, it would probably come out all right anyway, whoever writes it."

Pemberton never gave much sign of taking in what was being said, but he'd come out with it later on. He was a success, but Reaney could see little in him to copy. Even if he wanted to, he'd never master that high-nosed, pseudo-military aura. He and Pemberton went up to the control room to watch Barry's run-through. A few lines with the resident disk jockey and then he went into his last recorded number. The new one wasn't to be released for two weeks, but the deal here was that he got this in-between records spot in return for the first telly presentation of the new one, which by any negotiable standard most folk thought would be wowsville.

The appurtenances of television did not thrill Reaney to the core. He studied the production assistant's knees as she sat beside the bearded director, flicking switches at his command. He felt vaguely sexy all over, not painfully lustful, a pleasant change, viewing without feeling agonising despair. Great what a night in cells and a good stiff bunk-up could do for a man.

So the run-through was over, Jake and Barry were going up to the canteen, Pemberton was going up to his office, it was only fifteen minutes short of four. Cash! He left them with pleasantries and felt pleasant himself as he came out of the main entrance into the sunlight. Already there was a knot of young girls on the pavement, waiting for the famous ones. He felt for a short moment like giving them a fatherly sort of lecture on what had happened to Mary Gray, but in his new tomato-juice benevolence he merely smiled inside as he dodged round them and waited at the kerb for a taxi. He felt so *well*. No more hangovers, he said to himself. I feel good, and I need all my wits for the decisions that are to come.

No taxi came immediately, so he started off walking. Friday afternoon, secretaries carry suitcases for weekend with mummy and daddy in the country, line-free faces of city types peer from taxis taking them to Waterloo and un-anxious afternoons on Surrey lawns, not a surgical boot in sight. Girls with bare arms, lots of chest and back displayed. If they made him dictator of Britain he'd order all women to walk about with nothing on (in good weather, of course) so that men would not be tricked.

Chapter Sixteen

Felix had that Friday afternoon feeling, too, and when it came to half-past five he suggested they have a drink in their Wardour Street pub. With another fifteen from the petty cash in his hip pocket, Reaney felt armed for action.

"I'll just make a phone call," he said. Felix prepared to shine his shoes. He'd been talking about finding a small flat in central London, give him a bit more freedom to see people on business in the evening. He was getting randy, poor old roses not the thrill they used to be. Reaney was feeling distinctly that way, himself. Katrina, for instance, looked distinctly haveable, sitting through there in her little office, summer frock softening her general outline. He dialled Val's number, wondering which voice life's great lottery would throw up.

"Hallo," Val's voice said.

"Peter here, how's it going?"

"Lousy."

"I've just been with Pemberton Mobley, he was asking whether you were good enough for the Barry Black show . . ."

"You said no, of course."

"Of course. Hey, they'll only go to a hundred a script. Top weight. Is that within your price range these days?"

"A hundred here, a hundred there, it all mounts up. When do we know if they're going ahead?"

"Next week sometime. Anyway, are you working tonight or what?"

"I should be. I was otherwise detained last night, ha ha."

"Well, I don't want to come between you and art. You'll be finished about ten, won't you? Maybe I could come back in a state of relative sobriety with a fifth of rye . . ."

"All my relatives are bigger drunkards than I am. Listen, would you do me a favour?"

"Yes, how much do you want?"

"Not money, actually. Jody's been moaning at me she can't get out to the pictures or anything. If you weren't doing anything particular, you might conceivably consider taking her to the movies. Eh? They've got *The Hustler* on at the Notting Hill Classic. You could brush up on your interpretation of Minnesota Fats . . ."

"Take your wife to the flicks, eh? You're not frightened I give her a sight of the old kidney-wiper?"

"I don't think you're her type. Come to that, I don't think I'm her type either, not the way she's been going on today."

"Oh?"

"She says she has an uncontrollable impulse to laugh out loud whenever she looks at me. Is that bad?"

"Mine used to cry. All right, tell her I'll meet her in Finch's about eight. I'll see you, Fast Eddie."

"You can hold her sink-reddened hand, if you fancy that sort of thing."

Val had sounded preoccupied somehow, less sure what part he was playing.

They walked in step through release-maddened crowds in Regent Street, Felix eyeing Bob Cratchit's descendants with a superior sort of amusement. Maybe it was just his defence against the knowledge that they were young and he was not old enough not to care that they were younger.

In the comparative quiet of Soho's cooling alleys Felix said that the trouble with these people was that they didn't realise life was just a game. They took it too seriously to be successful.

"You should've been at that inquest with me," Reaney replied, going into the gutter to allow two young girls to pass. Felix went in for no such bogus gestures. "I got the impression that everybody's struggling to keep in a sort of vast safety net. A helluva lot get pushed over."

Felix grunted, prior to statement.

"If nobody fails, nobody succeeds," he said. "I had nothing when I started. I wanted to get somewhere, most of them don't—or they won't put in the effort. So I should worry what happens to a lot of lazy bums. They don't keep the country going, do they?"

And I should worry what happens to last year's top stag. You made the rules, dad. You don't thank me for bringing in humanity, will you thank me for playing it *your* way?

At first when you walked into a Friday evening bar you could see only the crowd, then individual faces. Was it— yes, Goddings, the angular profile, the thin shoulders. He didn't want to see who Goddings was with. He followed Felix through the press to the bar.

Of course, he'd had nothing to eat all day. When the hell *did* he last eat? Hunger could well be the reason for the sudden shakiness, imminent knee-collapse and trembling hand. Caught in the shock of this totally uncalled for disintegration, he asked for a pint of bitter before he could remember that this was tomato juice resurrection day.

He managed to get a hand on the bar, hoping Felix would not notice.

"Cheers."

"Cheers."

Beer was food, it might reassure his frantic belly. He drank to drown the messages for sustenance. A good half of a pint, down in a oncer. The small chat with Felix, rest on

the man's solidity, crawl up on the beach of his self suffi-
ciency. But eventually he would have to look. Belt the pint
down, same again, Alfred?

So his head turned as if *it* wanted to see, the hell with
what the lodger said, and, of course, she was looking at
him, over Goddings' shoulder.

Whatever strength was left seeped away as their eyes
met, not reproach, not fun, not dislike—knowledge. Some
enchanted evening!

The look was too long to require any other sign.

He broke away to pay for the drinks, dipped his face to
sink his lips into the cool beer.

". . . you, find them, I said, show me somebody I can use
and I'll do the rest, just show . . ."

Did the body have its own ideas? It didn't seem to want
to breathe. His whole lower jaw tried to shake loose. Of
course, Goddings wanted to know where she'd been looking and he was now pushing towards them, he could *feel*
him. Twitching noses, rats at maze corners, one great joint-
pulverising flow of volts.

"We're all over there, hiya Pete, you don't look so dusty,
just a minute, you know Maggie, don't you?"

WHY?

The body's fault.

Not even in the mind.

The body was taking over.

Wasn't even thinking about it.

STOP SHAKING, STOMACH!

Was she a magnet, to draw the life out of him, standing
so close, so lady-like? Yes, Jolly Jack, get the drinks in, this
pint hasn't drowned a single tremble.

He avoided her eyes in the business of accepting the third
pint. He looked at the beer bubbles, he fished around clum-
sily for cigarettes, he saw a clock-face at twenty minutes past

six, he saw jumbling, jawing, moving men as if back again in the silent film.

HE DIDN'T WANT HER.

Of all the things he needed, she was not it.

He'd found his person.

One was the ration.

She caught his eye when he pushed the fags. She might have been smiling, back there, in the blonde seal head, behind the big eyes, beneath the smooth cheeks. Young girls had different lips from old girls. Soft lips, no cracking, no suggestion of redness where lipskin meets faceskin. Young girls were flowers, old girls were marble columns.

"How are you making out?" Felix asked them both. Goddings said something about seeing TV contacts, building up, usual gabble of complete failure. Maggie turned her Labrador's head towards Felix.

"Girl singers don't seem to be very popular just now," she said. He didn't have to look at the rigid neck-twist, the strong white hand on the glass, the outward swell under the fawn jacket. He guzzled for strength. Their chatter was not even words, just noises from fish mouths.

Halfway through his fourth he found he was able to think again. The tremble was still there, the deadly paralysis, but he could think. Jody in Finch's at eight. Walk away from Maggie . . . walk away, like that, *yes.*

"And how are you, Peter?" she asked. Maybe her kind of broad Scandinavian face always carried a suggestion of a smile.

"Fine, thank you," he said, raising the defensive glass. So there was another way the bastard could get you, keep you miserable for years, then turn it on the other way, so many chances you were torn in little bits.

WHY?

"I had to put Peter up the other night," she said, looking

233

round the male trio. "Or maybe I should say, I had to put up with Peter the other night."

So it was a joke now, safe to broadcast to other people. That made him feel slightly better, not much.

Twenty to seven. Jody, you are the person, my person. I don't want, my brain doesn't want, this person, the body wants this person, the body is electrocuted by this person, it's nothing to do with me, not *me*, I've lost control, stomach no longer listens to my orders.

Then the alcohol began to hit the blood and he found that the trembling had been over for some time, the shakiness, but not the electricity. Again and again, the hand stretches out to touch the live wire, rat nose twitches tentatively, desiring the pain.

"I think you should bring Maggie round to the office, Jack," Felix was saying. WHAT? "You've been working with too many sweaty young louts. Perhaps we could help you, we're a bit smoother with the ladies, aren't we, Peter?"

The fifth pint brought him to par. Five to seven. Why did he find himself thinking about a toy soldier on a paper-boat, floating down a gutter?

"Better ask Maggie," he said, now closing his eyes and squirming, as if shaking clear of cobwebs. "I think I behaved like a dastardly cad the other night."

She smiled now.

"It wasn't too bad," she said. "He tried to get me married off to the boy next door. We live on a farm in the wilds of Somerset. The boy next door is ten miles away."

"Better than being at harm's distance, eh?" Felix enjoyed his own joke.

Seven. What to do?

Walk away!

Sorry.

No can do.

234

"May I say that Maggie took me in a strictly Florence Nightingale capacity," he said. "Not that her purity could ever possibly be in question, but knowing your dirty minds I'd better kill any nasty lurking thoughts."

She laughed. Goddings looked happier. He'd never been asked by Maggie, although it was true that his own wife was rather good-looking, indeed, few people could understand why she'd ever married the miserable git.

It's ten past seven now, twenty minutes more at the most, what's the move? Felix wanted to talk about the clever way of launching a new girl singer. He knew bloody well the chances were meagre, but maybe he fancied Maggie for his new town pad?

Goddings licked the unbendable upper lip, his contemplative gesture. Wheels whirred, electronic tumblers clicked, computers hummed. Reaney the Computer, able only to make decisions on information fed in by others, which woman meant most, no computer answer to that, which one gets the last life-belt, no answer to that one, both both both both.

Time. Wait and see.

How things work out.

Keep in both races.

"You ever go to football matches, Maggie?" he was asking.

"No," she said, shaking her head, which he wanted to feel between flattened palms, run knuckles over outswelling cheek bones. "I've often wanted to, I think those footballers you see in newspaper pictures are very sexy."

"Would you like to go tomorrow by any chance?"

"It would be lovely. Do we have to stand up and wave rattles and things?"

Up you, too, Goddings. Six pints it'd taken to get on par, but by Christ he'd made it.

So he was to meet her at Queensway tube station at one

o'clock, and the move over he now had to take care of the second, planned, instalment of the night's pleasure.

Leave when you're on top, retire as champ, bye bye, see you on Monday, Alfred, don't look so jealous, Jack, tomorrow then, Maggie, out out, isn't the first darkness exciting, the lights wink warmly and the sky is a dark, dark blue.

Another man thought he was in first with his wave for the taxi, but Reaney had the door open and was inside before the twit could catch up, the driver didn't care, off into the night, bold charioteer, take me to the orgy.

In those nights they used to shout things like "Honey pears, get up them stairs" . . . hey, bab a reebab was the thing you said as you clicked your thumb and middle finger, but it was all shy boy-gang stuff and they always walked home without girls, wondering *when*. This was like that.

For her night at the Classic, Jody was wearing a brown suede jacket over a thin black sweater, black ski slacks and high leather boots. Amid the tumult of Friday night Irishmen in Finch's she looked like the bar-experienced wife of a drunken Celtic poet, her red hair pulled back in a pony tail, her left boot on the brass rail, her right hand (not sink-roughened, Val, how blind the accustomed husband becomes) round a whisky glass.

"D'you come here often?" he said, standing behind her. She turned, smiling, the face of every man's dream wife, the shape of youth, the light of youth, the magically synthesized flesh and skin, the gray-green eyes that knew and still smiled, beauty that had nothing to do with crushable flower-flesh but was real, mature. To want younger flesh was a perversion.

"Are you the blind date my husband arranged for me?" she said.

"No, it's your mother I'm meeting, you're too young for the description I was given."

No draining away of strength with her, no trembling paralysis, merely warm certainty. He didn't even consider the betrayal factor as they left the crowded bar, her giving a cheery smile to a bell-bottomed Irishman who stumbled backwards into her path.

"A lovely woman, surr," the Irishman called to Reaney as they reached the door. He nodded back, winking.

On the bright pavement they looked left at the cinema queue and they both started laughing as they looked at each other.

"You know the plot, of course?" he said, taking hold of her strong, warm arm.

"I've had to see it twice and live with Fast Eddie for a year or more," she said. "Why is it all the men I know are so childish?" In those boots and slacks he felt prancing was imminent. Or wild Cossack dancing. She was a strong mare and the sooner she was harnessed the better.

"I'm not childish," he said. "And to prove I'm above the age of legal consent I will now hie me into that off-sales and purchase nectar."

The barman who wrapped up the half bottle of Bell's had red hair, too, and when he came back out on the pavement he half-expected her to speak with an Irish accent, the wild Celtic poet's widow that she was.

"Well then," he said, taking her firm, wifely hand. "Where to? I take it we're playing truant from The Hustler."

"I'm tired of making decisions for child-men," she said, her solid shoulder leaning into his chest.

"All right then, Sheik Haroun el Reaney will whisk you off to some lustful oasis, infidel virgin."

They had to cross the busy junction to get a taxi. As they stood on the kerb, under the skyscraper flats, he squeezed her hand.

"I'm glad I've got the flat now," he said. "At my age the

erotic possibilities of the office floor are a little too Spartan."

"I lost my virginity on the office floor," she said looking up at the sky, naughtily. "I was eighteen, my boss was like Craig Fairheart in one of those women's magazine stories. Funny, isn't it, I thought it was all highly illicit and romantic and now I look back and wonder how sordid could you get and yet, I dunno, it's beginning to seem like a marvellous romance all over again. That's a fine comment on your life, isn't it, your most nostalgic moment of romance on the office carpet!" She tried to free her hand.

"Youthful romance is for the birds," he said. "Where have all the taxis gone, gone gone forever?" He held on. This seemed to please her.

"You know something, it would be rather sexy to go back to the office floor again, after all these years . . ."

The taxi slid into the kerb. He gave the office address, and asked the driver to make it as fast as he could.

"So nice to be rushed off your feet by a masterful man," she said, leaning her mature weight into his side. He held her hand, matching hers now for firmness. He hoped the man would hurry, he was gasping for a leak. She was so *grown-up*. It was *she* who was masterful.

He had a key for the small side entrance of the block. The stairs were still lit, although most of the offices were dead for the weekend.

"I never use lifts in empty buildings," he said. "It can be very embarrassing, all that publicity."

She came into the men's washroom with him, standing by the mirrors above the basins while he went into the stall. At times like these he wondered how the body could hold so much. She was rather strong, wasn't she?

Then it was the darkened silhouettes of Linda's desk, the low leather furniture, the flood of light, the feeling of abandon created by being in the unusually dead rooms.

"This one, I think," he said, leading her by the hand into Felix's room. "The carpet's thicker." He pulled the Venetian blind cord before putting on the light.

"Let's have a drink," she said. He took the position of power, after pulling a chair close to Felix's desk for her. "Out of the bottle will do, I'm not the fancy type any longer." When she crossed her legs a strong calf stretched out her trouser leg. Powerful, woman—powerful.

He tore off the silver paper, pulled the cork, leaned over the desk. She took the bottle, swigged like a man, broad white throat. He could almost feel her warmth.

"So here we are," he said. "You want to be a star? Let me see now, what's your name? Don't tell me, it doesn't matter. It's a girlie show, you know that. All right, let's see your legs, girlie. Come on, babe, you wanna part or doncha?"

She stood up, taking off her suede jacket.

"Are all auditions like this?" She played the shy girl, hands folded defensively across her sweatered bosom. He put the bottle on Felix's clean blotting pad and stood up. For a moment he was going to carry on the silly game, then it came over him hot and strong, he walked round the desk and took hold of her hands, pulling them apart. This was how the position of power *should* be used. Big men playing silly games! Rubbish, sublimated rubbish.

"When Craig Fairheart ruined me he never even took off his trousers," she said. Eyes, that's what you looked at. The mouth acted but the eyes, the eyes had it.

The gathering, thundering, maddening rush to take off clothes. Then the unyielding hardness of the floor felt through her body. This is what it's all really about, office! Dry-stick men suddenly freed from their constipated suits. Thighs like these would demoralize armies.

To kiss the loved one, on the arm muscle, on the ear, on the wifely belly, to feel no shame in the strong neon tube-light, to be allowed intimacy with this grown woman and to attack her, at the same time, the mind's flickering newsreel closed down in blinding darkness. The ache, the whole body ache, to have known this body all the time and strive, strive to become part of it. Smaller than him, yet oh so much larger.

"My big man," she said in his ear, so close he felt the warm air words and the wetness. Cheek on the carpet trod by Felix, Black, Mathie, Braid, Val. What think ye now, chain-mailed souls? The wifely flesh, adorable cracked nail, washed-red lips.

Again. There would be no finish with this woman. Magic name, Jody, Jody Face, Jody Hair, Jody Ears, Jody Thighs. Jody feet. Nymphs and satyrs, cavort in woodland dales high above Regent Street.

So much so he took her out onto the landing when she had to go to the lavatory, nakedly, brazenly, keeping watch at the top of the stairs while her white wifely buttocks disappeared into the men's ablutions. The naked truth, shrivelling up the silly farces of men who tried to escape in rented hutches. The oldest magic-truth of all, the only one left. My male body, your female body, the very atoms convulsed with glee. All else—charades.

She slapped him quite hard on the beer belly when she came back, he returned the slap on her bum as she went back into the office. He locked the door again with her arms round his waist.

"Put out the light," she said. "I don't have to see you to know what you look like."

Then she was lying on his stomach, fingers feeling his eyebrows.

"Everything else seems very silly now," he said, kneading the loose wifely flesh of her back. "I feel like crying for all the poor bastards who aren't making love to you. You know I went to that inquest the other day? I came away from it wanting to blow up the world, all the cruelty and misery. This is the only thing, isn't it?"

"Val cries," she murmured. "The world won't let him write what's in his heart, he says. He doesn't mean it. He cries because he tries to write serious stuff and he knows it isn't in him. I love you because you don't want to be my son." Her words vibrated, chest to chest.

He put his fingers on her lips. He was her son. Such was her power, it didn't seem to matter that he would not be able to let her know that, not ever.

"I'm feeling very grown-up now," he said. "Shall we go back and tell Val that we're in love? The sneaky part can grow on you, you know. It can get to be a habit."

They dressed side by side, kissing occasionally, handing garments to each other. When she was fully dressed he held her tight in a last, long kiss. To *know* and not discuss! Warm, tired, grateful, two fulfilled bodies in a taxi, soft city lights applauding gently on either side.

It was quarter past ten when they reached the house. She had her key. He didn't feel frightened of what was to come. They closed the door quietly, not to wake the children. The children? Only a frightened man needed the blood link, he could be father to all children. A good father, because he still knew what it was like to be a child.

Val was not in his downstairs work-room. They climbed the stairs in silence. She looked into the children's bedroom, while he stood on the second top stair. It was then he heard the voices and the movement, feet on floor.

She looked at him, then went quickly to the door of their bedroom. She opened it wide, reaching for the light switch. Reaney followed.

The light came on. Val was jack-knifed, bending over his crumpled trousers. Frozen camera still of his face, wide-eyed, trapped. On the bed lay a naked, dark-haired woman. Reaney knew immediately this must be the much-discussed Frances—so that was why Val professed to hate her so much. She sat up, without undue panic. Reaney noticed she was still wearing her watch.

Jody looked and then began to laugh. She laughed and laughed, leaning against the wall, pointing helplessly. Val pulled up the trousers. Frances made a brave front, yawning even. Reaney just stood. Why did this phrase run through his mind—"loving care costs money"? What a funny thing.

"For God's sake wait downstairs," Val said, covering embarrassment with anger.

Jody slapped Reaney's back as they went down the stairs.

"Did you see Val's face?" she gurgled. "And that slut Frances! Wait and see how she tries to act her way out of this."

A great jape. So why did he feel a slight disappointment? He'd been all ready to play the plundering homebreaker and now it was all out of his control again.

Chapter Seventeen

He kissed Jody quickly while they were alone in the telly-sitting-room. She was enjoying the joke so much her lips seemed preoccupied. It was a nice room. On one wall shelves of orange Penguin paperbacks. Big, oldish armchairs you could almost lie back on. Walls painted white, nice, interesting lamps, no brutal ceiling main light. And, accentuating the soft glow of the room, the brilliant midnight blue of the outside night. All very jolly, but it wasn't his house, was it? Was he always to be a carefree lodger in the great matchings of men and women?

"I think I'll make myself a sandwich," he heard himself saying. "God knows when I last ate anything."

"Let me, darling," Jody said. She stood at the fireplace, booted for high-kickings. Then she changed her mind. "You know where everything is. You soon will, anyway."

She smiled. He knew what she was thinking, he said to himself as he went into Val's kitchen. He was always saying things to himself. He could have talked it all out to Jody, but the importance of talking was a private thing, wasn't it, and you had this feeling that to talk to a woman instead of rejoicing in finding a person out of the impersonal anthill was a sign of weakness. To tell a woman you needed her was to admit to weakness no real woman liked in a man. It was a big conundrum. He found the bread, buttered it unevenly, looked round for a filler, found a bag of tomatoes on a linoleum-covered shelf, sliced them with a blunt knife, pressed the slices on top of each other, ate the four slices in about five gulping bites, swigged half a bottle of milk and, bingo, the belly could shut up for a while. When he went back into the room Val and this Frances bird were milling about, looking at invisible objects of fantastic interest, continual throat-clearing prior to italicized silences.

Reaney brought the half bottle out of his jacket pocket. "Let's all have a snifter," he said. Val seized on the excuse. He busied himself with getting glasses and a jug of water. This Frances had a thin, hookish nose, a fine-boned bitch-face, slender brown hands with smoothly-red talons, very good legs in milkily translucent stockings. Total effect, blood-sucker. He could imagine *her* burning initials on a man's arm. Thank God, this particular vulture at least would have no chance to claw into his life.

"So," Jody said, raising her glass, pulling away the suede jacket to show the mummy-woman breasts on which his face had found heaven only half an hour before. "Good health."

It was like going to that Arnie guy's flat again, the sense of being a square at a secret meeting of secret people. Val had eyes for nobody. Frances, yes, very deadly legs, you could imagine them actually shaving a man, drank coolly.

"So where do we begin?" Val said, eventually.

Jody giggled. Frances looked at her with irritation, as though she was the injured party. She was very haughty, quietly desperate to look uppah-class.

"I happened to drop in," this Frances bird said. "It just happened on the spur of the moment, it always does. Let's not get all middle-class about it, a man and woman can have a perfectly normal fuck without turning it into *East Lynne*, can't they?"

Val was waiting for Jody's reaction. Reaney had a good mouthful of whisky and water. Don't be middle-class about it, chaps. You could be hanging upside down under a tube train, or trying to chat up a bird who'd never met a cleft palate before. An evening with the creative classes. Is that Jody trying to grin a secret message to me across a crowded room? My darling, *I* remember. The talk came loud and clear when it did start.

"Look, do we have to get all worked-up about something that was just a stupid impulse . . . ?"

"We're always joking about orgies, why do we have to be so damned working-class about the reality . . . ?"

"You're being working-class about it, not me . . ."

"You think I'm a sneaky husband-stealer, don't you . . ."

"It was my fault, she didn't really want to at first . . ."

"Who do you think you're kidding . . . ?"

"I know, you've always thought I was some kind of cheap whore . . ."

"Expensive whore, darling . . ."

"It's no laughing matter . . ."

"On the contrary, it's a positive scream . . ."

In a corner of the room Val and Jody (it was strange now to think of them together) had a very large narrow-necked chemical bottle. The glass was thick and lustrous, slightly greenish. Val originally intended to fill this glass monstrosity with sixpences, now it just stood there, empty, meaningless unless the ownership of former chemical containers was supposed to give one's home that essential touch of industrial élan. We're all workers now.

So *his* life was to be edged out again, suppressed at the moment of truth by the egocentricity of other persons, egocentrics who insisted on dragging their own dreary little affairs across his eyeballs. What dull, pointless, dusty trivialities occupied these feeble fools when *he* was not among them. Silly question, of course, when he wasn't there they went down like punctured balloons.

"You're mad because I'm not screaming at you, aren't

you? You think I'm cheating you out of your big melodrama, don't you?"

Now it's Val's turn. God, if we were real men we wouldn't make excuses.

"Look, Jody, you laughing won't help matters any. I'd had a couple of drinks, it just seemed to happen, we didn't plan it or anything if that's what you're thinking."

"No? Why did you suggest Peter taking me to the pictures? Not that I care, I don't like being made a fool out of, that's all."

What does Frances think? Haughty face. Probably insulted because Val's making out she's just a stray bang. Let's study her . . . knees to match her nose, fine bones, not thin, *fine,* cutting edges of the terrifying nyloned legs. Gaol with Frances would be a three-star nick, fifty years hard labour, hard anyway, with cruel, cutting Frances slicing your nose off with her thin nose, making fine cuts on your face flesh with the smooth razors of her shins and ankles, lovely mummy-wifely Jody, one boot over the arm of her chair, wifely hand dangling towards floor, sort of woman you got so friendly with you thought she was a bloke, and wee Val, onetime integrated person, now a small nasty little boy whose face was ghastly, the young-old face, little boy with devil's horns, lord of the flies, (a flash in the pun, ha ha) I'm Reaney the Flasher, I flash at the girls, the old and the young, and with someone I hate I sticks out me tongue, meanwhile back at the queen ant's egg-laying compartment three high-class drone ants drivel out their miserable preoccupation with the nasty possibilities inherent in possessing a human body, to get that body close to a strange smelling body, that's the battle. My daddy was a shunter, the poor ould sod, he shunted up and down, what he shunted nobody knows, why he shunted nobody cared, so one day he was shunted off into the damp wormy earth, forever a part of that green and pleasant land where men with splendid hearts may get crumpet still for tea with Frances, thin, fine, dark razor-woman, cut me with a million warm-slice kisses. Her teeth are the most voluptuous thing about her!

"I'd have thought we were above this peasant nonsense, the woman is always the whore but the poor innocent husband, oh no, he's just been led astray. My God, some people have the weirdest notions about morals."

"Morals! Don't lecture me on morals, Frances, what you don't know about morals would fill a very large book. It's nothing to do with morals—this is my home!"

Ah, so it's not such a joke with Jody after all. I love her for it. The lovely lying bitch that ye are, appearing straight from a command performance on the carpet of Alfred S. Felix, a wife who needs no introduction . . . nothing known about Frances, the secret of much-sought-after orifice hidden by fine skirt of an almost white colour, contrasts well with the plushmilk of her lovely legs, for me it does nothing, too chiaroscuro if that's the right word, now Val is going to cry a little, he's being dramatic as a writer, make like F. Scott Fitzgerald, Val, give us that line of yours, I'm a writer not a bloody bank clerk.

"I didn't plan it, I'm tired of telling you that, Jody, for Christ's sake don't you believe anything I say?"

"Why should I? You said you'd a lot of work to catch up on and then I find you naked with *her*. What were you writing, *The Turn of the Screw*?"

"Ha ha, very good."

"Shut up, Peter, for God's sake, it's got nothing to do with you."

No? Little do you know, little leprechaun, that I, too, am a card-carrying Judas, fully entitled to a vote at this conference. The exhibitionist in me wants to tell them what *we* were doing. That would betray Jody. Why not? I've already betrayed Val, my platonic love. Salt caked smoke-stacks and cheap tin betrays, why bless my soul, Val's springing another fifth of bourbon, Beauregard Clemens suh, it's muh pleasuh they're not going to hear about me after all just as well really, these well-planned moments of truth and revelation never actually work out.

"I'm damned if I'm going to say I'm sorry for something that wasn't really my fault, if you can't keep your man satisfied don't take it out on me."

Round three to Frances, she leads narrowly in this three-cornered tag match. What would I have done in her place? Tried to leap out of the window while pulling up my trousers? In her place I probably wouldn't have gone to bed with Val, I find writers lacking in erotic appeal. What would they say if I suggested we all shake hands and get into bed together?

"I don't care if you say sorry or not, Frances, I couldn't care less what you do—"

"So what's all the fuss about then?"

Poor Val, he's trying to make it all sound like an everyday incident in the everyday story of everyday city-folk.

"I'll tell you what the fuss is about, I don't care how many stray sluts you have outside this house but you're not going to turn my bedroom into a whorehouse."

"Oh yeah, I can remember a time when you were quite happy to turn Karen's bedroom into a whorehouse."

Nasty, Val, nasty. Let's keep the first Mrs. Tanqueray out of this. Any bedroom she was ever in was already a whorehouse. I should know. Now that I think of it, Val isn't really so manly after all, is he? They thought I was mad (you are mad, Uncle Louis) but they're all mad and I'm just sane enough to know that they're mad, me too, let's have a party, our rock singers sweep America proving once

248

again, oh yeomen true whom Nelson flogged, flogged, round every ship, flogged the great cat goes back and the murderous pain is relished by that one-eyed git as he ponces round Emma while the ratmen chew on their maggots, gad man, those were the days of the bulldog breed, we showed the gyppoes and the wogs and the krauts and the eyeties and the nasty nasty chinkeymen the opium war we don't hear much about that little trade war Britain gave the world its drugs, sir, we invented the junkie trade so shut up and invent the paper-clip again, prehensile woman-steel of a knee-joint, lick that knee, Daddy-oh, nothing known about Frances in bed, does she scratch, bite, whisper sadistic threats in your ear, wrap wax-smooth legs round your middle and squeeze you like a big bass fiddle does she rake her talons down your cheeks cos that's what we Englishmen want, suh, a good vicious school marm, heydey hey, thanks for the drinko, Val of tears, your head is filling the room but Frances now, she'd not want a master, but a boy-slave. Is she interested in me? Shall I stand up and neatly, without fuss, slip down my zip and flash the crown jewels in her direction, bowing slightly from the waist?

"Have another drink, Jody, the world hasn't come to an end."

"No, but our marriage might have."

Is she going to tell them what we did? Oh no, I must stop that.

"I've always thought that a good argy-bargy makes for real togetherness among friends. Sort of group therapy, isn't it? Who knows, if we go on like this we may all end up in bed together. Do any of you lot snore—it's the one thing I hate. My wife Angela, now she snores, she won't admit it, of course—"

"Your friend has a very funny idea of being helpful."

Val is glad of any interruption, Jody looks at me in a

funny way, Frances doesn't really know why I'm here at all. It's a good question. Am I here? They look at me as though I was the Ghost of Canterville, acknowledged but not feared, I am a helpless spectator floating above my own life-like corpse, it was dynamic at times but my connection with this anthill was always tenuous and now slipping away, the women are the clutching cliff hands, but each hold is only temporary as my own weight drags me down another foot or so, the tiny stones and dirt-rushes of my feeble thoughts falling away into the void behind and below, all right, I may as well drink, it is not making me drunk, thanks Val, little do you know I am the spirit who needs to invade your house and take your place in your wife's body and over the top of your children's cots, I am a foreign intelligence invading earthly bodies. Is it too late to warn you? Why is everybody so hateful to each other? Are we rutting chimpanzees to fight for the sanctity of body proprietorship? Boy-men never grow up.

"The Kraken awakes, well well . . ."

"Are you feeling all right, Peter . . . ?"

He blinked. The sound of his own voice had pierced the dreamy quality that had blanketed their conversations. He shook his head, raising himself in the armchair. Val's nervous habit of rubbing his head had produced a spiky, jagged hairline, with one tuft looking like a shorn peacock tail.

"I beg your pardon," he said. "I was almost asleep. What stage has the battle reached?"

Frances made an impatient face, obviously it was none of his business, who the hell was he anyway to sit through their sophisticated little scene? Jody smiled, openly not trying to convey any secret understanding. Val snorted down his nose.

"I wish I could cut it off altogether," Val said. Reaney

laughed, his little friend now looked positively gnomish, young shape in wizened skin.

"You *look* as though the stuffing's gone out of you," he said. "I don't mean to intrude on private grief, but you two seem angrier about it than Jody does. I suppose you need the guilt to complete the thrill, eh?"

Frances blew thin smoke from a thin mouth. Fine and dark and angry, a vicious woman all right.

"Men can be such clowns," she said, now looking at Jody, as if to re-arrange alliances. "Honestly, I often think one goes to bed with them more out of sympathy than anything else."

Jody swung a gay boot. A full thigh and calf pressed against the black slacks. She smiled gently to herself. Reaney felt an uneasy tremor. He could count on her, couldn't he? He had looked at Frances' legs only out of abstract interest. The body's fault, actually. He had to speak again. Had to.

"If anybody's interested in the wisdom of the older man, may I say that no red-blooded heterosexual could possibly not want to go to bed with either of you lovely ladies."

Did this create an impression of silliness? He was only trying to smooth over things, to help them. Frances gave him a thin look.

Val clucked. Jody stretched her arms. Yes, silliness. What did he care? He was free, white and ninety-one. These serious people could get on with their serious wranglings over the tiny machinations of their trivial lives. Get on with it, I am too big for them to understand. Nothing known. Posterity would recognise him, only what had he ever done for posterity?

The play ended in a series of short stabbing scenes. Val suddenly left the room. Jody finished her drink, stretched

—and while wifely arms were still above her head, looked directly at Frances and said:

"If you want him have him. If it was only a quick screw get out. You're a dirty little vampire."

She, too, left the room, without even looking at Reaney.

"Well . . ." Frances exclaimed. Now she needed reassurance, even from Reaney. "She's just a big *mother*." Insulted, she looked demoniac. A fine, vicious woman who needed kneeling homage. Reaney stood up. He heard Jody calling something. He went out of the room and up the stairs. Jody was trying to turn the handle of the bathroom door.

"Come on, Pringle, don't be so stupid," she was saying.

"What's up?" he asked.

"He's playing suicides again," she said. "He won't come out if there's anybody still here. You'd better push off."

"But . . ."

"PLEASE! Just go."

"Are we still . . . ?"

"I don't know. Of course we are. Just go, I'll see you tomorrow. Have a walk or something." She banged on the bathroom door.

So he went back down the stairs. Frances was in the hall, putting on a black and white striped coat. He didn't know whether to kick her or scream.

"All this because of feeling sorry for him," she said. "Now it's after two and I've got to walk home on my own."

"It's only prostitutes who get murdered," he said. But he had to leave anyway for a bit, so he went out with her, down the street-lit garden, lighting a cigarette, taking care not to touch her. The streets are calm at night and the rooms are dark, the lonely traveller's time, the hunched men who look with dead eyes into the memories of Christmas decorated rooms and turn away into the lonely night, away from the log fires, the silent jumping of the children, the blue eye of the iridescent set, says he with a hollow laugh for the part is supposed to take over the actor, as roles and jokes will.

"You're married, aren't you?" he asked.

"We live our own lives," she said. "It's the only way to keep a marriage alive."

"I suppose so. Specially if you never see each other."

She sniffed. He was obviously too much of a peasant for her tastes. It was sexually ecstasy, to be scorned by a vicious woman, to be a toy. That was what was wrong. But could you control it?

She lived in a solid block, the rows of resting cars containing a majority of large, expensively shining models.

"You may as well come up for a drink," she said, not looking at him. Did he suggest a suggestion of strained casualness? What the hell, he was a soggy log floating up and down in the poisonous tides of the Thames, condemned to an eternity of ebb and flow, once reached the Medway towns but the flood subsided before I made the sea.

African carvings, Persian rugs, he knew it all, he was bored, please be bored, stay bored, body. It's all too much. He flopped down baggily in some kind of futuristic flying saucer.

She threw her zebra-crossing coat on a low table by the wall, said "oh my God, what a mess", went behind a queer sort of bar, poured whisky with the air of exasperated fortitude, a sort of Mrs. Miniver of the sex war, not so vicious-looking now, perhaps needing fresh homage to replenish her strength. Too bad, vampire lady, I'm fresh outa blood.

"Cheers," he said. "Been quite a night, hasn't it?"

"Oh, it'll be forgotten by morning," she replied, flopping down sideways on a slimline couch which looked more like a bunk from a padded cell, or maybe a millionaire's morgue block. This way her legs faced him, knees slightly apart, whitish skirt in a series of sand-ripples. He crossed a ponderous thigh, noting how blunt was his knee. He was floating in some chemical, mind levitating all over the damned place. Her voice seemed slightly *caught*.

"It's typical, isn't it, Jody sleeps around all the time and then she turns nasty when that poor little husband of hers shows any sign of independence."

"Oh, I see. *She's* the nympho, *you* were just playing Florence Nightingale? I'm very insensitive in these matters, I thought she took it very well."

"Pretending, it was obvious, perfectly obvious. Still, that's all over now, thank God. I was getting tired of playing silly aunties in that dreary little nursery set-up, anyway. Tell me about yourself."

"I'm big alcoholic uncle Peter. The man who comes to dinner. The wandering Jew."

"Oh? You're not Jewish, are you?"

His nose snorted wind in a dying series of mirthless exhalations.

"You're against Jews?"

"Oh no, not at all, I know some very sexy Jewish men actually." He got up on the silly Swedish lamp standard and watched the two bodies. Then he swooped down close enough to see if her teeth had been filed, like her nose. Ruminative, that was how he left the body. Float high, high, high, the lights fall away, how high *does* the city noise flow, now it's just a dot down there, we just passed Africa, down there Pinocchio Peter in the glinting shadows of the fires, dance little puppet, dance, tomorrow you go to the night-island of donkeys, the whips crack and the big snarling boots loom up in the grim light, all little boys turned to donkeys, cry cry.

254

". . . I believe in taking the most out of every minute, I am repelled by peasants, any kind of peasants, for instance, I see you as a peasant, you'd be shaken out of your wits if I asked you to go to bed with me . . ."

Zoom down quickly. Re-enter ruminative body.

"You think so? Maybe you're right. I suppose you could call it a principle, really, never make love on top of another man's semen. Luckily it isn't a common temptation. No, I don't think I would be surprised, I had you marked down as a very physical person the first moment I clapped eyes on you."

"Oh. You looked like a cabbage sort of person to me, actually."

So she was a nymph, the initial coldness, the brittle, composure, then the catchy edge in the oh-so-casual voice, come up for a drink, come up for a blood-letting, might as well die that way as under a tube, it didn't matter any more, even Jody must have a personal profit-motive or she wouldn't have given herself so easily. But being relieved of the pressure gave you *some* independence. For a while he had felt quite strong.

"Are you *asking* me to go to bed with you?" he said across the wealth-proving room. Childless, money, possessions, cheque-book's more fertile than your ovaries, so life's a non-continuing charade. YES! CHILDLESS. HIM! She was him, in a skirt. A vampire. Giving nothing. Needing children, wanting to be a child. And knowing that death would be the end, because nobody else had been given life. You don't die if you have given new life. She was dead, she knew it, her vampire body knew it, a woman of our city, no children, deaddeaddead, the walking dead, needing his blood, meeting me at a point in time when I want to stop being a son and become a father, never having quite made it as a man. My blood may warm her, but I need my blood to give somebody new the chance you have denied. Posterity will be what *I* tell my son.

". . . difficult for women the way men have restricted them, kitchen slaves, but never me, not for any man, I want to live myself, my own life, I'm not ashamed to enjoy the pleasure of sex."

"Do you burn your initials on a man's arm with the lighted end of an exotically perfumed Turkish cigarette?" he asked, grinning.

Nymphs have no time to laugh, sex-junkies who must go on searching for *the* pain-killing connection. She nodded aside his question, relentless now in her need, not caring if he talked jonglyboggiegabble, does the insect-eating orchid consider the fly's colour?

"No, I enjoy it and why shouldn't I?" He thought of his tirade to Maggie. The self-revolving world of the little girl who wants to dress up and be clapped by grown-ups, her deadly little preoccupations turned into matters of planetary significance, this vampire-woman with her legs open to receive the never-ceasing flow of Aztec sacrifice, oh, to be a woman and to know that the world revolves round *you,* all else is nothing. And yet, didn't the self-mutilators run to the temples in a frenzy of ecstatic self-torture? Could he be stronger than that age-old impulse?

"So do I," he said. "Actually, I think you're about the most attractive woman I've ever seen. I suppose"—self-deprecating grin here, look slightly ashamed of your boldness—"you hear that all the time? Still, it's true, I was very jealous of Val's good luck."

The slave cringes. The goddess smiles. Give me your unborn babes to eat to prove I am still loved. Cut out your hearts and beg me to devour them. Run to your temples and cut off your male appendages that I might know you adore me. She is on a wavelength of her own understanding now.

And as love flows, so she gathers close the skirts of her tantalising self, maybe I won't eat your silly little heart after all. So there!

"You're only saying that because you think you've a chance of making me, aren't you?"

Oh no, divine Frances, I beg to be allowed to join the queue of victims. So what does the great actor-manager do now?

"Don't tease me, please, I'm a broken man as it is. No, speaking objectively, I know you don't find me very attractive, I can see it on your face, but take it as a compliment from a ship in the night, you're a very lovely woman. I want nothing in return."

She crossed her legs slowly, her downcast eyes inviting you, too, to worship. Am I not lovely beyond the cruel dreams of tortured men, she says, smiling, are you not lucky to be allowed to crawl across a field of broken bottles to kiss my hem? She looks up, poor Goddess, if only she *was* remote, but her own need is choking her. How long can she play high priestess to her own aching body?

"You're subtle, I'll give you that," she said, lowering her chin to give him meaningful eyes, my God, which came first, Hollywood or people? Then she stretched out her hand, palm upwards, gesture requiring his panting scurry across the carpet, preferably moaning 'ohmydarlingfrances'.

"No," he said, shaking his head, pretending to concentrate on his glass. "I'm not subtle. I think people should pay each other compliments without looking for something, don't you? There's so much nastiness and selfishness in the world already, isn't there? I think about these things, actually, silly isn't it, but I had to go to an inquest this week, you ever been to a London coroner's court, oh my God, it's enough to make you weep, there was one poor bloke, Irish, he was on the platform at Stockwell tube and—"

"Come here," she said, her hand more insistent. He tried to express a certain kind of bewilderment. She should be fairly panting by now.

"Do what?" said in the most moronic cockney, nasal and brutish.

"Don't be so thick." She patted the sofa, or Swedish-style trolley.

"You mean—?"

"Of course."

He lumbered to his feet, lumber, big man, great folds of cloth falling into place. He walked over. Her head was back in the corner, feet still on the carpet only by dint of a revealing twist of thighs and knees. Fine nose presented a cutting edge as he looked down, hip bones standing up through skirt. Not much breast at all. Eyes too intent. On something going on at the other side. Almost closed as she raised arms to welcome him to the priest's offering table.

"Ohhhh."

"Oh what?"

"Quickly, quickly . . ."

He took the hand that felt for his. He closed his fist round fine bones, slash me cruel goddess. I am bad, bad, I am betraying the only person I ever found, betraying her already, oh my God, I deserve punishment. I ache for it.

"What are you doing? Come up here."

Of course. His only chance. To play *his* fantasy, she didn't want a slave kissing her fine-boned feet, she wanted the services of a heavy stallion, her fantasy. Two separate plays going on at the same time on the same stage, different scripts, over-lapping casts.

"Stop slobbering on my stockings, I want you to make love to me."

"I adore you. Let me be your slave. I'll do anything for you."

"Make love to me, be a man, ohhh hurry."

"I'm not fit to touch you. Let me adore your feet."

"For God's sake!"

The very thing that the goddess wants is the one thing the slave cannot—or will not—do. He wants to grovel. This is his passion. She doesn't understand that. She doesn't think of herself as a goddess at all, she is, in fact, just as much of a slave as he is, a slave to her own insatiable starvation. She wants a function from him, he wants her to deny him, viciously, the right to fulfil that function. Perhaps if she cracked a whip—but she has no script, she is totally unsuited for the part her shape and form suggest in his mind. But he has another motive, he is burying his head in the sands of his own, temporary, role. This is his only chance of protecting himself from the screaming desire to yield, to betray. Her body needs the whole army to rape it, squaddy by squaddy, it's a bag of potatoes as far as she's concerned, itching potatoes, and me, the hero, kneels at her feet, pressing kisses on her disinterested shins.

"I adore you."

"MAKE LOVE TO ME! ARE YOU A PERVERT OR SOMETHING?"

Then she was crying with the rage and the frustration. He could not bear to see her cry. Crying was too terrible. Even the mangled dead didn't cry, not in your face. But what can a groveller do for a crying goddess? All very well to bleed for the tortured dead, she was here, in desperate need.

Wouldn't it be easier to play bleeding hearts for a crying goddess than an old dirty man?

Unfortunately, no.

Chapter Eighteen

"I'm sorry. It's no good."

"I need it, I need it. Try again."

"I want you to—"

"That's no good. I want—"

"It's no good, I'm no use, not that way."

"You're not a man. Come on, if you adore me so much."

"Help me. Scratch me."

"Oh, very well."

"Harder."

"It's stupid."

"Please. Treat me cruelly."

"You're *perverted*."

"I want to kiss your feet."

"How disgusting. Are you, or are you not—"

"I'm sorry."

"I hate *that*."

"Go on, you're sadistic, I *know* it."

"I am not. I don't like that funny stuff."

"It offends your puritanical conscience?"

"I just don't like it. Why can't you behave like a man?"

"No, you behave like one for both of us."

"How disgusting!"

"You're a fine one to talk."

"What's wrong with me? I'm perfectly normal, thank you."

"Thank God we're normal."

"I don't like sarcasm."

"Beat me."

"There are no real men left."

"If you want a billy goat I'm no good to you."

"I can see that."

"All right then."

"Please. Just try again."

"You don't care whether it's me or a horse. You wouldn't have to even speak to a horse. You're *selfish*."

Tears could not keep him now, not when his legs felt raw where trouser touched skin. Escape, escape, from her from me, the me that was revealed in there. Hurry away, before the hands reach out, the eyes not caring which face I own. I am not *all* like that, I am not. All men are capable of all things, at some time. Confirm this, please, confirm this, never mind, I will shut it out of my mind. It never happened. The imagination, that's what it was. Forget it. I kept my innocence—ho ho—no, I can say I never betrayed my Jody, I can say that, I threw-up a smokescreen and it worked, never mind that the smokescreen was part of me all the time. Never mind. Nothing known. Except in here. Walk away quickly from the flats, cross between parked cars, she may follow, it is night, walk along a high garden railing, from lamp-post to lamp-post. Not a cat or dog in the street, not a movement in the shadows, not a light in a window, just the lamp-posts lighting pavements, not a policeman, not a bird. Ears hum with absence of city sound. So still, the last waking man. Nothing known, eh, houses, just you and me and you say nothing known. At Val's house Jody knows me, she'll speak in my defence, she won't close her eyes, she'll speak for me. Hurry to Jody, just to be in the same house is safety, the streets aren't deserted, there's someone following, *they*, experts in following that man. Look back and they've quickly hidden in gates. Walk quicker. The Belisha beacon flashes to an empty road.

Orange, night, orange, night. The traffic lights change, red, red-amber, green, amber, red, the city machine goes on and only I know it's living, wires hum beneath the street, telephone wires hum above me, the lights change, the beacon pulses its orange message, the people think they're sleeping, they're waiting, if only they knew, waiting for the city to eat them, hurry to Jody's house, the orange flash follows me, is the city machine ready to pounce, is it hungry? *It* knows about me.

They, it, a few yards behind, hurry the last few yards, in, they, it, stretching arms, get the key out now, Val's key, find the keyhole, quickly, key, turn, thank God, inside, close the door, barricade, the vampires hurl themselves in the face of the closed door, a second late, but there's always tomorrow night.

His pyjamas felt warm, as they did when he was a boy on cold nights. He pulled the blankets up to his ear. There was a choking impulse to cry or pray or shout for mum, but he had to remember he was sleeping in the house of his best friend, whom he was betraying and this, if anything did, meant he was grown up. Surely now he could sleep as men did, honourably tired? The dirty bitch.

When he awoke the sun was shining through the window and for a moment he felt innocently happy. In the old days it always shone on wonderful Saturday mornings. This was Saturday morning. In Val's house. Was it safer to stay in bed, until trouble found him, or get up and meet it face to face? Whatever else the woman had done, meeting her had told him something. He could not help her. Was it too late to help himself? If only he could find simple decisions to make. He got up, found the bathroom empty, ran the bath, lay in it limply, as though newly pulled back from an extended campaign in mud. There was a knock at the bathroom door. It was Val. He leaned across to slip the bolt, flopping back in the bath. Maybe Val would push him under.

"Hullo," Val said, not very sure of himself. He came into the bathroom, hands in pockets, looking at Reaney's feet. "It's after twelve."

Maggie, when was he supposed to meet her? One, was it? Oh God, she'd be all girlish and happy.

"How are you this morning, Val?" Strange, to speak to him without being facetious.

"Hellish. Jody isn't speaking to me. I think we've had it. The worst of it is, I've got to go out, this bloody police series, they're having a script conference this afternoon, I can't get out of it."

Say it now.

"Pity about last night. Still, it'll seem like a big laugh in a day or two, it always does."

"That's why Angela walked out on you, I suppose. Maybe she didn't have a sense of humour. Peter, I—tell me something, I need somebody to talk to . . . does Jody still love me?"

Say it now.

"How do I know, Val, she didn't say anything to me, I don't know, do I, she's bound to be a bit upset, finding you in kip with her mate, isn't she? Do you still love her?"

Val shuffled about, looking at the floor, out of the window, at Reaney's cloudy navel.

"I don't know. Before last night, I mean. Oh Christ, what a mess! Look, Peter, I'm not the ideal husband, by any means, I know that. It's the kids. Oh Christ, *why* did you have to come back so early!"

But he was too depressed to consider that question. Reaney tried to press himself down into the water, knees, feet, shoulders, belly. It was warm in the bath. Filth was pouring out of him. He needed time.

"She won't leave you just like that," he said, not looking

at Val. "Best just to push off, give her time. If she's going to forget it she will, if not, there's not much you can do about it, is there? Especially if you don't even know if you love her yourself."

Val seized on this way out with reluctant agreement, the silly little twerp only wanted to be told what he was going to do anyway. It was the inconvenience he was worried about, either finding a new cook and mother or having to move out with all his gear, all his papers. Move out? Don't we know an ideal bachelor establishment, vacant now, as it happens? No, not even Judas Reaney could manipulate the poor bastard *that* coolly. Val went away, saying he would see him sometime, he hoped. There was a doominess about him that irritated Reaney. Nobody had ever helped him . . .

Reaney let him leave the house, listening for the gate to slam. Husbands knew not the sexy days of their unseen wives. Then he got out of the bath, rubbing himself with a cold cloth. He was starving. He found a shirt that Jody had washed and ironed, on a coat-hanger in the wardrobe. He went downstairs, wondering how he'd get out in time to make his date with Maggie, couldn't let her down, sort of owed it to the girl. He wanted to inspect Val's children. Think of Maggie as a breathing space.

Jody was doing something domestic around the kitchen sink, a cloth in her hands.

"Morning," he said. She put the backs of her wrists on her hip bones. She wasn't exactly smiling, but she seemed to be looking in the direction Val had gone, so maybe he would escape without criticism. Having seen the Boy-Reaney he could now make a better attempt at being her masterful man. The Boy-Reaney had disgusted him.

"He's gone to his script conference," she said. "He thinks I'm going to leave him. Him! He's not worth the effort."

Oh. So who was leaving who? Sorry, whom?

"He was a bit unlucky, you must admit," he said. He didn't feel so bold as to walk right in and kiss her. Time to box clever. You had no idea, no idea whatsoever, how women thought from one minute to the next. Presume nothing. "He asked me if I thought you still loved him." He sat down at the shiny kitchen table, a blue top, the sort of place kids would eat at.

"What did you tell him?" She still hadn't let on what she now thought about him and her, as opposed to Val and her.

"How could I know?"

"You? *You* know how I feel. Don't *you* start playing silly boys!"

"I wasn't sure, I mean, we hadn't talked about it, had we? I wasn't going to break the bloke's heart on the strength of a quick bump on the office floor, was I?"

That was a wrong thing to say, provided he wanted to say the right thing. Where the hell were the kids, the old one anyway, he knew what the baby looked like. Her face flushed.

"So that's all it was, a quick bump on the office floor! Thank you very much!"

"Now, now, I was only joking, we're not past the joking already, are we? Christ, I'm starving, Missus, you got any grub, actually, I've arranged to take a music publisher to the football, I've got to, can't get out of it, I've got to meet him at one, oh well, I don't want to spoil good digs, maybe I'll snatch a bite outside."

She walked towards him, grabbed a handful of hair, pulled his face round and up, looking down at him, a bit of red hair hanging down the side of her wifely face. He could feel her warmth. He grinned. She narrowed her eyes but there was no viciousness in her face. He wanted to please her—always.

"Take care, Reaney," she said. "I'm an old hand at handling husbands." She let him go, wiping her hand from his still bath-wet hair on her apron. He'd had enough sex for a couple of years, it was good to have a rest and a joke. "I suppose you hopped into bed with that nymphomaniac slut last night, don't lie—*men*—you're so easily taken in by sluts."

"Who me? I walked the city streets, the lonely man who walks away from well-lit windows. Listen, Jody, what *are* we going to do?"

"I'll see," she said. "Just stick around, Reaney, I'll have to make up my mind about you." But she was smiling now and he knew this little corner of England would forever be waiting, provided he really loved her, provided the older child was fatherable.

He kissed her this time, grabbing her round the buttocks, pulling her heavy body into his face. He stood up, liking the solidity of her waist between his arms, the way her freckly skin dropped away into the breasts, kissing her lightly on the nose, very friendly.

"It'll work itself out," he said. "I must go. Do you think I should be missing this evening?"

"Be missing for a week if you like. I'm not tying you down. Not until I'm ready and then, watch out, sonny boy, watch out. I have my children, you know. I'm like a female wolf for them. Isn't that what mothers are supposed to say?"

The perfect arrangement. For why is the sun shining on plumping Peter Reaney, 37, this spring morning? For why? For because thirty consecutive minutes have gone by without one crucifixion, that's for why because. He felt young as he walked away from the house towards Notting Hill Gate, young and free and off on a picnic. He was being forged into a man of steel by life's great forge. No drink today, not a drop.

It was a sunny, safe city the taxi took him through on

his way down Bayswater Road. People who didn't make it could blame themselves. Each man had to be his own tiger. Maggie was wearing a mod girl's trouser suit, quite young-making for him, he'd seen thousands of them but he'd never seen himself taking one of them out, they were part of the market, not inner party material, sort of thing Barry Black would hang about with, he'd always thought. It was a light mustard colour, sunny colour for a sunshine outing. NO SEX!

To him there was a magic about her, standing on the busy corner, as though she shone with fame, the aura that catches the public eye when professional models pose in public places. Why was the evil blonde *still* the figure of whole-some desire?

"Sorry I'm late," he said, taking her elbow. "We lonely bachelors tend to sleep late, y'know."

"Five minutes, that's nothing," she said. The sun made a fuzzy halo close to her creamy cheeks. She smelled of flower-water. There must be *something* wrong with her or she wouldn't be spending Saturday afternoon with him. She had eaten, so he bought two pounds of Granny Smiths at a stall, it being health day. He covered the first minutes talking about which game she might like best, how Spurs was difficult to get at, West Ham too much like foreign travel, she didn't care either way, he decided on Chelsea. Don't come back for a week, Jody had said. No point in going all the way north to Manor House on the Piccadilly Line when Chelsea was practically within walking distance of a certain basement flat, where a girl could knock up an omelette and an ageing Lochinvar could play the gay bachelor, even if only in his own mind.

"You'll have to stand, of course," he said. "I mean, we probably could get seats but I think it spoils it, sitting down. Get with the people, I say."

She didn't mind. They crossed the Bayswater Road

and entered the park. Couples (the blokes generally younger than himself, the girls not nearly so lush as Maggie), Indians in groups of five, children, dogs, prams, boys playing football, couples lying on the grass, Irishmen playing cards in a Red Indian circle, a model-type girl and a hacking-jacketed Steerforth with an Afghan wolfhound, an unshaven man in braces flat on his back, sunbathing or sleeping it off, pairs of not-so young girls in deckchairs, grass worn smooth as ice, dog dirt everywhere, the plump elbow in his fingers, softer than Jody's matured flesh, soft, flower-water, a kite high above the Round Pond, the ghost of the night walking among you all, estimating your happiness-ratings, wondering if the couples will end in slapping matches, wondering if the children were being taught the posterity things, wondering if the Cypriots yearned for Cyprus, the Irish for Ireland, the Indians for dusty roads and bazaars, the English for—what did he yearn for? This? This was now. But it wasn't now. It was feeling the sun, sparkle of water, people laughing, this was not *now* it was *then*. Twenty years ago this was what he had yearned for and now he yearned to be back there yearning. Happiness was always in the past, never now, for if it was now it only reminded you of then, it never satisfied you as it was.

"I keep wondering what a lovely young girl like you is doing with a dreary old fool like me," he said. "You know, I wouldn't go out with the kind of girl who would go out with me, ha ha."

Always the reason, ruin everything asking for the reason. She seemed to beam on people as they moved across the grass, although she was not actually smiling.

"You asked me, that's why," she said. "Why did you ask me? The other morning I thought you thought I was a proper little horror."

No, you must give me the reason.

"It just seemed to happen," he said. "Like the other morning."

"But you meant all that, I know you did. Then the next thing, you and your Mister Felix are talking about taking me on! Perhaps it's best, to go out with people who're more mixed up than you are yourself. You feel quite normal."

So she didn't know either, it had just happened to her as well. What the hell was the use of *that*? Nobody he knew seemed to make any conscious decisions about anything.

They came out of the park, crossed over Kensington Road into Queens Gate, she was content to be led and he needed to walk—to call a taxi or sink into the awful day-night of the underground would bring back all *that*.

Down broad, cool Queens Gate, across Gloucester Road when the lights held up the city-fleeing traffic, still only two o'clock, talking about nothing in particular, her elbow not as Jody's but softer, requiring a grip that would not bruise, as though there were no positive strength in her girl plumpness, the passive girl who went along with a man because he had asked her. Presumably her degree of positivity ended with the initial decision to have or not have any contact with the man at all. From then on—why me, I have no strength to be making her decisions? There was something wrong with the men of England—even in films they didn't know what to do with Diana Dors. Too many wars had drained off their manliness.

Brompton Road, his own territory, houses that once measured the imminence of the hate situation, now just houses, make of them what you feel like at the time. Girls in headscarves, not-quite lovely long legs of the English middle-classes, no bosoms worth mentioning, voices that cut cloth at forty yards. Low sports cars leaving a wake of virile fart-exhaust—is each postal district populated by extras from The Great Casting Department? Then into Redcliffe

Gardens, the first football walkers, men with a purpose that took them through any enclave, the cars whizz down one-way Redcliffe Gardens, home of exiled Poles of the officer class, music teachers and student architects, hiding behind heavy curtains as the football men invade their territory. Maggie gets whistles and waves from men kneeling at the windows of a supporters' coach, red and white scarves are waved back at the coach by bands of paper-hatted youths who come from Manchester—what think ye of tall South Ken?

"They must have a lot of money to come all the way from Manchester for a football match," Maggie says.

"It's all part of the capitalist opiate," but that was not what he felt. To be from Manchester and to walk through South Ken wearing Manchester insignia—you'd know who you were then. A supporter. Mindless? Some people remained who supported something, alive for this moment at least.

In Fulham Road the crowd was thicker, the English crowd in the novel sun, pouring along the road, men, men, not fashionable men, not smart men, not superior men nor men of power, just men, men with their mates, men with their sons, men alone but together, men not wanting money or women or whipping or promotion or fame—not now, anyway—just men. He was introducing Maggie to men, he wanted to tell her that these were the drilled men, the Naafi men, the smoking men, the ordinary men, out of uniform now yet not quite out of uniform, never quite out of uniform. Here, by God, nothing needed to be known, nor did he want anything to be known, for it was enough to be one of them, they could look at the trouser suit but when they saw him, well, old Pete Reaney knows how to pull 'em class birds, don't he? Val would be rabbiting away with the slicksters, desperately trying to think up, out of their personal vacuums, what would appeal to us men of England. Val had been brought up one of us men, but he was easily led, he'd fallen for all that pink-shirted crap.

He stood in line to buy a programme. Maggie waited. He looked at her. There's our daughter, men of England, she's got style, hasn't she, but she hasn't left us, not yet, anyway. Take her elbow again, make little jokes about being trampled to death under football-maddened hordes, in line towards the battery of turnstile gates, men joking, the younger ones, time in plenty for them to join us, horsing about, if they lock us out now we go over the top, lads, we all smile, it's Nobby Clarke whispering loud cracks about the co from the rear rank, great to be back with the mob again, don't close the gates now, let Maggie go through first, the gateman smiles behind his mesh, the turnstile creaks forward, we're in. Thank God.

"I never knew so many people went to football matches," she says.

I'm glad you like it, daughter, what am I saying, let's get up the steps. *All human life is here,* proclaims the giant *News of the World* hoarding which looks down over the great bowl. Move round the terraces, nearer the middle, facing the un-smart, un-slick stands, nearer to the centre of the action. Men have been here for some time, making an effort to grab advantageous positions, but they do not mind us arriving now, they do not claim to own the ground they stand on, Maggie's blonde head makes them look, look again, they think—why is that fat geezer with that lush piece? Remember me, lads, Pete Reaney of 'B' Coy? Sure you do.

The great roar. Explain to Maggie about the magic of Manchester United, point out the shimmering head of the great Law, the prematurely bald Charlton, it would be better explained to a son, but probably a son would know more about it than me for I haven't been much, not since I got married eight years ago and Angela said it was silly to waste a Saturday afternoon. Chelsea in blue, they seem typical of London, shortish, youngish, darkish, cheeky almost beside the self-contained stylists from the north. Who was greater, Matthews or Finney? Why was Len Shackleton kept out of the England team? Nights in the Naafi, Jock taking it so seriously he'd want to belt geezers who said Glasgow Rangers couldn't beat the lot of your English poofs, we're lucky we got in, the gates must be closed now, worst thing in the world to get locked out, excluded from the great community, we're in, though. Maggie says it's much the same as hockey, she's enjoying it, the man in front is cheerily apologetic for blocking her view, he offers to let her stand in front of him, she's not tall enough to see over his head, she's only young, I smile at her, she's all right, Maggie, she's one of us. Am I one of us? Say I am, lads, this civvy-street's been a right mess, but it hasn't been altogether my fault. Are those twenty-two out there, professionals, are they Barry Blacks or our sons? Barry Black is somebody's son, surely. Nobby Clarke got a bint in trouble once, didn't he? What's so nasty about Barry Black? The money? The selfselfself? Nobby pulled his bird in Blackpool, when he was wearing bd, boots and beret, with a cropped head and eight bob in his pocket. Barry Black is famous. Nobby used to hide under the table in the boozer when his bint came looking for him, Barry Black was surrounded by grown men, who paid Mary Gray to crawl off and die. These lads out there, *we* all played this game once, we're all playing it now, we're not subjects and rulers, stars and slobs, we're all part of it. The men. Law is Scottish, his hair is the same colour as Maggie's, not the poison dwarf Glasgow Scot, the Viking, his body is electric, Barry Black's hair is whiter than that, a painted thing in a screaming world of make-believe, Law and Maggie are real, Maggie's being told by another man why the referee blew for a foul, the man is fatherly the way he talks, of course he wouldn't kick her out of bed, he's a man, isn't he, but he's not an alligator, blue versus red, primary colours, nothing is fashionable here, the iron stands and the primary colours, haircuts from barbers, suits even laughable; half-time and Maggie and the man swap places again, she loves it, she isn't tired standing, she wants to know which player is nicknamed 'Ruby' and why, she thinks it's funny for she's heard of Ruby Murray, of course, she wants to be a girl singing star, doesn't she? But if you're a star, Maggie, you won't be here with us, it wouldn't be safe—at least that's what stars say, it wouldn't be safe. Do they think we men of England would jostle them and rub off the magic aura? Are they Rommel's men, to be frightened of us? Yes, but which side is Peter Reaney on?

What is Val talking about now? What is Frances thinking about? Who is moving forward on the tube platform, cut off from us, desperately cut off? Whose life is so tortured —at this very moment—that he or she could not shout—with us—as cocky number ten in blue, Venables, robs Law? Can Chelsea score? No, they do not. Are we the same faceless crowd who roared at Nuremberg? No, we were never faceless, not *that* way. It's a game. We like it, we played it when we were young, we admire the skill, we wish it was us, we shout but no man orders us to shout. What slick people are up in that jet, leading lives of such barren artificiality that they are travelling when they should be on the terraces? We are all specks to them, but to us they don't exist. Who cares for those who are not with us? By choice, of course. Our feet are solidly on the terracing steps, we do not buy first-class tickets to avoid ordinary men. Have another apple for God's sake, I'm tired of holding the bag, chew the sweet healthy acid. Maggie doesn't want the last apple, holds it to the man who gave her his place, to give and to accept, no suspicion (well, just a little in his eyes at first) for why would we be suspicious of each other? We are not looking for advantage over other men. Can I trust myself to remember this when the game is over?

Chapter Nineteen

They took their time walking round the terraces to allow the worst of the crowd to subside. Maggie had enjoyed it and Reaney felt relaxed, light even, the apples working their good work. A beer can rattled from concrete step to concrete step, a small boy threw the last toilet roll of the afternoon towards the goal, a gang of whooping youths ran like Red Indian braves playing tag.

"Well then, what's the programme now?" He asked her as they made the Fulham Road. Her elbow expected his hand now.

"What would you like to do?" she said.

He hadn't thought that far ahead. Actually, he was beginning to feel somewhat weak. His legs were not used to static marathons. There was nowhere he particularly wanted to go, nothing he particularly wanted to do. They ate in an Italian cafe-restaurant near South Kensington tube station. He had spaghetti, slices of bread, three cups of coffee, anything to fill up. The point about Maggie was that she didn't need to say very much, she was happy if the person she was with was happy. He supposed. Silences were not strained, small-talk was easy. Yet . . . he snorted involuntarily as the name of Brästweiber came to mind. What had all that been about? Difficult to remember these ghastly mental writhings in this straightforward situation.

"Now then," he said, vaguely, when they had finished the apple pie. "I hate making decisions. What would you like to do this evening?"

"Whatever you'd like to do." No hostility in her cream-surrounded eyes.

"Tell me, Maggie, straight out, don't you have a boy-friend or anything?"

She smiled as she inhaled.

"I've only been in London a month, you know," she said. "Jack's been taking me so many places . . . I had one, at home, I write to him but he's going to a technical college for three years so . . ."

"Do you see me as a boyfriend or an uncle?"

"I hadn't thought about it. Well, a boyfriend then. Uncles are older, aren't they?"

Uncles are older! Stap me, how old can you get?

"The imminence of the grave is my greatest obsession," he said. "When I'm with you I feel younger and older at the same time. I'm thirty-seven."

"That isn't old."

"It isn't young either, believe you me. Anyway, I've got a good idea. You ever see a film called *The Hustler?*"

Again, in the cinema, he felt he was introducing her to his man's world, showing her *his* life, wondering how she would react. He held her hand, but still there was only blessed friendship in it, no sign of creeping cannibalism. Was he Fast Eddie Folsom or Minnesota Fats? The wandering boy or the old pro? He looked not dissimilar to Jackie Gleason, that was for sure, but his life was more like the wandering boy of the pool halls. She said she liked the atmosphere but she didn't understand about billiards. They were out in Notting Hill Gate again, not nine o'clock yet, the sky going deep purple, standing on the same bit of pavement where twenty-five hours previously he had stood with Jody, who now waited in a house over thataway, waiting for her husband to come home or not come home, so that she could work out what to do about him and everything.

No, he didn't fancy a drink, no more drink, the projector kept trying to come in with clips of tomorrow's return to business and Dorry, no drink. Eyes, tired. Feet, tired. Sex—asleep now, for a blessed miracle.

They walked away from the cinema, holding hands. Young lovers usually bought ice cream this kind of moment, but he couldn't quite shut out the watching eyes of those who knew the other Reaney: Imagine Minnesota Fats pushing a pram.

"If you met Mister Right would you chuck in all these show business ideas you've got?" he asked her as they came to the archway at the entrance to millionaire's row.

"I don't know," she said. She had a funny little mannerism, when she walked, of holding her head low, twisted slightly to one side, as though it was a little too heavy. "I haven't got much to give up, have I? You can't say in advance, can you?"

In a less relaxed mood his irritation might have meant something, now it was merely a mental note, Maggie gives nothing away.

"Anyway," she went on, "how do you recognise Mister Right? Are you Mister Right? Is this some enchanted evening I will meet a stranger?"

"I am Mister Wrong," he said. "I need a wife called Susan, then she can be Suzie Wrong. Pardon me. The only advice I could give a young girl on the threshold of life's great adventure is so nasty I wouldn't even tell you."

"Go on, shock me."

Please understand this is genuine advice. How to make her understand? He stops, pulling her hand back so that they are facing each other, his big black head looking down at her broad seal-face.

"Please take me seriously, promise, I mean this straight out, genuine advice, I found out the hard way. Now, you promise? I'm being perfectly honest, not hinting at anything?"

"I promise. Goodness, you're so suspicious."

"All right then. Anybody can look like Mister Right. Or Miss Right. But marriage has nothing to do with looks, absolutely nothing, not after you've met anyway. My genuine advice to a girl is to try him out in bed first because that's where it goes or it doesn't. If it goes you've got a chance. If it doesn't, God help you. Everything else is propaganda put about by sex-starved God-botherers. Love comes after, real love, I mean, not temporary infatuation. At least I think so, I've never had any." He shrugged. It was really just a weary little seduction gambit he'd tried often enough in the past.

"What if you try it and it doesn't work but you're pregnant anyway?" She sounded genuinely interested.

"I don't know. You don't go to a backstreet hairpin artist, that's the worst thing of all. Never do that, it doesn't matter how bad things are, never do that. Anyway, you'll never have to do that. People don't get pregnant all that easily."

Don't they? How about you-know-who? Was that Maggie, flower-blood drip-dripping onto cigarette ash? No, not her. She had something special, things like that never happened to special people, the lucky ones.

Along the side of the park now, she's thinking, head forward, I'm a conniving rat like the rest of them. Well, at least I showed you a time when men were not conniving rats.

"We might as well go up to my flat," Maggie said as they approached Queensway. "If you think I'm safe, of course." A cheeky girl's laugh or a tease's laugh? The spaghetti and bread still lay heavy in him. Somewhere he could lie down, sleep between cool sheets, no action of any kind whatsoever, heads down early lads, tomorrow it's the big one.

We're fighting the frogs and you know how long Olivier's bloody speeches take.

She made coffee, while he sat at the same table, now keeping his eyes open by concentration. Soft, warm air came through the window, the night was soft and dark, the kitchen was lit only by a raffia lamp on a chest of drawers, Maggie had the air of a woman who pulled off long white gloves to serve at soup kitchens, a picnic girl for summer grass. He drank the coffee. The cigarette tasted metallic, he stubbed it out after a couple of drags. Resting on his elbows, he blinked and his eyes tried to stay closed.

"Oh, I'm sorry," he said, shaking his head, "it's been a lovely but tiring day, I think I'd better push off, I'm working tomorrow . . ."

"Where do you live?"

"Well, that's a good question. I'm staying with that guy Val and his wife but they're having a row, I think I'll go back to my own place."

"Stay here," she said. She wasn't smiling, she wasn't deadly serious either, not like grimly casual Frances. She was just—well, stay here. It's an invitation, not a clue for Krafft-Ebing.

"You're quite safe, I can promise, I'm nackered, Maggie." So he washed his face and hands with her sweet soap, dried himself on her soft towel, went to say goodnight to her in the other bedroom, where she was already in bed.

"You can't sleep through there, she's coming back to-night," Maggie said. Her face, her blonde hair against the pillow, her creamy neck, her shape under the pink blankets. He was too tired. He put off the light and crept into bed beside her, still wearing his Aertex pants and vest. Her arm forced its way under his neck, her other arm went over his shoulder. He put his right arm over her waist, gently.

It's nice to be friendly, she said in the darkness. If only

people were more friendly, if only I was nice enough for you, Maggie, if only, if only . . .

There were six of us when we found the great iron door which led to one of those open-sided industrial lifts, we went up, stens ready, not knowing where more of the bastards might be hiding, I remember it as clearly now, even the splinters on the heavy wooden slats of the lift floor, I knew that kind of splinter, rasped by steel-tipped boots, see it in the army all the time, the lift stopped and the little gate went up, it was a place without windows, like a boiler-cellar only it was at the top of the place, the walls were lined with asbestos, light gray originally but there had been many fires up there in that burned place, the remains of the bodies were still on the asbestos walls, charred gristle, blackened bones, you couldn't tell if they'd been men or women, I remember Sarge, he was breathing heavy as though he was whistling, we saw where they had put them on tables, the black boiler-doors, a flapdoor which when pushed opened up a metal-lined chute, you couldn't see the bottom, there was even blood on the low asbestos ceiling, Sarge closed his eyes, somebody said it made you want to die to think of what'd gone on in here before we came, Sarge said we should all look and never forget, this was what they were all about, politicians would try and cover it up and say it wasn't that bad, but we'd know, I kept thinking of the burned ones on the walls, if only we'd got there earlier, they must have gone mad, are there really human men alive who'd do this somebody asked Sarge, he said yes, they're down in the yard, they look just like us, somebody else said, that's the trouble, my God, we'd seen a lot but we were like ghosts when we went back down the lift, Sarge breathed as though he was in a fever, his jaw was leaping up and down, what'll happen to them, Sarge, they'll get hung, maybe, it was funny, I'd always thought we'd put them up against a wall before the bloody lawyers got hold of them but when we got down in the yard I couldn't look at them at first, sneaky glances, I tried to see what was on their faces, but they were just like men, only we knew what they'd done up there in the asbestos room, but they were just like men, I kept crying, for months, I kept thinking that if we all cried and cried it might help, because if you imagine the worst thing that could ever happen to anybody it was nothing to what we'd seen, I used to wake up at nights, shivering, why didn't we do something about it earlier? It changed my ideas about death, I realised that there were times when death would be the greatest miracle any human being could ever imagine, sometimes I can't believe it was real, but it was, I swear it was, it was, it was, THEY WERE JUST LIKE MEN.

"What's wrong?"

"Just like men, what's happening, what's happening, Maggie, Maggie . . ."

It was *true* of her to hold him close to her breast, he'd known she would take care of him, Maggie's loving care doesn't cost money, doesn't cost mon . . .

He woke first. She had freed her arm, lying on her back, the creamy girl flesh warm from the night. He kissed her arm. Later he told her it was some silly old nightmare, it was quite a jokey time with her and her flat-mate, Bobbie, a jolly sort of girl who kept laughing about the drunken visit. Gay, young, pure, Peter Reaney has enough fantastic insight into the human condition to know that every combination of people will automatically form into a family grouping and it suited them for him to play the big brother home from the bad world with many wondrous tales and jokes for his oohing and aahing sisters. Maggie went about it in a short dressing-gown that showed off her plump calves and sturdy girl's ankles, there was a difference in liking to look and burning to look, he loved looking at her legs, maybe when he was back to that so-called real life out there it would not be nice but . . . On the phone he arranged to meet Dixon at the airport, wanting to travel by himself.

It was half-past eleven when they had another of Maggie's blow-out breakfasts, easy to see she was none of your clothes-horse city brats but a farmhouse girl, if only she'd never left her lovely farmhouse, bet her mother's a dish, too. Then he was ready to go.

"Thanks, Maggie," he said at the door, holding her hands, looking down into the blue of her pupils. "I'll be working late, maybe I'll see you next week? You and Goddings are coming to the office anyway."

"Whenever you like, Peter," she said. "Thanks for a lovely time."

He couldn't have made love to her, she wasn't of the barnyard.

On the BEA coach to the airport he saw a man with a bitterly tightened mouth and he wondered if Maggie could make it soft. The papers were full of the usual drivel. He looked out of the window. London was getting up with the times now, fly-overs and motorways and all that jazzy twentieth-century stuff, did it add to anybody's happiness, suppose it must, somehow. They reached the airport. He didn't rush to be first out of the door, letting several business-type men go first, doggy-faces, carrying briefcases like brandy barrels, then he moved towards the door.

"Don't shove, *if* you don't mind." The tight-mouthed man had been sitting down and then made a very quick movement, looking viciously at Reaney as he pushed past. It was so uncalled-for Reaney almost kicked out, what right had the miserable bastard to spoil a lovely day? Some people! He met Dixon up on the great first-floor lounge, big as a hangar, all glossy people from advertisements jetting in and out of London, England, my God, was there nobody left to spend an August Sunday in a field? Dixon was all tensed up for his big moment in the public relations business (Felix became very angry if anybody said they were press agents).

"We've got a good turn-out, all the nationals, BBC and ITN as well," was his greeting.

"There's something I forgot to ask Felix," Reaney said, feeling the good part slipping away. "Oh yeah, what did he do about Rahilly, do you know?"

"He's coming, Felix said he could have the exclusive if he did it today and they used it on Tuesday. We've got to fix him up with an hour with Dorry, maybe back at the hotel, after the others have gone?"

"Yeah, that's best. Now listen, the personal assistant, you know nothing about him, absolutely nothing, remember? Tell them they've got to ask me about him. We'll play him very cagey, if Joe Alterberg's right they'll go mad about him, he looks like something dragged out of a gangster movie, but you know nothing. Right?"

In the half hour before the New York flight arrived he forgot all about the good part. The ones he didn't know had to be met, the least important provincial chain men given most encouragement for they didn't have the same push as the national hands, anyway he always had this idea of helping young blokes, the older ones were there for a few pars, it was a picture job really, the trades and show biz writers would only be here to make sure there were no angles about the arrival, they'd gather round Dorry in earnest at the hotel, he had to borrow a fiver from Dixon, were the cars laid on, where was that girl from what's-it bloody magazine, she was new and he'd promised her editor he'd let her get some colour taken at the airport, they could just make some production deadline with it, thank God the beauty queen wasn't here, Dixon could handle Manchester on his own, yeah, Dorry's the greatest guy in the business, not big-headed in the slightest, boy does he know where to put it, remember last time in the Dorchester he's out in the corridor, good job he's a mate or we'd have used that, Peter, I always knew you were a decent kind of rat, now, anything forgotten? Phew, it was worse with two of them, he had to check on Dixon as well, keep him sober, too, if Dixon got carried away at the reception, as he well remembered doing all those how many years ago at his first reception when it seemed like a glorious party only he was supposed to be working, ah well, who needs fields?

With ten minutes before the arrival his mouth was hot from non-stop smoking and he was slightly dry inside and wet outside. Time for a quickie? He went to the vip lounge bar, most of the men here knew him or who he was, not one of your stuffy publicity men, a real raver when you get him going.

So what, if he was starting he might as well have a Scotch on ice, plenty of water. Cheers, chaps, here's to the traditional English Sabbath.

"The office said Dorry made a hundred thou last year," one of the photographers said, half-interested which was burning enthusiasm for a photographer.

"More than that," Reaney said. "That didn't include record royalties, it was just box office receipts. Add another hundred thou at least on records and merchandising—he's sold about twenty million lp's. Not bad, eh?" Eager support of the client was not his style. "For a piss artist," he added. The photographer made a knowing grimace, but had Reaney ever seen how so-and-so swilled it down, by Christ, there was a . . .

Then Dorry was coming through, led by a girl in uniform and an airport official, the smoother-outer, great big Dorry towering behind them, suntanned, very fit if you didn't see the belly, string tie, pale blue suit, his big outdoor face lighting up.

"Hiya, Pete old man," he said, the big hand out.

"Welcome to England, Dorry, you're looking great, man, great."

Like all stars, the entourage: Cholly Aberdeen, the personal manager who'd found Dorry in a small Texas town and brought him into the big world and now came along, indispensable friend and percentage collector, a man who'd got that rope-like throat barking at a million country fairs and who now wore mohair imported from England; Jake the Rake, the dresser, errand-boy, girl selection board and Alka Seltzer man; and this time, instead of wicked little Joe Alterberg, Franks, the gorilla with the nursing diploma. Reaney started them towards the bar, holding back himself to get a look at Franks.

Joe had, of course, been exaggerating. He was only a small gorilla and he wore a neat suit, very neat, three-buttons, tight on his chest and sides. It was his shoulders and his eyes—the shoulders held low, straight, the eyes a lightish shade of gray, eyes that swept round like a stalag search-light. Hair cropped in American astronaut fashion. White shirt with a high white collar. The real point came to Reaney as he moved across to introduce himself. Head on, Franks was as wide as he was long. He looked along the shoulder ridge to see where the padding began, but when he reached the end of the shoulder he could see more shoulder pushing out against the top of the jacket sleeve.

"You're Franks, aren't you?" Reaney said, putting out his hand. "I'm Peter Reaney, pleased to meet you. Joe Alterberg maybe told you he would write to me and explain your ehm, part in the proceedings?"

Franks didn't smile. He shook Reaney's hand and if

Dorry was big in the Texas style, Franks seemed to be an iron man operating under careful mechanism. There was nothing soft about the hand, nothing.

"I'm delighted, Mister Reaney," he said. "Perhaps we can have a longer talk a little later, I think I'm needed now."

He went past Reaney, low, like a well-tailored tank. From the back the impression was that he had metal suiting keeping him in a dead straight line from neck to heel. He went into the knot at the bar. One thing, you knew something about being English when you were with Americans. You knew your hair was too long, your voice was too high, your mannerisms were downright foppish. At least with this kind of American. So, Dorry was so bad now on the booze they'd had to send human handcuffs. How far would Franks go to keep Dorry off it? Hit people? Hit Dorry? Reaney went into the knot. The accredited photographers would have done Dorry on the aircraft steps, now it was straight stuff for Monday's first editions, Dorry had his elbow on the bar, the girl was doing her best to throw the booze around, Dorry with his entourage, the girl puts glass after glass on the bar beside Dorry, but he waves a big brown hand, a big American was really something, really big. Stock questions, stock pictures, some photographer starts taking names for captions, 'how do I describe Mister Franks?'.

Mister Franks had nothing to say, he was just behind Dorry, looking through between the big man's shoulder and Cholly's ear.

"He's the assistant personal manager," Reaney said.

"He looks more like a wrestler to me," somebody says. Suddenly preoccupied photographers fiddle with their cameras as they move, ever so unobtrusively, into an angle for a shot of Franks. Dorry turned and put his hand on Franks' shoulder.

"Glen wrestles all right, he wrestles the wimmin away

from my door, don't you, Glen?" Dorry is laughing, everybody is laughing. Franks isn't laughing. He may have nodded slightly, but he doesn't laugh. He is, after all, guarding a million dollars and if his job depends on stopping that million dollars from the first taste of wine, well, who's laughing?

Dorry has a large orange juice for the cameras.

"My, I just love being in little old England again," he says, raising the glass. He smiles as he makes the toast gesture, but what he says is strictly for laughs among the gang. "You English sure piss a lovely shade of yaller."

So Dorry is on top form, the first stage has been all right, nothing great, nothing disastrous, now then, lads, you know where the cars are, the chosen ones depart, tell the others to stay and drink the bar dry as Dorry's guests, knowing they'll be out of there in five minutes.

The cavalcade down the motorway. Dorry only likes to sit in front, Cholly, Jake and him are in the back of the Rolls, Dixon looks so weak and boyish in the English manner between Dorry and the driver.

Dorry washes up in his suite and then the second stage, everybody's smoking, Reaney has heard it all a hundred times, he chats softly to Cholly while they stand watching the show biz writers try to get through Dorry's massive benevolence, got to get something new, Dorry's been around a long time, not quite a Bing Crosby institution, not long enough or just too long, Franks sits away to the left, not too far away, the drink-table is behind the press chairs, cloth-covered trays go round all the time, Sunday is now a smoky room, Rahilly tries to take part but he's concentrating on noting what the others ask, so that he can get different stuff for his column, he's desperately hoping the drink bit doesn't feature too large, he doesn't know yet about the orange juice, a hell-raiser gone wrong, will *he* be disappointed, who needs a reformed lush, we want lushes, two-fisted tigers from the Hollywood pool-surrounds, men who battled with Errol Flynn, Dorry never even met him, Dorry's only fight is with the bottle, a fight to get it all to himself, he's so cheery, Cholly whispers back that some people think he's off it for good, Cholly's expressive mouth spits metaphorical tobacco juice, he knows his boy, he's off it as long as Franks is there, the drink comes up, Dorry deals easily with that, didn't we all hit the bottle a bit too much when we were young and wild, the business is too competitive now, he's got too many people depending on him, Judas Priest if I piss longer'n two minutes ten people are outa work, sorry ma'am to the ladies present, they love it, Reaney hesitates, then takes a whisky off the waiter's tray, Cholly lights a cigar, that guy with the glasses, he seems to be trying to needle the boy, what's with him, oh, he's just like that, the stuff he writes is never as bitchy as the questions, so then who is your Mister Franks, does he talk? Glen Franks, male nurse, sits easy, like a guard not listening to the condemned man's last chat with his wife, it's only duty that brings him here, play your silly little games, come on, he's a bodyguard, isn't he, boy, do I look like the kinda fairy who'd need a bodyguard, keep them laughing, Dorry, you've been around, the big money's in keeping around, all things to all men, no I don't pay too much attention to civil rights, I'm too busy trying to make as much money as Sammy Davis, what's that, do I regret my three marriages, no ma'am, I don't regret them, they were all nice women, that was the trouble I reckon, what do I think of the Beatles, I think they're wonderful, all that hair, to think I went bust trying to breed hounds that looked like that, I was before my time I guess, no seriously, they're wonderful artistes, I admire them but I admire so much about this country, hey, Cholly, this is Paris, France, isn't it, big laugh, Dorry can do it all right.

Then they begin to drift, a few more pictures, the ladies want a few words, Dorry frees himself from one, Dixon introduces another, Reaney hovers, Dixon has to learn and this is easy. Then the only drunk wants to challenge Dorry to an argument about Negro singers not getting a fair chance in the States, wasn't Nat Cole better than anybody, why was he neglected for films, how about Lena Horne, Dorry gets help from Reaney, Reaney tells the man that Cole was worth billions when he died, the drunk says he was still victimised, Dorry slips away, imperceptibly, then Reaney uses the watch-look, the gradual withdrawal, Dorry is in the next room with Rahilly, Cholly going along for support, Dixon helps Reaney with chit-chat, thank God, they're all gone. The waiter, Dixon, Jake's away pressing suits, Franks.

"Would you like something?" Reaney called across the room to Franks. He shook his head. "Cholly will see him all right in there," Reaney added, trying to be friendly. Franks made a very small mouth movement. But the thought disturbed him. He got up and went across to the connecting door. "They'll be all right, maybe better not to disturb them."

Franks came across to the bar table.

"Some soda water, please," he asked the waiter. Dixon handed Reaney a large Scotch. Ice, lots of water, just a snifter in the line of business. We aren't *all* lushes. "Mister Reaney I don't even like leaving him to go to the john. In Pennsylvania he got an elevator jockey to carry a pint so that he could drink going up and going down, I wasn't with him fifteen minutes and he was trying to get out of a tenth floor window. He's a real alcoholic, Mister Reaney, he isn't just a big lush any more. He'll kill you if he gets *one*. They're not paying me five hundred dollars a week to get my picture in the papers."

Reaney nodded. Franks was educated, one step only from being downright smooth. So Dorry's industry depended on keeping him in a straight-jacket and this was it and that was where your money got you. He swallowed his whisky just as quickly as he could drain it through the ice. Keep sober, your industry needs you. It was like that guy Arnie's bedroom drug lay-out, something at the heart of things, something that was obscene. Isn't that a very moralistic judgement for me to make, of all people, he thought. Are the white drugs any more obscene than the white whisky label? Is Dorry being kept off the booze any more obscene than Dorry lushing himself out of his mind? No, but there was something about the motive for keeping Dorry off the booze—in the interests of money they were going to save Dorry's life whereas his body, presumably, wanted, for some mysterious reason, to die. Is every drunk committing nightly suicide? Knowing he will arise again in the morning? There was no fathoming these affairs of men. He was not any more than any other man, so why should he tear himself in pieces trying to work things out. The Niagara of greasy days—or the mainstream of life, it was all the same, we were all ruined from the start because we grew up to believe we were special, we *were* more than other men. A widow woman had bad breath, so? He should bleed to death? She had bad breath, that was all. Toothpaste would cure her, or a glass of water every morning, or a slower eating rate. She didn't need the man on the cross, she needed a bag of peppermints.

"You might as well have another drink," he said to Dixon. "It's all on the firm." He had another himself. Franks knocked on the connecting door and went inside. Him and Dixon and the waiter, Rahilly, Aberdeen, Franks and Dorry, the scribe, the usurer, the policeman and the clown, all of us needing each other. Ha bleeding ha, the feebler the brain gets the more it clowns about in search of allegory. There is no deeper meaning, we are here to do our jobs and that is all. And seeing there's no universal symbol in my perfectly human liking for a drug that sweetens life, I can have a few more.

Around six Rahilly had finished the formal interview, but he had all Monday to write it, his kick was hanging about with stars so that he could write about them as though he shared their most private moments. Cholly liked a drink, Dorry seemed quite happy to gargle in orange juice. Then he went to lie down and it was Cholly, Dixon and himself, the waiter having left them to pour their own, Rahilly going to phone his wife.

"So," Reaney said. "You're quite happy so far?"

"Sure, sure," Cholly said.

"He's terribly good with the press, isn't he?" Dixon said.

"He likes all that," Cholly said. "It makes him feel he's more than just a pair of lungs. Y'know what his number one obsession is? You won't believe it. He wants the guys he was in the army with to think well of him. He'll never see any of them in a million years, but he's always worrying in case they read about him and think he's gone on the big star kick. You understand that, Peter?"

"Yeah, I think so. Is this why he's gone on the booze so badly, he thinks he's just a big face in the papers, a rubber man that other people blow up and push in the direction of the mike?"

"Who knows?" Cholly said. "Sometimes I wish I'd gone in for fighters. If they ain't idiots when they start they soon get their brains beaten in. Fighters would be easy to handle. Anyways, let's get the cards out for an hour, eh, less you two got something else on? The female scene won't be till later."

"Are you organised?" Reaney said. Cholly made his spitting mouth, this time grinning a little.

"Jake said on the plane, if you can't get it in London you can't get it anywhere. Switch on the teevee, son, I don't like all this silence."

So they put a coffee table between the armchairs, put a bottle and three glasses on the edge of the table, Cholly found his cards and began a game of gin rummy.

On the TV it was the early evening no-man's land of oblique Christianity, clean folk-singers introduced by a secular in a dark shirt. Cholly kept glancing at this. They played for small change. Rahilly came back from phoning his wife. Reaney felt sorry for him, she must be a cow or he would have been able to speak from the phone in the room. He knew about these things. Rahilly said he didn't care for gin but he'd join in anyway. Dixon and Rahilly were both star-struck, in their different ways. Whereas he was—? Self-struck? It all boiled down to the same thing, the "star" was a human spotlight in which all hangers-on felt important. Heydey hey, whoever cooked this supper should be crucified.

An hour and another bottle later Dorry appeared, refreshed, the sleeves of his open-necked white shirt pulled halfway to his elbows revealing wrists like planed logs. Franks had also removed his jacket. Again Dorry had orange juice, again he made a joke about it. Jake was downstairs, fixing up the female scene. Rahilly told several anecdotes in all of which he proved that he knew all about the secret lives of the stars, most of whom were his very dear mates.

Franks sat quietly, reading an *Observer* left behind from the reception. Cholly chewed non-existent tobacco and punctuated the handwork of cards with glances at the set. Dorry picked up his first hand, said that the guy who dealt this load of crap should drop dead, throwing them down face up, so ending the game. Rahilly wanted to row himself in on the female scene, he showed absolutely no reaction to any stretches and yawns and other hints that the party was breaking up. Dixon had not gone silly on the whisky, which impressed Reaney. Yet, if the new young no longer played the fool, what would they be like when they grew up? He began to feel restless. Colourful Americans playing cards and drinking whisky in smoky hotel rooms was all right in the movies. Certainly he had no insensate yearning for the doubtlessly sordid female scene that was to follow. That was for gypsy-stars and limpet-scribes and the young, who could be excused for wanting to wallow in life. But this was the dead end of the week, early Sunday evening, always the dead end, since he was a boy, never escape it, even if they turned all the churches into orgy palaces. He needed a lifeline to get him out of this smoky room. Had he had too much whisky to have another boy-meets-girl session with Maggie? Probably. Back to the flat? No, it would be dark and cold and lonely. So, it was back to Jody and Val, either one of them might be better than drifting along here to certain oblivion, depending on the reaction when he phoned.

He was picking up the phone when Jake came back, Jake the Rake, tiny master of humanity's rat-runs. He stood watching Jake, the receiver at his ear while the hotel switchboard dialled Jody's number. Jake wouldn't announce details with Rahilly and Dixon in the room, rat-run men followed stiff protocol. Cholly went off into the bedroom with him. Dorry had his feet up on the sofa, hands behind his head, staring blankly at the screen. Rahilly was obliged to talk to Dixon, but his eyes rarely left Dorry's face, waiting for the star to react to his witticisms. Franks went on reading the *Observer*. Reaney had a strong image of suits hanging in plastic covers, of underwear strewn round hotel rooms, of cartons of American cigarettes, the five-star gypsy caravan scene. He heard Jody's phone ringing.

"You're through now," said the switchboard girl.

"Hullo?" It was Jody.

"It's me," he said. "Peter. I thought I'd give you a call, see how things—"

"Peter." She sounded peculiar. "Peter, you've got to come back here."

"What's wrong?" he asked. Cholly came back through from the bedroom.

"You've got to come, Peter, now," she said, her voice rising. "I need you here, Peter."

"Tell me what's wrong," he said, impatiently. The new phones were made of lightweight plastic. They felt like toys.

"Just come, Peter," she shouted. She slammed down the phone. Something was wrong to make her carry on like that.

Now what? He'd wanted to get away from this scene, but he could feel apprehension in his stomach about what might be happening at Val's house. Why couldn't she tell him? Val must be there. He'd found out. He was standing beside her with a bread-knife, telling her to get Reaney over there so that he could cut out his lights . . . he was trying to break the door down, ready to strangle her. . . .

Wasn't it just enough that *she* wanted him to go to the house? To be honest, no. A quick bash with some women and they thought they had the harness on you. Who was Jody, anyway? His best friend's wife. Not a young girl, either, a well-used woman. You couldn't afford to be soft, you got trapped. But suppose Val did her in and then did himself in and left one of those notes, telling the world how his best friend had betrayed him? Suppose he'd really gone berserk and was murdering the kids? He'd have to go. At least, if he was first on the scene, he could destroy any incriminating notes.

He made sure that Dixon would stay around until Cholly said it was all right to leave them, said he would try to see them in the morning before they left for Manchester, even managed a joke about the imminent female scene.

Suppose she'd gone bonkers and was waiting with a gun when he got back, blank-eyed, press the trigger, the man who'd broken her happy home slumps to his knees, blood trickling from his belly?

Chapter Twenty

"You see that?" the taxi-driver shouted through the narrow connecting panel. "Bloody madmen about, in't there?"

He didn't care any more about taxi-drivers.

"You're driving too fast," he shouted back. The cabby thought it was a joke. Slumped down in the seat, jacket shoulders pressed up almost to his ears, Reaney ignored what he said. He had to be ready for any situation. Val with a blood-dripping knife, Val swinging gently on the end of a rope, scenes of utter carnage, and a note, maybe a message written in indelible blood in foot-high letters on the walls: REANEY BROKE OUR HOME. REANEY IS TO BLAME. And underneath, the bodies of the children, insensately mutilated. And himself, going through the rest of his life with the Judas mark, the man who betrayed his best friend.

He gave the driver ten bob and walked away without waiting for change, letting the garden gate swing behind him. It had been night when he last came to this house, now it was late evening, not yet lighting-up time. He saw nothing through the windows. His whole body tingled, waiting to be struck with murderous force.

He found Jody in the kitchen with Mark, the first, his resemblance to Val being stupefyingly obvious. Jody looked up at him, the baby in her arms. There didn't seem to be any expression on her face at all.

"What's wrong?" he asked. "Where's Val?" He looked round, in case Val was sneaking up behind him, axe above his head.

"He's dead." Jody's eyes didn't blink, nor did they leave his face. Behind his dead-pan mask his brain worked like lightning. She'd killed Val, he knew it. Why? He'd tried to kill her because he'd found out about them. That meant it would all come out at the trial. He was finished.

"How d'you mean, dead?" he asked, to give himself time to think. Pretend not to believe it. Be dumbfounded. People always were—if they were innocent.

"He's dead," she said. "He was killed this morning."

Was killed? What did that mean? She'd had help? Were there other people in this? He'd been drawn into a fiendish plot by a scheming wife, now she was going to announce that his fingerprints were on the weapon. He'd been tricked.

He said nothing. Her accomplice, her *real* lover, would be listening, taping their words, drawing in the trap.

"Oh Peter," she said, still staring at him, open-eyed. "I can't believe it, I can't believe it . . ."

"What happened for God's sake?" he said, his hands clenched.

"He didn't come home last night and the police came this morning and said he was in an accident and then they said he was dead."

"In an accident? What kind of accident?"

They often called suicides accidents, until the coroner's court. The coroner's court. It would be him this time, *really* involved, on the other side! Val must have left a note, he was a bloody writer, wasn't he?

"It was those script people he went to see, Val and some other man were in the car, the police said the other man was driving, I've forgotten his name, they told me what it was, they were drunk, the police didn't say they were drunk but I know they must have been drunk, they were in Swiss Cottage, the other man is dead, too, the police said I'd have to identify the body, oh Peter, I can't believe it, he went out to get drunk, I know he did, it was my fault, I shouldn't have—"

"Don't say that," he said. He clenched his teeth. Dead in a car accident! He had a terrible impulse to burst out grinning and shout 'IS THAT ALL'?

Oh my God, what kind of man am I?

You're evil. For God's sake don't show *her*.

He went to the sink and rinsed out his mouth with cold water. Then he drank some. Putting down the glass he turned and walked towards Jody and the baby. Mark hadn't looked at him at all. He looked down at the girl. It was a happy little creature, it always gurgled back when people, even strangers, came near.

Mark looked up at him. He grinned.

"Uncle Peter," he said. "Naughty Uncle Peter."

"He doesn't really understand," she said. Her hair was no longer in the pony-tail, it was a dishevelled flow of red down each side of her face, each side threatening to fall across her face. She had not been crying. Maybe she was numb, as people were supposed to be at times like this. Was he numb? He was sad. Really sad. What an obscene thing to have shouted out, *Is that all*? He put his hands under Mark's armpits and lifted him to his chest, turning him so that his face came near his own.

"It's all right, Mark," he said, feeling stupid yet obliged to sound like this. The kid didn't look upset in the least. What was death to a child? How would he have reacted at four if told that his own father had been killed? *Can't we go to the zoo on Sunday then?* Yes, probably. He'd never grown up. Or else he'd always been grown-up. A changeling. No real human instincts at all. No, he had to pretend, to say the things that sounded right. "Daddy said I was to take care of you, Mark," he said. "You'll be all right. Uncle

Peter will look after you and mummy and the baby. Daddy told me to."

"Daddy's dead," Mark said. Reaney tried to see into his baby blue eyes. He could remember things from the time when he'd been four, he'd known a lot more than grown-ups would have believed. Was Mark playing out this scene as well? God, it was all a great mystery.

When they'd put Mark to bed, Reaney sat beside him, telling him that he would have to help to look after his mother because that's what boys and men did, they looked after their little sisters and their mothers, they were ladies and couldn't look after themselves. Mark listened, his father's blue eyes fixed on Reaney's mouth.

"Do you think you'll like me taking care of you?" Reaney asked.

"Yes," Mark said. "Is Daddy in heaven, Uncle Peter?"

"Of course. He was a good daddy, wasn't he?"

"Daddy said there wasn't a heaven," Mark said.

"Nobody really knows, Mark."

"Daddy will know now, won't he, Uncle Peter?"

"I suppose so. You say a prayer for him, won't you? You do know some prayers, do you?"

"Thank you for the flowers so sweet," said Mark.

"That'll do fine," Reaney said. "Now you go to sleep, you'll have to be up early in the morning to start looking after your mother, won't you?"

The baby—must find out her name now—was already asleep in her cot, sucking her thumb, the other little hand thrown back on the pillow. He put out the lights. Jody was in the front room, looking down at the empty grate.

"They're asleep," he said, not going too near her. "I'm very, very sorry, Jody. I don't know what to say . . ."

She shrugged.

"I won't start crying," she said. "It's just the shock, I'm not the stricken widow."

"Don't let's talk about it, eh? I think I've got Mark to feel—"

"I never really loved him," she said. "I'd never met a man before who came straight out and said he wanted to go to bed with me, first time we met. The men I knew didn't say it straight out. He was so desperate. I started Mark before we'd hardly known each other. There was something funny about him, he wanted me and then he wanted the children but he didn't really want any of us. I could never get it out of my head that it was just an episode, he never really seemed like a husband, do you know what I mean, he wasn't really like a husband at all. What was it he wanted, Peter?"

"I don't know. How the hell *should* I know, anyway? He was only my so-called best friend, I didn't know the first real thing about him. Sit down, would you like a cup of coffee or something?"

"That would be nice, I've been in a dither, I didn't feel like eating. Nobody has telephoned or called, Peter, nobody. Just a newspaper. He had lots of friends, hadn't he?"

"They won't know yet, will they?" he replied.

"No, I don't suppose so."

As he made the coffee he wondered if the numbness was the new people's lack of feeling, or was it nature's buffer? He gave her a cigarette, then he switched on the hot-air heater and sat down on the sofa. So this time he would be personally involved in an inquest. Or would he? Was there any difference—wasn't it just another situation into which he'd been artificially grafted?

She sipped her coffee. It seemed to shake her out of the dreamy state. By concentration he'd thought himself into something which felt like real sadness.

"I'm sorry, did this interrupt you, you were meeting Dorry, weren't you, you shouldn't have—"

"Jody, listen, that doesn't matter. I was phoning up to see if he had come back and then I'd have come back here for a drink-up, or if he hadn't then I'd've, well, I wondered how you felt about everything. You know . . ."

"You're not to feel trapped here, not because of this," she said, two hands united, cigarette burning in one, coffee mug in the other, head up, you-will-have-to-convince-me-with-difficulty-that-you-really-want-me in her eyes. "What we did was—"

"Shut up," he said. "There's no use feeling guilty now. We both meant it. Now it's happened, so don't let's have a lot of recriminations and rubbish. Will you marry me? I love you and I want to be with you and be a father to the children and have more of our own. I've always loved you, even if I didn't know it."

My God, woman, I was going to ask you and him to let me become the third marriage partner only a little time ago, when was it now . . . ?

"Don't do anything out of pity," she said, shaking her head. Her hair, being down, made her different, less sure of herself, somehow.

"All right then," he said. "You've got time to decide whether I mean it or not, I'm still bloody married, aren't I? If you don't know by the time I'm divorced you're . . ."

She began to cry a bit when they decided to go to bed, at first he went to go to the spare room but she held his hand. They went to bed together in *their* room. But it was him and her now, not—

She cried herself to sleep. He held her tightly until he, too, fell asleep.

When they both lay awake in the morning he found himself moving so that his head was higher on the pillow, looking down at hers. In her eyes he could see no doubt, no question about his right to be there. He wondered, would there be any pain? *Was* pain necessary for reality? Val's story would be one of the scenes at the coroner's play now, poor, struggling Val. He had wanted to bleed for those other people, yes, to bleed, to scream out. But now it was Val, somebody he knew, part of his own life. There was no need to look deep down in the shadows with which we surrounded our shameful self-knowledge, he did not want to bleed for Val. Death had been quick. Perhaps all death was quick. More important, he was profiting by Val's death. In some way it had saved Val pain, for he would never know now that he had been betrayed.

Was this what you had to do? Let people die so that you could be happy? He remembered now, the real shame, he had been glad when that man had died, glad. That man, the anonymous shunter from whose world he had escaped. Glad. That was why he wanted to bleed for the city's victims, he didn't know anything about them, except that they were tragically dead, safe to weep over because nothing was known.

"Jody," he said, his voice a deep murmur round the bed. "What do you think I should do about my job? I hate it, you know, really hate it. The trouble is, I don't know what I really want to do. There isn't anything else I really can do, anyway, not that I could make a decent living out of."

Eyes, so close, come apart. They are not eyes, they are wet orbs, skin junctures, lashes, mosaics of coloured glass.

"There's any amount of things you could do," she said. His desire was so complete there was no need to express it in sex. Or so he felt, their legs and feet pressing together, arms round each other. "If you hate it give it up. Val always said he hated what he did, but he didn't mean it. Do you really

302

mean it? We don't need much to live on, not now that the house is paid for."

"I never know what's best for children," he said. "My family had nothing, I always wanted more than they had, that's why I got into this business in the first place. If we'd had money I might have done something else, something I wanted to do, not just for money. Yet . . . it's often just as bad for the children the other way round, isn't it?"

"I suppose so. Why worry about it now? Don't you feel it's like a dream? I do. I can't believe I'm lying in bed with you and Val's dead and we're talking away. I keep thinking I should be having hysterics."

They smiled sadly at each other. This was it. You profited from the dead. One way or another, every death meant profit for someone still alive. Mrs. Gray took five hundred, he took a woman. Mrs. Gray was, somehow, responsible for her daughter's death. He was—there was no point in thinking about that, Val was dead, now he meant no more than the dish-washer, a memory only, something that raised echoes, something that couldn't be allowed to affect the life that remained. The dead were nothing. Memories. The tragedy was in yourself. Could you *really* profit by their deaths?

He left about nine, not wanting to rush in too fast on Mark. The boy had to have some time between fathers, otherwise . . . He thought about Mark on the bus. What would it all be like when Mark was thirty-seven? Could he help the boy at all, was there any way of passing on your own lessons to save precious time for the young?

He noted Queensway on the left. Maggie, at least their memories would be *kind*, she would understand, if she ever learned, how he felt about Jody and Mark and the baby. (It was a girl, he knew that.) She was young, she had time.

He didn't have time, not to spare on a new adventure. It was a question of making a concrete decision. Eliminate.

To go on with Felix as before didn't seem right. No, he didn't want to go on as before. He wanted to give it all up, didn't he? Yes, but—

It was the only real world he knew, wasn't it? Ironic, to waste your life in artificiality and then wake up one day and realise the artificiality was your own, only reality.

The sun made Regent Street sparkle.

When had it last rained?

There was almost too much freedom about sunshine. It made the English spirit artificially buoyant. *His* English spirit, anyway. Life was not sunny. Bad weather was like pain, it gave things reality.

Chapter Twenty-one

He took the coffee from Katrina, maintaining a smile, hoping the message would travel between their eyes, this is me being friendly, the war is over. She smiled back, after a second, her hardening face lines relaxing slowly and then disappearing.

"You're looking rather lovely today, my dear," he said, trying to get the correct note of jokey-sincerity. Miss Rimmer did not look up from her inevitable array of day-books, expense chits and invoices. "Oh, Miss Rimmer, if you could give me a note of how much I'm into the float for I'll settle up with one lightning cheque." He beamed at them both. This was not a sign of weakness, but of strength. Hitherto he had been a card-carrying malist now he was going to run non-stop flag days for the human race. Next thing he'd be singing *If I can heeeelp somebody as I go along then my living will not be in vain,* as once he had picked up a phrase from an American novel and had gone round thinking of himself as *The Good Humour Man.* I can afford to turn both smiling cheeks towards Katrina and Miss Rimmer, let's confront big daddy and see what he has to say. Carrying his cup and saucer in the delicate way a cup and saucer have to be held he found Felix going through the morning papers.

"Got a good showing, didn't we?" he said, looking up. "This chummy Franks takes a good picture. If I didn't know what he was I'd say it was a publicity stunt."

Safe-making, low-gear humour, men sharing the cosy fun of their own trade. The coverage given to Dorry would be of concrete assistance in a deal Felix was currently negotiating with the American agency, a healthy new area of profit, handling their artistes exclusively in Britain. Printed evidence of their efficiency, aren't we clever chappies, all Monday mornings should be so free of anal-seated depression, Felix is really chatting brightly as his way of telling Reaney he has done a good job, the bright boy.

Yes, he had seen the small piece about Val's death, my God, wasn't that a real shocker, he couldn't believe it, you never could when it was somebody you'd been drinking with just the other—when was it, my God, you never know, do you?

". . . and it had to happen just now—I mean, it'd be tragic anytime, of course—but to happen *now*, just when Barry's show was at the crucial stage . . ."

Reaney prepared to unveil his information. Even then, he was still trying to decide what he really thought about Felix. Was he angered by the typical businessman's reaction, the death was sad because it hindered our machinations? Was Felix a goody or a baddy? Was there still just a tinge of cringe as he looked at the smooth, dark head? No, it seemed to be missing.

"Actually, Alfred, I'm going to marry Val's wife," he said, looking down at the remains of the coffee, downcast eyes underlining the significance of what he had just said. Look up, see how the man takes it, see how he took how the man took it, wait and watch and hope self is not attacked.

"That didn't take you long," Felix said. No, there was no trace of a leer, nor of nastiness. "Still, I had a pretty good idea you weren't staying there just for the breakfasts."

A nice, snide crack. (Where had he come in contact with that phrase, recently?). Was there, in men, some physiological defence-mechanism fending off the jolly-boat called togetherness? Do I have to prove I'm as strong—or as nasty—

as you before you let me close in? Or do I have to wait until you're dead before you let me love you?

"Funny, we were going to tell Val, this week actually," he went on, giving Felix another chance. "Still, I won't bore you with the messy details of my private goings-on, there's something else I want to talk to you about."

"Fire away. Let me be your father, if you remember that ad."

Quite so. Is this a day with an ur in it? Do I know if I am going to be strong and nasty? My nose twitches forward, sniff, sniff, ready to bolt.

"Alfred, I've been thinking a lot about things in general, frankly I'm not very happy about my current position in life's great drama, that resignation I gave you last week, you laughed it off as a drunken impulse, well, it wasn't, not really. I meant it when I typed it . . . still, you've *always* been able to change my mind for me, haven't you?"

"You're not happy?" Felix said. How does his face punctuate his words? Still safe, it's the sardonic Jew again. "Who *is* happy, may I ask? I'm not happy. I can't think of anybody who *is* happy. Only fools are happy. I'm well off, but I'm not happy. Do you want to be well-off, too? Believe me, money doesn't make you happy. I know, it's a silly old cliché, but it's true. Four thousand, twenty thousand, once you've got enough more means nothing. Not a thing."

We're all working-class now. Money means nothing as long as you've got it. Of course, you're right. But it's the only way I can measure myself against you. Isn't it?

"You may be right, I've never had twenty thousand so I don't know." He put the cup and saucer on the edge of Felix's desk. "Maybe it's jealousy. Why should I spend my life cavorting about for the Barry Blacks and the Dorrys of this world, grubbing about for morons and lushes, and not even getting enough money to make up for the grubbing?

For my four thou I have to grub, for your twenty you only have to make decisions. Maybe that's it, I want to make the decisions and not have to grub about in the mire. I dunno."

Felix sat back in the position of power, hands coming together under chin, his chance to play priest-psychiatrist, staring at Reaney as if trying to sum him up for the first time.

"It's more than making decisions, Peter," he began. At last. "It's being a businessman. That's what I am, a businessman. It's what I do, what I was cut out for. If it wasn't this business it'd be selling cars or soap or something. It's just what I am. Now you're not a businessman, Peter, you never will be—"

"What if I said I wanted to be a businessman?"

"I would tell you to go out and get pissed and forget it. Believe me, I'm trying to give you a compliment. I know the truth about myself, believe me, making money's all I can do. You, well, I know for a fact that the money-making bit bores you, doesn't it? Come on, own up, I know more about you than you sometimes give me credit for."

Something known? Yes, but not a very important something.

"Perhaps you're right," he said. "But business isn't all making money, you know." Now there was just a faint tremor of self-defence, the hackles stir infinitesimally, you don't know everything daddy otherwise I'm nobody. "I'd say, for instance, that you were a bit short on imagination. This business could be twice as big as it is, the printing, for instance, printing's like a goldmine these days but you've let old Farmer jog along for years not even scratching the surface of what that shop could be making. And Braid. You've been talking about getting the skids under him for long enough, why don't you do something about it?"

Felix shrugged. No anger. The young—don't make me

laugh, it's the casting, you see, in a land of seniles the middle-aged is juvenile—always burn with ideas, it was not a personal attack, it was a safe situation.

"Braid? What can I do? He's got the boy signed and sealed, legally water-tight. For the moment he's just a cross we've got to bear."

"I don't think so. You could put the squeeze on him today. You're such a hard businessman, Alfred, why don't you tell him you want Barry's contract or you turn him over to the law for conspiring towards an abortion? He's told me all about it, easy to prove, see how he feels about going down for a couple of years in the Scrubs . . ."

Felix made a face. Actually, there was the possibility that the position of power could work the other way. To be high up could be a disadvantage, the raised perch always involving a certain risk of ridicule.

"So what good would that do? Barry would get as much stick as Braid, wouldn't he? In any case, it's a very nasty idea, especially coming from you. My God, only a minute ago you were saying you didn't like grubbing about in the mire! Now you're suggesting blackmail! Really, Peter, sometimes . . ."

Oh no, big daddy, not that easy. Think of me as the town drunk who has suddenly sobered up and surprised Tombstone by proving he's the fastest gunslinger in the west.

"Well, then, that's what you point out to Braid. He either sells out to you at a reasonable figure—reasonable on your side, of course—or he and Barry both go down the river. He gets a fair sum or he gets two years in the nick. I know which he'd choose, don't you?"

It's all a bloody game anyway. The successful men don't take it seriously, not personally, the serious reverent ones stick up there on the high stools, shining their arses for peanuts. The top men played at it, hard and cold-blooded *because* it was a game, *because* they could afford to be irresponsible when it suited them. Emotions were for bank-clerks. Felix is musing now, little wheels revving into a good whirring rate. His whiskery twitching nose detects a trace-scent of danger somewhere in the air.

"I don't know if you're serious or not," he said. "One minute you're too high and mighty, the next you want to play it vicious. Do you know yourself what you're really getting at?"

"I don't know if I know or not. Maybe I'm just trying to make out I could be a businessman if I wanted. I'm fed up with things as they stand, that's one certainty. It's probably got something to do with being Number Two. Most normal men want to be Number One, don't they? You know, I might get married and be happy this time and have kids and all that family nonsense, but you think I want to be the under-paid nonentity who's king of some tiny suburban empire and Mister Nobody outside?"

Felix made a face, I-understand-what-you-mean-but-let's-be-practical-what-do-you-expect-me-to-do?

"Whatever way you look at it, you're Number One here," Reaney went on. The plastic Venetian blinds still allowed in enough diffused sunshine to make it difficult to spot ex-actly what was being shown in Felix's eyes. But this again might be a reversal of the power position, for not to know became eventually not to care. "You own this set-up, I don't. Whether I'm as good at business as you or not doesn't matter, does it, you own it and that's that. Why should you give anything away because I'm fed up? It'd be simpler to let me clear off, you could easily hire a dozen blokes like me—lots of sober, industrious lads like Dixon around, as we know."

That was left hanging in the air, a smoke-ring into which

Felix would, or would not, be tempted to stick his index finger, as men do with smoke rings.

"Perhaps I haven't paid enough attention to you recently, Peter . . ." This part was waffle, the man is thinking, wheels whirring, click-click, what comes up on the fruit combination, millions and billions of moments when men (and old ladies with a cat) wait to see what fruit comes up, eventually the losing streak becomes part of your very flesh, you *feel* hopeless, you see yourself with the eyes of a winner and you know you're no bloody good, so step forward to the edge of the platform, maybe the winners will be sorry but it will be too late then, won't it, you may even cause them a little bother or is that too much to hope for? ". . . twenty-six years. Maybe I am a bit stick-in-the-mud but when you start with nothing, it's a long haul, you get to the stage where you're content with what you've got. Listen, Peter, I don't want to sound like a feeble old fool, but I've always thought of you, somehow, as a sort of son. Ha ha, all right, don't laugh at me but it's true. I've no family, just the wife and she knows nothing about anything. I've always intended to see you all right. After all, I don't want to go on forever, do I? What do I do with this business when I want to swallow it and grow the bleeding roses and nothing else? In five years, maybe a bit longer—well, you'd be the natural candidate to take over, wouldn't you?"

Would I? Do I wait, as you waited? Go on, tell me nice things, daddy. Tell me why I should spend my juice years doing your dirt so that one day you *might* be inclined to do me a great favour, when my juice, too, is gone. Maybe I am just cut out to be a secondhand father, at least my secondhand wife is a woman who excites me mightily into sincere renditions of the male act. Should I want more? Is it just ego and pride that makes me sit here and wonder, what will Mark think about me when he's thirty-seven and

I'm mouldering in the grave (if they still allow precious land to be wasted that way by then); will I be *his* shunting nobody? The stepfather who never quite made it? What does Jody think of me, she says she doesn't care about money, is that because I don't matter, just another episode, another stray event? Felix, you sit here and tell me sweetly why I should be happy to be less than you, less of a man, dirt and all. If I choose now to challenge you, who will have been responsible? To be friendly was all *I* ever wanted.

". . . then again, knowing you, blackmailing Braid might have been some kind of joke?"

"Perhaps. I get funnier notions than that at times. Don't get offended, Alfred, but I even thought in a moment of hungover madness to put the bite on you, too. I mean, it would be easy, wouldn't it, you send five tons to Mathie in cash, he got it to Mrs. Gray—two minutes with a couple of CID lads and she'd cough her guts all over the place, you'd be right in there with Mathie, conspiring to pervert the course of justice or whatever they call it, wouldn't you? Oh yes, I get some very funny ideas at times, silly isn't it?"

No, not really. I wasn't supposed to know that you paid the five tons, Alfred. Now you're getting a message, all right. I know, and you know that I know I'm not supposed to know, so why have I brought it up, how did I get to know, why did I want to know? I've made a joke of it, but that's part of the game, isn't it? Never say it out loud, fence round, mongoose and snake, I'm boxing clever by making it a joke, you have to decide what I'm getting at, there's still time for me to show that my bullets are blanks and my bayonet made of rubber, but you have to evaluate the chances. This is your real war, a silly boy's game. No, it's to do with Chinese, in every convoluted flow of a million words there is one oblique, inscrutable, feathery threat of real meaning.

So let's see who can stay silent longer. Who wins, the man of natural power (who does it without knowing why), or the clever mimic (who doesn't have real nerve but may be stronger because he understands the role)?

"What *would* make you happy, would you say?"

Ah, Alfred, I know that one, too. To stumble out some unrehearsed statement now would put me back at the bottom of the snake. Shrug. Self-deprecating, I am not important enough to know what I want. Daddy.

You've got to think now, really think. Can you let me go off into the city bearing such a secret, me, the great saloon-bar oracle? As well trust your secret to a daily paper. Then again, how much will it take to keep me here, a loyal part of the team? Not too much, you don't want to give me too much, for that might make me think you were scared to hell. In any case, you're not entirely sure that I am consciously going through this rigmarole. Can you afford to call the bluff? Funny, I'm not frightened at all. Funny, isn't it? Just shows you the miracle effects a good woman can have. Or was it Val? Or Mark? All these people are watching me. Suddenly, Alfred, you don't seem to loom so large.

"Peter," Felix said, squaring up to his desk, palms being placed firmly on the blotting pad. "I think I see things more clearly now, it's been very useful this little chat, helped to clear my ideas up. I've made a decision . . ."

When you are actually listening to good news, well, it's like actually hearing the person is dead, you don't feel the significance, that comes before or after. You half-listen. Later you throw your arms up (or weep), but at the time it never seems quite real. Perhaps because it is *déja vu—* you've already heard the good news in a thousand dreams.

He was to get twenty per cent of the existing business and fifty per cent of all the new business he brought in. Profits, you see, all to be coldly worked-out by the accountants, no charity, no sops, all business-like, the need to expand (not the need to buy off blackmail), look ahead, build for the future . . .

"But Alfred, you really don't have to—"

"For God's sake, what more do you want? You wanted power, didn't you? All right then, it's yours, don't tell me you're going to go on playing the fool all your life."

Thank you, Alfred. In one giddy sentence you've told me I *was* a fool and ordered me to become rich. Small rich, but it's a change from being big-fool.

A little thankyou speech? My contribution to the fairy-tale, that you did it out of spontaneous combustion and not out of blackmail? No, I shall light a cigarette and puff away in a terribly offhand manner, I am not a little squirt at prize-giving, not any longer.

"Mind you," Felix said, "you may come to remember everything before today as your best years. You'll find out, Peter, my God you will, once it's yours you'll never stop worrying. Happiness! You'll forget what the bleeding word means. Still, it's up to you. I'm not giving you a partnership so's you can live it up on the grand scale, remember that. You're in business now, mate, right in it." Felix smiled. Reaney thought of the printing shop. How would he *actually* begin to double its turnover? Surely he'd be able to think of something!

They had started to chat about general outlines when Katrina rang through. Felix listened. He looked up at Reaney and again there was the knowing smile. Reaney was beginning to dislike that smile already. It was as though Felix knew he was in for a hard time and was going to enjoy every minute of it.

Well, he'd just have to keep on his toes and that was one way of losing weight.

"No, I don't want to see them," Felix was saying to

Katrina. "Tell them they'll be dealing with my partner. You don't know who my partner is! Tuts, tuts, who else could it be but—Peter Reaney, of course. Yes, Mister Reaney will be out to take care of them."

Felix put down the phone.

"Well, you wanted to expand, get out there and get on with it." He was all mischievous now. Reaney stood up. Standing at the desk, looking down, Felix was smaller, older than he had been against the light.

"Who is it?" Reaney asked.

"It's your friend and mine, Jack Goddings, with his brilliant new discovery, Maggie Greenhough," Felix said. "As you recall, I said to Goddings we might consider taking her on. I leave it all to you. If you think she's any good we'll do a deal with Goddings. There's just one tip, from an old man, Peter—" again he was the grinning imp, this was going to be a helluva set-up if that was the attitude he was going to take—"there's plenty of crumpet about without getting it on the books. You follow me? Audition them all but remember, the profits don't come from *that* kind of talent. Best of luck, my old mate."

So. This was going to be a great bloody help. Yeah, that was all he needed, Maggie on the books! He'd have to see her all the bloody time. And Felix, jumping about like a kid going on holiday, he'd go on seeing it as a big joke. Every single day he'd be shoved up against Maggie, knowing what he knew, knowing what Felix was grinning at . . . as he went out into reception Katrina came out of her office to tell him that Cholly Aberdeen was on the phone, Dixon *had* got drunk and stayed the night in the hotel and was too ill to get the Manchester train, Cholly sounded very annoyed, who *was* going to Manchester with them . . . ?

He'd shoot Dixon out on his ear, he vowed to himself, seeing no way out except by rushing off to Manchester himself, unless they could bring Dixon round in three quarters of an hour, yeah, ring me back in twenty minutes, now then, Maggie, what will it be like when I walk in there and see her, what will happen?

He took a deep breath. This was what you had to do, wasn't it? This was why some men were shunters and other men made decisions, wasn't it? Try and think of Jody and Mark and the baby (still can't remember its blasted name) —and the money.

Ha bloody ha.

Loving care cost money, isn't that what it had said?

~~Radiology~~

Oct 10th   Radiation

Chok 10:15
ın   10:30

11:00

Cancer Center
490
A West 219
Road

Frets
Door To
Right